MIS
IN S

Mark Harrison

Copyright Mark Harrison 2013
Mark Harrison has asserted his right under the Copyright, Designs and Patents Act 1988 to be identified as the author of this work.
This book is sold subject to the condition that it shall not, by way of trade or otherwise, be lent, resold, hired out, or otherwise circulated without the author's prior consent.

CHAPTER ONE

'Ah, Fernandez, just the man.' Chief Superintendent Philip Bowater OBE, QPM, glanced up. 'Take a seat, I'll be with you in a moment.' He went back to scribbling.

So this was the inner sanctum.

Detective Inspector Michael Fernandez sat down and looked around the office, noticing the commendation for bravery signed with a squiggle of blue ink above the words, "Home Secretary."

Michael crossed his legs, straightened his back and adjusted his tie. He glanced at the knife-edge creases in his grey woollen trousers and brushed away an imaginary piece of fluff. At least his black slip-on shoes were shiny. He had polished them that morning before leaving for work. The Chief Super's shoes protruded beneath the antique mahogany desk; tasselled oxblood loafers glistening in the light, revealing the faintest of cracks where constant bending had caused a crease to form along the base of the toes. The hard leather soles were almost as polished as the uppers, from miles walked over carpets but rarely outdoors. Huge shoes, size eleven or twelve and in perfect proportion with the rest of Bowater's frame. Michael often said he could read a person from the shoes they wore and these shoes, though old, exuded quality and style and gave the wearer an aura of authority.

But why had the Chief Super asked to see him personally? He couldn't think of anything he'd done recently that might have landed him in hot water. That was not Michael's style. He hated those clichéd TV caricatures of detectives who were always at loggerheads with the top brass, always cutting corners and taking risks. Some might have called him a plodder, but to him, process and attention to detail were the watchwords in any successful investigation. The only hint of unorthodoxy was his willingness to rely on his own intuition even when it flew in the face of the evidence. It was something he had developed throughout his ten years in Nottingham CID. He had a nose for the job that others found difficult to fathom.

Two pairs of eyes caught his attention. They seemed to be gazing out at him from a silver picture frame. Twin daughters, their long blond locks draped symmetrically across their shoulders, formed mirror images in their mortarboards and gowns. Distinguished parents flanked them, their pride epitomised by beaming smiles.

Conscious of staring, he looked away.

Bowater leaned over the pages, his pen hovering and his eyes flicking from side to side following lines of text. Michael noticed a bald patch on top of Bowater's head. He'd started combing his hair forward in the last few months and colleagues had remarked on it. The colour had also changed from brown to black coinciding with the disappearance of grey hair from the temples.

Michael's anxiety turned to impatience. Was this one of those "mind games" detailed in the Manual of Interrogation Techniques?

'That's done,' said Bowater, rising to his full six foot six inches to look down on the Inspector. He buttoned the double-breasted jacket of his blue pinstriped suit, strode across the office and stepped out.

'There you go, Penny. Just a few changes. Then get one of the constables to run it over to HQ this afternoon please. Oh, and make a pot of tea for Michael and me. Soon as you can. Thanks.'

Michael? The Chief had never used his first name before.

'Let's sit over here. More comfortable.' Bowater gestured toward the coffee table set beside an L-shaped sofa as he collected a blue folder from his desk.

'How's your Spanish these days?' he said. 'You do speak Spanish, don't you? It's on your file. How is it?'

'Fine. I mean, it's – it's all right.' Michael felt himself stutter. 'Pretty good I suppose. I don't use it much.'

'But I'm right in thinking you're quite fluent, aren't I? We're not just talking schoolboy Spanish, are we?'

'No sir.'

'That's what I thought. How would you like to get some practice?'

What the hell is he on about? Michael thought. He had better be careful how he answered or he could find himself volunteering for something he might not want to do.

'Not sure I really need to practise. I mean it would soon come back to me if the need arose.'

'Good, that's what I wanted to hear.'

Michael's heart sank. This had all the hallmarks of a set up.

'Tell me Michael, are you married?'

'Divorced.'

'Children?'

'No sir.'

'Live alone?'

'Yes sir.'

'So no family ties?'

'Depends what you mean.' *And what did he mean?* Michael's suspicions were now fully roused.

'You know, no one you're responsible for. Ageing relative, sick auntie, crippled dog, that sort of thing?'

'Not exactly.' Michael flushed and stiffened as if to protect an imaginary aunt or dog. But it was difficult to be evasive short of telling the Chief to mind his own damned business and say he had plenty of friends and family, thanks.

However... 'Look, sir, do you mind telling me what this is all about?'

'Sorry, Fernandez – Michael. You're right to be curious. I just wanted to know how things stood. Have you seen this?'

Bowater pulled a copy of the Nottingham Evening Post from the folder and slid it across the table. Michael caught it before it fell to the floor. He read the headline: NOTTS COUPLE DISAPPEAR IN SPAIN.

'Know anything about it?'

'Only what I've seen in the papers.' Michael stopped reading, put down the newspaper and looked at the Chief Super. Was this a chance to impress? 'A local couple left for Alicante two or three months ago. Retired in search of their dream home. Not been heard of for a few weeks. Relatives getting concerned. Money still being withdrawn from the bank. Hire car overdue. Spanish police suspect foul play.'

A knock sounded at the door, three gentle taps.

'Come in Penny. Splendid, we'll have it over here please. Just leave the tray. Thanks.'

Penny Edwardes wriggled demurely toward them, her tiny steps determined by the circumference of her tight skirt. She lent forward carefully, bending her knees to prevent showing more of her shapely legs. Sitting at the low table, the two men were in direct eye-line with her cleavage. Michael blushed and reached for the tray.

'Here Penny. Let me take that.'

'Oh, thank you Michael.'

Penny turned and tiptoed back toward the door, her high-heeled stilettos leaving pin-point imprints in the thick woollen carpet.

'I forget, you two know each other don't you? I mean, outside the office.' It was Bowater's turn to stutter. 'Not much escapes my notice. Office gossip, I mean.' He reached for the milk jug.

Michael felt his cheeks glow as they reddened. 'That was all over months ago. It never really got started.'

'Actually, it was almost four months ago,' said Bowater to Michael's surprise. 'I mean, since the Harringtons left for Spain,' he added quickly. 'And twelve weeks since they were last in contact with anyone over here.'

Michael remained silent. He began to realise where this was leading.

Bowater poured the tea from the stainless steel pot, careful not to overfill the Royal Worcester cups. The gold rims were a little worn, but they would still create exactly the right impression, Michael imagined, for the elite who crossed the threshold.

'Help yourself to milk and sugar.'

Michael usually took his tea with lemon, but thought better than to ask. He added a generous splash of milk.

'Any ideas?'

Michael paused for a moment.

'Sometimes people want to disappear, of course. Start a new life. Lose the baggage of their past. That sort of thing.'

Bowater sat back in his chair, cradling the bone china saucer in his left hand and lifting the cup with his right. 'That's exactly what I thought. But we're both missing something.' He took a sip.

'What's that?'

'It's happened before.'

'What has?'

'Last year another British couple left for Spain. Roughly the same area. Disappeared for months. Then they were found dead, tortured and murdered for their money by a gang of Venezuelans. The Spanish cops caught them eventually, but took a lot of flack for not taking the case seriously in the first place. So did the Foreign Secretary for not putting pressure on the Spanish authorities. The Foreign Sec's PPS has already been on to the Chief Constable. He wants things handled carefully this time. Covering his back if you see what I mean.'

'I get the drift, sir.' Michael knew what was coming next.

'So you're the obvious choice. What do you think?'

'I suppose I could take a look. See if there's anything I can suggest.'

'I don't think you quite understand, Michael. The Foreign Secretary wants someone in Spain to work with the Spanish police. And the Spanish authorities are worried about the effect on tourism and property sales. The Guardia Civil think it's a good idea, as well. They're not daft. Having the British police involved will share the responsibility, and the blame, if anything goes wrong. We need someone who can deal with the relatives at this end and who can work with the police in Spain. The Guardia Civil isn't exactly flush with fluent English speakers, so they've asked for someone who can speak Spanish. So you see? You fit the bill perfectly. What do you think?'

Michael took a long draught of tea and nearly choked. How

could anyone drink this lukewarm creamy stuff? He returned the cup and saucer to the table and pushed it to one side.

'Do I have a choice?'

'Not really. I'll put it this way, the Chief Constable would be very disappointed if you refused. Anyway, what's the problem? I thought you'd jump at the chance of visiting your homeland, all expenses paid, get a bit of spring sunshine.'

'What makes you think Spain is my homeland?' Michael managed a tight smile.

'Well, I just thought... With the Spanish, and a name like Fernandez.'

'Yes, the name comes from my father. He was Spanish. I'm British.'

'My mistake. Sorry, but all the same it'll be good to go back. See the relatives perhaps.'

'I'm afraid I've never been to Spain. I speak Spanish because my father taught me, but that's as far as it goes.' If it wasn't in the file he wasn't going to mention that Spanish was always the first language spoken at home in his childhood.

Bowater straightened, removed his rimless spectacles and tossed them onto the table. 'You're joking. I thought everybody had been to Spain, even if only on a package – to Benidorm, or Majorca.'

'No, I've never set foot in Spain and I'm not sure I want to go now.'

'Is there something I'm missing here? Something I should know? You're not wanted by the Spanish police are you? An illegal immigrant or something?'

'No sir.'

'Look, cut the "sir" crap, now. Let's be straight with each other. Unless there's any good reason why you can't, you're going to Spain. There's too much at stake here for you as well as for me. Now, for the last time, what's the problem?'

Michael hesitated to consider his options. There were none.

'I'll be frank with you. I'm not personally interested in going to Spain, especially on a wild goose chase. I don't see that anything could come out of it. But if there is no alternative, I will go.'

'Of course you will. That's the spirit. I knew you'd do this, Fernandez. You never know, it could be the making of you. After all, you've been an Inspector for how long, eight years? That's quite a long time. A successful outcome in a high profile case like this would give you a little limelight and there's a lot to be said for that you know.'

Michael sat back in his chair. A thousand thoughts ran through his mind, not one of them to do with David and Alison Harrington.

Bowater slid the folder across the coffee table.

'Here's what we have so far. You're booked on the 15.25 EasyJet flight from East Midlands on Monday. That gives you the rest of this week and the weekend if you need it.'

'EasyJet? Your not pushing the boat out are you?'

'Short flight. We need to be seen to make economies. There are a few leads to follow up before you go. A couple of property companies were contacted by the Harringtons before they went in search of their dream home. Oh, and you'll need to speak to the brother and sister-in-law, it was they who raised the alarm. Well, it was the sister-in-law, Linda Harrington, who made the first contact. The brother didn't seem too concerned.'

'Well, I would have to say, if the immediate family doesn't seem too concerned, then surely – '

'No, that's enough, Michael. This is a high profile case and we need to respond. The Foreign Secretary, the Chief Constable and I myself, for that matter, think there's enough evidence to give cause for concern. So I don't want it to be a half-hearted effort on anyone's part. If you're right they'll turn up as soon as the word's out that the search party's on its way. Then everyone will be happy and you can come back home. Until then I want one hundred percent from you and your Spanish counterpart. Did I tell you the Guardia Civil have assigned their own officer to work with you? Captain Josie somebody-or-other.'

'Jose' Michael stressed the 'H' sound.

'Yes, all right. The name's in the file. He's picking you up at Alicante airport. Make sure you're ready. We need to be careful. Can't afford to do anything to upset our Spanish colleagues.'

Michael opened the folder and Bowater returned to his desk. He sat down in the high-backed leather chair.

'That's all for now Fernandez. I'd like to see you on Monday before you leave. Let's see...' He turned the pages of his diary. 'Yes, ten-thirty will do. Just before the weekly briefing at HQ. You can bring me up to date and I can put the Chief Constable in the picture while you wing your way to sunny Spain.'

Michael stood up, tucked the folder under his arm and headed for the door. 'Thank you, sir.'

'It's Miguel-Ángel, isn't it?' Bowater said behind him. He pronounced it Mig-wel Angel (as in the Angel Gabriel). 'Your original first name. It's on your file.'

Michael turned. 'It's Mig-el sir. I've never used the Ángel.' He stressed the hard G.

'Just wondered,' said Bowater closing the pink personnel file. 'You're very lucky you know. Beautiful country Spain. Gaudi's Cathedral in Barcelona. The Alhambra Palace in Seville. You don't paint ceilings in your spare time, do you?'

'I'd like to sir.' Michael opened the door. 'But Michelangelo turned out to be Italian and the Alhambra Palace is in Granada.'

Bowater continued cheerfully, 'What part of Spain is your father from?'

Michael glared at the photograph of the Chief Superintendent's twin daughters. 'My father came from Alicante Province. Is that all for now sir?'

'Just one other thing. We need to email a copy of your passport to the Guardia in Alicante so they can arrange some kind of ID for you when you arrive. Pop it in with Penny in the morning and she'll do the rest. You do have a passport don't you?'

'Yes sir. I have a British passport.'

Michael shut the door sharply. Penny and the other two secretaries in the outer office looked at him. Silence replaced the usual chatter.

'Some people have all the luck,' said Penny. 'I don't suppose you get to take a partner on your Spanish escapade, do you?' She adopted a provocative pose, mimicking a flamenco dancer.

'Is nothing confidential?'

'Ooh, what's ruffled your feathers?' Penny laughed. 'Sorry, Michael, only joking.' The other secretaries giggled.

This time it was the turn of the outer door to rattle as Michael slammed it behind him and marched down the corridor toward the lift.

But by the time he reached the office of the Criminal Investigation Division he was concerned only with: Why did it take so long for the family to come forward? Why was the brother seemingly so unconcerned? Could this really be a copycat of the earlier case?

He strode toward his desk in the corner without lifting his eyes from the file. A humming from his work mates gradually rose to a crescendo.

'Oh yes we're off to sunny Spain, y viiiiivah España.'

'Ah, get lost the lot of you.' Michael picked up his bag. He turned to leave. 'Pack of gringo bastards.'

'Have a beer in me you lucky bastard. How about a San Miguel?' someone shouted.

Michael marched out to the street.

CHAPTER TWO

He almost missed the office of Saunders & Shaw, Spanish Property Agents. Looking for a shop window, he was surprised to find only a small plaque directing him to the first floor office above a hardware store in Nottingham's Broadway.

'Please sit down Inspector. How can I help you?' Susan Shaw sounded more excited than concerned about the presence of the detective.

'I won't take up much of your time Mrs. Shaw. There are just a couple of things I'd like to run through and there are other property agents I have to see before next week.'

'Please, call me Susan. I don't know what more I can tell you. I told everything I know to the sergeant last time.'

'I know it's a bit of a pain, but there are just a few questions.'

Susan Shaw flicked her wispy blond fringe back from her eyes, but it returned to the same position. She looked prim and professional in a lime green skirt and jacket. Her cream silk blouse, accentuated by a double row of pearls, accompanied the outfit with style. As she flicked her hair again Michael caught a glint from a ring on her left hand. Three enormous brilliant diamonds stood proud of her finger and dwarfed the plain gold wedding band. A diamond solitaire on the third finger of her right hand confirmed that this was a lady of substance who liked to show it ostentatiously.

'Not at all Inspector. Only too glad to help.'

She flicked her head this time so that her hair fell behind her shoulders and revealed more of her powdered face and the wrinkles on her neck. Her heavy perfume was beginning to irritate. She pushed her chair away from the desk that separated them and crossed her legs. The suit skirt was just a fraction too short and gave a hint of slightly bulky thighs above the hemline. They were carefully covered by sheer, skin-coloured tights. Or were they stockings? Michael's eyes were drawn to the peach-coloured slingbacks that adorned her feet. The elongated toes culminated in vicious points that made her feet appear much longer than they were. Expensive.

Susan licked her lips lightly and offered a hint of a smile as she caught Michael's gaze.

'How do you make your money Mrs Shaw?'

'What?'

She stopped flirting now.

'Well, I know you advertise property for sale in Spain, but you don't seem to have a shop window, just this office. And I can't see any photos or brochures of property for sale. I just wondered how you manage to sell anything and where the money comes from.'

Susan relaxed.

'Ah, I understand your confusion. You're thinking of us like an English estate agent. The Spanish market doesn't work like that. We don't actually have any properties on our books, so to speak.'

Michael let her continue despite his confusion.

'You see, anyone wanting to sell a house in Spain, new or resale, would appoint a Spanish agent. The Spanish agent does the usual stuff, valuations, photographs, brochures, that kind of thing and most have a shop window somewhere. But they rely on other people in the UK, Holland, Germany, wherever. That's where we come in. We advertise extensively – *Sunday Times, Mail on Sunday*, property exhibitions and events. When we get a response we ask people what kind of property they're looking for – size, price, location, etc. Then our man in the Costa Blanca contacts all the local agents and sends us details of properties that might interest our clients. We used to do it all by fax until a few of years ago, now it's all done by email. Sometimes we just download details from web sites and send them on. If the details we send clients are of interest, we arrange for our man to meet them in Spain and show them round. You see, we are really just an intermediary between the client and the Spanish agent.'

'Yes, but how do you make your money?' Michael tried not to look perplexed.

'Ah, yes. Well you see, Spanish agent's fees are much higher than is normal in the UK, sometimes as high as ten percent of the sale price. If we introduce a client and the sale goes ahead, we take a share of the fee. There's plenty to go around, even after we've paid our man over there.'

Michael stood to leave.

'That's very helpful Mrs Shaw. Thank you.'

'Is that all?' Her disappointment was obvious. 'Don't you want to know about the Harringtons? About the properties we offered them?'

'It's all in the file, thanks. Sergeant Rawlinson made extensive notes. I assume I can talk to your man – Brian Small isn't it? – when I get to Spain. I've got his details.'

'Yes, of course. He's an interesting character you know. Lived in Spain for years. Not your typical property salesman, but the clients seem to like him and he knows the Costa Blanca like the back of his hand.'

'I just hope he can shed some light on where the Harringtons are, assuming they're still alive.'

Susan looked serious. 'I hope to God they are. Another murder would be very bad for business.'

'And for the Harringtons, poor devils.' Michael moved toward the door. 'Thanks for your help Mrs Shaw.'

'By the way, are you Spanish or English, Inspector Fernandez?'

'Yes,' Michael replied. 'Good afternoon.'

He was already on his way out.

The Hilltops Estate was as drab and dreary as he remembered from his childhood. Block after block of identical terraced houses lined narrow roads. The town planners of the 1950s had not anticipated the spread of car ownership to the working classes when they designed this particular patch of social housing. Pennine Way, Cotswold Road, Cheviot Avenue, gave a clue to the well-intentioned post-war dreams of Nottingham's city fathers.

It would be easy to get lost in the rabbit warren of culs de sac that were linked to the main roads like tributaries to a river, but

Michael knew the way to Brecon Road. He passed the Harringtons' house on the left and drove by in search of a parking space. With some reluctance, he left his car in a garage forecourt where he'd kicked tin cans as a kid. Always a scruffy backwater, it had deteriorated into a dumping ground. Half the garage doors were missing, the others kicked-in or obliterated by graffiti. An old Ford Escort sat abandoned in the corner, its wheels missing and the hubs perched on four columns of bricks.

He walked back toward number 22, passing four blocks of red brick houses with grey slate roofs. Gone was the uniformity when the colour of a front door was the only distinguishing feature on a house. Standard doors and windows had been replaced by residents anxious to express individuality and display their status as property owners – all thanks to Margaret Thatcher's Right to Buy.

He opened the rickety gate and walked up a weed-lined path. Linda Harrington opened the door before he had a chance to knock.

'Come in Inspector. Thank you for coming.'

'Not at all Mrs Harrington. Sorry to disturb you, but it's important I speak to you and your husband before I go to Spain tomorrow.'

'John, the Inspector's here. We're in the kitchen. Coffee Inspector?'

'Yes – yes, thank you.' Michael was still surprised by Linda Harrington's pixie cut brown hair with an ultra short fringe that accentuated her elfin face. 'That would be nice, thank you,' he answered, noticing the torn and faded jeans stretched tight over her skinny legs. She turned and Michael followed as she sashayed down the hallway, her blue suede ballerina pumps sweeping silently across the brightly patterned carpet.

John Harrington was quite a contrast. He shuffled into the hall in pair of grubby, lace-less trainers worn without socks. A grimy white t-shirt stretched around a prominent paunch that sagged over the waistband of his track-suit bottoms. Michael had never quite fathomed the trend for trainers, or sneakers as the Americans would call them, to be worn with everything. Invariable they were scuffed and dirty within a few weeks of being new and never cleaned until they were disposed of for another pair of the same. You wouldn't go out in a dirty shirt or trousers he often thought, so why go out in a dirty pair of trainers?. Give him a pair of leather shoes and a tin of Kiwi polish any day.

Several photographs of David Harrington were in Michael's file, and in them all, David was tidily dressed, clean-shaven and carefully groomed. John looked an inch or two shorter than the five foot ten inches recorded on David's file, but though David was more slightly built it wasn't hard to see a resemblance in the sleepy eyes, square jaw line and short forehead. However, John's recalcitrant expression and ruffled mop was in complete contrast to David's precise side parting and close-cropped back and sides and his warm, somewhat shy, smile. David was a handsome man.

'Pass us the fags love.' John slumped into the chair opposite Michael at the formica-topped table and ran a hand over the grey stubble on his chin.

Michael leaned back to take the report pad out of his briefcase.
'I don't need to go over everything. The sergeant's put me in the picture, but there are a couple of things I'd like to clear up. According to the file, your brother and his wife left for Spain on 7th January.'

John pulled hard on the cigarette and expelled a cloud of smoke.

'Something like that, can't remember exactly.'

'After looking at properties, they were due back here on the 21st.'

'Not necessarily.'

'Sorry, I don't understand. What do you mean?'

'Well, they were booked for two weeks, right, but that doesn't mean they were coming back.'

'I'm still not sure what you mean Mr Harrington.'

'They booked the hotel for a couple of weeks, but David said something about renting a place after that so they could have longer to look round if they needed it.'

'Why didn't you tell this to the sergeant?'

'He never asked.'

'Mr Harrington, is it possible your brother might want to

disappear?'

'What, like he's robbed a bank or something? You must be joking. You don't know David, do you? Everything carefully planned, everything worked out. Good job, steady wage, bought his house, saved his money, didn't smoke or drink. Then the bugger drops lucky and gets a redundancy payout. Before you know it, he's off to Spain with the painted princess and doesn't give a shit about anyone else.'

'Painted princess?'

'That wife of his, Alison.'

Linda placed a cup and saucer in front of Michael. 'John, whatever you think, it's not like David and Alison not to be in touch, and I'm very worried. As you'll have gathered Inspector, we're not the closest of families, but even so it's over ten weeks since we heard from them. And now we hear another couple was murdered over there only last year.'

Michael sipped his instant coffee and coughed. 'You shouldn't be too alarmed Mrs Harrington. There's probably some logical explanation and they'll turn up before I get to Spain wondering what all the fuss is about.'

'That'll spoil your holiday.' John opened *The Sunday Sport*.

Michael began a sigh, but left it. 'I've got details of properties they were interested in and I'm meeting agents out there. But I've been wondering, where did the money come from? I mean, some of the houses they viewed were over three hundred thousand pounds, and they'd need money to live off.'

He had John's full attention now.

'Three hundred grand? Jesus, I knew they had a bit tucked away and then there was the money from the house, but three hundred grand?'

'Don't get me wrong Mr Harrington, some of the properties were much more modestly priced, but a couple were in that bracket. I'll have a better idea when I get to Spain...You mentioned a redundancy payout?'

'Yes, my brother worked for the Council in the Printing Department. They were getting rid of people and David volunteered to go. Tell you the truth, I was gob-smacked. He'd been there about seventeen years, but they must have made it worth his while to leave.'

'Any idea how much?' Michael knew the answer to that one.

'Like I say. You don't know my brother, the secret squirrel.'

'And you mentioned selling up. What do you mean?'

Linda jumped in as John returned his attention to the back page.

'They lived just round the corner in Mendip Road, overlooking the playing fields. They decided to buy from the Council about ten years ago. Got the place for next to nothing what with the discount and all that. They did it up, put in a new kitchen and built an extension to give them a dining room and an extra bedroom. Sold it last October for almost one hundred and fifty thousand and no mortgage to pay off. Of course, we could have done the same thing, but John wouldn't have it. "Better to rent," he said...'

John slapped the newspaper on the table and stood up to leave the room. 'Don't start all that again.' Seconds later the television roared as someone scored in a football match.

'Sorry about that Inspector – they're like chalk and cheese, David and John, not that close really but John's as worried as me deep down.'

He has a funny way of showing it, Michael thought. 'Tell me about Alison. John seems to have a critical opinion.'

'Bit of jealousy I expect. You see David was a bachelor until he was thirty-five. Never seemed interested in taking a chance on marriage. More of the serious type, set in his own ways. Then he met Alison at the amateur dramatic society and we were all shocked when they announced they were getting married. She's an attractive woman, eight years younger than David; outgoing and she likes to dress – well, let's just say – a bit younger than her age. Mind you she's got the figure for it. Not expensive stuff you understand, couldn't see David paying for that, but fashionable. You know, the sort of stuff the kids wear.'

'Does – did she work?'

'Yes, she had a job in a trendy hairdressers in town, but only part-time for the last couple of years.'

'Did she have any money of her own? Inheritance, anything like that?'

'Not that I know of. Her parents died, I think, some years ago. At least that's what we understood. Put it this way, they weren't at the wedding.'

'Any children?'

'No. That's another sore point with John, especially when our two boys start playing him up and asking him for money.'

'Anyone else they were particularly friendly with?'

'They had a few friends from the dramatic society, but no one they met on a regular basis. I've spoken to people from David's work and from the hairdressers, but no one's heard a thing.'

'Did they contact you regularly when they first left for Spain?'

'Well, they phoned three or four times in the first two weeks while they were in the hotel, but after that there was nothing for a couple of weeks. Then they phoned in early February. I was out at bingo and they spoke to John one Saturday evening. John was watching football and he'd had a few beers. He said David hadn't had much to say, except that they were still looking at properties. I asked if David mentioned where they were staying, but John said they didn't talk about it – or if they had, he didn't remember.'

'What about Alison? Have you talked to her at all since they left?'

'Oh, yes. David would talk to John for a few minutes and then I had a quick word with Alison, but I was aware of the cost and didn't speak for long.'

'Did she say much?'

'Not really. Just that the weather was great and they'd looked at some very nice houses.'

'Did she seem different to you? Excited, anxious, apprehensive, anything like that?'

'No. Just the same old Alison as I recall. It was almost as if they were just on holiday out there again.'

'Again?' Something else not in Sergeant Rawlinson's notes. 'I hadn't realised they'd been before.'

'Yes, they had a holiday in Benidorm last August. They really liked it, though there was no mention of going to live out there at that stage.'

'So when did they first mention the idea?'

'I think it was around September. Yes, that's right, David had been offered the redundancy and that seemed to spark things off. It all happened so quickly. Before we knew it, they'd sold the house and off they went looking for their dream home.'

'So they hadn't talked about Spain before?'

'No. Even going to Benidorm was unusual for them because they'd always gone to France before. David loved it. He's a bit of a wine buff. He liked touring, visiting vineyards, tasting wine, that kind of thing. Though I'm not really sure it was what Alison wanted.'

'Why do you say that?' Michael asked.

'Well, sun, sea and sangria was more Alison's idea of a holiday. You should have heard her when they came back from Benidorm. All tanned and full of the nightlife, restaurants and shows they'd seen.'

'And David?'

'That's the oddest thing of all. I don't think he enjoyed it much. That's why we were so surprised when they went to look at houses out there. We assumed that it was all Alison's idea.'

Michael raised an eyebrow and Linda caught the question.

'Oh, David was the steady one,' she said, picking up her cup. She took a sip of coffee and continued in her slow, slightly husky voice. 'He liked to think he was in control, but Alison ruled the roost. She could twist him round her little finger when she wanted to. I told you, Alison was younger than David and she wasn't always happy just to stay round the house. Dinner at home with a decent bottle of wine was David's idea of a good Saturday night and he liked to cook – he was a marvellous cook. But that wasn't for Alison, unless they had friends over. Music and dancing was more her idea of fun. David went along with it, but every now and then he'd put his foot down. Even so, Alison usually got her way in the end.'

'So you think moving to Spain was Alison's idea?'

'I expect so, but it still seemed strange. You see, Alison would pester and push for her own way and, like I say, it worked most of the time. But not where money was concerned. David always had control of the purse strings. But he must have gone along with the Spanish idea otherwise they wouldn't have gone, would they?'

Michael paused, trying to find a way of framing his next question.

'This is awkward, I know,' he finally began, 'but how were they together? Would you say they were happy?'

Linda ran a hand through her short cropped hair.

'Happy?' she gave a smile. 'Not many of us could say that, but – yes, actually, I think they were. They had different ideas, but they were close, a unit. They discussed everything together. And they seemed very happy about going to live in Spain. I was quite envious and excited for them.'

Michael flicked through the sergeant's notes. 'They moved out of their old home on 20th October, I see. Where did they live after that?'

'They rented a furnished flat in Regents Park where the students stay. Alison enjoyed it, but it was only short term until they could go to Spain.'

'And what did they do with their own furniture?'

'It's in storage with Gleesons. They paid for three months, but that's up now and Gleesons have been on to us to ask what's happening. They want someone to pay for another three months, but John's refused.'

Michael made a note to make sure Gleesons held on to the stuff. There could be something useful in there.

Linda looked up slowly. 'Are you sure nothing's happened to them Inspector?'

'Well, that's what we have to check. That's why I'm going to Spain.'

'But that other couple last year – the couple who were killed?'

'The culprits in that case were apprehended and they've been locked up in jail all this time, so they're not involved at all.'

'Yes, but what if it's a copycat case? You read about that sort of thing all the time. It's horrible. I just can't understand why they haven't phoned.'

Linda's eyes looked moist and she pulled a tissue from the box on the shelf by the table. Michael was tempted to comfort her for a moment, but thought better of it when he heard another roar from the football crowd.

'I really must go,' he said. 'Thank you again for seeing me on a Sunday. We're doing everything we can and so are the Spanish police. I'll know more when I get there tomorrow and the station will keep you posted from this end. Thank you for the coffee – it was very nice.'

CHAPTER THREE

The EasyJet flight from East Midlands Airport on 4th May was forty-five minutes behind schedule, "due to the late arrival of the incoming aircraft."

Michael had opted for a window seat and was hemmed in by an overweight possessor of sleeveless vest, shorts, trainers with black socks, and white legs. Blue and red tattoos ran up and down the man's arms. He had cropped red hair and a heavy gold earring and he was beginning to snore.

The man's wife occupied the aisle seat. She leaned back to tell three kids for the fourth or fifth time to stop kicking. Michael put his head down. He wanted to take off his jacket, but settled for loosening his tie before leaning toward the window and opening the file.

David Harrington, forty-eight years old and his wife, Alison, forty, had flown to Alicante on 7th Jan for a scheduled two-week stay, returning to East Midlands on 21st Jan. They were booked at the Hotel San Marco on Benidorm's Levante beach. The hotel had been suggested, but not paid for, by Susan Shaw as a good base from which to view property in both south and north Costa Blanca. They had an appointment with Brian Small on 9th Jan. and Small had set aside two days to show them round. Susan Shaw had warned that they seemed a little vague about their requirements in terms of both location and price. This was not unusual, especially for people on a first time inspection trip, and Brian was well used to dealing with this. His purpose would be to give a feel for the area and the lifestyle. More importantly, he would build their trust and confidence so that, if they decided to buy at some time in the future, they would do so through Saunders and Shaw.

David Harrington hired a car at Alicante airport, reserved in advance through Aurega and collected on the day they arrived. A cobalt blue Renault Clio, registration number 1004 BYZ. It had never been returned.

Brian Small had kept the appointment and spent the next two days driving the Harringtons around the Costa Blanca from as far south as Torrevieja to Javea and Denia in the north. He had taken them to three new developments with plots for sale, four newly built villas, two apartments and five resale properties. The prices varied from 100,000 to 350,000 euros. Most of the properties were close to the coast, but a couple were inland from Calpe/Moraira in the Jalon Valley. Brian left them at the end of two days. They said they were planning to look around some more properties over the next week or so and would be in touch.

Another British property agent, Spanish Home Sales, had arranged for their contact, Matthew Summers, to meet the Harringtons at their hotel on 14th Jan. He had gone to the Hotel San Marco, but they failed to show up at the appointed time. He had checked with the receptionist, who said they were still staying there, but the concierge thought they had left in their car earlier in the day. Summers had left a message asking them to contact him by telephone, but they had not been in touch.

Inquiries by the Guardia Civil had revealed that the Harringtons had visited a property exhibition on 15th Jan. at the Hotel Perdiz in Benidorm. They'd collected brochures and leaflets from a number of stands but, so far, no one had come forward to say they'd made further contact. There were also a number of possible sightings between 15th Jan. and 6th Feb. at the offices of Spanish property agents spread right along the Costa Blanca. None of these had been verified.

A Dutch couple, Jacob and Helena Gessels, who'd advertised their villa in the Costa Blanca News, had contacted the Guardia to say a couple resembling the Harringtons had viewed their house after telephoning to make an appointment for 23rd January. They'd been shown an old photograph of the Harringtons and confirmed a strong likeness, though they could not be absolutely sure. The couple had given the name Johnson and appeals by the Guardia for them to come forward had drawn a blank. The Gessels' villa was on the outskirts of the village of Alcalalí at the western end of the Jalon Valley, known locally as the Val de Pop. It was on the market for 300,000 euros.

A nodding head of close-cropped ginger bristle came to rest on Michael's shoulder and he nudged it gently inducing it to flop to the other side. He resumed his focus on the file and turned to another section.

David Harrington had worked for Nottingham City Council for the last sixteen and a half years. He had joined them as Production Manager in the printing department, but for the past five years he had been Head of the Department. He was described as quiet and conscientious but reluctant to embrace change. The introduction of digital printing equipment and the outsourcing of much of the routine work had prompted a slimming-down of the workforce in the department and a call for volunteers for redundancy. Everyone was surprised when David came forward because, at forty-eight, he would not qualify for his pension straight away, but would have to wait until he was sixty. His salary was £38,000 a year and his redundancy payout came to £24,330. He had left Nottingham City Council on 30th November without much ceremony.

Inquiries at his bank in Nottingham showed a well managed account, never in the red and with regular withdrawals in the form of cheques made out in favour of the Midland and West Building Society. The Building Society confirmed a gradual accumulation of £16,788 over the past five years. No significant withdrawals until recently. On 21st October the account was boosted by a cheque for £147,541 from solicitors, Warren and Barton, who had handled the sale of the Harringtons' house. There was a further addition of £24,330 on 1st December when the cheque from the council had been paid in. At this point the joint account stood at £188,659, but not for long. On 17th December David Harrington had arranged an international money transfer of 155,000 euros (£129,000) to an account that had been set up in October in his name with the Javea branch of the Banco de Bilbao. A week later he had asked to withdraw a further £55,000 in cash from the building society account. He had collected the money on 5th January, leaving a balance of just under £5,000.

There had been two withdrawals from the Spanish account. The first, on 12th January was for 70,000 euros and the second, on 13th March, was for 75,000 euros, both in cash.

'Anything to drink, sir?' interrupted the flight attendant.

It took Michael a few seconds to gather his thoughts.

'A beer, a vodka tonic, three Cokes for the kids,' said Ginger.

Michael closed the file and put it by his side.

'Just a mineral water, please.'

'Fizzy?'

'Si, con gas.' Michael surprised himself, though not entirely. He'd been mentally practising his Spanish for the past five days. 'Thank you.'

'De nada.' The attendant placed the glass on Michael's tray. She smiled and Michael wondered, too late, whether and how to respond.

'Not on a holiday then?' said Ginger.

'No.'

'Thought not. You don't look like a holidaymaker. And that file isn't exactly light reading, is it?'

Michael grabbed the file and covered it with his hands.

'We're off to Torrevieja for two weeks. My sister's got a place and we come over four times a year. Lovely place, right by the beach, close to the shops and bars, there's even a McDonald's. Prefer a curry myself. Little place in town does a lovely Chicken Madras. Whereabouts you going?'

'Alicante.'

'Nice place. Lots of people I know never go there. They think it's just the airport, see. But I like it. Lots of shops for the missus, nice marina – and there's a beach as well, you know.'

'Yes, I know.'

'Where are you staying?'

'In the centre. It's a business trip. In fact, I've got a quite a few business papers to catch up on – sorry about that.'

'Don't mind me mate.'

Michael did his best to angle his body away from Ginger. He

opened the file, holding it upright to prevent prying eyes and turned the page to read the inventory prepared by Sergeant Rawlinson that morning when he examined items left in storage by the Harringtons at Gleesons Furniture Store.

The list contained a full range of household furniture: three piece suite 'of nice quality artificial leather, almost new', television, video recorder, radio, dining table and chairs 'which could be pine', coffee table, two double beds ('plus complete sets of bedding, one almost new'), kitchen equipment, crockery and cutlery. There was also a collection of garden furniture: plastic table and chairs, a parasol, sun-beds and a gas-fired barbecue. A plastic document folder contained an assortment of papers: bills, bank statements, 'nothing we don't already know about,' which Michael glanced through to confirm: insurance documents, letters about the sale of the house and some personal correspondence relating to David Harrington's redundancy. A 'large but battered' suitcase, the list stated, contained several pairs of ladies' shoes and a few ladies' clothes. There was also a man's heavy winter coat, three jackets, two pairs of trousers and a cardigan. The sergeant had been very thorough, going through the pockets to turn up sixty-seven pence, a credit card slip from a garage in Nottingham, a receipt from Tesco's (also in Nottingham), an out-of-date library card, a crumpled lottery ticket, a business card from Sanders & Shaw, one postage stamp, two ticket stubs from the Odeon in Nottingham, a restaurant bill from La Farola in Derby dated 21st August last year, and a punched railway ticket from Nottingham to Derby, return, dated the same day. It was all routine stuff, and not very revealing, except perhaps for the restaurant bill and train ticket, Michael thought, but it confirmed that the Harringtons had left in storage some papers that people did not leave lying around – bank records; insurance documents; letters... And then there were household items. Surely they must have planned to return at some stage... Otherwise, why not sell the furniture?

Michael turned to another page and then another. It was no use. His concentration had slipped and he was just staring at the pages. Eventually he closed the file again, pushed his head against the back of his seat and shut his eyes, trying (pretending) to sleep, but his thoughts were racing.

Why the rush to get to Spain? Why not find the right place and then sell the house in Nottingham? Why had David Harrington opened a Spanish bank account in October? How had he opened it? Why was it only in his name and not in joint names, like the English building society? Why the cash withdrawals – from the English account, as well as the one in Spain? Where, why, who, when, how...?

A fog of facts, suppositions, possibilities and unanswered questions. And he felt as if his nose was twitching. But something was wrong and it stemmed from the way the Harringtons had just upped and left England. Was this the behaviour of two normally careful and rational people? He wasn't sure, but then, he thought, half-asleep, he had never taken a risk in his life. Never been a dreamer...

Heat from the door of the plane blasted him awake and he was soon herded onto a transit bus with excited tourists. Minutes later the tourists were rushing down a corridor, leaving Michael to amble thoughtfully behind.

In the baggage hall, Ginger and troop were barging to the exit, five pairs of trainers jogging alongside a trolley of cases and bags. Michael pushed his trolley down the ramp to the arrivals hall of Alicante's El Altet airport. He removed his jacket and placed it neatly over the handle of the trolley. His tie still hung loosely round his open-necked shirt.

A sea of faces crammed the other side of the barrier. Excited relatives and friends called out, jumping and waving then hugging and kissing. A more subdued group, mainly men, held up cardboard placards with names written in large heavy letters. Michael scanned the line as he approached looking for "Fernandez."

He pushed his trolley to the end of the line, more self-conscious with every step. As the crowd dispersed, his composure slipped. He was a foreigner, out of place in a strange land. He stretched his arm to bring his watch into view from under the cuff of his long-sleeved shirt.

A voice rang out in Spanish: 'Inspector Fernandez, sorry I'm late. Parking's terrible.' The immensely tall man took control of the trolley. 'I've been circling the car park for ages. I'm Captain Jose Luis Perez. Here, let me help you with your bags. The car's just outside. I gave up in the end and parked on the road, told the traffic cop I'd only be a minute, but I don't trust those bastards.'

Michael grabbed his jacket as he hurried along behind.

'How did you know it was me?'

Jose Luis stopped and looked back to answer Michael, showing himself to be plump-cheeked and friendly-faced. Another group of tourists poured past down the ramp. 'You don't look much like the average tourist.' He nodded toward red and white soccer shirts. 'Manchester flight. Come on, I don't want to get a fine.'

Jose Luis strode ahead and Michael had to jog, almost, to keep up with the dusty, brown leather slip-ons clipping across the marble floor. Probably Italian. Small for such a large man. Though large men did sometimes wear surprisingly small-looking shoes and it did depend upon make and style...

The wide glass doors slid open and they crossed over uneven paving to a silver Seat parked untidily and jutting out into the road. The traffic cop stood in attendance and Jose Luis nodded his thanks. Michael's suitcase was deposited in the boot.

'Wrong side,' said Jose Luis to Michael who was standing at the driver's side door waiting to get in. Michael smiled in embarrassment and switched to the other side. Jose Luis turned the air-conditioning to full blast. An icy draught hit them in the face.

'It is Michael, isn't it?' inquired Jose Luis.

'Why do you ask?'

'Well, the email from England said Michael, but the copy of your passport they sent had Miguel-Ángel as your first name. I just wondered which, or what.'

Michael fiddled with his seat belt strap. 'Michael will do fine.'

'Well, Michael, have you eaten?'

'Not a bite. No food on EasyJet.'

'Me neither, so let's stop somewhere. Then I'll take you to the hotel.'

Driving away from the terminal and out toward the A7 motorway, Michael spotted a blue Ford Mondeo parked behind a green and white Guardia Civil car with blue lights flashing.

The driver of the Ford stood anxiously as the Guardia officer clasped a sheath of papers. Two tourists standing by the car gripped their hand luggage, watching events.

'They never learn,' said Jose Luis. 'Easy pickings.'

'Sorry?'

'You must have seen them in the airport, holding up names, waiting for passengers. Mostly unlicensed taxi drivers charging to take people to their villas or hotels. The Spanish taxi drivers hate them because they undercut the licensed fares. They complain like mad, so every now and again we pick up a few drivers, impound their cars, slap on a fine as a warning to others.'

'How do you catch them?'

'Easy. We have a couple of plain clothes officers in the terminal. They look out for people with name placards and follow them to the car park. Then they radio ahead the registration number and a description of the car and we have someone waiting outside the airport ready to pick them up.'

'But what if they say they're just collecting friends or relatives?'

'Most of them are stupid. They leave the name placard in the car. We search the car and if the placard matches the name of the passengers, we've got them. You wouldn't need a name placard if you were picking up your friends or family, would you?'

'Suppose not, but it doesn't seem like the crime of the century.'

'Of course, it's not. But we have to be seen to respond to legitimate complaints, even if they're not top priority. It's a game, but don't tell me it's different in the UK.'

'I know what you mean.'

Jose Luis collected the ticket from the toll machine and they joined the A7 heading north for the city of Alicante. By now the car was icy cold and he turned down the fan. They'd been driving barely five minutes when Jose Luis pulled into the service area at Campello and parked.

'It's not brilliant, but we can get coffee and a snack.'

Michael sat at a square plastic-topped table with hard seats and Jose Luis returned with two tiny cups of café solo and a couple of bocadillos containing cheese and dry-cured ham. The place was almost empty, the nearest customers several tables away. Jose Luis clenched the bocadillo between his teeth and tugged until a chunk broke away, scattering crumbs all over the table. Michael tried to be more refined, grinding his teeth to sever the crunchy bread and chewy ham, but was forced to tug the bread until it broke away, leaving a slice of jamon serrano dangling from his mouth. He pushed it in and continued to chew, but the dry bread seemed to go round and round in his mouth until he was forced to slosh it down with coffee to get rid of it. He left the rest on the plate.

Jose Luis had finished his sandwich. He lit a cigarette.

Michael glanced round, looking for a NO SMOKING sign. There was none. An awkward silence fell. Jose Luis made the first move.

'Your Spanish is excellent. Where did you learn it?'

'My father was Spanish.'

'Really? Where was he from?'

'He... I'd better explain. I'm British and I'm only here because I speak Spanish and I'm a bit uncomfortable about it because I don't know Spain at all. This is my first visit. But I've got a job to do, the quicker the better, and then I have to return home at once. I'm afraid that's all I'm able to say.'

Jose Luis bristled.

'Well, let me tell you something. I never asked for help on this case. If two stupid English people come to Spain and get lost, that's their problem. But the powers-that-be are worried about the effect on tourism and, from what I gather, your bosses are keen to avoid criticism if it all goes wrong. So we're stuck with each other. Like you say, sooner it's sorted the better and we can both get back to the real work... Anyway, come on, we'd better check you into your hotel. Busy day tomorrow.'

The Seat rejoined the A7, approaching the outskirts of Alicante. Michael became uneasy with the tension. He wished he'd not been so abrupt. He spotted a road sign with the word "Alicante" crudely painted out in black aerosol and replaced with "Alacant".

'I see that some people still want to stick with Valenciano?'

Jose Luis responded quickly, as if relieved the silence was broken.

'Yes, Valenciano is the first language of many in this region, especially in the more remote parts. Everyone speaks Castilian, of course, but a few are sensitive about losing their identity, so they demand road signs are in both languages. If only Castilian is used for the signs they get changed in black spray paint. Looks a mess, but to some people it's important.'

'Do you speak Valenciano?'

'I can, but I don't unless I need to.'

Jose Luis was suddenly distracted as the steering wheel began to judder violently and the car swerved toward the metal barrier separating the two carriageways. He braked gently and wrestled with the steering wheel until he had the car under control. Michael was clasping the dashboard in front of him but looking behind at the same time.

'It's all clear on the inside, you can move over.'

The car came slowly to a halt on the hard shoulder, accompanied by the sound of metal on tarmac. Jose Luis switched the engine off and released his seat belt, glancing in the rear view mirror.

'Are you all right?' he asked.

Michael tried to look calm.

'Fine, thanks. You did well to get us here in one piece.'

Jose Luis was still looking in the rear view mirror, watching a dark blue Toyota pull up behind them.

'Open the glove box will you?'

Michael did as he was told.

'Pass me the pistol.'

Michael hesitated for a second then gripped the black leather holster and passed it to Jose Luis. It was heavier than he had expected. His eyes widened as Jose Luis removed the pistol from its sheath, leant forward and stuffed the barrel down the back of his trousers. Only the grip was protruding above his belt as he turned toward Michael.

'In a moment I want you to get out of the car and walk round the front to look at the off side wheel. I will do the same. Try to look as if you're rattled. Okay?'

'Okay.'

'Right, let's do it.'

Jose Luis slid awkwardly from the driver's door, careful not to expose his back to the two men approaching from the parked Toyota. Michael stood by the wheel, examining the shredded tyre and puffing his cheeks. One of the advancing strangers called out in heavily accented Spanish.

'That was a close thing. We saw the blow-out. You did well to keep it under control. Need any help? Where's the spare? In the boot?'

Jose Luis approached the back of the Seat and Michael followed, trying not to glance at the pistol.

'Er, yes, thanks for stopping.'

Michael was still bemused. He looked at the two men. Both were dark skinned; not black, but more than just sun-tanned. They were smartly dressed in tailored trousers and open necked shirts; one a patterned blue, the other dazzling white. They both wore reflective dark glasses and had similar mops of almost jet-black hair. Then he noticed the shoes. Cheap, rubber soled, heavy, dusty and badly scuffed. His intuition was just kicking in when he saw the knives, pulled in unison from behind their backs. He was just a fraction too late in realising what was going on and felt the cold touch of steel pressed against his throat as the white-shirted attacker slipped behind him. Jose Luis was much more aware and had stepped back. Even so he was staring down the long blade of a kitchen knife being waved just in front of his face.

'Give us your money and the keys,' said blue shirt.

'Okay, take it easy,' replied Jose Luis. 'We don't want any trouble.'

He reached behind his back as if going for his wallet, then swiftly brought his right hand back and clamped it with his left, holding the pistol firm and pointing it straight in the face of blue shirt. 'Police!' he shouted, 'Now drop the knives.'

White shirt was temporarily distracted. Michael slammed his right elbow into the man's rib cage with all the force he could muster and grabbed the knife hand, pulling it away from his neck. His assailant doubled-up in pain as Michael took the man's arm with both his hands and cracked it over his knee. The knife fell to the ground and Michael followed up his move by ramming the man's arm up between his shoulder blades and pushing his face to the tarmac.

'Here, put these on,' called Jose Luis. He tossed Michael a pair of handcuffs removed from his side pocket. He was still in a stand-off with blue shirt who'd viewed his compatriot's fall from the corner of his eyes.

'Now give me the knife,' demanded Jose Luis.

Blue shirt seemed frozen to the spot for a moment then raised his arm and threw the knife toward Jose Luis who jerked to his left to avoid it. The man turned tail and started running toward the Toyota as Jose Luis recovered his balance and raised the pistol.

'Stop or I shoot!'

'Don't shoot,' cried Michael, already in stride and gaining on the fleeing attacker.

Suddenly a shot rang out and blue shirt seemed to falter and buckle at the knees, losing his momentum for a second. Michael lunged forward and clasped the runner around the thighs with both arms before slipping his grip to the man's knees and bringing him crashing to the ground with an agonising yell as his elbow smashed into the tarmac. Before he could recover, blue shirt found his head pressed against the road with the barrel of the Jose Luis' pistol shoved in his ear.

Michael released his grip and dusted himself down. There was a tear in the knee of his trousers and the toe-caps of his black shoes were deeply scoured where they'd dragged across the rough tarmac. He looked at Jose Luis, now pulling blue shirt to his feet, gun jammed against his neck.

'Jesus! What the hell were you shooting at? You scared the shit out of me,' said Michael.

'I fired in the air, but it worked, didn't it?'

'I would have got him anyway.'

'So you say.'

A squad car and two sergeants arrived to take the villains into custody and the two detectives returned to the Seat to change the wheel.

'Sorry Michael, but we'll have to make a detour to the barracks to file a report. They'll need a statement from you as well.'

'Barracks?'

'Sorry, of course you wouldn't understand. I mean the central police headquarters. We're likely to be there some time, you know, paperwork. I'll take you to your hotel later on.'

'Oh, I know all about paperwork.'

'That was pretty impressive back there, the way you brought him down,' said Jose Luis.

'I played scrum half for Notts Police until last year.'

'Scrum half?'

'You know, rugby union.'

'What's rugby union?'

'Never mind.'

'The Colonel will be delighted. We'll be heroes. We've been after those two for ages. They've turned over at least twenty cars in the last six months with four woundings. Always the same scam. They look out for cars pulling into a service station and watch the drivers go inside. Then they stick a knife in the tyre and follow until you pull over. Usually they pick on tourists, but this time they made a big mistake. This will do our promotion prospects no harm at all. Oh, sorry, I mean my promotion prospects. Even so, I'm sure your bosses in England will hear all about it.'

'What would you have done if I hadn't brought him down?'

'Shot him, of course.'

'In the back?'

'I didn't say that.'

'Can I claim for a new pair of trousers?'

'What?'

By the time they'd finished at HQ and reached the Hotel Ramis on

Alicante's sea front, it was past midnight.

Jose Luis lifted the suitcase from the boot of the Seat and set it at the side of the road.

'You don't mind if I don't come in, do you? Only I need to get home. I'm already in trouble with my wife for too many late nights and I hardly saw the children last week. You've got the file, so if anything occurs to you give me a ring in the morning, otherwise I'll see you on Wednesday.'

'Wednesday?'

'Oh, didn't I mention it? I've arranged for you to see Brian Small tomorrow morning. He's set the day aside to show you around. I suggest going to the places he showed to the Harringtons, but it's up to you.'

'How will I know him?'

'You can't miss Brian Small. Anyway, he'll see you in the bar at ten-thirty. By the way, thanks again for today. I mean it; I couldn't have done it without you. See you on Wednesday. I'll pick you up here. Ten o'clock.'

Michael looked for a porter, but there was no one about so he carried the suitcase through the automatic doors and dropped it in front of reception. He looked around the dimly lit lobby hoping to see some movement, but there was no one around. Everything was neat and tidy with armchairs arranged symmetrically around polished coffee tables. He could see the bar at the far end of the lobby, though it was in darkness. The reception desk was illuminated by a row of chromium spotlights set into the ceiling. There was no one behind the desk, so he thumped the bell and waited. He was about to ring again when a light flickered in the back office and he heard the creaking of bed springs followed by a shuffling sound. The night porter brushed down his crumpled shirt and rubbed his eyes as he emerged behind the desk.

'Fernandez. You have a reservation for me.'

'Ah, Señor Fernandez, we were expecting you this afternoon.'

Michael took his passport from his jacket as the night porter ran his finger down a computer printout. 'Here we are. Room 711.' He scanned the pigeonholes. 'You'll have to carry your own bag I'm afraid. I can't leave the desk. The elevator is in the corner.' He picked up Michael's passport and peered. 'But this is a British passport.'

'So!'

'Your Spanish is excellent.'

Michael didn't bother to say thank you as he carried his bag wearily toward the lift. The night porter didn't bother to say good night.

CHAPTER FOUR

The bar was empty next morning and Michael seated himself on one of a long row of stools to wait for Brian Small.

He'd breakfasted early and to contend with the heat he'd opted for a short-sleeved shirt and light weight trousers. Now, just as he was thinking he was ready for work and it was late, a man appeared at the entrance to the bar. Short, slim, bald, tanned – in pink polo shirt, green checked trousers, and white slip-on shoes that matched his belt. A heavy gold bracelet hung from his wrist, held up as he spoke into a mobile phone.

Michael walked over. 'Brian Small?'

'Sorry, mate,' the man said. He flipped the phone shut. 'John Evans.'

'Oh, my mistake. I'm expecting a property agent, Brian Small.'

'I know him well, but you obviously don't or you'd never have made the mistake. As it happens, we're both in the same business.' Evans glanced toward reception. 'Ah, here's my punters. Look, here's my card, if Brian can't help you, give me a call. Bye.'

Michael returned to the barstool and finished his café solo. He was about to look at his watch again when he heard a voice.

'Inspector Fernandez?'

'Yes.'

'Brian Small.'

They shook hands.

Looking to be in his fifties, Brian had thinning hair, whisked to one side. His checked shirt and beige corduroy trousers would not have been out of place at an English county show and the knitted cardigan with chunky leather buttons looked as odd in this setting as the two pairs of spectacles dangling from cords round Brian's neck. His light brown suede desert boots appeared incongruous with the rest of the outfit. The jumble of styles was baffling. Michael's impulse was to play it safe and distrust the man.

'Anything wrong?' said Brian. He sat down and ordered coffee.

'No – it's just... meeting a stranger. I'm never sure who to expect.'

'Neither am I. Your English is excellent.'

'Thank you. How's your Spanish?'

'Oh, I get by... To tell the truth, I didn't know whether to expect an English-speaking Spaniard, or a Spanish-speaking Englishman.'

'Definitely the latter – though now I'm in Spain, I'm not so sure.'

'So, Inspector, where do you want to start?'

'Please – call me Michael.'

'I'm Brian.' He sugared his coffee. 'Be Small, be a property agent.'

'I wouldn't have said you look like a typical property agent.'

Brian smiled. 'You're not the first to say that and pretty soon you'll be right. I retire next year. I've never really liked the property business.'

'Money, you mean?'

'Lord no.' He took a long sip. 'I could make money anywhere. The property business just means I can live my life in Spain. I love it here.'

'Well, many would agree with you, of course.'

'Right. Am I a suspect?' Brian asked.

After the confusion of the man's appearance, Michael wasn't going to let him off the hook too easily. 'I suppose so, since you were one of the last to see the Harringtons, but I'm not planning to arrest you just yet.'

'How do you want to play this?' Brian drained his coffee. 'I've made a complete list of the properties I showed the Harringtons and I can take you to each one if you want.'

'That would be fine – and I'd like to understand a bit more about the property market out here and how it works. I'd also like to know about the Harringtons. How they struck you. We'll have to use your car I'm afraid. The Guardia Civil haven't provided me with transport.'

'All part of the service,' Brian said. 'We've a lot of ground to cover. I suggest we start in Torrevieja, about half an hour south of here and then we can head north to somewhere a little more exclusive.'

'What do you mean?'

'You'll see.'

They were soon heading south in Brian's green, four-wheel-drive Renault Scenic with 'Saunders and Shaw' painted on the sides.

Just a few wispy clouds speckled the vivid blue sky. After the urban sprawl of Alicante, the countryside flanking the motorway was arid and dusty. Great hollows seemed to have been gouged out of the rock where stone had been extracted to fuel the construction boom. The few surviving trees were taking on the shape of skeletons as they shrivelled in the water-starved landscape.

Emerging from a short tunnel, they cruised round a long gentle curve and the skyline suddenly changed. A forest of building cranes rose from a sea of pastel coloured properties stretching as far as the eye could see.

'Welcome to Torrevieja,' Brian said.

'Jesus, it's monstrous.' Michael had seen urbanisations along the coast, but nothing on this scale.

'That's exactly what it is. From tiny fishing port to one of the biggest development sites in Europe in just fifteen years. Population in excess of fifty thousand. Takes some getting used to, doesn't it?'

'You can say that again.'

They left the motorway and swung down toward the outskirts of the town, passing a McDonald's and a Lidl superstore. A dual carriageway took them closer to the coast, flanked by new car showrooms selling every make and model from Mercedes to Mitsubishi.

'I'll pull off and show you the place I viewed with the Harringtons,' said Brian. 'It's just along here, about ten minutes from the sea front.'

A huge hoarding marked the entrance to Vista Verde development, the giant letters surrounded by pictures of beaches, boats, parasols, surfboards, sandcastles and sun. At first they drove along tarmac roads, piles of rubble alongside. Then they turned left and Brian pulled up alongside a quadrangle of three-storey linked houses, newly painted white with terracotta roof tiles. They were separated from an identical block by just forty metres of newly planted gardens. A Pickford's International removal van was parked by the entrance to one of the ground floor apartments and two men were humping a settee through the doorway.

Brian climbed out of the car. 'This is phase three. I showed the Harringtons round phase two, but that's sold now. They're all pretty much the same. Wait a moment, I need to see the site agent and get the keys.'

Michael sat in the car, still cool from the air conditioning. He'd pictured the dream life in Spain to be a pretty villa with carefully tended gardens and a view of the sea. Instead, he was reminded of Hilltops Estate as it gradually emerged from the green fields on the edge of Nottingham in the late 1960s. The only difference was the sun.

Brian was returning from the office, rumbling along with a slight limp.

'Okay, I've got the keys, let's take a look.'

Michael followed Brian through the entrance to a quadrangle alongside an unfinished swimming pool and then up the stairs to the top floor apartment.

'This show unit is roughly the same condominium I showed the Harringtons, only theirs was on the north side. More sun, but hot in summer. You pays your money and you makes your choice.'

'And what sort of money are we talking about?'

'They start at 150,000 euros for two bedrooms, one bathroom, fitted kitchen, balcony, air conditioning and central heating.'

'Central heating?'

'Yes, of course. It gets cold here in winter.'

'And what did the Harringtons think of it?'

'Difficult to say at that stage. They looked round the place, but were non-committal. I guess they knew they had more to look at. Seen enough? Want to buy the place?'

'Yes, and no thanks. Where to next?'

'Lets head back north and I'll show you some more inspiring properties.'

On the A7 again, they skirted Alicante before seeing the towers of Benidorm's high rise hotels with the Hotel Bali dominating the skyline. At a glance, it looked like Manhattan.

'Are we going there?' Michael asked.

'Can if you want to, but I didn't go there with the Harringtons, except to pick them up from their hotel. Would you like to look round?'

'Some other time, perhaps. What's it like?'

'Benidorm? Ask the thousands who come back year after year. It's really two resorts in one. In winter it's like the Costa Geriatrica. The grey pound goes a long way and some people come for months on end to escape the British winter. Cheap food and drink, tea dances every afternoon and plenty of day trips. Around Easter it changes. The families arrive, beaches are crammed, the pubs are packed and so are the burger bars. But this is not Ibiza or Ajia Napa – it's basically a bucket and spade holiday for the kids and the beaches are wonderful for that.'

'Where to next?'

'Moraira first, then Javea. The house in Moraira is still on the market so we can look around. I phoned the agent and he'll meet us there. Do me a favour though. When we get there, act as if you're a potential buyer. You know, act interested, ask a few questions. He's a busy man and I don't think he'd take kindly to being dragged out solely for the benefit of the police.'

'Well ...' This sounded like the ridiculous role-play sessions on the equal opportunity training courses. 'I'll do my best, but you'd better give me some help. For a start, how much are we talking about, for this place?'

'It's on the market for three hundred and twenty-five thousand euros, but we could probably shave a bit off that if you were interested.'

'How much?'

'Property on the coast is always more expensive and Moraira is a very popular area. The place has boomed in recent years, but it's all done very tastefully. There's a new marina and promenade, posh restaurants, walk ways and lots of chic little shops. I'm sure you'll like it.'

'Not at that price.'

A series of small signs appeared at the side of the road: Partida A, No's 1 to 57, Partida B, No's 58 to 103. They had just reached Partida E when Brian turned off the road.

'Here we are. It's number 237, right at the top. Spectacular views.'

They climbed in a series of zigzags, passing gate after gate on both sides of the road until they reached the summit of the estate.

'Ah,' Brian said. 'Vinnie's here already. Now remember what I said.'

'I'll try. But do me a favour and don't drop in any Spanish when you speak to me. I should be totally English don't you think?'

'Totally English it is.'

Vincent Roberts was leaning against the bonnet of a blue Mercedes Cabriolet; its roof dropped down to expose cream leather upholstery and burr walnut dashboard. Approaching, Michael began to weigh him up. Everything about him was casual but expensive: tailored blue shorts, Calvin Klein T-shirt, heavy gold necklace and a Rolex watch that Michael doubted was fake, until he spotted the rubber flip-flops.

Vinnie pushed himself away from the Mercedes and walked toward them.

'Hi, Bri. Still rustling up the punters?' He spoke in a broad northern accent. Probably Lancashire, Michael thought.

'Thought you'd have retired by now with all the fees I've given you over the years.'

'Unfortunately, you're the one making all the money by the looks.' Brian nodded toward the Mercedes.

'Who've we got this time?' asked Vinnie.

'This is Michael Fernandez.'

'Fernandez?' queried Vinnie. 'English or Spanish?'

'English,' Michael said brusquely.

'I hope you're not wasting my time like the last lot Brian showed round. Funny couple, hardly said a word. I usually get a sense of what people want, but not those two. Ever hear anything of them, Brian?'

'Not a thing.'

Vinnie led the way into the villa and rushed from room to room as if he was in a hurry or had done this too many times and was fed up with having to explain things to half-witted punters.

'Built about six years ago. Just a holiday home, hardly been used. Nice kitchen, three bedrooms, two bathrooms, big naya. Air conditioning in the bedrooms. That's all you need, really. No central heating, but then you don't need it out here.'

Vinnie pushed open the double doors leading to the terrace and pool. 'Here's the best bit. Just look at that view, one of the best in Moraira. This is the thing I like.'

Vinnie walked across the terrace and around the pool He inserted a key in a small box on the side-wall and pressed a button. A wide roller shutter rose to reveal a large bar with a row of optics on the back wall. A shiny chrome beer pump was clamped to the ledge, a steel barrel underneath. Michael noticed the stacking hi-fi system resting on a shelf in the corner wired to two large speakers at each end of the bar.

'What do you think, Michael? Impressive isn't it.'

Michael was looking down from the far side of the terrace to see the neighbouring house about ten metres below. The villas on either side were separated by just a low, open-block wall and a few climbing plants.

Brian nudged him.

'Oh – yes, very impressive...'

'So what are you looking for, Michael? A holiday home or are you thinking of joining the exodus from the UK?'

'Well, just a holiday home right now. To start with. I mean, I may spend more time here later on.'

'You'd love it. Thousands of expats live here already – English, German, Dutch, some from France and Belgium. The weather's great, cost of living's cheap and let's face it, Britain's going to the dogs. So, what do you think?'

'Brian said it was three hundred and twenty-five thousand euros.'

'That's right. A snip at that. Prices have rocketed in the last couple of years. I'm telling you, you won't get a better bargain anywhere on the Costa Blanca.'

'Is the price negotiable at all?' Michael asked.

'Just leave that to Brian and me. We won't quibble over a few hundred euros. So you're interested, are you? The place is empty. You could be swimming in the pool in less than a month. What do you say?'

'I'd like to think about it.'

'That's what they all say. I'm telling you, it's a bargain. Don't think too long or it will be snapped up. I've lost count of the number of punters who dither then come back too late when their dream home has already been sold. Ain't that a fact Brian?'

Brian had wandered into the garden with his hands behind his back.

Vinnie continued the patter.

'Cash is it, or do you need a loan? I can fix you up with a mortgage if you want. Interest rates have never been lower.'

This was a charade and Vinnie was beginning to irritate.

'Did you ever see the Harringtons again Mr. Roberts?'

Vinnie was knocked off his stride.

He stuttered, 'No. I mean, what the fuck's going on here? Brian, who the hell is this?'

Roused from his reflections, Brian came rushing round the pool.

'Sorry, Vinnie,' Brian said. 'I – ah, just happened to mention to the Inspector...'

'Inspector? Who the fuck is this Brian?'

'Sorry Brian, but this is a waste of time. Mr. Roberts, my name is Michael Fernandez as Brian told you. I'm a British CID officer working with the Guardia Civil in the search for David and Alison Harrington. Now, did you see them again after Brian brought them to see this place?'

'Don't know who you're talking about.'

'Then why did you say "no" the first time I asked?'

'Look, everyone knows about the Harringtons. It's been splashed all over the Costa Blanca News. They've even got their own reporters on the case after that couple were murdered last year. It's a bloody nuisance. People are saying it's not safe to come here any more. It's ruining business. Look, are you accusing me or something?'

'I'm just trying piece together their last movements and the people they met. I assume you have already contacted the Guardia?'

'No. Look, I only saw them for a couple of minutes. Brian's the one you should be talking to. I've had enough of this. I'm off. Brian, you bastard, don't bring any more punters to me. You're finished.'

Vinnie was striding toward the road as Michael called out, 'The Guardia may want to talk to you, Mr Roberts.'

The engine of the Mercedes was already revving.

'They can piss off,' yelled Vinnie as the car screeched away.

Michael turned to Brian. 'I'm sorry about that Brian, but I needed to ask the questions. I've put you in a bit of a spot.'

'Don't worry about it Michael. He's an arsehole.'

'Couldn't have put it better.'

'Do you really suspect him?'

'Can't say as yet, but he seems a bit of a shady character. It wouldn't do any harm for the Guardia to have a little chat.'

'He'll love that.'

'My thoughts exactly. Where to next?'

'Javea, that is Xabia in Valenciano. It's just along the coast heading north, but shall we stop for coffee first?'

'Sounds good to me.'

They parked on the outskirts of Moraira and walked along the seafront promenade, Brian leading the way to a restaurant overlooking the sea.

'Sun or shade?' he asked.

'Shade please, if that's all right with you.'

They sat at a small table under a large green and white parasol.

Michael got back to business.

'What did you make of the Harringtons?'

'Hard to say really. At the time they were just two more potential clients and you meet all sorts in this game. I've stopped being surprised by anyone, but there was one thing.'

'Yes?'

'I only thought about it afterwards, but I never really got a feel for their budget.'

'What do you mean?'

'Well, normally I like to find out at an early stage what sort of money people are looking to spend. It's not that I'm nosy, but it saves a lot of time if I know they have an absolute limit. Sometimes I have to talk them up a bit. You'd be surprised how many people still come here expecting a nice villa for a hundred grand, but those days are long gone, at least in this part of Spain. So I talk them up to a realistic price level for the type of property they are looking for and then tell them how cheap it is to live here. If they are only looking for a holiday home I tell them how much they could expect to make from letting it out, if that's what they want to do.'

'And the Harringtons?'

'That's what I mean. I pushed them, gently of course – that's usually enough – but they never gave anything away. Even when I showed them some of the more expensive properties, they never seemed to be put off.'

'And yet they started in Torrevieja?'

'Not that surprising. They seemed to know a bit about the place as if they'd been before. Perhaps it was just a starting point. You know, to see – well, let's just say – the cheaper end of the spectrum. But they definitely gave me the impression that they were looking for something a little more – shall we say – exclusive.'

'What made you think so? You said they didn't discuss their budget.'

'Just that they didn't linger for very long at the condominium in Torrevieja, but showed much more interest in some of the other places I took them to. As you will see later on there's a vast difference.'

'What did you make of them as a couple?'

'They seemed nice enough, but they were very quiet. I never got to know them really, which again is quite unusual. I get to know something about most of the people I show round. Not that I pry, but it's inevitable when you spend two or three days with someone, in the car, over meals, they often open up. You'd be amazed at what some people are willing to tell me. I've had complete life histories and witnessed several blazing rows. But the Harringtons were different. They asked all the normal questions about prices, the cost of living, the process of buying a house, that kind of stuff. But they never opened up about themselves; never mentioned family or friends. It didn't bother me at the time. I just thought they were very private people and that's their privilege, of course.'

'Tell me about buying a house. How does it work?'

'You might be better speaking to an asesoria, a lawyer, but basically an informal contract is drawn up by the asesoria and the buyer pays a deposit – usually ten percent of the purchase price, but it's negotiable. Before completing you need a Numero de Identificación de Extranjeros – NIE. It's a simple process; you just fill in a form with a few personal details and provide a copy of your passport. The form is taken to the local police station and stamped and then you are issued with an NIE number.'

'Do you need a bank account in Spain?' Michael asked.

'You don't need one, but most people set one up. The asesoria will normally take care of this. All that's needed is your NIE number and, again, a copy of your passport.'

'I see. What next?'

'The asesoria carries out a legal search on the property, mainly to establish the property is free from debt. It's important, because in Spain any debt is passed on to the new owners.

'Then an appointment is made with the Notario and everyone meets on the appointed day. The rest of the purchase price is handed over and other things are sorted, like bills and local taxes.

'The Notario signs the escritura (deeds) and the place is yours. You get a copy of the escritura there and then and the original goes off to the Central Registry in Madrid. You get it back some weeks or months later when your ownership has been officially registered. It's a bit more complicated if you're buying a plot of land to have a house built because there are stage payments to make, but that's about it.'

'So how long does it take?' Michael asked.

'It varies. Sometimes the sellers want a long completion period, especially if they're looking to buy another house, but it can all be done in less than a month if everyone is happy.'

'And what does it cost?'

'You sound as if you're interested.'

'Just humour me.'

'Well, let's see. The asesoria's fee, Notario's fee, bits and pieces for paperwork. Let's say, a thousand euros. Then there's the purchase tax, seven percent of the declared value of the property. The buyer has to pay this.'

'You said "declared value"?'

'Ah, yes. It's quite common for the value to be under-declared on the escritura. It saves the buyer a slice of the purchase tax and sometimes the seller wants to avoid capital gains tax.'

'Is that legal?'

'Strictly speaking no, but everyone knows it happens. The declared value is usually paid by cheque in front of the Notario and the rest is handed over in cash – it's called "black money".'

'Doesn't the Notario check?'

Brian smiled. 'Lord no. You really don't know much about Spain, do you?'

'And what about your fee?'

'You mean the fee for Saunders and Shaw, don't you?'

'Whatever.'

'That comes later. We claim our share from the seller's agent when everything is done and dusted. It can take weeks, sometimes months, depending on the agent.'

'And what does it amount to?'

'That would be telling. It can vary, but it's usually a percentage of the sale price.'

'Is that the actual sale price or the declared value?'

'What do you think? Come on, time we were moving. We've

still got a lot of ground to cover. We may not finish today at this rate.'

They haggled over the bill though it was just a few euros. Brian won when he said that Saunders and Shaw would reimburse him for expenses.

'And now for something completely different. Let's skip Javea; it's pretty much the same as Moraira. We're off to the mountains where the best people live.'

'How so?'

Brian grinned. 'That's where I live.'

They joined the N332, the old coast road, and headed south again through Gata de Gorgos to Benissa.

Brian explained this wasn't the quickest route to the mountains, but he wanted Michael to get his bearings by viewing the area from the top of the slopes. A moment later a giant builders' yard appeared on the right. Stacks of concrete blocks, gravel and bricks sat shrouded in a cloud of dust. Fork-lifts buzzed around, feeding a fleet of lorries. A modern red brick and glass office building looked out of place, as did the cars – BMWs, Jaguars and a Porsche – in the executive car park. A cement wagon lurched round the corner in front of the Renault almost forcing Brian into the ditch.

A few minutes later they arrived at the tiny village of Lliber and were halted by traffic lights.

'Could be a long wait,' Brian said.

'Why's that?'

'Most of these villages have main streets just wide enough for two donkeys to pass carrying panniers. They're gradually building by-passes, but not here. So there's a single track road through the village with traffic lights at each end. We'll have to wait a while.'

After what seemed like and age, five cars came through from the other end of the village. The traffic lights changed to green, but Brian was prevented from moving off by a delivery truck rumbling toward him. When it had passed, the lights turned red again and the driver of a blue BMW behind Brian sounded the horn. Brian jumped the lights, followed by four more cars.

'Bloody Germans – sorry, BMWs,' he said, 'always in such a

hurry. We'll have to gun it, otherwise we'll meet the next lot coming through.'

Halfway through the run, the road widened at the side of a tiny square and this created a dogleg in the route. Brian slowed, but the BMW returned to his horn so Brian pressed on. He'd just cleared the bend when a frozen food van tore up from the opposite direction, followed by three cars. The van driver joined the horn thumping, and gestured that Brian must reverse along with the BMW and two more cars behind that. Ten minutes later, chaos resolved, they escaped into open countryside.

'What a palaver,' Michael said. 'It's a wonder anything gets done.'

'Well,' said Brian. 'This is quite normal in Spain. It works perfectly if you're Spanish or if you like it here. And there's always mañana.'

'Wouldn't be allowed in England by the traffic engineers.'

'Precisely! Anyway, here we are. Welcome to the Jalon Valley.'

A vast tract of flat land lay in vine-planted plots, criss-crossed by meandering tracks. A few tiny buildings pepper-potted the landscape which otherwise was a sea of uniform green. The bed of the valley was about two kilometres wide and flanked by jagged mountains which tapered to a point in the far distance.

'Jalon ahead, Xaló in Valenciano,' said Brian. 'See the blue domed church? And beyond that Alcalalí and then Parcent. Look, you can just about see the village on the hill with the church spire sticking up.'

Michael stared straight ahead. His heart skipped a beat.

'Sorry Brian. I have to get back.'

'But you haven't seen the houses I showed to the Harringtons. There's a new development in Jalon and a resale villa just outside Alcalalí – and a very pretty town house in Parcent. We've got plenty of time.'

'Not today though – sorry about this. Take me back will you?'

'You're the boss.'

Brian reversed the car and returned through Lliber, this time without incident. Michael broke the silence.

'You said you live in the mountains?'

'Yes, in a tiny settlement – Castell de Castells.'

'You didn't mention it. I mean, when we were looking up the valley.'

'No. We couldn't see it from there. It really is in the mountains, right at the top of the valley. Real Spain.'

'How long have you lived there?'

'Oh, about eighteen years.'

'You obviously like it.'

'Wouldn't want to be anywhere else in the world.'

Brian glanced over at Michael, took a deep breath and said casually, 'Tell you what, it's a bit early, but how about stopping for a bite to eat. Do you like fish?'

Before he could think of an excuse, Michael had said, 'Yes'.

They left the N332 at Calpe and dropped to the coast. Calpe was a bustling town dominated by high rise buildings, but even they were overshadowed by a gigantic rock, the Peñon d'Ifach, jutting above and far out into the sea.

After rounding a lake where pink flamingos waded at the water's edge, they entered the old town and parked by a fish market. They crossed the street and approached a row of restaurants each fronted by open air displays of fresh fish on platters. A glass of sangria was thrust in Michael's hand by a waiter.

'Give it back,' Brian said. 'He's trying to get you to sit down.'

They moved on.

'What's your poisson?' Brian grinned. 'Sorry, I mean your pescado.'

Michael followed Brian to the penultimate restaurant in the row. They took their seats on a sunlit terrace and Michael agreed with the suggestion that they order a platter of fish and shellfish for two.

'How's the sangria?' Brian asked, after they'd been served.

Michael took a sip. 'Seems all right.'

'They usually water it down.'

'I've never tasted it before.'

'You're joking!'

'No. Never been to Spain. Never tasted sangria.' *Best to*

anticipate the questions. 'My father was Spanish, but he left here before I was born. He never wanted to return and I never felt the need to come. I'm only here now because I'm on this missing persons case.'

Brian took a sip of his sangria and screwed his face. 'Your father taught you Spanish?'

'Taught, no. It was our first language at home when I was young.'

They looked about in silence for a moment until Michael glanced behind to see a waiter carrying a platter toward their table.

'That was quick. It looks good.'

'Smells good, too.' Brian lifted some griddled sardines onto his plate along with a fillet of sea bass, a wedge of swordfish, a heap of giant prawns and a few mussels before passing the platter to Michael and helping himself to salad and a chunk of bread. 'Don't be shy, take plenty,' he said.

Noticing Brian's overflowing plate, Michael took more modest portions that left the platter still half full.

'Alioli?' Brian said, pushing a brightly coloured bowl in Michael's direction. 'You do know what alioli is?' Brian enquired.

'Of course,' Michael said with a hint of annoyance. 'My mother used to make it all the time with fresh garlic and mayonnaise.'

'So your father didn't completely abandon his Spanish roots?' Brian said, sucking the head of a prawn.

'Why do you say that?'

'Well, the language and, of course, your name was kept. Fernandez isn't commonplace in England or the easiest name to pronounce correctly. Some people might have changed their surname to Francis or something like that.'

'Never really thought about it that way.'

'So why did your father leave Spain?'

'It's a long story.'

'How's the fish?'

'Wonderful. In fact I've never had anything like it.'

Bones and shells gradually mounted on the platter in the centre of the table. The waiter removed an empty wine bottle and replaced it.

'So how did you find your way to Spain?' Michael asked.

'That's a long story as well. I was divorced in 1973. No one's fault really, but it didn't end amicably. I travelled for a few years, had my share of adventures, but never really settled. Then I came to the Costa Blanca in 1984 to do some photography and I fell in love with the place.'

'And the property business?'

'Just a means to an end. I knew John Saunders from way back and he was just setting up over here. He needed someone to deal with the customers at this end so I said I'd take it on. Never looked back.'

'You still don't seem like a typical property agent to me.'

'I've never seen myself as a hard sell merchant, if that's what you mean. Don't get me wrong, I like to clinch a deal, I need the money. But mostly I see myself as the middleman, helping people fulfil their dreams. The last thing I want is to put square pegs in round holes. I live here, remember, so I'm always bumping into old clients and it would be awful to find they weren't happy.'

'Does that happen?'

'Rarely used to, but things are changing.'

'What do you mean?'

'Until a couple of years ago, most of the people I met wanted to come to Spain. They knew something about the country, the people, the history and the way of life. Many chose this part of the Costa Blanca because they'd been before and not just for a day trip. But it's changed. Half my buyers don't have a clue about Spain; they just want to get away from Britain. It's sad, because Spain is magnificent, but you need to adapt. You need to want to adapt. If you come here simply to escape from somewhere else you'll probably be disappointed. After all, Spain isn't paradise. Sorry... I'm rambling.'

'No, please carry on. I'm interested. Why do you love the place so much?'

'Well, firstly it's the scenery. You saw the mountains. How could you not be inspired? And the climate's one of the healthiest in the world. But it's much more. The people are so... at times chaotic and disorganised – they're Spanish, after all – but always astute, thoughtful, and warm. If you adapt, they make you welcome. You can't expect people to change for you, especially up in the mountains. The way of life is what's precious, though you'd have to live here a while to fully appreciate it. Sorry, I'm rambling again. Anyway, you were telling me about your father, and why he left.'

Michael sat forward. Whether it was the wine, or a sense of camaraderie, he wasn't sure, but he felt like opening up.

'He was ill and he had to go to England.'

'What part of Spain was your father from?'

Michael hesitated, and the waiter returned to clear the table.

'Parcent,' Michael said, breaking the silence.

'What?'

'My father came from Parcent.'

'Christ! No wonder you looked so shocked – surprised – when I pointed it out. Of course, you've never been there. Never seen the place before.' He continued, allowing his enthusiasm to take over. 'It's a beautiful place. I've been there many a time. Even sold a few houses in the village. You'll love it.' Brian was now in full flow and had obviously lost all sense of inhibition as he posed the next question.

'When did he leave?'

'In the early fifties.'

'And you say he was ill and *had* to leave?'

'Yes.'

Brian seemed momentarily lost in thought before he spoke again. 'Wait a minute. Your father wasn't a leper, was he?'

Michael looked up in horror.

'He suffered from leprosy. If that's what you mean.'

'No – sorry, I didn't mean to pry. It's just that when you mentioned Parcent... you know... when you said your father was ill in the nineteen fifties.'

Michael had one question. 'What made you think of leprosy?'

'There's a history of leprosy round here. In the nineteenth century it was almost an epidemic and there was another outbreak in the fifties. Living in these parts, you get to know about these things. There's even a sanatorium in the mountains which has patients to this day.'

'Fontilles,' Michael said.

'You know about it?'

'Yes. I know all about the sanatorium at Fontilles.'

With that, Michael had said enough. He'd never told anyone and now he'd talked about it to someone he barely knew.

'Better get the bill,' he said. 'And I do need to get back to Alicante.'

CHAPTER FIVE

After reflecting on his day with Brian Small, Michael mused on what might have happened to the Harringtons. He needed to prepare something for his meeting with Jose Luis in the morning and think through the steps he would have taken if he'd been running the investigation from the start.

It was nearly midnight. His concentration slipped, his mind took him back to the view of Parcent in the far distance and to Fontilles. He wished he'd never met Brian Small, wished he'd kept his mouth shut, wished he'd told Brian not to say anything to anyone, wished he could sleep...

Jose Luis arrived just as Michael was finishing breakfast. His outfit was the same as before, except the shirt was short sleeved, pyjama stripes – and he had sunglasses on top of his head.

'You look tired,' Jose Luis said cheerfully.

'I didn't sleep well. Too hot.'

Jose Luis pulled up a chair at the breakfast table and summoned the waiter to bring him a cup of coffee. The dining room was almost empty.

'Let's get down to business.' Jose Luis rummaged through a cardboard folder he'd taken from under his arm. 'Here's your ID. It's only a civilian ID card, we couldn't give you a proper warrant card and badge, but this will get you into most places you're likely to go.'

He slipped the laminated card across the table and Michael picked it up, surprised to see his own photograph in the top right-hand corner.

'Where did you get the photo?'

'The wonders of email. Your station sent it yesterday. Make sure you carry it with you whenever you're on duty. By the way, it doesn't give you police powers, so don't arrest anyone. We can't issue a gun either. I'm sure you understand, but then you wouldn't have a gun in England, would you? Can't understand that in this day and age. I mean, with the crime in England I'd have thought you'd need all the help you can get.'

Michael didn't rise to the bait.

'Right,' said Jose Luis, 'so what do you want to do now?'

'You make it sound like I'm on holiday or something. But let's keep it reasonably straight. You're no happier having me here than I would be if this were my investigation in England, but we're stuck with each other, so the sooner we clear this up the better. Why don't you start by bringing me up to date on what your team's been doing?'

Jose Luis smiled. 'Team? There's no team, just me I'm afraid. And I have a full caseload already. If a couple of foreign dreamers come to Spain and get lost, that's their business. My bosses are panicking because of heat from the Ministry for Tourism. I've made all the usual inquiries, followed up all our contacts and come to a dead end. As far as I'm concerned, it's now a question of wait and see.'

'Is that what you thought about the couple murdered last year?'

Jose Luis leaned forward so that his face was close to Michael's. 'For a start, that wasn't my case. And another thing, right from the start it was clear that the couple had been abducted. This is a completely different case. There's no evidence at all to suggest anything other than that the Harringtons have just disappeared. Who knows, perhaps they don't want to be found. Anyway, we got the last lot and they're locked away in Alicante prison, so it's no use looking there for clues.'

'Are you sure you got the right people?'

'Dead sure. They confessed, didn't they?'

'I know, but I just wondered. The confessions weren't – let's say – "helped," were they?'

Jose Luis slammed the folder shut. 'For your information, Detective Inspector Michael Fernandez, the Spanish Inquisition ended in 1780.'

'I know,' Michael said, folding his arms, 'and the last victim somehow confessed to having had carnal knowledge of the Devil before he was burnt at the stake.'

Jose Luis smiled. 'You know your Spanish history.'

'A little,' Michael said.

The waiters were re-setting tables for lunch and Jose Luis suggested they move to the terrace by the pool. They found a table in a quiet corner and sat in the shade. It was too early for sunbathers, but a grey-haired old man ploughed up and down the pool.

Michael asked, 'I understand you need an NIE – a National Identity number – before you can buy a house in Spain. Have you checked if the Harringtons applied?'

Jose Luis raised his eyes to the sky. 'Yes, we've checked, and yes, Mr Harrington registered for his NIE number in October last year. You see, you also need a NIE number to open a bank account in Spain.'

'He wasn't in Spain last October, so...?'

'It was all handled by James Weeks Associates, asesorias in Javea. The forms were completed by post and James Weeks took them to the police station with a copy of Mr Harrington's passport. The forms were stamped and the NIE number issued on the spot. It's just routine. We have copies of the forms. They're in the file if you want to see them.'

'Later, perhaps. I'm surprised you can open a bank account by post.'

'Well, actually you can't, but the asesoria can do it for you and then you can transfer money into the account. Then you have to visit the bank and prove your identity – usually by showing your passport – before you can make any withdrawals. Like I say, it's all pretty standard stuff. Is this leading us somewhere?'

'No, I just want to understand the process. Would you need a NIE number to rent a house?

'No, thousands of people rent villas every week for holidays.'

'There's no way of checking whether the Harringtons rented a place?'

'We've trawled all the known letting agencies in the area and drawn a blank. But there are lots of other ways to rent a place, especially if you have cash and we know Mr Harrington had plenty of that.'

'Yes,' said Michael. 'What was it? Fifty-five thousand pounds from the English bank and another seventy thousand euros from the Spanish bank in January while they were staying in Benidorm. Then seventy-five thousand euros in March. That's a lot of money to carry around and that's what puzzles me. You see, if they'd been carrying the cash then we might imagine they had been robbed, possibly by a gang like the ones we picked up on Monday. That would be straightforward and they would surely have reported it. But why would someone abduct them if they had already got their hands on so much money? It doesn't make sense.'

Jose Luis looked interested, or pretended to. 'Perhaps the abductors knew they had more money tucked away.'

Michael considered the suggestion. 'It's a possibility, but I still think a robbery for that sort of money would be enough for most people. Just take the cash and run. Why take the risk of abducting two people when you already have the best part of a hundred and fifty thousand euros in the bag? Not to mention the fifty-five grand in Sterling. It doesn't add up. Have you checked to see if there are any other bank accounts in the Harringtons' name?'

Jose Luis raised his eyebrows at the continued probing – as if he was used to asking the questions not answering them.

'Of course,' he said abruptly. 'Why do you think they looked at properties that seemed to be well outside their resources? Are you sure they don't have more money in the UK that no one knows about?'

'Sure as we can be. As for the houses, Brian Small says it's not that uncommon for time-wasters to take a guided tour without ever intending to buy. You know, have a good look round, enjoy a free meal or two. It's better than a coach tour.'

Jose Luis looked smug. 'You English never cease to amaze. By the way, how did you get on with Brian Small yesterday?'

'Fine. Didn't really learn much, just went over the same ground that you did three weeks ago, but we didn't see all the properties the

Harringtons looked at because we ran out of time. I may have to meet him again at some point. By the way, I don't suppose the Guardia could provide me with a car? Only I feel a bit dependent stuck here with no wheels.'

'I can recommend a cheap car hire company,' said Jose Luis. 'I'm sure the Nottingham County Constabulary can run to that.'

Michael didn't answer directly, but stared across the terrace as he continued to pull the threads together, searching for leads. 'That other agent, Summers, the one who says the Harringtons didn't show up for their appointment. Have you checked him out?'

'Of course. His story holds up. The hotel receptionist remembers and confirms what he said. We're sure as we can be that he never met them.'

'That reminds me,' said Michael. 'I came across another agent yesterday who'd met the Harringtons in January, but never came forward. His name's Vinnie Roberts. I think you should pull him in.'

Michael sat back as if indifferent, but enjoying an image of Vinnie in shorts and flip-flops, sitting in a cold damp cell at Alicante police station.

Jose Luis seemed to read his mind. 'Look, I don't know how you operate in England, but we don't go around arresting people just because they've been in contact with the missing couple. If you give me his details, I'll talk to him this week, but I don't expect anything to come of it.'

Michael tried not to let his disappointment show. He considered telling Jose Luis what a shady character he had deduced Vinnie to be, but thought better of it.

Jose Luis continued to spar. 'You really are wasting your time looking at known property agents.' He leaned back as if to drag out his spell of superiority. 'There are so many other ways,' he said, restraining a yawn, 'of buying houses in this part of Spain. It's highly unlikely any of the known property agents would get involved in something as sordid as an abduction.'

He paused, forcing Michael to ask the next question.

'What other ways?'

Jose Luis smiled. He'd regained the initiative.

'Houses change hands all the time, especially where there's cash involved. People do deals in bars on the shake of a hand, you know, "a friend of a friend has this place he wants to sell, strictly cash, no questions asked, no tax". Then there are property auctions where a group of villains set up in a room somewhere, purporting to sell-off repossessed houses. It's a scam, of course, but you'd be surprised how gullible some people are, if they think they're getting a bargain. We have a saying here: "people in search of their dream life often leave their brains at the border". Not just the British. The Germans and the Dutch are just as bad. Normally cautious people come to Spain and do things they would never dream of doing in their home countries. I think it's the sun or the cheap booze more likely. So you see, following up on contacts with property agents, at least bona fide property agents, is unlikely to lead you anywhere other than on an inspection tour of some very nice and very expensive houses.'

He sat back further looking triumphant.

'But what about the paperwork, the escritura, the Notario, NIE numbers, all that sort of stuff?'

'My dear Michael,' said Jose Luis, tapping his companion on the shoulder, 'you really do have a lot to learn about Spain and about human nature come to that.'

'Well, a bit of study can't do any harm. Thanks for the tip.' But it was getting hot on the terrace and Michael's head was spinning again. It was as if, removed from his familiar surroundings, he was unable to function. Perhaps it was lack of sleep. Or the heat. Perhaps it was Spain.

'So where to now?' he asked, trying to sound businesslike.

Jose Luis shrugged.

'It's up to you. I've just about exhausted all my leads. Like I said, I've got other crimes to solve. Here, you can have my file if you want it. You've seen most of it already but there are notes in there of all my interviews. Perhaps you can come up with something. Feel free to ask around some more if you want or just enjoy the sun.'

He slid his chair away from the table and began to stand.

'Oh, I forgot to mention, there's a press conference at eleven-thirty on Friday. We've reserved the business suite here at the hotel. All the local press are invited, and British papers are sending reporters as well. Apparently, the story's hit the headlines in Britain and everyone wants in. Spanish TV and radio will be there and the BBC. John and Linda Harrington are flying in tomorrow. It's your boss's idea, what's his name – Bowater. He's been talking to my Colonel and they set it up between them. Just a publicity stunt I expect to show how well the Guardia and the British police are working together. That's all right with you, isn't it?'

Jesus. Michael visualised the packed audience, John with fag and rolled-up newspaper, Linda weeping, reporters firing off questions, trying to trip him up, exposing gaps in the investigation.

'Ah – hmm, yes. Probably a good idea. Renew interest in the case, get some fresh coverage, see if we can get some new witnesses to come forward, that sort of thing. But, ah... will there be a briefing beforehand?'

'What, to get our stories straight, you mean?'

'No, I mean... Well, sort out who – who does the introductions, that sort of thing. You can't go into these things cold, you know.'

'Of course not,' said Jose Luis. 'And what I mean by that is, of course there will be a briefing. My Colonel's running the show. His name's Cardells, Antonio Cardells, but for Christ's sake don't call him Antonio. Never. He'll be here at nine-thirty Friday morning and we can run through the details then. The Harringtons will be here at ten-thirty with someone from the British consulate. Don't worry, it's all arranged.'

'Who said I was worried?'

Jose Luis flicked a name card onto the table and started toward the sliding doors of the hotel lobby.

'Anyway, I've got things to do. I'll see you on Friday. If you want me, I'm here.' He added, 'Just think – you could get your picture in the papers, maybe on TV.'

Michael didn't say goodbye. He stared out over the pool and the turquoise sea to the horizon for a while and then ordered a pot of coffee and a bottle of mineral water to be delivered to his room. He retired there for most of the afternoon, skipping lunch while he pored over the files again.

The Harringtons had checked out of their Benidorm hotel as scheduled on 21st January. They left in the hired blue Renault Clio, but didn't catch their flight home. The car had never been returned. Could they have been robbed on the way to the airport? But the Gessels in Alcalalí said that a couple called Johnson (almost certainly the Harringtons?) viewed their house on 23rd January. If this was true, then the Harringtons obviously never intended to catch their flight home. They were moving around in January, so if they'd been abducted it was some time later. But where had they been staying? Another hotel perhaps, a rented villa, somewhere else? There had been a few more possible sightings over the following weeks, and the phone call home in early February. Then, on 13th March, David Harrington had visited his bank in Javea to withdraw seventy-five thousand euros in cash.

Michael turned the pages of Jose Luis' file to find the notes of the interview with the cashier. The money had been ordered five days in advance and David Harrington had been alone when he collected the cash. The cashier had confirmed his identity by asking to see his passport. He had signed for the cash and left with a large bundle of five hundred euro notes. The signature had been confirmed as authentic. The cashier said it appeared to be a normal transaction (large cash withdrawals were not unusual for visits to the Notario) and Mr Harrington had seemed perfectly calm and relaxed, as far as anyone could remember. So, Michael surmised again, by 13th March, David Harrington was still around and doing business as usual. But where was Mrs Harrington? Could it be that she was being held by abductors who were forcing Mr Harrington to withdraw the cash under threat of violence to his wife?

At this point the trail went cold. Repeated appeals through the press had failed to turn up a single new sighting since the trip to the bank nearly two months ago. If the Harringtons were hiding then they had been very careful and discreet otherwise someone would surely have spotted them. On the other hand, if they had been abducted there was every reason for them to be well hidden. Indeed, Michael thought, with the Spanish bank account virtually cleared, there was very little reason to keep them alive, especially if they could identify their abductors.

Though he'd never admit it to anyone, he was at a dead end and he sympathised with Jose Luis's predicament. What more could he do? There must be something he'd failed to notice and he was still puzzled about why they'd viewed properties that seemed well beyond their means. A free inspection trip at an agent's expense was one thing, but what about their trip to see the Gessels' place in Alcalalí? Assuming it was them, of course.

Bereft of other ideas, Michael decided to pay Jacob and Helena Gessels a visit. He telephoned and made an appointment for 11am the next morning and then arranged a hire car for a week. It would be delivered to the hotel first thing in the morning.

He ate in the hotel dining room that evening and finished with a coffee and a large brandy in the hope it would help him sleep. The brandy was a Gran Solera from Jerez called Grand Duque d'Alba, and the waiter looked surprised that Michael asked for it by name.

He lay on top of his bed staring up at the cracked white ceiling. The air conditioning unit rattled over the door and wafted barely chilled air over his near naked body. He was fighting for sleep, but his mind was still working overtime. He tossed from side to side, trying to find a comfortable position as he wrestled with ideas. It was as if someone was flashing a series of photographs before his eyes. As soon as he managed to delete one picture, another one came in to replace it with increasing rapidity. It felt as if he was sitting in front of a computer, clicking the mouse to clear the screen only for another image to pop up in front of him. Click, click, click... only the computer was beginning to anticipate his moves. And one image kept returning with escalating frequency until, suddenly, it stopped and the image remained fixed on the screen. Click, click, click... but the image was frozen and could not be removed. He seemed to be able to view it in three dimensions, moving around to see it from different angles and perspectives and zooming in and out. But it could not be erased.

A higgledy-piggledy collection of colour-washed houses rose

around a hill surrounded by much taller mountains. The random roof lines of weathered terracotta tiles seemed to form steps as they climbed to the summit of the village, punctuated by a few round green trees and thin pencil pines. An irregular pattern of spaces marked the position of narrow streets all appearing to culminate at the top of the hill. And protruding high above the rooftops was a white church tower with a fretwork spire of Moorish design, silhouetted against a clear blue sky. Parcent. Michael had only taken the briefest of glimpses from his distant viewing point on the outskirts of Lliber, but it had left an indelible impression seared within his mind like the patterns on a memory chip.

Michael rose early the next morning, feeling surprisingly fresh. Before breakfast he made another telephone call.

'Brian, it's Michael Fernandez. I'm coming to Alcalalí this morning and wondered if we could meet, if you're free.'

If Brian was surprised it didn't show. 'Delighted. I'm with some people this morning, but I can meet you for lunch about one o'clock.'

They agreed to meet at Bar Porche in the centre of Alcalalí, adjacent to the church and where Brian said they could sample some authentic tapas. He warned Michael not to attempt to drive into the centre of the village. The streets were extremely narrow and parking was impossible. He suggested parking on the outskirts and walking.

Following the directions to the Gessels' house, Michael approached Jalon, finding its road sign spray-painted to obliterate 'Jalon,' leaving only the Valenciano 'Xaló' to confuse visitors. He bypassed the town centre and drove past several bodegas on the left-hand side of the road. He paused at a crossing and watched a group of tourists tumbling out of the Cooperativa. Laden with five-litre plastic wine bottles, they headed back to a coach parked under riverbank trees. A sign on the coach announced: Benidorm. Between the bodegas, a new shopping arcade presented a 'Lawson's of London' window displaying hundreds of properties for sale. And two doors along from that a bright new awning announced the availability of fish and chips. Over to the north, two large urbanisations were being developed on the slopes of the mountains, sprawling toward the summit.

He crossed the narrow bridge over the dried-up River Jalon and could now see Alcalalí about two kilometres away. The road twisted and turned, opening up new views toward the top of the valley as he wove through the gentle hills. A glimpse was all he saw of the distant church tower, but it was enough for him to match it with the imprint etched on his mind from the previous sleepless night.

He followed the directions he'd scribbled in a notepad the previous evening when he'd spoken to the Gessels.

"Turn left just after the entrance to the Almazara urbanisation, cross the tiny bridge and follow the road for about five hundred metres through the almond and olive groves."

They had said the road was a little bumpy and it was. He feared he might rip the sump from the engine as he steered between pot holes and rocks. At one point he was forced to pull over to allow a small tractor and trailer to pass in the opposite direction. The trailer was laden with long bamboo canes bearing leaves and it bounced up and down on the uneven surface. The driver wore a tattered straw hat and had the stub of a torpedo-shaped cigar clenched between his teeth. He gave a cheery wave as he passed by. The scene looked so typically Spanish that Michael imagined he must have seen it before in a holiday brochure.

"Turn right at the fork in the road and keep straight on until you see a black wrought iron gate on the left."

The road continued to deteriorate and there was no sign of a house. He was just concluding he was on the wrong road when he spotted it.

Jacob and Helena Gessels greeted him at the gates and offered coffee. They were both remarkably tall, about six foot six inches in Mr Gessels' case, his wife only a fraction shorter. Helena Gessels had tightly permed hair; grey, dyed light brown. She wore a cotton print top, with teenager-ish calf-length slacks and open-toed pink mules. Jacob, in a stiff-collared pinstriped shirt, looked as if he'd seen time in an office. His neatly laced shoes were made of interwoven strips of polished brown leather. They belonged with the shirt, Michael thought, and reflected a man of substance and good taste, though the effect was knocked off-balance by white sports socks and baggy shorts. They looked to be in their mid- to late-seventies.

He followed them round the house, past a pool and into the garden. This was a tropical oasis, delineated by tall hedges of oleanders just coming into bud. There was a patch of green lawn that could have come straight from suburban England – except that it was dotted with orange and lemon trees.

They sat down at a glass-topped wicker table in the shade of an open-arched naya. The coffee was perfectly dark and syrupy and Michael took a sip before going through the usual preamble, apologising for having to ask more questions and getting down to business.

'How certain are you that the couple who viewed the house, the Johnsons, were in fact Mr and Mrs Harrington?'

Mrs Gessels answered, explaining that her husband did not speak much English. 'We were quite sure from the photographs the Guardia showed us even though they were not very good. The man in the photograph was quite ordinary looking, but it was the woman we recognised. Petit, very beautiful with long blond hair and very distinctive eyes, like doe eyes, if you know what I mean, slightly sad.'

Michael complimented Mrs Gessels on her English and continued, 'Did you talk to them much?'

'Quite a lot, yes. I remember they asked a lot of questions. They seemed very interested.'

'What sort of questions?'

'The usual, you know, about how old the house was, how far to shops and restaurants and if it was cold in winter. We don't have central heating, you see. Oh, and Mr Johnson also asked about neighbours. I thought it was a little strange because it's only too obvious when you drive out here. We told them that no one else lives nearby. Our closest neighbours are on the edge of the village about one kilometre away.'

'Was that the answer he was looking for?'

'I'm sorry, I don't understand.'

'I mean, did he give you the impression that he was looking for somewhere so isolated?'

'He commented on how nice and quiet it was, so I guessed he liked the idea of being away from people. That's what attracted us in the first place, sixteen years ago when we bought the plot and had the house built.'

'Did they say anything else?'

'Not that I remember. We left them to wander on their own for most of the time. They spent time in the garden. I remember Mrs Johnson saying how lovely the garden was, but that was about it – wasn't it, Jacob?'

Mr Gessels responded grumpily, in Dutch, to his wife who interpreted. 'He's saying that they asked why we were selling. Jacob thought they were being nosy.'

Michael phrased his next question carefully, aware that Mr Gessels was following every word of the conversation.

'Did you give them an answer?'

Helena ignored a muttered comment from her husband.

'We love it here, but the garden is hard and it's a long way to the village. I don't drive and if Jacob became ill I couldn't manage alone. We plan to buy in Calpe, close to the shops, somewhere with a terrace but no garden.'

'I can see why you fell in love with the place, it really is beautiful. By the way – is it still on the market?'

Mr Gessels sat up. 'You want to buy it?'

'Out of my league, I'm afraid. I only asked because it was the end of January when the Harringtons, if it was the Harringtons, came to see it. It's now May and I wondered why it hasn't sold.'

Before her husband could say anything, Mrs Gessels answered.

'Something to do with the euro, so they say. The English pound has gone up or down, so it's more expensive for English people. I told Jacob we should put the house with agents but he didn't want to pay their fees. So we advertised it in the Costa Blanca News. Anyway, we've put it with agents now, only I feel we have wasted three months.'

The answer hit Michael like a boxer's right hook.

'When you say you advertised in the Costa Blanca News, do you mean the English version? It's printed in Dutch as well, isn't it?'

'And German,' said Mrs Gessels, 'but we put it in the English version because all the houses round here seem to be bought by English people. Ten years ago it was different, it was mainly Dutch and German people who wanted to come to the mountains, but now the place is gradually being taken over by the English. It seems they're the ones with the money now, especially since prices here have rocketed in the last couple of years.'

Michael remembered the fish and chip shop in Jalon and understood what Mrs Gessels meant. But he was still missing something. He asked the next question to buy time, anticipating the reply.

'The German and Dutch versions of the Costa Blanca News, do they have advertisements for houses for sale?'

'Of course,' said Mrs Gessels, as if it was obvious.

Michael almost ignored the answer. He was still ruminating... pattern, process, procedure, deduction.

'Are these advertisements in Dutch and German, rather than English?'

'Of course they are. Why would anyone English read the foreign versions of the Costa Blanca News?'

The coin dropped and Michael gave a brief smile.

'Tell me Mrs Gessels, when you contacted the Guardia, where did you hear about the Harringtons?'

'I read about them in the Costa Blanca News.'

'The English Costa Blanca News?'

'Yes. I don't usually buy it of course, but I was buying it then to check that our advertisement was in.'

'Have you read anything about the Harringtons in the Dutch version?'

Mrs Gessels hesitated and asked the question of her husband. The answer was clear from the shake of his head.

'Now that you mention it, I don't think there's been anything in the Dutch papers.'

Michael needed to make a phone call. He thanked Mr and Mrs Gessels for their time and the coffee and wished them success in selling their house. He opened the door of the hire car, intending to make the call on his mobile phone. It was like an oven, so he set off back along the bumpy track with the air conditioning blasting on full power. By the time he reached the main road the car had cooled but his back was wringing wet. He parked in a cart track and left the engine running while he made the call. Jose Luis was not too pleased with Michael's demand that Dutch and German reporters should be invited to tomorrow's press conference. Colonel Cardells would be furious at this last minute interference with his carefully laid plans, but Jose Luis agreed to put the suggestion to him.

At 12.45pm, following Brian's suggestion, Michael parked his car at the entrance to the village of Alcalalí. He could see the church tower in the distance and headed off in its general direction, surprised to see a modern bank and a sign for the municipal library.

He walked beneath an impressive stone arch and entered the tiny square, spotting Bar Porche immediately. He felt nervous about entering a Spanish bar alone and hoped that Brian would already be there. Through the open doorway he could see a few people on barstools, but no Brian.

He hesitated for a moment and then continued walking, pausing in front of the church to read an inscribed tablet explaining the origins of the village dating back to Roman times and mentioning the Reconquest of the Moors by King Jaime I in 1238.

'Interesting, isn't it,' said Brian, appearing at Michael's side. 'Most of the villages round here were ruled by the Moors at one time or another. Until the Reconquest, Moors and Christians lived side by side for centuries, but there was always distrust and the Moorish people were finally sent packing by the Decree of Expulsion in 1609.'

'Yes. And the valley was repopulated with Majorcan farmers.'

'You certainly know your history,' said Brian.

'Bits of it.'

They walked back to the bar where a chalkboard with a menu for tapas hung on the wall and sat down at a corner table.

Michael ordered quickly, but found himself sitting back to eat slowly, watching tiny dishes of tapas arrive two at a time, all freshly cooked and served with crusty bread and alioli. The bar gradually began to fill with 'tradesmen looking for lunch at the start of their two-hour break before taking their siestas,' as Brian explained. Soon the place was a noisy, heaving mass of people, shouting orders, greeting friends, chatting, eating and drinking beer or wine. Michael expected to feel uncomfortable, yet there was an air of conviviality about the place and he felt curiously at ease. It was not until a waitress asked if he had enjoyed the tapas and remarked on the excellence of his Spanish that he felt like a foreigner again.

Brian had discarded his woollen cardigan in deference to the heat, but in all other respects his outfit was in the same style as before – country gentleman meets desert trekker.

'So what's it to be?' He wiped away a few morsels of tapas that had fallen onto the spectacles dangling on the cords around his neck.

'Sorry?'

'Well, I assume you didn't just want to meet me for lunch.'

'Oh, no. No, not at all. You mentioned some other properties the Harringtons had looked at.'

'You mean the town house in Parcent?'

'Well, yes, but you said something about ...'

'Come on, let's go,' Brian caught the waiter's eye, scribbled with his finger in the air and mouthed the words, '*la cuenta.*'

They met up again at the edge of Alcalalí and Michael followed Brian's Renault as it headed further up the valley. A few minutes later they rounded a sharp bend and the village of Parcent came into view, every detail just as Michael had visualised it the night before. Brian drove almost full circle around the base of the hilltop village then turned sharp right into the settlement itself. They parked in a tree-lined street, much wider than Michael had expected to find.

'Come on, follow me. It's a bit of a climb,' said Brian, striding up another tree-lined street and turning left up an even steeper one.

'Where are we going?' asked Michael, struggling to keep up as he tried to take in every detail of the surroundings.

'To the town house I showed to the Harringtons. It's been sold to another couple now, but they use it just as a holiday home. They're away at the moment, but I have a key so you can have a look round.'

Anxious again, having that feeling of being railroaded into something he was not sure he wanted to do, he thought about turning back, but curiosity overcame unease.

They turned into another two-donkey street, this one level and lined by walls of different pastel shades and textures. Carved doors opened onto the pavement, inches from the street. Behind window grills, the shutters were closed and it was easy to imagine dark little rooms starved of sun.

Most houses were two storeys high with two or three balconied windows hanging over the pavement. A few were taller with more balconies at a higher level. The soffits had been colonised by swallows with two, three, or more mud nests clinging to the undersides of the eaves.

Halfway along the street an old lady, perhaps four and a half feet tall, swept the pavement with a hand-crafted besom. She was dressed in black – skirt, blouse and cardigan – with woollen bedroom slippers, also in black.

She paused to return Brian's greeting of, '*buenas tardes*,' obviously recognising him and then turned away. A little further up the same street, Brian stopped, gesturing for Michael to take a peek inside an open door.

'This is it,' he whispered, opening the narrow front door.

Michael put his head inside the door and a waft of cool air hit him as he adjusted his eyes to the dim light. The flagstone floor of the short entrance hall was dominated by a dark oak sideboard and the scent of furniture polish filled Michael's nostrils.

They moved on to a large lounge with a high moulded ceiling and stone framed fireplace. The furniture was rustic Spanish, mainly in dark wood with a warm patina. Carefully placed ornaments decorated the shelves and mantelpiece, mingling with a collection of old oil paintings. An expansive woven rug covered the centre of the mosaic-tiled floor.

'The place came fully furnished,' Brian explained and the lady next door looks after it when the owners aren't here.

They passed through the lounge to a set of double doors that opened onto a white-walled courtyard that stretched back almost as far again as the house. In the bright light of the early evening sun a collection of pots and tubs could be seen, overflowing with geraniums and petunias. Through an open door to the right, Michael spotted a modern fitted kitchen with walls dominated by a series of hanging paella pans descending in size from that of a cartwheel to one the size of an ordinary frying pan.

'Would you like to take a look upstairs?' Brian asked. 'There are four double bedrooms on two floors and two bathrooms. There's also another small terrace at roof level.'

'No, I don't need to see any more, thanks. Are they all like this?' Michael asked Brian, as they paused at the foot of the stairs. 'I'd imagined these places to be cramped and claustrophobic.'

'Claustrophobic houses? Brian replied. 'We'll be giving them cognitive therapy next. But yes, some are bigger and this one is particularly nice. I know other people in the village, we can have a look at some more if you like.'

'No, not right now. I don't want to intrude. I just wanted to get an idea of what these village houses are like. But how much would something like this cost, approximately?'

'Just over two hundred thousand euros, give or take.'

'How much?'

'The expat boom has arrived in Parcent. Two years ago you could have picked up places like this for next to nothing, but prices have rocketed. The coastal towns are overcrowded, especially in the summer.'

'And what do the locals think of it?'

'Some are happy to take the money, for the time being at least. You see, not so long ago people here scratched a bit of a living off the land and foraged in the hills for wild plants and herbs. Many of the men hunted – still do today – rabbits, birds, wild boar. But the expats have changed all that. Foreigners are welcomed for their money, of course, and the value of property has soared. Whether it'll stay this way remains to be seen.'

'It's changing though?'

'Inevitably. Most of the elderly people keep to the old ways despite their new wealth. But foreign influences have an impact on the younger generation and there's not a lot of money to be made from a few hectares of olives or oranges.'

'I don't know,' Michael said, stopping to look back. 'But I sort of resent the destruction of a sound way of life.' He turned to walk on. 'How far does it go, in the valley, with these foreign buyers?' he asked.

'This is about the limit, for now at least. There are a few small urbanisations further up, around Benigembla, but after that they begin to peter out. A few intrepid expats have settled in the more remote villages, even in Castell de Castells and that's about sixteen kilometres from here.'

'Castell de Castells, that's where you live, isn't it?'

'That's right, want to take a look?'

'I do, but I'll have to make it another time.'

They walked on down the street past more narrow houses and emerged into the village square, littered with parked cars and vans. A tobacconist stood in one corner of the square near several grand, balconied houses. Another corner was occupied by a collection of red plastic tables and chairs. A faded sign above lace-curtained windows read, "Bar Moll."

The square was centred by a drinking fountain and four trees protected by wrought iron rails. Opposite, a heavy metal-studded wooden door straddled a stone archway. Above the door, a small cross had been cut into the façade and above that sat a clock face set into the tower. Below a small niche containing a bell there was a simple inscription that read: "Parcent 1949".

As Michael lifted his gaze, his eyes fixed on the white fretwork spire framed against the clear blue sky, just as he had dreamed.

'Sorry, Brian,' he said, 'but I have to go now.'

At almost 7.30pm, Michael arrived back at his hotel. The concierge called out from the reception counter and thrust a note into Michael's hand. A few minutes later he was on the phone.

'Where the hell have you been, Fernandez? I've been trying to contact you all day. You're not on a bloody holiday jaunt, you know.'

'Sorry, Chief Superintendent,' Michael said half-heartedly, proceeding to explain some of his movements.

'And what's all this about wanting to invite the Dutch and the Germans to the press conference? I've had Colonel Cardells on the phone. He's livid. You'll want to involve Interpol, next.'

Chief Superintendent Bowater seemed just about satisfied with Michael's explanations, but still wanted the final word.

'Look, just don't go upsetting the Spanish Police. It's their show. Remember you're only there to lend a hand, not to take over the whole bloody shooting match. And keep your mobile switched on – day and night. Is that clear?'

CHAPTER SIX

Michael breakfasted early having slept well for a change. He was thinking about the press conference when Jose Luis marched through the door looking smarter than before in grey trousers and a sharply ironed, dazzling white shirt. His shoes had been polished and were without a trace of dust. He seemed edgy.

'Colonel Cardells should be here in ten minutes. Just remember, he likes things on a formal footing so don't get familiar. And whatever you do, don't spring any more surprises. It's his show; let him run it his way.'

'You make him sound like an ogre.'

'I work for him, you don't. Here, he wants everyone to wear these.' Jose Luis handed Michael a name badge and clipped his own to the pocket of his shirt. Michael looked at his badge: "Detective Inspector Michael Fernandez, Nottingham County Constabulary". The blue insignia was reproduced in the bottom right hand corner. He was about to clip it to the lapel of his Prince of Wales checked jacket when Jose Luis commented.

'Do yourself a favour Michael, dispense with the jacket. This isn't England you know, and it's likely to be hot in there.'

'If you're sure.' Michael slipped the jacket from his shoulders.

'And the tie isn't strictly necessary,' added Jose Luis.

'I'll keep it on if you don't mind.'

'The Colonel has asked if you'll act as interpreter. He wants all the questions to go through him, so if any of the British reporters ask questions in English you'll translate. Only answer yourself if he tells you it's okay.'

Jesus. Michael finished his coffee. *Right farce this could turn out to be.* He nodded as if he thought it an entirely practical plan.

Jose Luis looked at his watch. 'Let's go, mustn't be late.'

In the hotel lobby, near the business suite, Jose Luis paused. 'By the way, I met Vincent Roberts yesterday. He didn't tell me anything new. I'm fairly sure he only met the Harringtons once, when Brian Small took them to the place in Moraira. He was furious about you though. He said something about acting under false pretences. He wants to make an official complaint of some kind, so I told him to speak to your Chief Constable.'

Jose Luis smirked, but Michael airily adjusted his name badge, straightened his tie and took a quick look at his shoes. The hotel polishing machine had done a great job buffing out the scratches from the earlier motorway skirmish.

Colonel Cardells was by the coffee trolley in the far corner of the ante-room, his vast frame casting a giant shadow on the stained beige carpet.

A uniformed waiter fussed at his side. Jose Luis waited for the Colonel to turn before introducing Michael. Perhaps it was the cup and saucer in the Colonel's right hand, but Michael's tentative offer of a handshake was brusquely ignored. The two men gave each other the once-over.

A sparse covering of glossy jet-black hair was evenly spread across the top of the Colonel's head, carefully positioned to give maximum coverage, a la Chief Superintendent Bowater. A pencil-thin moustache, coloured to match the hair, sunk into flabby jowls beneath the Colonel's cheeks. The buttons of an epauletted white shirt just about managed to contain the Colonel's paunch which drooped over the front of dark green trousers that looked to be part of a uniform of sorts. The shoes were rubber soled with dull black leather uppers and fraying laces... Augh!

Before Michael and Jose Luis could get coffee, the Colonel ushered them to a small table in the centre of the room. They took their places, the Colonel sitting beside a fidgety young man who was shuffling files. He was introduced as Sergeant Ramirez, the Colonel's personal assistant.

As Jose Luis had anticipated, this was the Colonel's show. He launched into commands about how the press conference should be run. He stressed the key themes time and again: the British police and the Guardia are co-operating fully; everything possible is being done to find the Harringtons; no one should give the impression that they had come to any harm; this type of incident is very rare on the Costa Blanca; tourists and potential homebuyers could come to the Costa Blanca in complete safety.

He paused at one point to check that Michael understood. Michael suspected the inquiry was not simply about his grasp of the language, but replied nevertheless: 'Yes Colonel, I understand your Spanish perfectly.'

Cardells grunted and continued to spill out directives before pausing to ask if anyone had any questions as he rose from the table.

Jose Luis looked skyward when Michael, with a vaguely apologetic shrug in response to the Colonel's glare, began to speak.

'Just one thing Colonel,' said Michael as Cardells resumed his seat. 'How are you going to handle John and Linda Harrington? I mean, it's going to be difficult to control what they say, isn't it?'

At once Cardells was out of his seat and moving toward the door. 'I think you'll find that's already been taken care of, Inspector Fernandez, but if there are any problems I expect you to deal with them.'

He left the room, with Sergeant Ramirez scurrying along behind.

John and Linda Harrington were in the adjacent room with Timothy Middleton, a British Consular Official from Alicante. He'd chaperoned them since their arrival in Spain the previous afternoon and picked them up that morning from their hotel in Benidorm. Colonel Cardells introduced himself briefly and headed for more coffee.

Michael greeted the Harringtons, expressing regrets for the lack of positive news. Linda, at least, had made an effort for the occasion – deep grey trousers, white sling-back shoes with a kitten heel and a lime green twin-set. Not so John, who sported a gaudy Hawaiian shirt with faded denims and trainers.

The consular official anxiously interrupted, handing Michael a sheet of paper. 'Chief Superintendent Bowater wants you to cast an eye over this before we start the press conference.'

Michael excused himself from the Harringtons and moved to one side to examine the document. Middleton clung to his side. Typed on official Nottingham Police stationery, it was headed: "Statement prepared by John and Linda Harrington". It should have read: 'Statement prepared by Chief Superintendent Phillip Bowater, OBE QPM' Michael thought as he hurriedly read the prepared script.

Two Guardia Civil officers flanked the doors as Colonel Cardells led the entourage into the business suite. Michael noted their black leather holsters and wondered if they were expecting trouble. Entering the room, he spotted a raised platform at the far end beyond rows of seats. A giant logo of Nottingham County Constabulary was draped above the stage alongside that of the Guardia Civil. Michael was contemplating the clash of designs when he was interrupted.

'Here you are Michael.' Penny Edwardes thrust a plastic document wallet into his hand.

'Jesus, Penny – what the hell are you doing here?'

'The Chief Super sent me with all the public relations material. He wants to make sure this is seen as a joint operation, not just the Guardia Civil. Have you seen? The BBC is here.'

He was already struggling to maintain equilibrium. Now butterflies converged. His palms were clammy and he felt beads of sweat on his forehead. Perhaps Jose Luis had been right about the tie.

Penny's sudden appearance did not help his composure and the sea of reporters and cameramen made him even more jittery. He took his seat next to the Colonel with John and Linda Harrington on his other side.

The chatter subsided as the Colonel made it obvious he was impatient to get proceedings underway; such was the air of authority he exuded.

He performed the introductions and perfunctorily thanked the assembled gathering for attending. Then he launched into reading in Spanish from a prepared script, re-running the rehearsal he'd been through in the ante-room. He thanked the Nottingham Police for sending Detective Inspector Fernandez to help with the investigation and added that the Inspector was working closely with Captain Jose

Luis Perez of the Guardia Civil to pursue a number of lines of inquiry. He hoped the press would give the widest possible coverage to the case. In particular, the police needed to hear from anyone who had seen, or thought they might have seen, the Harringtons or their hired car since January. He gave the registration number of the blue Renault Clio and said photographs of the missing couple were in the press pack. He ended by saying the pack contained a transcript of his statement, in Spanish as well as English. A Spanish reporter rose, but the Colonel brushed him aside saying questions would be taken at the end. He handed over to John Harrington, inviting him to read his statement.

John Harrington sat facing the assembled press corps, squinting into the glare of camera lights and confronted by an array of microphones. Oblivious to the Colonel's invitation, he failed to respond. There was a brief pause until Michael said quietly to John that it was his turn to speak. John stood, shuffled the papers in front of him and spilled them onto the floor.

Michael retrieved them, whispering, 'Don't worry, take your time.'

With a pair of steel-rimmed spectacles perched on the end of his nose and his hair flattened, John Harrington looked almost scholarly as he began to read the prepared statement.

In a monotone voice and with a ponderous cadence he began to speak.

'I would like to start by thanking the press and television for the interest they have shown so far in the search for my brother David and his wife Alison. I would also like to thank the Guardia Civil and the Nottingham Police for everything they have done to investigate the disappearance and to follow up on the information they have received.'

He coughed, twice. Michael passed him a glass of water.

John resumed. 'My wife and I are seriously concerned about David and Alison, as are family and friends in England. It is most un-char-ac-ter-ist-ic of them not to be in touch for such a long time. However, if, as we hope, they are simply keeping out of contact for some reason, I urge them to get in touch with me or the police so we may know they are safe. Anyone who has seen or heard of them in the past few months, please contact the police. Any information, however in-sig-ni-fi-cant, could help solve the mystery of their whereabouts.'

John paused again, distracted by camera flashes.

Colonel Cardells interjected abrasively to say, 'No photographs until the end.' Everyone complied.

'Our worst fear,' John said, 'is that David and Alison may have been abducted. If anyone is holding them against their will, I appeal to them directly not to harm them, but to return them safely to their family and friends. The continued uncertainty about what has happened to them is causing us enormous stress and worry, so please, if you are holding them, make some kind of contact if only to let us know they are safe.'

John's eyes began to glisten. He lifted his spectacles to rub his face. Linda Harrington blew her nose softly and wiped her cheeks with a tissue. A camera flashed followed; one professional photographer risking the Colonel's wrath, knowing this was the picture his editor wanted. John sat down, pushed the papers to one side and looked toward Michael. No longer playing the nonchalant lout with the fag, all his fear was exposed on his face.

Michael patted him on the forearm. 'That was fine.'

To everyone's surprise, Linda Harrington grabbed one of the microphones and the attention of the audience. 'David and Alison, if you're watching or if you read about this, please get in touch. We need to know that you're safe. We hope to God that no one is holding you, but if you are please, please let them go. They have done you no harm. We just want them back safe and sound. This is destroying our family. I don't know how long we can go on like this. We just want it to end. It's a nightmare. Please let them go. Please, someone must know what's happened to them. Please... '

John Harrington halted Linda's rambling, placing an arm round her shoulder in an awkward display of affection. She sobbed uncontrollably, her shoulders bobbing up and down. More cameras flashed. An embarrassed-looking Timothy Middleton pulled a handkerchief from his pocket and thrust it in front of Linda.

Colonell Cardells took command once more.

'We'll take questions now. Please bear in mind that this is very stressful for Mr and Mrs Harrington and address all questions to me.'

At least half the audience failed to understand what he'd said and Michael didn't think to interpret until someone stood up. An impatient Spanish reporter was first off the mark, asking if there was a link between this case and the one last year. Cardells brushed aside the idea. A couple more questions from Spanish reporters received reassuring replies. Yes, everything possible was being done to find the missing couple. No, there was no firm evidence to suggest they had been abducted. Yes, it was perfectly safe to come to the Costa Blanca.

The Colonel stiffened, but looked composed as the team from Spanish television put him in the spotlight to pick up more platitudinous remarks.

A BBC reporter, John Lynes, was the first of the foreign contingent to enter the fray. His cameraman swivelled to get him into the frame. He had a smattering of Spanish and seemed to have understood most of what the Colonel had said. Even so, after his self introduction he framed his question in English for the benefit of viewers back home.

'Colonel Cardells, is there any truth in the rumour that the Guardia Civil failed to assign an officer to this case for three weeks after the Harringtons were reported missing?'

The camera swung toward Cardells who had a look of calm innocence on his face, oblivious to the reporter's accusation. His expression changed profoundly when Michael interpreted without attempting to tone it down. In return, Michael received the Colonel's glower as his dark eyes turned to thunder. By the time he returned to the BBC man, he'd regained composure and responded with a masterly side-step, ignoring the question and delivering a long-winded 'no stone left unturned' diatribe which Michael interpreted verbatim.

Lynes' attempt to follow up was studiously avoided as the Colonel scanned the audience for a sympathetic questioner. He found the familiar face of the reporter from the Spanish equivalent of the Police Gazette.

A reporter from the Spanish Daily, *El Pais*, was next, more by the force of his voice than any invitation on the part of the Colonel.

'Inspector Fernandez, since you joined the investigation in Spain, have you been satisfied with the steps taken by the Guardia Civil, and are they co-operating fully with your own inquiries now that you are here?'

About to respond, Michael felt the force of the Colonel's stare, saying: 'You may answer, but you had better be very, very careful.'

Michael made the right kind of noises, responding in Spanish.

A reporter from *The Times* posed a similar question in English and Michael gave a similar reply, noticing from the corner of his eye that Sergeant Ramirez was whispering in the Colonel's ear.

A Dutch reporter, Jan van Orterloo, posed the next question in perfect English. 'Colonel Cardells, why did you specifically invite Dutch and German reporters to this press conference?'

Again Michael interpreted the question for the Colonel's benefit, and in turn he was required to interpret the answer.

'As part of our investigations, information came to light suggesting the Harringtons may have been in contact with Dutch or German property owners or agents. There has been little coverage of the case in local Dutch and German newspapers and we' (Michael nearly said 'I', but was conscious of Sergeant Ramirez hanging onto his every word) 'thought it germane to extend the press coverage to include the Dutch and German media. A special telephone number is in the press pack for people to call and the lines will be manned by Dutch and German speaking operators.'

The next questions were aimed at John and Linda as the British tabloids probed David's and Alison's personal lives. A thinly disguised question from *The Sun* reporter suggested they might be hiding from the British Police with the rest of the fugitives on the Costa del Crime.

This brought a resounding table-thump from John Harrington as his wife blubbered at his side.

Timothy Middleton interceded to call for decorum and led the

Harringtons away with muttered comments about, 'understandably upset, distressed, all very traumatic.'

As he was ushered from the room, John Harrington turned and jabbed a finger in the general direction of *The Sun* reporter.

'I'll get you, you bastard,' he shouted.

Middleton's firm hand in his back finally saw John Harrington leave the scene, but not before a myriad of flashlights popped in unison.

The Colonel allowed one more question as a sop.

The *Daily Mail's* Mark Slaughter grabbed the opportunity. 'Inspector Fernandez, is it true that you were instrumental in the capture and arrest of a notorious gang of motorway robbers on the day you arrived in Alicante?'

Ramirez whispered furtively into the Colonel's ear. Michael shrugged and shook his head in response to the Colonel's piercing glare.

'We're here to discuss the disappearance of the Harringtons,' said the Colonel. 'This is not helpful.'

He slammed his folder shut, shoved it toward Ramirez as he descended from the platform and marched between the aisles of seats to the door, muttering to Ramirez and ignoring shouted questions from reporters.

Jose Luis gathered Michael by the elbow and propelled him forward. 'Come on, and for Christ's sake don't say anything on the way out.'

Michael did as he was told.

Ramirez was waiting just outside the door of the business suite.

'The Colonel wants to see you both in the ante-room.'

'That went rather well, I thought,' said the Colonel, puffing himself up to even larger proportions. 'Pity about John Harrington's outburst, but it will capture the headlines if nothing else. We'll just have to wait and see if we get any new leads. Thank you all for your help. Now I must get back to the office. Keep me informed if anything turns up.'

As Ramirez hurried out, shadowing the departing Colonel, Michael called out in English, 'Thank you for your help, Sergeant

Ramirez.'

'You're welcome,' he replied in English, with barely a trace of accent.

Penny was in the lobby when Michael and Jose Luis came through from the ante-room. She had been busy stacking the surplus press packs and rolling up the Nottingham Police banner and now crouched to cram it into a heavy cardboard tube. Jose Luis spotted her in a tight-fitting skirt that stretched virtually to breaking point around her trim hips. As she bent on one knee, the soles of her white ankle-strap stilettos appeared ready to split. Michael had seen them before and thought they were graceless, even vulgar. But then, Penny's inclination to dress provocatively was just one of the things that made Michael feel less than comfortable in her presence and contributed to the demise of their ill-fated relationship.

Behind him, Jose Luis spoke in faltering English, 'I help you?' he said as he bent to help Penny slide the banner into the tube.

'Ooh, that's a tight fit,' Penny exclaimed.

She rose to her feet and wriggled to straighten her skirt. If the words were lost on Jose Luis, the innuendo certainly wasn't especially when reinforced by Penny's flirtatious grin. Jose Luis took a step back.

'Now, which of you handsome men is going to take me to lunch? I'm back to England tomorrow and it would be nice to see a bit of Alicante before I leave.'

'Sorry, I've got things to do myself,' Michael said before Jose Luis had fully grasped the invitation, 'but I'm sure Jose Luis will be delighted to take you out to lunch.'

'Si, er…yes.' Jose Luis was finally up to speed with the conversation. 'I know nice restaurant.' He took another step backward.

Penny stooped again to pick up the folders and the cardboard tube. She dumped them on the reception desk. 'I'll collect these when I come back,' she said to the startled concierge before linking through Jose Luis's arm, looking back as she marched him to the door.

'And Michael, I will be having supper with you tonight!'

'You're staying at this hotel?'

She walked away with metal heel tips clicking on the marble floor like a stonemason's chisel. 'Of course,' she replied without breaking her stride.

Michael took a salad for lunch and returned to his room, channel hopping on the small wall-mounted television. Only BBC News 24 offered any respite from the seemingly endless stream of commercials on the Spanish channels. By five o'clock the news editors had sifted the day's events and the morning press conference was second only to Spain's Prime Minister attending a summit meeting in Rome to discuss the latest round of reforms to the constitution of the European Union.

Colonel Cardells featured prominently in the slot and Michael realised it was true what they said – television did make people look fatter. His platitudes about efforts being made to find the Harringtons were heavily edited, but the message came through. A brief snippet of John Harrington followed, with Spanish subtitles and a close up of the weeping Linda. They had tactfully omitted the outburst directed toward *The Sun* reporter.

The report continued and the Nottingham Police logo now appeared in the background as the announcer spoke.

'As a measure of concern by the British Police, they have sent one of their own policemen, Detective Inspector Michael Fernandez, to work alongside the Guardia Civil. Here's what he had to say.'

The camera zoomed in on Michael speaking in Spanish and answering one of the reporters' questions. First time on television and different to the image he was used to seeing in the mirror. His Spanish sounded fine to him though he wondered if he had picked up a British accent over the years.

The report ended with a still shot of David and Alison Harrington above the telephone number of the Alicante Police incident room.

It wasn't long before BBC News 24 caught up, though the item merited just a brief slot towards the end of the revolving half-hourly news summary. Michael featured again, this time answering in English and then a short clip showed John Harrington reading from the prepared script.

In a statement that would not have pleased Colonel Cardells or his bosses, the correspondent closed by saying: 'This is the second incident of its kind after another British couple were found tortured and murdered in the Costa Blanca last year. There are fears that this might be a copycat crime and there must be questions about the safety of Britons travelling to this part of Spain with a view to buying property.'

Five minutes later the phone rang in a long high-pitched electronic chirp that woke him from a heat-induced state of drowsiness.

It was Chief Superintendent Bowater. 'Just seen it on the BBC. Good show Michael, I thought you came over well. The logo looked good, don't you think? All good publicity. Any coverage over there yet?'

Michael put him in the picture and told him about the outburst by John Harrington, warning him to look out for *The Sun* in the morning.

Bowater seemed to think Michael should have prevented the incident.

Michael didn't bother with excuses.

'So what's next?' Bowater enquired.

Michael hadn't given this much thought but blustered through, saying he had a couple more people to see in the morning before he went to Alicante police station to await responses to the news coverage. It sounded plausible to him and the Chief Superintendent had no better suggestions.

'Penny's not with you by any chance?' said Bowater.

'No.' Michael bristled. 'What makes you think she might be?'

'Oh, er… it's just that I've tried calling her room and there's no answer. Any idea where she might be?'

'At lunch, sir. It's lunchtime here in Spain, and...' Bowater must have called Penny before calling him, perhaps hoping to get a report on proceedings from his spy. Michael was tempted to say she'd gone off with one of the Spanish policemen for a free lunch; but the gentleman in him, or the caution, led him to make excuses. 'She said she wanted to do some shopping as well.'

'What!' Bowater exploded. 'You let her go out on her own? Alicante's a dangerous city by all accounts. What on earth are you thinking of to let her wander round a place like that alone? She could get lost, mugged, even abducted. I expected better of you, Fernandez. You'd better find her and make sure she's safe. And for Christ's sake, make sure you stay with her and get her on that plane tomorrow. We're going to look pretty stupid if anything happens to her.'

'I'm sure she'll be fine – she's not exactly the shy retiring type.'

'You'd better bloody hope so. Now get off your arse and find her.'

The phone slammed down and Michael shouted back at the receiver, 'f... you too,' though he could not quite bring himself to say the word.

After six or seven repeats of the same news broadcasts, the novelty of seeing himself on the television was beginning to wear off. He dozed and woke to find it past seven-thirty. He telephoned reception to ask if Ms Edwardes was in her room but the receptionist was unable to help. A call to room 318 failed to produce a response and, with Bowater's words ringing in his ears about danger on the streets, even knowing better didn't prevent a flutter of anxiety.

His first timid tap on the door of room 318 would, he realised, have failed to disturb a slumbering dormouse let alone someone sleeping off a Penny-style shopping expedition and wine-soaked lunch. He knew from experience that Penny rarely said 'no' when there was anything left in the bottle.

So he rapped harder, surprising himself with the volume produced by his knuckles on the hardwood door. Finally, he was relieved to hear movement from inside and Penny's voice.

'Just a moment.'

As he waited, he suddenly realised he could be recognised from television by anyone passing – and here he was, calling on a woman in her hotel bedroom.

The door opened and Penny appeared in an oversized bathrobe. From her damp tousled blonde hair, it was obvious she had just taken a shower.

His embarrassment increased when a door opened at the far end of the corridor and a couple walked toward him. They glanced at him and into the open door as they passed.

His rehearsed lines deserted him and he stuttered, 'Ah, Penny, er... is everything all right? Only the Chief Superintendent was worried, er... and I wondered if you wanted to have that supper tonight.'

Not wishing to stare at Penny's proudly displayed cleavage, he shifted his gaze to the background. Penny had just started in with her flippant response, 'Why, Michael, I didn't think you cared,' when he spotted the brown leather size seven slip-on loafers at the foot of the dishevelled bed. He looked at her, then at the door, then the floor, then toward the end of the corridor.

'Sorry... I see you're busy.' He began to move away.

'Michael!' called Penny, now speaking sing-song to the back of his head, 'Where do you think you're going? What about the Chief Superintendent?'

'Don't worry, I've covered for you,' he answered without turning around.

CHAPTER SEVEN

There was no need to look up from his breakfast cup to know Penny approached. She joined him at the table and caught the waiter's eye to ask for tea.

'So Michael, are you going to run me to the airport?'

If Penny felt any embarrassment about the previous night's events, it was impossible to detect.

'I thought your Spanish consort would take you,' Michael said peevishly.

'Don't be like that Michael. It was only a bit of fun.'

'He is a married man, you know.'

Penny giggled girlishly and touched the back of his hand. 'Oh Michael, you're such an old prude. Anyway, what did you tell Bowater?'

'I told him you went shopping in the afternoon, but you'd better say we had dinner together last night. He thinks I should be looking after you.'

She giggled again and squeezed his hand. 'You are sweet Michael.'

He withdrew his hand.

'What time's your plane?'

He deposited Penny at the departure point of El Altet airport a comfortable two hours before her midday flight. Her suitcase and the collection of public relations material were taken from the car and loaded onto a luggage trolley, but that was as far as courtesies extended.

She'd pecked him on the cheek by way of farewell and he was still wiping away bright red lip-gloss as he drove toward Javea to meet James Weeks, Asesoria, who was free for lunch. They'd agreed to meet at the Christobal Colon Restaurant on Javea's Arenal beach.

Michael took a table facing the promenade beneath a striped canvas canopy that offered shade and a cool breeze. He scanned the beach, trying hard not to stare, but staring, at topless sunbathers strolling at the water's edge. He tried to conjure up a mental image of James Weeks, whom he'd spoken to only once on the phone. But it was difficult to untangle his image of the man from the topless bathers, brown slip-on shoes, Penny's lip-gloss and a feeling that he should have done something to protect Spain from Nottingham. However, in James Weeks, he was expecting someone with a bit of dignity for a change.

His quiet contemplation was disturbed by the rumble of a Harley Davidson sweeping into a narrow parking space at the side of the restaurant. A portly figure in a black helmet dismounted from the black and silver machine. The helmet was discarded and draped over the handlebars to reveal a head of wispy brown hair stuck to the forehead. Beads of sweat trickled down sideboards and disappeared into a thicket of whiskers. The man's generous frame was not flattered by a loose-fitting T-shirt, faded denim jeans and open-toed canvas sandals.

James Weeks had obviously conjured up his own mental picture of Michael as he strode directly to the table and introduced himself.

'Let's sit inside,' he said, rolling his eyes. 'These stalls are for tourists, it's much cooler inside at the back.'

They relocated to the air conditioned rear of the restaurant and took a table with a pink linen tablecloth and matching napkins neatly folded and placed in polished wine goblets. A frozen glass tankard filled with icy beer appeared in front of James Weeks as he sat down. Michael declined the offer of the same in favour of another mineral water. An ashtray appeared next, placed alongside a packet of Mehari's cigars and a silver Dunhill lighter.

Though the beard made it difficult to be precise about his age, Michael put James Weeks at around thirty-five. Their initial exchange had told Michael that this was a well-educated man, but now, 'I'm an air force brat,' James said, 'in case you're wondering. My father retired early from the RAF and came to live here in Spain.

I spent all my school days here in various international schools and then at university. I guess you could say I'm British by birth, but Spanish by nature. And what about you, Inspector Frenandez?'

Michael was still scrutinising the stranger opposite, trying to make sense of the confusing impression he presented.

'Please, call me Michael. I guess you could say the converse is true in my case.'

James looked slightly perplexed, but didn't want to pry. 'I usually take the menu del dia.' he said. 'There's wine included but it's not the best so I order something a little better. Is that all right with you?'

Michael nodded and within minutes faced a glass of Rioja Reserva.

Time for business. 'You set up the bank account for John Harrington, I believe, and obtained his NIE registration?'

James took a gulp of his Rioja. 'Yes, it's standard practice. You see, lots of people come over for a couple of weeks to look at property without intending to buy. But they fall in love with a little villa in the sunshine with a view of the sea. They get home to dreary old England and decide they just can't wait to get back. So they contact me, or another asesoria, and we set the whole thing up at this end. It's all done by phone, post and email. That way, when they return to Spain, everything is in place for a quick purchase.'

Michael continued, 'You need copies of their passports, I believe?'

'Yes, for the bank account and the NIE registration. If the people are here at the time they usually pop into the office and one of the girls will take the copies. If not, I usually ask people to post me a photocopy from England. It would be impracticable to ask them to put their actual passports in the post.'

'Does anyone ever ask to see the originals? The actual passports?'

'I don't need to see them, but the bank would. It's possible to transfer money into an account created in this way, but the bank would ask to see the actual passport before any money could be withdrawn.'

'Doesn't anyone ever check the details on the photocopied passports?'

James frowned. 'What do you mean?'

'I mean, doesn't anyone ever check that the photocopied passport is valid? To see if the passport number tallies with the name?'

The frown turned almost to a scowl. 'Do I? No. Why should I? But as I said, the originals have to be produced to the bank. Look, are you suggesting there might be a forgery or something?'

'I'm sorry.' Michael nodded. 'I didn't mean to imply anything about the way you conduct your business. I'm just trying to understand the process. Forgery is always a possibility of course, not necessarily to commit a fraud, but sometimes just to disguise someone's real identity.'

'But it can't be that easy to get hold of a forged passport, surely?'

'No, but it's easy to tamper with a photocopy,' Michael said, before changing the subject. 'So how's business at the moment?'

James smiled. 'The last few years have been exceptional. I sometimes wonder if anyone wants to stay in England. But the last couple of months have been fraught with problems. Since the recession started, money is tight and the pound has weakened against the euro by something like fifteen percent. When you're buying a house for two hundred and fifty thousand euros, that's a lot of extra money to find. I've had at least half a dozen clients pull out in the last few weeks.'

'Really?' Michael sat back as lunch arrived.

'It's a typical problem. People come over with a budget of, say, one hundred and fifty thousand, but these days that's not really enough in this part of the Costa Blanca at any rate. Then some quick-talking agent persuades them to extend their budget with scares about rising house prices. So they stretch to two hundred thousand and that gives them no leeway. Next minute, the pound sinks and they're in a mess. Of course the most cautious people reserve their euros in advance as a hedge against this kind of problem, but you'd be surprised how few people think of it. If only

Britain would join the euro life would be much simpler, but you little Englanders think you're so different to the rest of Europe.'

'I trust you are not including me in that description.' Michael said.

'I don't know you well enough to answer that,' James replied.

Michael changed the subject. 'I understand it is common practice to under-declare the purchase price of a property when the official documents are drawn up in order to avoid tax. Is that true?'

James bristled. 'I hope you're not accusing me of anything.'

'No, no. Of course not. I'd just like to understand the process.'

James relaxed and smiled. 'I think, Michael, it's not the process you need to understand, but the culture. You see paying tax here is – how can I put it? – well, more of a voluntary event. A certain amount of tax avoidance is tolerated, even accepted. In the case of the property market, prices have risen so rapidly that the tax revenue produced is beyond anything that might reasonably have been contemplated. So people find their own way of reducing their liability.'

'And is that legal?'

James spluttered. 'Of course it's not legal, but the Spanish are phlegmatic about such things. Let's just say there is no real effort to clamp down, so naturally people take advantage.'

'I doubt that would happen in Britain,' Michael said.

'Indeed not, but perhaps that's one reason why there are so many expats living here in Spain. That and the excellent wine.'

James chinked Michael's glass and took another gulp of the Rioja.

'Cheers,' he said.

'*Salud*,' Michael replied.

Michael looked out for a supermarket on the way back to Alicante. He'd exhausted the supply of mineral water in the mini-bar in his hotel room and, conscious of the hotel's inflated prices (and the rate at which he was drinking the stuff), he thought he'd stock up.

Passing through Benissa he noticed a sign for Mercadona so he followed the directions to the car park. Being a Saturday afternoon, it was crowded and two laps around the fume-filled, grimy underground car park left him wishing he hadn't bothered. He was about to leave when he spotted a car reversing from a space next to the exit ramp. He pulled into the tight – very tight – space between two concrete columns and then walked to the steps that led to the store.

A few minutes later he found the water and placed a dozen bottles in the trolley. He was on his way to the checkout when he noticed a special promotion on Cardinal Mendoza Gran Solera Brandy de Jerez. This, he knew, was like nectar and knocked the spots off even the very best French Cognacs – though it was just as expensive. He couldn't resist.

Exiting the lift, pushing a trolley over the uneven car park, he had a sense of movement behind and turned to see two sharply dressed young men leaving the stairwell. They turned to the left, heading for the far side of the car park. As he moved toward his car he was gripped by a sudden sense of unease. The two men carried no shopping, had no trolley, basket or bags. Why had they descended the stairs from the supermarket?

He deposited the brandy and bottles of water in the boot of the hire car and returned the trolley to the bay, recovering the euro coin from the slot. The car was stuffy and hot so he started the engine, turned on the air conditioning and opened the windows. He engaged reverse gear and took a careful look in the wing mirrors to make sure he didn't take a further chunk out of the already gouged concrete columns. Over the revs of the engine a shrill cry came from the vicinity of the lift.

'Help! – they've taken my bag,' shrieked an English voice.

Almost immediately he heard loud revs from another motor, followed by a screech of tyres from the far side of the car park.

A black four-wheel drive lurched from a parking space and rounded a row of parked cars at speed, heading for the exit.

Sensing something was wrong, Michael slammed the accelerator to the floor. The hire car lurched back. He stamped hard on the brake pedal, bringing the car to a halt in the path of the on-coming jeep. By now he could see it was a Subaru.

The rest seemed to happen in slow motion. Blue smoke emerged from the Subaru's tyres before the sound of screeching rubber reached his ears. He braced for the collision, gripping the steering wheel and straightening his elbows, jamming his back against the seat. He screwed his eyes tight shut and tensed the whole of his body. 'Shit, no seat belt,' he realised a fraction of a second before the impact.

The sound of crumpling metal was surprisingly quiet and soft, as seemed the force of the crash. But gradually it reached a crescendo of cracking, jangling, twisting, tearing, shattering metal and glass. Michael's head remained motionless as the rest of his body, braced against the back of the seat, lurched sideways once the metal had crumpled to its full extent. The muscles in his neck stretched and tore as his right ear thumped against his shoulder. Like the recoil of a gun, his head snapped back in the opposite direction, smashing his left ear against the sill of driver's side door with a thud that echoed through his brain. The pain came slowly, rising and ebbing then rising again, each time to a new level of intensity. He waited for it to peak as he made a mental assessment of the extent of his injury. The noise of the crash passed as abruptly as it had arrived and the sound of tinkling pieces of metal and glass gradually subsided, like the last few drops of rain at the end of a cloudburst. Silence returned.

He gathered his wits and gingerly turned his neck. The contour of a man's head bulged from the passenger side of the Subaru's crazed but unbroken windscreen.

Despite the pain, Michael leant against the door until it fell open. Still dazed, he walked around the front of his car to the driver's side of the Subaru. The front seat had jerked forward and was pinning the young driver against the steering wheel. Even so, the man had managed to shove the twisted door open and, with his hand on the roof of the car, he was trying to lever himself out. With all the force he could muster, Michael shoved his right hip against the partially open door. The man let out an ear-piercing scream as his forearm crunched between the door and its frame. It signified the end of the struggle.

A voice said, 'Are you all right?' A woman's face leaned over him.

That was the last thing he remembered.

'You're a regular Superman, Michael. What are you trying to do? Solve the Costa Blanca crime wave single-handed?' said Jose Luis, bursting through the doors of the private room in Denia's General Hospital at eleven o'clock on Sunday morning. 'Nothing but the best for you, I see. We must look after our celebrity detective.'

Michael smiled weakly, but that sent a searing pain down his neck, now cocooned in a cushioned brace that restricted his head movement to little more than a nod. His left ear was throbbing inside a padded bandage and he didn't need to look in a mirror to know he had a black eye.

'What chaos you've caused,' said Jose Luis. 'Two villains in hospital, one with head injuries and the other with a broken arm that he insists was not caused by the crash. Two vehicles written off – I hope you had full insurance on the hire car by the way – and a Mercadona supermarket closed for half a day. The Colonel will be delighted, especially as you have no jurisdiction over here. What on earth did you think you were doing?'

'I didn't think,' croaked Michael.

'I guess we'll have to call it a citizen's arrest, but there could be repercussions, especially if the two villains decide to sue.'

'Is that likely?'

'Only when they get out of jail and with a bit of luck you'll be back in England by then. By the way, they recovered this from your car.'

The Cardinal Mendoza was safe, protected by its soft cork box.

'You have excellent taste. Here, take a look at these.'

Jose Luis tossed the morning papers onto the bed. There was coverage in both the British and Spanish press, with most showing John Harrington comforting his tearful wife, though *The Sun* had opted for a close-up of the finger-stabbing John, eyes bulging, mouth wide open, face contorted with anger. Michael was mentioned in most of the coverage and, in the British press at least, he received more column inches than Colonel Cardells.

A couple of phone calls had come in, with possible sightings of the missing couple in Denia and Calpe. It was too soon for the weekly foreign language papers and Jose Luis thought these might provoke more interest in the case, but they would have to wait until the middle of next week.

In the meantime he suggested Michael take a rest. The doctors had said he should remain in bed for a couple of days at least.

'By the way, your Chief Superintendent has been trying to reach you. We told him you were alive and well, but he still wants to talk to you. Perhaps he wants you to go home.'

Michael thought he detected a hopeful note in Jose Luis's voice.

'Anyway, I must go now. If there's anything you need, let me know. Just take it easy and don't go making any more citizen's arrests.'

Jose Luis eased himself off the bed and moved toward the door.

'Oh... I almost forgot. We had a call from a woman. She wants you to call her. Says it's personal.' He withdrew a notepad from his pocket and turned the pages. 'Here you are, Rosana Ferrando Moll.' He tore the page from the pad and placed it on the bedside table. 'Anyone you know?'

Moll? Where had he heard that before? Cogs were whirring but the accident seemed to have put them out of synchronisation. Output zero. He stuttered, 'No. I don't think so.'

'Perhaps our intrepid hero has a fan,' said Jose Luis as he headed back to the door. 'Just stay out of trouble. If anything happens, we'll let you know. Take it easy. Bye.'

Michael stared at the paper, trying to unscramble his brain. Concentration deserted him, replaced by inexplicable foreboding which only relented when tiredness took over and he drifted into an uneasy sleep.

He woke with a jolt an hour and a half later when a dark haired nurse whose sturdy white shoes he'd noticed earlier, prodded him apologetically.

'Sorry, but I have to take your blood pressure and pulse. Head injuries, you know. Can't be too careful. Anyway, it will soon be time for lunch.'

Michael complied meekly, dazed from disjointed sleep and disturbed dreams. Sleep had not alleviated the anxiety induced by the name on the paper that still lay at his bedside, but gradually the mists rolled away and an image came into focus... Moll? Bar Moll. The church square in Parcent.

'Get me a phone, will you?' he snapped, before recognising the tone in his voice and adding, 'Please.'

'You're supposed to be resting,' the nurse protested, only to be persuaded by several repeats of "please" as Michael attempted charm.

He waited until the nurse had left before punching in the number. As the ringing tone chirped in his ear he almost hoped that no one would answer. His throat was dry and though he sensed what was about to happen, he had no idea what he was going to say.

'*Si, digame*,' the woman responded in a quick, matter-of-fact voice. Michael was still getting used to the Spanish way of answering the telephone. Literally translated it meant "speak to me," but it was framed in the imperative and sounded more like an instruction than an invitation.

Michael's reply was much more politely put. 'Please – may I speak to Rosana Ferrando Moll, please.'

'Speaking.'

'This is Michael Fernandez, you wanted to speak to me?'

Rosana's voice slowed. 'This is rather difficult, Señor Fernandez, I'm not sure where to start. Your full name is Miguel-Ángel Fernandez?'

'Yes.'

'Was your father's name Francisco?'

'It was.'

'He came from Parcent?'

That seemed hard to deny at this point. 'He did.'

'Then your grandmother was right. She saw you on the news last night and even before they mentioned your name, she recognised you.'

'My grandmother?'

'Maria Carmen Fernandez. Her son was Francisco, your father.

She wants to see you. She hasn't stopped talking about you since last night. You look exactly like your father, she says. She's so excited.'

Michael played for time. 'What's this to you?' Too late came the realisation that this was a tactless remark.

'I'm sorry. Of course, I understand this must be a shock. My grandmother and yours are best friends and cousins. When Maria Carmen saw you on the television she asked me to call you. We tried to put her off, told her she must be mistaken, but she's adamant. Crying, joy, excitement, disbelief – call it what you want, but she knows it's you. You have to see her. She's eighty-seven you know and very frail. It was a shock to her. If you don't come, it would break her heart. She needs to see you urgently.'

Michael rarely failed to rise to a challenge. Though there were many things in his life that he'd rather not have done, when faced with the inevitable, he'd get on with it. But this was different. This was not just a few minutes or hours that he could write off before returning to matters of more importance.

'Look, there are things you don't know about, that happened years ago. My grandmother, if she is my grandmother, will understand all this.'

'What do you mean? *If* she's your grandmother? There's no possible doubt. I know all about what happened with your father. That was fifty years ago, it broke your grandmother's heart and... I'm sorry, but you can't do this. What kind of a man refuses to see his own grandmother?' Her voice tightened. 'I know it's none of my business, but if you'd seen her elation when she saw your face, as I did, you would understand.'

'And if you know about my father, you must know why I can't go back to Parcent.' As soon as he had said it, he realised his mistake.

'Back? What do you mean, back? Have you been here before?'

He needed a way out while he had the chance. 'Look, I have to tell you I'm in hospital at the moment, so it's out of the question, anyway.'

This sounded like a feeble excuse, since he'd been talking

vigorously, and obviously would not remain in hospital forever.

'But I'll give it some thought,' he said. 'That's the best that I can say. I can't make any promises. I have to go now. The doctor says I must rest.'

That excuse was as feeble as the last, but it produced hesitation.

'Goodbye,' he said. 'I will call you again.'

As he replaced the receiver he thought he heard a faint voice saying, 'But, Miguel-Ángel...' and it left a feeling of desperate ill-ease impossible to cast off. There was something in Rosana's voice, something in the words, 'But Miguel-Ángel,' that began to haunt him.

He wrestled with the stiff white bed linen for the rest of the afternoon. The pains in his head and neck reached an intensity that could not be subdued by painkillers. Every attempt to blank out his mind was frustrated by Parcent zooming in and out of focus. This time, he also saw his father; an image that had once peered out from a silver picture frame on the cabinet at the side of his mother's favourite chair. Dark hair slicked down tight, precise parting on the left. The slight sharpness in the cheeks softened by the smile and the dimpled chin. The eyes, large, round and deep-set beneath thick eyebrows that appeared at first glance to sparkle for the camera.

Another image flashed across Michael's mind.

An old woman with a deeply-lined complexion. She came closer. Her eyes stared back at Michael as if he were looking into a mirror.

By evening, Michael was still considering his next move.

It had been wretched, the way he'd handled the telephone call, but he despaired at the idea of acquainting himself with a part of his past that he knew he should never explore.

Perhaps his injuries provided the justification he needed. Yes, that was it – call Bowater, catch the next plane home and slip back into work.

Whether he could have taken this course, he would never know, because he was interrupted whilst debating with himself.

'You have a visitor, Señor Fernandez.' The nurse bustled importantly into the room, pulled him up, fluffed his pillows and straightened the bed.

He flopped back and then sat up bolt upright to ask about his visitor.

Before he could get out a word, the nurse departed with a very unsubtle wink and the visitor had appeared at the door.

Michael surveyed his guest with caution, starting with dainty cut-away pink leather sandals, moving up to a sylph-like, belted waistline and on to a startling head of strong dark auburn hair.

'Are you Rosana?' he asked in what he hoped was an unknowing, invalidish tone.

'You sound as if you were expecting me.'

'I'm sorry... ' Michael continued weakly. 'Please... sit down.'

Rosana pulled the hard plastic chair closer to the bed and crossed her legs, straightening the creases in her figure-hugging cream trousers.

There was a soft rustle from her white silk blouse as she settled back in the chair and tossed her wavy locks back behind her shoulders in a pose like someone, it suddenly struck him, on the cover of a romance novel.

He wanted to laugh for a second, but was suddenly conscious that he was staring at her face, studying the harmony of her features.

An instant later he became aware of his own pose, with the neck brace pushing his chin up and the heavy bandage still clamped against his ear. He was sitting on the edge of the bed in a hospital gown tied at the back and ending just above his knees. His bare legs and feet dangled in mid-air. He put his knees together and tugged at the gown.

'They told me about the accident,' Rosana said. 'Are you all right?'

Rosana's arrival had distracted him from the pain.

'Oh, yes. As you can see, it's nothing really.' He tried to grin. 'I'll be running round in a couple of days.'

'You don't seem too popular with the Guardia Civil,' she said.

'You've heard.' He continued, 'Look, about this afternoon, on the telephone, I behaved rather badly. It's just that...'

'No need to apologise. I don't think I handled things very well myself. I know what a shock it must have been.'

'Actually, it wasn't a shock. I mean...'

'You expected a call?'

'No, but as soon as I got the message to ring you, I suspected what it might be about. Your name, Moll, I saw it outside the bar in the church square. It didn't take much to put two and two together.'

'Bar Moll, that's my uncle's place. It's been there for years. So I was right, you have been to Parcent before?'

'No, well, only once, a couple of days ago as part of my investigation.'

'So where do you go from here?'

'My grandmother, you mean? Of course I'll see her.'

Rosana's eyes widened. 'Oh, Miguel-Ángel,' she said. 'That would be wonderful.'

'You don't need to call me Miguel-Ángel. Just Michael will do.'

'When will you come?'

'It's rather difficult at the moment.' He had genuine excuses. 'I'm stuck here in hospital for now and of course I'm working, so I can't just swan off when I feel like it. And I have no car. Well I did, but I wrecked it.'

'You could always hire another one.'

'That might be difficult.'

'Miguel-Ángel Fernandez.' She raised her elbows and placed her hands on her hips. 'I'll drive you there myself – and as for work, I'll speak to Captain Jose Luis Perez. I'm sure we can arrange a few days sick leave. When are you coming?'

'No, don't speak to Captain Perez. Is tomorrow all right?'

'Tomorrow,' she repeated, as if she'd anticipated the answer. 'It's the start of the fiestas and the whole family are having lunch at Restaurante L'Era.'

'Oh.' *The whole lost tribe...* 'Perhaps some other time... '

'Tomorrow it is. I'll pick you up at ten o'clock.' She turned and left the room leaving a trace of perfume; a sort of polished mahogany.

The next morning Michael's suitcase and clothes had mysteriously arrived from his hotel in Alicante. By ten o'clock he was shaved and dressed carefully in sports jacket, white shirt and tie, grey flannel trousers and freshly polished black Oxfords. The neck brace had been discarded, despite protests from the nurse and the wound on his ear was covered with a small piece of Elastoplast. He'd been pacing up and down the room for half an hour. He wasn't sure he could face Parcent and the thought crossed his mind that he might escape the hospital and leave a note for Rosana making work an excuse. But he had lingered, indecisive, for a moment too long. Here she was.

Today Rosana wore a short-sleeved peach cotton two-piece suit with a skirt just above the knee. Her elegant matching peach shoes with pointed toes and low oblong heels told him this was a woman of exquisite taste. He stood up and she greeted him with a stab of a kiss on both cheeks before stepping back to scrutinise him.

Michael stood to attention and adjusted his tie. 'Will I do?'

'Perfect.' She linked her arm through his, grabbed his suitcase and marched him out of the room.

On the journey to Parcent, Rosana pried, casually, but with a glance at him after each answer, as if to check his sincerity.

'Your accent?' she said after a while. 'I can't quite place it. Have you spent time in South America?'

'No... ' His answer hung in the air. 'Well, my ex-wife was Argentinean. I suppose it rubbed off.'

'That explains it.'

'About my grandmother,' he said quickly, 'You said she's very frail?'

'I may have exaggerated a little. She suffers from diabetes and has a few aches and pains, but she does quite well for eighty-seven.'

'Where will I meet her?'

'Don't worry,' she replied. 'We're going straight to her house where you can meet her alone. Then after half an hour or so we'll go to the lunch.'

'I'd prefer not to be alone when I meet her, if that's all right with you.'

'Of course, I'll be with you if you want. You've caused quite a stir, you know.'

'What do you mean?'

'It's nothing, just don't let any anyone bother you.'

'All right. And you say there's a lunch?'

'At two, at Parcent's famous paella restaurant, L'Era. You like paella?'

'I've never tasted paella.'

'Miguel-Ángel Fernandez,' she said in that now familiar psuedo-sisterly tone, 'you've never tasted paella?'

'Why do you keep calling me Miguel-Ángel? I use Michael, I always have, from school on up.'

'Michael is such a plain name and not the least bit Spanish.'

That's the whole point, he thought.

'And besides, Miguel-Ángel is a lovely name. Don't you think?'

He didn't answer.

Rosana parked in the Placa del Poble, the square next to Bar Moll and they walked the short distance to the home of Maria Carmen Fernandez. Rosana linked her arm through Michael's as she strode purposefully down the narrow street. It wasn't clear whether she did this to support him or to prevent him from running away and, against a rising tide of nervousness, he struggled to remember what he planned to say when he entered the house.

Halfway along the street they stopped at an ancient wooden door centred between a pair of grilled and shuttered windows. Without thinking, he lifted his head skywards to view two more storeys of balconied windows. The pain in his neck made him wince. He took a deep breath and felt to see that his tie was straight.

'Ready?' Rosana tapped on the door and stepped inside the cool, dark interior.

'Maria Carmen,' she called out, 'Miguel-Ángel is here.'

Through a short vestibule and across a larger living room, he saw his grandmother rise from a high-backed chair. She squinted through gold rimmed spectacles as he walked up to her and reached to clasp his face between her hands. She pulled his head down, kissed him on both cheeks and rested her head against his chest. He put his arms round her.

'Thank God,' she whispered.

After a moment he eased her back into the chair. She raised her spectacles and wiped at tears. 'You are so like your father. You have his eyes.'

'Sit down.' Rosana moved a chair behind him. 'I'll make coffee.'

Michael lowered himself into the chair. 'Grandmother.' Now he half-remembered what he'd planned to say. 'I don't know what to say.'

'Say nothing,' she said. 'It's enough that you have come.' She was silent for a few seconds. 'Susan, your mother?'

'She died two years ago.'

'I'm sorry to hear that. What age...?'

'She was sixty-seven.'

Maria Carmen shook her head slightly. 'The young English nurse... later I recognised her courage. You must miss her. Both your parents.'

'I do.'

'Susan wrote to me when you were born and occasionally after that. They were very warm letters. I often wondered if I should...'

'There's no need to explain anything.'

He didn't know there had been letters.

'Coffee,' Rosana said, coming in with a tray. 'How do you like it Miguel-Ángel?'

Michael cringed again at the use of his Spanish name. It felt as if he now had two personas – one Spanish, one English. 'Black with plenty of sugar,' he said at length.

Rosana placed the cups on a small table next to Maria Carmen's chair.

They drank the coffee in silence and Maria Carmen's eyes remained fixed on Michael's face.

They left the house with Maria Carmen clinging to Michael's arm. She stepped out with surprising vigour for someone so tiny and 'frail'. A stout black leather handbag hung over her left arm and her matching low-heeled court shoes tapped smoothly along the road.

Her deep blue outfit with the broad-rimmed hat and soft coat combined with her proud demeanour to give her a regal air.

Several neighbours had appeared on the street and they looked up, seemingly casually, as if saying to themselves: 'So this is the long lost grandson...'

'*Bon dia*, Maria Carmen,' they called out.

Maria Carmen smiled up at Michael. He glanced round, catching faces at windows and doors, and noticed how Rosana clipped along behind Maria Carmen, looking neither right nor left, like a protective chaperone.

Everyone else in the village seemed to have gathered at Restaurante L'Era and the place was buzzing with excited conversation which seemed to lull as Maria Carmen and Michael entered the dining room. Rosana led them both to a long table at one end of the room that was set for twenty. Introductions began. Uncle Jose Maria was first, offering a handshake that turned into a hug. He was Francisco's younger brother, he said, though a resemblance was hard to detect.

'They call me Pepito.' He introduced his wife, Lorena.

Pepito's eldest son, Pedro, was next.

Well scrubbed and pressed, Pedro shook Michael by the hand like a wet dog shaking its head until the ripple reaches its tail. One collar of Pedro's shirt turned up, outside the lapel of a jacket with too short sleeves. His crooked tie hung awkwardly and his brown hair went its own way, despite flat areas proving an attempt had been made to bring it under control.

'Pleased to meet you, Miguel-Ángel,' he said in faltering English.

Other introductions were quickly made.

Michael was led to a chair at the centre of the table next to Maria Carmen with Rosana sitting opposite. The other chairs filled. A young boy and girl, children of Rosana's brother, wore outfits reminiscent of Michael's Sunday school days. Rosana's mother and grandmother sat nearby; her mother nursing a lifeless left arm, the after-effect of a stroke. There were just two vacant seats.

'Oh well,' murmured Maria Carmen. 'God tries our patience.'

The gathering was completed with the arrival of a buxom, heavily made-up blonde in a short red leather skirt stretched over disturbingly bulky thighs. Lofty white heels were obviously intended to compensate for a lack of stature. Her partner, in a pale grey suit over a dazzling white shirt and paisley silk tie, swaggered in. His dark hair was manicured to a predetermined profile that had defied the breeze outside. For a second, Michael thought there might be a family resemblance, but quickly dismissed the idea. He didn't need to examine the man's shoes (though he noticed they were grey, chisel-toed slip-ons in mock crocodile) to form an impression of the latest arrival.

Maria Carmen introduced them. 'This is your cousin Julio, Pepito's youngest, and his wife, Teresa.'

'Hello, Grandma.' Julio kissed her on both cheeks.

As soon as they'd taken their seats, paella arrived, steaming in three black bottomed pans the size of dustbin lids. Everyone began to lift portions onto plates using long-handled spoons.

Several bottles of red wine arrived next, placed at intervals along the table. The bottles were scratched, slightly dusty and devoid of labels. 'It's from Pepito's bodega,' Maria Carmen said.

And then the inquisition began. What brought him to Parcent? How long was he staying? Had he ever been to Spain before? The atmosphere sometimes implied questions unasked and Michael fended off the enquiries with vague responses. He noticed that Julio's eyes flashed away whenever he looked toward him.

At last Maria Carmen scraped a large spoonful of burnt rice from the bottom of the giant pan. 'The best bit.' She tapped the sticky brown lump onto Michael's plate.

'I know. It's called *socarrat*,' said Michael, glancing towards Rosana to see on her face the anticipated look of surprise at his knowledge. 'I read about it.'

The meal ended with fresh fruit, coffee and sweet Mistela wine made from dried muscatel grapes (again from Pepito's bodega).

A handful of strangers wandered over to Michael to make his acquaintance. A few even recalled his father, though without effusing in his memory. Julio watched each encounter as if making mental notes.

It was Julio who felt it was time to bring proceedings to a close. 'Come along, Grandma, I'll walk you home.'

'No. Thank you, Julio. I'd like to walk back with Miguel-Ángel.'

She rose so awkwardly from her seat that Michael felt obliged to take her arm. Julio glowered as if regretting a decision to leave the daggers at home and marched past Teresa who was in conversation with her father-in-law.

'We're leaving,' he pronounced.

Heads turned. Silence was followed by whispering.

Back at Maria Carmen's house, Pepito and Lorena, with Rosana, led Michael out onto the rear walled terrace to sit with them in the fading light of a slowly sinking sun. But Michael's neck ached and the small talk had been tiring – as had the endless remarks about his miraculous appearance, the whispering, and the unasked questions.

He leaned over. 'It's time I started back,' he said quietly to Rosana.

She stood up, beckoned him inside to the kitchen and closed the door.

'What are you talking about?'

'I have to leave now – I have to get back to Alicante.'

'Don't be absurd.' Her fists went back on her hips.' Leave? You think you can just pop in, say hello, then turn around and disappear?'

Michael leaned back against the worktop. 'Look, I'm glad I came and I intend to keep in touch with my grandmother, but I don't belong here. I never planned to come to Parcent, or even to Spain, for that matter. I have work to do, I'm tired, I'm ill, and I need to get back to my hotel.'

Rosana folded her arms. 'You just want to slope back to your dark little closet, Miguel-Ángel Fernandez, with some theory about your father.'

'Not in the least. And it's not a theory at all. You have no idea what happened or why my father rejected this place and why I never wanted to come here.'

'Your father never rejected Spain or Parcent. He called you Miguel-Ángel, after your great-grandfather, and he taught you Spanish. And you, you've never been to Spain and you claim you never wanted to come, but you know as much about Spain as most Spaniards. *Socarrat* indeed. And now you come here dressed like some English gentleman, calling yourself Michael and acting like some out of place foreigner, but you don't fool me. It's all a façade.'

'Let's just leave this, Rosana. Some things are best left alone.'

'No, they are not. Your grandmother needs you, and you need to talk to her or you will live the rest of your life based on a misconception; full of anger and hatred.'

'I am not full of anger and hatred,' he said, glowering. 'I simply have my own feelings and opinions.' He wouldn't be pushed around, but apart from that, he was right. This could only end in trouble. 'I'd like to talk some more with my grandmother, of course, but…'

Rosana's face lit up. 'So you'll stay?

'I didn't say that, no. In any case, where on earth could I stay?'

'Here of course.' She led him back to the terrace. 'Maria Carmen, Miguel-Ángel has decided to stay to the end of the week.'

His grandmother bobbed to her feet. 'The bed's made up.'

'I'll get your bag from the car,' said Rosana, rushing into the house. 'Tell him about tonight, Maria Carmen,' she shouted back.

In a few short moments, it seemed he'd been turned into a forlorn schoolboy on holiday with relatives, itinerary pre-arranged, every move mapped out.

'It's fiesta week in the village,' Maria Carmen said enthusiastically, 'and tonight there's a Mass for our patron saint, San Lorenzo. It starts at eight and then there's a candle-lit procession and fireworks. Come, I'll show you to your room. We need to get ready.'

This was turning into his worst nightmare. All the thoughts and feelings he'd fought to suppress were being prised into the open. But still he failed to protest.

Completely out of place and uncomfortable, not just because of the hard wooden pews, Michael sat halfway down the church, grandmother on one side, Uncle Pepito on the other. Outside, across the Placa del Poble, suited, embroidered, laced and cummerbunded villagers were still converging on the tiny flower-adorned Church. Latecomers brought their own household chairs, folding picnic chairs, or red plastic chairs from Bar Moll advertising *Mahou Cerveza*. Inside, Aunt Lorena fussed over Pedro's collar. Cousin Julio was still in his sharp suit. Teresa had changed into a longer skirt and knee-high boots. Rosana sat in front, her long wavy hair lifted from her shoulders, held up either by magic or a comb.

The Mass proceeded; the community practising the rituals of Catholic belief. *A community that had failed to find compassion for his father.*

After Mass, boys in sailor suits and girls in long white dresses with blue sashes and tall black mantles of lace, filed out, the rest of the congregation following. A procession formed, its centrepiece a plinth holding the statue of San Lorenzo carried on the shoulders of eight stout men. A clergyman in gold braided costume, a mitre perched on his head, began the slow march. The village priest in a plain black robe followed and then the band, playing sombre music. Villagers, carrying candles, fell in behind and together they criss-crossed the village before returning to the square.

For a few minutes a crowd lingered in the square and Michael was standing with Maria Carmen when Rosana came up. 'I know a better place to watch the fireworks,' she whispered in Michael's ear. 'All right, Maria Carmen?'

Maria Carmen smiled as if she'd been expecting this move.

Rosana led him down a narrow side street and opened the door of an empty house. He followed her through the half-light up two flights of stairs to a rooftop terrace with a view over the chimneys and across the valley. The jagged ridge of Carrascal mountain range formed a dark silhouette in the distance, framed against the night sky and a full moon.

Across the valley floor, house lights flickered. To the east was the outline of Alcalalí, dominated, like Parcent, by a church tower. To the west Benigembla. On the outskirts of the village a crowd had gathered in the dusk.

Suddenly, a rocket soared and exploded softly with a glare that illuminated the whole of the valley in a myriad of colours and drifts of smoke. Michael clutched the wrought iron balustrade at the edge of the terrace and watched in silence. A breeze cooled the night air to a chill and the faint waft of Rosana's perfume was overpowered by the acrid smell of spent gunpowder.

Rainbow showers flared and faded. The display seemed to be reaching a climax as the frequency of the flashes increased – until a moment of silence heralded one last giant sky rocket that shrieked heavenward with a high pitched whistle, leaving a trail of smoke and sparks.

Rosana clasped Michael's arm. An ear-piercing boom split the atmosphere and resonated around the valley before bouncing back off Carrascal. The echoes faded, replaced by a faint ripple of applause from the crowd in the distance. Rosana eased back and looked up into Michael's startled face. He returned her look, his mind a jumble of emotions.

'That was loud,' he said foolishly.

'That's the whole idea.' She smiled up.

He held her gaze momentarily then turned his eyes to the panorama in front of them.

'This is a spectacular spot,' he said. 'The house, I mean. Whose is it?'

Staring out over the valley toward the mountains in the far distance, she answered.

'I think you'll find it's yours.'

Michael spent a restless night in his father's old room. I own a house in Parcent. What am I supposed to do with it? My grandmother, what am I going to say to her? What will she say to me? Where is all this leading? How can I get out of this mess? I wish I'd never come.

This was his father's home; his father's room; his father's bed. His father was a leper. Michael remembered when he had found out what a leper was; cried in his room; stood stiff in his father's presence; cringed when his father touched him.

He saw his father's face...

Saw himself take his father's hand in the days when he was getting weaker; speaking Spanish... and knowing he could never atone for the years of rejection and denial.

CHAPTER EIGHT

A chirping phone roused Michael from a fitful sleep – Jose Luis.

'How's the patient?' he asked.

'Ready for work,' Michael replied. 'Any news?'

'Great news,' Jose Luis said enthusiastically. 'We've arrested a couple of Dutchmen. They're being questioned right now. A stroke of luck really. We had a call from a Dutch couple in Holland, Mr and Mrs Ruiter. It seems your hunch was right about the Harringtons possibly contacting foreign agents. Anyway, the Ruiters were out in Spain in March and they contacted these two supposed agents through an advertisement in the Dutch edition of the Costa Blanca News.

'The agents took them to see an old finca near Orba. Well, they call it a farmhouse, but it's little more than a ruin. They were interested in the place, but got cold feet when the agents became aggressive.

'They wanted to drive Mr Ruiter to his bank to withdraw ten thousand euros for a deposit. One of them bundled Mr Ruiter into their car and drove him to Denia while the other one stayed behind with his wife.

'On the way to Denia, Mr Ruiter says the man made vague threats, saying he'd better not back out. Luckily, he had the sense to create a fuss inside the bank and the man ran off. Then he called his wife on her mobile. She managed to get to their car and drive away.

'They didn't report it at the time because they felt a bit stupid, but they've just read the story in a Dutch newspaper and contacted us. We managed to track the men down through a mobile phone number which the Ruiters gave us and then I posed as a potential buyer and set up a meeting. We picked them up last night in Orba, and here's the best.

'We confiscated the mobile phone. It's a pre-paid line and it's not been registered, but we checked calls made from the hotel in Benidorm where the Harringtons stayed and the number came up. It's clear that the Harringtons contacted the two men and they probably met. My guess is that the Harringtons visited the place in Orba so now we need to find out what happened after that. We're searching the finca this morning; sniffer dogs, digging equipment, the lot.'

Michael listened intently, but something didn't ring quite true. If these two had met the Harringtons and robbed them, or worse still abducted them, why were they so easy to track down? They'd surely have ditched the mobile phone, especially if they'd got their hands on the Harringtons' money.

'I'd better come over now. I'd like to be there when you interview them.'

'No need, Michael. You've no jurisdiction over here and we don't want to foul things up by breaking rules. We'll handle it. You're on sick leave, remember. Make the most of it. You could be on your way home in a couple of days. I'll be back in touch as soon as we have any news.'

'Have you told Chief Superintendent Bowater?'

'The Colonel spoke to him first thing. Don't worry, we gave you the credit for bringing in the foreign press. We told him what a great help you've been and he knows you're recovering after the accident.'

Michael disliked the brush-off and he would have been more insistent if he thought this was a real breakthrough, but somehow he doubted it.

He didn't mention his misgivings when he spoke to the Chief Superintendent.

'Well, Michael, looks like they've cracked it,' said Bowater, sounding smug, 'and it's all down to you. Well done. How are you, by the way?'

'My neck's still giving me a lot of pain, I think I may have whiplash.' He decided to lay it on a bit thick. 'But I should be well enough in a couple of days to stop relying on the crutches.'

'Well, take it easy, everything seems to be under control. With a bit of luck, we'll have you back here by the end of the week. By the way, where are you staying? I called your hotel last night and they said you'd checked out.'

Michael hesitated. 'Er... with my grandmother.'

'Oh, very nice – so you do have a family! It's turned out to be a bit of a holiday, after all?'

'Well, no sir... I simply thought I should perhaps...'

'Don't worry, only joking. Officially you're on sick leave so you're probably in the right place, recuperating with family. Get some rest, but keep in touch.'

In the kitchen with his grandmother half an hour later, before he'd finished his coffee, Uncle Pepito, dressed in faded jeans and work shirt, appeared at the door.

'Come on, let's go, Miguel-Ángel.'

'Where?'

'The *campo*. It's all arranged, isn't it, Mama? I'm going to give you a tour,' said Pepito, ushering Michael in the direction of the door.

After leaving the house, he led Michael a few hundred metres to one of the steep streets leading down and out of the village.

'Hop on!' Pepito slid onto the hard metal bench-seat of a small open trailer, hitched to a kind of giant garden rotavator. Michael looked baffled; he'd never seen such a contraption. 'It's a *mula mecánica*,' Pepito said. 'We did away with the real mules years ago. This one is vintage 1954.'

Michael slid aboard and Pepito set the rumbling, rattling machine in motion. They chugged down the hill leaving a cloud of blue smoke behind them.

'Watch your knees!' Pepito pushed the handlebars out wide to negotiate a bend. It was nine-thirty and the sun was beating down. Pepito reached behind to the trailer for a frayed straw hat which he plonked onto Michael's head. 'You'll need this.'

'Thanks' Michael removed the hat and used it to fan his face.

They trundled onto a cart track, the trailer bounced up and down for fifty metres until the engine spluttered to a halt. Pepito dismounted and waved his hand over a plot that resembled an English allotment. The rich red-brown earth was freshly tilled and planted with tomatoes, peppers, beans, onions, aubergines, courgettes, peas and pumpkins, all lined up in neat rows.

'Well now, what do you think?' Pepito pulled a handkerchief from his pocket and mopped his brow.

'It's all very nice.' Michael climbed down. 'I'm impressed.'

'There's more.' Pepito marched off along the long thin plot, leading Michael into a terraced olive grove at the far end. 'A lot more. Seventy-four trees at the last count,' he said. 'Good trees, as well, but there's no money in olives these days. The vineyard's over here.'

They crossed the olive grove and scrambled up a low stone wall. Row after row of lush green vines stretched out before them. Michael made a quick calculation. Fifty rows of fifty vines – two thousand five hundred.

'Pepito,' said Michael, 'what's all this about?'

'It's yours, Miguel-Ángel. Yours and mine. And there's more. Six plots like this on the other side of the village with almonds and olives. And a large orange grove. Then there's mother's house, of course. That belongs to us as well, but Maria Carmen has the right to live there for life – and there's the other house too, the one Rosana showed you.' Pepito took off his hat and twisted it thoughtfully. 'Oh, and there's an old *riu rau*. I'll show you that later. It's the arched building where we used to dry the grapes for raisins. These days we use it for storage.'

'But Pepito, how can any of this be mine?'

'When my father, your grandfather, died eight years ago, under Spanish law everything came to your father and me as the direct descendants. When Francisco died, his half automatically passed to you. So it's yours.'

'But I don't want any of this.'

'No – no, it's yours, ours. We have joint ownership and nothing can be done with it unless we agree. But come along, let's have some breakfast.'

At the side of the olive grove, a dry stone wall made a seat. Pepito fetched a basket from the trailer and lifted out freshly baked bread drizzled with olive oil and layered with wedges of hard goat's cheese and slices of tomato. He produced a chilled bottle of beer and poured two glasses.

'It's a little early, isn't it?' Michael reached out a tentative hand.

'You English,' replied Pepito, 'you drink more than any other nationality I have come across, but pretend you don't. Beer isn't alcohol; it's sustenance, a part of the meal.'

Michael sipped the beer and pictured Nottingham City centre at closing time. 'So if all this is ours, what do we do with it?' he asked.

'It's hard to know where to start.' Pepito scratched his chin. 'Ten years ago land here had no value, except for crops. But property development in the valley has gone crazy. Now it's reached Parcent. Plots like this are fetching more than sixty thousand euros if you can get permission to build. And the houses in the village, some sell for two hundred thousand, or more. It's ridiculous.'

'So what's the problem? It sounds like you're onto a good thing.'

'Oh, some people can't wait to sell, especially the younger ones.'

'How do you feel?'

'I've worked this land all my life, so did your grandfather,' Pepito said slowly. 'I could sell, but then what? Sit back and watch the destruction?'

'Perhaps that's progress?' Michael said, looking around.

'Not to me. Land isn't like a car or a machine to be traded in. You have land once and when it's gone it's gone forever. This land has been in our family for generations. They shaped the landscape, cut the terraces, moved the rocks and planted the trees and vines. The land is soaked with their sweat. Who am I to end all that? No, this land should be there for the next generation and the generation after that... though not everyone agrees.'

'Who do you mean?'

'My boy, Julio, for one.'

'He doesn't work on the land?'

''Ha! Not interested. Too hard, too little reward. He runs his own construction company. It's only small, but he's got big plans. That's why he'd like to get hold of this land. He wants riches so he can squander them – and what would that leave for his children and grandchildren?'

'My appearance has complicated things...'

'You can say that again. Julio's been pestering me for years to release some of the land for houses, but I've resisted. He wanted to take over the empty house in the village, but I told him it wasn't mine. Until recently, the old Mayor refused to allow any new building around the village. But there's a new Mayor now, backed by Julio and a bunch of builders and speculators. He jumps to their tune.'

'And what about Pedro?'

Pepito paused and then spoke carefully. 'Pedro... he's a good son, but he's a little... slow and set in his ways. He works the land every day. It's his life. He's never done anything else. When I go, my half will pass to Pedro and Julio. It wouldn't take Julio long to persuade Pedro to sell. But now you've appeared on the scene and they can't do a thing without your agreement. That's the law.'

Michael took another sip of beer.

'What do you think my father would have done?'

Pepito looked at first surprised and then he smiled. 'Francisco? He'd keep it. He used to rush here after school every day to tie up the tomatoes, prune the vines, collect the olives. Your grandfather pretended he was a nuisance, but he loved having Francisco come over. The two of them would sit on that wall over there talking until dusk about the state of the olives, when to plant tomatoes, how to know when the grapes were ready for harvesting, but...'

'I'm sorry, Pepito, I know this is difficult, but I would like to know what happened.'

'I know.' Pepito blew his nose on the crumpled handkerchief. 'I'll tell you. I was fifteen. Francisco was nineteen. They said he had to go away for a while. Then kids said my brother was a leper. At first I hated him. I hoped I'd never see him again, because of the shame. But I grew older and I missed him so much. Believe me, I often wondered about him. My parents, your grandmother and grandfather, suffered most. For years they cut themselves off from almost everyone. Mind you, it suited some people to keep away from the family. Some believed the disease was hereditary.'

'But couldn't they have stood against the village, so my father didn't have to leave?'

Pepito's chin dropped to his chest.

'Don't you think I've asked that question a thousand times? It's impossible to know what it was like back then. Talk to your grandmother, see if she'll explain... She's always refused to discuss it with me.'

At the *riu rau* on the edge of the village, carts and farm implements littered a yard looking as if they'd gathered dust for a hundred years.

Inside five arched vaults lay a vast collection of dusty wine bottles, neatly stacked on shelves with faded scraps of paper denoting the years. Michael noticed one shelf labelled 1955.

'This is the family bodega,' Pepito said. 'Nearly a thousand bottles at the last count. The late bottles will be shipped out in the next year or so to a handful of local restaurants we supply, but there are a few good vintage years at the back and we save those for special occasions. I'll show you if you want.'

Michael was bewildered. One day he was plain old Michael Fernandez, detective with Nottingham CID; now he was Miguel-Ángel Fernandez, property owner, land owner, farmer and wine entrepreneur. It was all too much.

'I have to go now,' he said. 'I can't take all this in.'

'I understand,' Pepito said. 'I'll give you a lift home.'

Home.

'I'd rather walk if you don't mind.'

He trudged back through the village streets, head down contemplating the import of what he had just learned – and the enormity of the consequences.

Rosana's voice interrupted his ruminations. 'Well, Miguel-Ángel,' she said cheerily, 'now you do look like a real Spaniard.'

'What?' He snatched Pepito's tattered straw from his head.

'You've had an interesting morning, I expect.' She raised an eyebrow.

Michael baulked. 'Jesus! Does everyone in this place know everyone else's business?'

'Pretty much. That's village life, you know.'

'Well, this place is just too prying for my liking. You can't move without everyone knowing what you're doing. It's like living in a goldfish bowl. I don't know how you stand it.' He continued along the street with determined strides.

'Miguel-Ángel, I thought we might have dinner tonight,' Rosana called out to his back.

'I can't. I'm busy.'

The door to his grandmother's house was unlocked so he stepped inside. Maria Carmen was standing there, smiling to greet him.

'I need to speak to you, Grandmother,' he said sternly.

He led her to the armchair, pulled another chair over and placed it directly in front of her.

'Why did you allow my father to be driven out?'

'I can't talk about it.' She turned her head to one side.

'No one understands. Father would never explain what happened and Uncle Pepito doesn't know. I have to hear about it from you.'

Maria Carmen looked back at him, her jaw set firm. 'It's wonderful you're here, Miguel-Ángel, but we must leave this.'

'I can't. I never wanted to come to this place. I know what it did to my father. But now I'm here and it turns out I own half the village. How can I deal with all this if I don't understand what happened?'

'It's not half the village,' she snapped.

'You know what I mean. I'm not leaving this seat until you tell me.'

Maria Carmen bowed her head and for a moment Michael felt guilty for speaking so harshly. He clasped her hands in his.

'Grandma,' he said softly, 'I know this is painful, but don't you think it will help if you talk to me? I understand guilt. I withdrew from father when I found out about the leprosy. I couldn't touch him.'

She stiffened. 'I never did that.'

'Then tell me. Please tell me.'

'I could try.' Maria Carmen sighed and was still for a moment. 'Oh... Miguel-Ángel... Francisco was such a beautiful boy. Not a day went by when I didn't thank God for the blessing He gave us when Francisco was born. Pepito too, but Francisco was our first born and he would always be special. We watched him grow, always happy...'

She took a deep breath.

'He was nearly eighteen when a lesion appeared on his right arm. It was small, but red and sore, though it didn't itch. Francisco said it had no sense of feeling, but we didn't even go to the doctor.

'Four months later another appeared on his shoulder and he complained of numbness in one foot. The doctor prescribed antiseptic cream. It was my mother who first knew. She was in her seventies and she'd seen it before. Leprosy used to be quite common around here.

'In the last half of the nineteenth century there were sixty-five cases in this village; more in the surrounding villages and the population was much smaller then. That's why they built the sanatorium at Fontilles.'

'My mother told me,' said Michael, trying to keep the dialogue going.

'Anyway, when my mother finally saw the lesions on Francisco, she recognised them straight away. There hadn't been a case in the village for almost forty years, but mother had seen the early signs before. She'd also seen the way the village dealt with the disease.

'Anyone even suspected of having leprosy was driven out, the entire family shunned. She warned us to keep quiet. But this was 1951 – leprosy was treatable and we hoped people would be more understanding. We should have known better.'

'We didn't dare go back to the doctor because we knew it would get round the village. So without telling anyone we took Francisco to Fontilles. They knew immediately. It was the worst day of my life. Our beautiful Francisco was a leper. Nothing would ever be the same.

'Francisco refused to accept it. He kept saying, "Why has this happened to me?" He even said it was our fault.'

'But leprosy isn't hereditary,' Michael said.

'Just try telling people that, when you have no other explanation.'

'What happened?'

'It got worse. Francisco had only a mild form of the disease, tuberculoid leprosy, but the doctors at Fontilles said it was contagious. It could be spread through prolonged contact with the skin and possibly through the air because the bacillus forms in the nose. But they said it could be cured and after three months treatment it would no longer be contagious.'

Maria Carmen stared at the floor, her mouth a tight line.

Michael had to get her to speak on. 'You have a good memory for detail.'

Her eyes widened and flashed. 'Do you think I could ever forget? Listen. At first, this was good news. Francisco could be treated and then return home; everything back to normal. How stupid we were...

'Francisco refused to accept it, that day. He wanted to get out of the sanatorium, but we stayed to talk to the doctors. They took Francisco out of the room. More tests, they said. Then they told us he couldn't leave. Your grandfather, Antonio, tried to fight them, but they pinned him down. The doctors said Francisco must stay. "For his own good and the good of the community," they said.

'Francisco needed to be kept in isolation for three months. Antonio still refused. "We'll take him away from Parcent," he kept saying.

'They showed us around the sanatorium. It was like a group of family home, nicely furnished and decorated, surrounded by landscaped gardens and open space. All the patients had private rooms. But a high stone wall encircled the whole area. The only way in and out was through the main gates. When we came back inside, the doctors asked us to tell Francisco what needed to be done. Antonio said he couldn't speak to Francisco about it, so it was left to me.

'He didn't want to listen, but I calmed him down. I told him he was in good hands; that he needed the treatment or the disease would get worse. I explained he'd be there only a few months and then he'd be home. He broke down in tears and sobbed like a little boy. I held him in my arms and felt his body shaking. He was still crying when he approached his father. But Antonio flinched. I know he regretted it for the rest of his life, but Francisco saw fear in his father's eyes and it was as if he realised what living with leprosy was going to be like.'

Michael nodded his understanding and Maria Carmen resumed.

'Francisco walked off with the doctors and the door closed. I told Antonio that I would never forgive him, but he never forgave himself. As we left, we walked between two of the blocks towards the main gate. One of the assistants was trying to reassure us that everything would be all right. And then I heard Francisco's voice. I looked round to see his face in a window opening, with his hands tugging the metal bars. "Don't leave me, mother," he screamed. I can hear it now. "Don't leave me, mother."'

Maria Carmen dropped her head in her hands and wept uncontrollably.

Michael put his arms around her.

After a few minutes, Maria Carmen's long, shuddering sobs slowed. She pulled herself upright, took a deep breath and continued with her story.

'We visited often,' she began slowly. 'Antonio came to begin with, but he started to make excuses. Francisco was hostile – I think because of the way Antonio had reacted that first time. We had to keep it a secret so we told people that Francisco had gone to stay with a cousin of mine in Galicia. It was summer and he'd been there before.

'Francisco said he hated Fontilles, though he seemed reconciled and he was free to wander round once they trusted him not to run away. He'd met Susan, your mother, but we never realised they were becoming close. Your mother was a nurse with the Red Cross and had come to Fontilles to learn about the treatment of leprosy.

'After two months, the treatment was going well. Francisco had to take a mixture of drugs every week and the doctors were pleased with his progress. We talked about Francisco coming home. Then someone discovered Francisco was in Fontilles. At first it was just whispers and I noticed people anxious to get away if I stopped to talk. One night, the village priest, Father Ramón, visited our house. He said he'd been approached by a group of villagers. He put it very politely, but made it clear these people would not accept Francisco back. He said there would be consequences if he returned and it would be better for Francisco to stay in Fontilles as others had in the past.

'Antonio was furious. He said that as a Christian, Father Ramón should persuade people to show compassion, instead of doing their dirty work. There was a dreadful scene. Father Ramón – he was in his seventies – said God had a purpose and we should look to ourselves for the reason why He'd brought leprosy to our family. It was the last straw. Antonio raised his fist and if I hadn't stepped between them, I'm sure he'd have killed him. As it was, the old priest was knocked over and I tumbled with him. Antonio picked me up then picked up Father Ramón and threw him out of the house.

'Antonio never entered the church again, even after Father Ramón retired a few years later. I went to the presbytery and pleaded with Father Ramón to talk to the villagers. I told him the treatment was working and the disease would not be contagious. I begged him to talk to the doctors at Fontilles. He could have helped. But he was from the old school. He'd seen leprosy before. I think he truly believed that the disease was a punishment from God and that the only way of dealing with it was to isolate lepers.

'He wanted me to persuade Francisco not to come back, but I said I wouldn't. He was livid and said, "Maria Carmen Fernandez, there will be dire consequences if Francisco ever sets foot in this village again. He will be shunned and so will you all. You are going against the will of God." And then he showed me out.'

Michael was stunned. 'Called himself a man of God... Jesus.'

'It didn't end there. A few days later, I went to see Francisco. I knew something was wrong at once. Father Ramón had been to see him and told him what he'd told me. Worse, he'd told Francisco that for the sake of his family he must never return to Parcent. I thought

Francisco would be upset, but he just shrugged and said, "Don't worry, mother." I didn't know what to say. I cried and he held me. For the first time in his life, Francisco comforted me, not the other way round. Then he kissed me and said, "You had better go." That was the last time I ever saw him.'

Before Michael could ask what happened, his grandmother pointed to the corner of the room. 'Pass me that bible.'

A leather-bound bible with gilt-edged pages sat on a shelf. Michael reached up and handed it down to Maria Carmen. She opened the cover and carefully removed a slip of yellowing paper.

'This was at Fontilles next time I went.'

Michael unfolded the note and read the familiar handwriting.

> Dear Mama,
> By the time you read this letter I will have left Fontilles and Spain for good. I have gone to England with Susan. Apart from you, she is the only one who accepts me for what I am, a leper. I am sorry for all the pain I have caused you. I think it best if I never return to Parcent, so please do not try to contact me. I will always, always love you.
> Francisco.

Michael looked up. 'Couldn't you stop him?'

'He had already left. And should I have forced him back to stay in Fontilles?'

'Did you try to contact him?'

'I thought about it many times, but I always went back to that letter. Perhaps I should have, but I always believed that if he wanted to, he would get in touch. He knew I loved him and thought of him every day. I had a note from Susan when you were born and we heard when Francisco died.'

'How could you stay in this village after what happened?'

'You must understand, Antonio's family, and mine, have lived here for centuries. Antonio made his living off the land. Without it, there was no way to survive.'

'But how could you live with these people?'

'It was not that simple. We did have a few friends; real friends. And we didn't know who told Father Ramón to expel Francisco. After Francisco left, a few people asked after him, but we just said he'd decided to stay in Galicia. We even lied to Pepito, but he found out when other children started tormenting him at school.

'Two years later, Father Ramón asked me to go and see him. He was very ill and close to death and he wanted me to know the truth. He told me he'd been visiting another patient at Fontilles when he saw Francisco. He talked to the doctors and they told him Francisco was planning return to Parcent after his treatment. He thought it was wrong. He said he knew the village would never accept Francisco back, so he invented a story about a group of villagers pressing him to talk to us. I was deeply shocked. It was terrible to think that it need never have happened. But Father Ramón was unrepentant.'

'That priest was evil,' Michael said.

'Don't judge him too harshly,' said Maria Carmen. 'He was just following his beliefs.'

'I believe in evil, and that priest was evil.'

'He was probably right. The village would never have accepted Francisco. Perhaps this way, we were spared the pain of finding out.'

If his grandmother had learnt to forgive the old priest, it would serve no purpose for Michael to express his feelings further.

He also sensed that Maria Carmen's story was at an end.

She sat quite calmly in her chair, her eyes fixed on the young man in the photograph on the table beside her.

CHAPTER NINE

The mobile phone woke him again. This was getting to be a habit.

'Good morning, Michael, you can book your flight home,' said Jose Luis with obvious glee.

'What?'

'It's all over, we've got them.'

'The Harringtons, you mean?'

'We've not found the bodies yet, but it's only a matter of time.'

'Bodies? Will you stop wasting my time and tell me what's happened?'

'The Dutchmen, Hagemans and Van Doorn, we searched the old finca in Orba and found their fingerprints. We found bloodstains as well. The results came through overnight and we matched them to the Harringtons. There's no doubt about it.'

'Have they confessed?'

'No, but it's only a matter of time. It's not the ending we would have wanted but, like I say, the case is all but over. We'll be charging them later this morning.'

'Has anyone spoken to John and Linda Harrington yet?'

'I don't think so.'

'Well, don't. I'm coming over.'

'There's no need, there's nothing you can do.'

'I'm coming over,' repeated Michael, before ending the call.

He said goodbye to his grandmother, promising he'd be back and noticing the doubt in her face. Next he called at Rosana's house.

'What do you want, Miguel-Ángel?' she said grumpily.

In a baggy T-shirt over faded denims with pale blue ballet pumps, he'd never seen anyone so beautiful. Her dark hair was tousled and hung randomly about her face.

'I need to borrow your car,' he said abruptly.

'What for?'

'To get back to Alicante. Something's happened in the investigation.'

'What if I say no?'

'Just give me the keys.'

She returned a moment later with a bunch of keys, removed one from the ring, and slapped it into his open hand.

'You've got a nerve.'

'I know,' he replied. 'I'm sorry about yesterday. Look, at least you know I'll be coming back... to return the car, I mean.'

'Is that the only reason?' She placed her hands on her hips.

'Of course not.' He leaned forward to kiss her, very briefly, on the lips, and then took off before there was a reaction. 'Bye.'

At the Guardia Civil Headquarters in Alicante, Michael's civilian pass failed to get him past the front desk. He was told to wait until Colonel Cardells was free to see him. He waited forty minutes in the public area while officers dealt with an assortment of villains and victims. Eventually a summons came and he was escorted into the Colonel's inner office. Jose Luis was there, looking nervous. The greeting was cordial enough.

'Good to see you again, Inspector. I hope you are fully recovered from your accident,' said Cardells.

'Yes, I'm fine, thank you.'

'Jose Luis says you insisted on coming over, but there really was no need. You see, we're confident that Hagemans and Van Doorn abducted the Harringtons and probably murdered them. It's a matter of time before we wrap this one up. It's a tragic ending, not what we would have wanted. They've been interrogated at length and we're searching the house in Orba and their apartment in Denia, but there's nothing for you to do at the moment.'

'Can I see the interview notes and the forensic evidence?'

'Of course you can, but there's not much point.'

'And then I will need to speak to Hagemans and Van Doorn.' Michael deliberately framed his remark as a statement, not a request.

Cardells stiffened. Jose Luis looked even more uncomfortable, as if he anticipated the Colonel's response.

'I'm sure I don't need me to remind you, Inspector, that you have no jurisdiction here. You're here by invitation and only because we thought it would be useful to have you. This is a Guardia Civil investigation and now that the case is as good as solved, I see little point in your continued involvement. In fact, you can make plans to return to Britain.'

Michael was in no mood to back down, despite the Colonel's authoritarian tone. 'You need to remember, Colonel, that I was sent here to work alongside the Guardia Civil and not in a token position. I will need to talk to John and Linda Harrington some time today and I would like to be able to satisfy them that everything possible has been done and that the real culprits have indeed been uncovered. What's more, when the news emerges, the media, at least the British contingent, will expect me to comment. I would find it very difficult to express my complete confidence in the investigation until I have seen the files and talked to the suspects.'

'Have you discussed this with Chief Superintendent Bowater?'

'I don't need to. I'm sure he would want me to be thorough.'

The Colonel's bloated face reddened.

'Give him the files Perez and arrange for him to see the prisoners, but I want you with him at all times. Is that understood?'

'Yes – yes, Colonel,' said Jose Luis, as if surprised not to have witnessed one of the Colonel's real rages. He raised an eyebrow at Michael and nodded towards the door, indicating it was time to depart. Michael accepted the invitation.

'Thank you, Colonel,' said Michael as he stood leave.

'And Perez,' said Cardells, 'tell Ramirez to get Chief Superintendent Bowater on the phone right away.'

Outside the office, Jose Luis rolled his eyes and gasped.

'I've seen people shot for less.'

'I don't doubt it.'

For the next hour Michael worked through the files and interview notes in a back office, while Jose Luis stood by, answering questions and occasionally popping out for coffee.

The finca in Orba, it turned out, was hidden away at the end of a dusty track and barely visible from the nearest property over a kilometre away. No one was sure who owned it, though it clearly did not belong to Hagemans or Van Doorn. A search of the two-roomed ruin had revealed several sets of fingerprints, including those of the two suspects, one set of David Harrington's and several others as yet unidentified.

Both rooms turned up several small bloodstains, though most were in the second room which contained an old bed. The stains were mainly on the floor, but a few specks in a spray pattern were found on one wall. The tests identified the blood as belonging to both Mr and Mrs Harrington. Most, but not all, of the blood on the floor belonged to Alison Harrington, while the blood in the second room was from David Harrington. There was no sign of a weapon. The second room was a kitchen of sorts with a stone sink, a work surface and a couple of cupboards containing a few old mugs and a collection of drinking glasses, none of which appeared to have been used recently. There was also an ancient two-ring gas hob (but no gas bottle) and a rusty old kettle which showed no sign of recent use. The suspects' fingerprints had been lifted from doors and door handles and from the dusty work surface in the kitchen. David Harrington's prints had been found on the walls of the bedroom, Alison's nearby.

Next, Michael turned to the interview notes. The interviews were conducted by Colonel Cardells and Jose Luis. Both suspects spoke little Spanish but were reasonably fluent in English, so Sergeant Ramirez had acted as interpreter. The Dutch consulate had provided an interpreter for the later interviews and a Dutch lawyer had also been present.

The two men admitted they had tried to use the Orba property for a scam. They placed advertisements in the Dutch edition of the Costa Blanca News offering a finca for restoration together with a parcel of land for development. Their plan was to persuade prospective buyers to hand over a sizeable deposit and then abscond with the money. They'd found two other remote properties and planned to use them in a similar way in the future. They'd shown three people around the finca in February and March, including a Mr Carrington, but were getting nowhere because no one expressed any interest in the place, even when they reduced the price. Then the Ruiters came to see the property at the end of March and seemed interested. By this time they were getting desperate for cash, but Hagemans blew it when he made threats to Mr Ruiter on the way to the bank. After that, they decided to back off because they were worried the Ruiters might report the incident. They claimed they had not been to the finca since the beginning of April. The police had searched the two men's apartment in Denia, but found nothing to link them with the Harringtons.

'Is this a mistake?' Michael asked, turning the file towards Jose Luis.

'What?'

'In the notes of Van Doorn's interview, where he refers to Mr Carrington, not Harrington.'

Jose Luis studied the notes.

'Just a mistake, I expect. Something got lost in translation.'

'I'm ready to see them now,' said Michael.

'Together or separately?' asked Jose Luis.

'Together, I think. After all, I'm only satisfying my curiosity. You've already done the interviews.'

Up from their basement cells, the two men looked tired as they entered the room. Van Doorn was a surly man of considerable height and bulk. His face was wider at the bottom than at the top; an imbalance exaggerated by the dense dark stubble on his chin and upper lip. The man's demeanour, size, and scuffed Doc Martins, laced above the ankles through metal clips, made it easy for Michael to imagine him guilty of kidnapping, or worse.

In complete contrast, Hagemans was nervy, fidgety, thin. He had fair, wispy hair and no more than a trace of blond bristle on his boyish face.

Both were in their late twenties.

Michael explained his position, emphasising that they were not obliged to talk to him, but he wanted to understand their stories.

They could have a solicitor present if they wished, but this was not a formal interview. He presented himself as 'their friend' and after his introduction they both seemed anxious to talk, preferably in English.

Jose Luis protested.

'I'll have to get Sergeant Ramirez, if you're going to talk in English.'

'Relax Jose Luis, or we'll be here all day. I'll tell you what's said, if there's anything significant.'

'Just don't tell the Colonel.'

Before Michael could start, Hagemans burst out hysterically, 'You've got to help us, Inspector Fernandez. They're trying to pin murder on us.'

'I see... It's Wilhelm, isn't it?

'Wil.'

'Like I said, Wil, we can all just relax. I'm here to get to the bottom of this and if you're innocent you've nothing to fear. First, you both agree you met David Harrington when he came to the finca on 27th January?'

'Yes,' said Hagemans, 'He called a few days before, but he said his name was Carrington.'

'Are you sure?'

'That's what it sounded like,' said Hagemans, looking towards Van Doorn, who nodded confirmation.

'But you are sure it was him?' asked Michael.

'Yes, they showed us his picture, but that was before they told us about the fingerprints and the bloodstains.'

'Did he come alone?'

'Yes,' said Hagemans.

'And you've never seen his wife?'

'No,' said Van Doorn, suddenly taking an interest. 'Look, what's the point of this? We've been through it all with the Spanish cops.'

'The point is, Johan, the Spanish cops think they have enough to charge you with murder. At the moment I'm your best hope of getting out of here, so it's in your interests to tell me as much as you know.'

Hagemans touched his partner on the arm.

'Please, Johan, let's try to help – tell him all about it.'

Van Doorn pulled his arm away and folded it across his chest. He leant back in his chair and slipped downward, stretching the Doc Martins out under the table.

'How did he meet you?' Michael asked Hagemans.

'We met him at a bar in Orba as arranged by phone and then he followed us in his car.'

'What kind of car?'

'I don't know. Blue. Small Renault, I think.' Hagemans looked at Van Doorn who responded with a shrug of his shoulders.

'What was he like?'

'What do you mean?'

'You must have talked to him. What did you talk about? Did he seem interested in the place?'

Again it was Hagemans who answered.

'He seemed pretty interested. He asked about how much land was included and we told him about forty thousand square metres – everything around the house. Then he asked about neighbours and we said there weren't any. I remember he wanted to know how soon we could complete the purchase. Johan said he could have it straight away, but that he needed to make his mind up pretty quickly because we had other people interested. We said we'd accept a cash deposit to secure the sale and then draw up the papers. It could be his in a couple of weeks. I was convinced he wanted to buy the place. I really thought he was going to pay the deposit.'

'He was never going to buy,' interrupted Van Doorn.

'Why do you say that?' asked Michael.

'Because he never asked the obvious questions about a water supply or electricity. Everyone else asked and we had answers, but he never mentioned them. He asked about the price and I told him, sixty-five thousand. There was no reaction. He never haggled or anything like that. He was just going through the motions.'

'What happened next?'

'He just said he'd think about it and then he left,' said Van Doorn. 'I was pretty pissed off with him. He was bloody rude, to be honest. Just wasting our time. I thought about grabbing his wallet or something, but he didn't seem the sort to be carrying a lot of money.'

'Why do you say that?'

'Oh, there was just something about him. He was kind of putting on an act, pretending to have funds – but any budget he might have had was kept a complete secret. I doubted he had money to buy anywhere. Like I say, he was just a time-waster.'

'Did he mention his wife?'

Van Doorn said no, and Hagemans nodded agreement.

'Why did you keep the phone?'

'What?' said Van Doorn.

'After that business with the Ruiters, surely you must have realised you could be traced through the phone?'

'It was just a pay-as-you-go. I didn't think you could trace those.'

'Well, the phone hadn't been registered, that's true, but when Captain Perez here phoned you, didn't you realise it might be a set up?'

Van Doorn looked a little less confident as he contemplated the question. 'Look it was a good plan. People come over here and do stupid things. I know, I've seen it. People buy houses like cars. Cash changes hands in bars and no one bothers about contracts or stuff like that. Sooner or later someone would have given us money for that place.'

'And in the meantime, how do you make your living?'

'We sell stuff,' Hagemans replied, almost childlike in his anxiety to tell the truth. 'At the rastro markets in Jalon and Teulada on Saturdays and Sundays. It's mostly junk, but people buy anything out here.'

Michael noticed Van Doorn twitch uneasily and flash a warning glance towards his partner, but Hagemans failed to pick it up.

'What sort of stuff?' Michael asked.

'Old china, copper and brass, bits of jewellery – just glass – a few books, even bits of furniture. Sometimes we go back to Holland to buy stuff there and bring it back to sell in the markets.'

Hagemans jumped as Van Doorn kicked him under the table and

shot him an angry glance, daggers in his eyes.

But Hagemans was keen to continue.

'Look Johan, handling stolen goods is a lot better than murder. Okay, so some of the stuff might be stolen. We buy it cheap in Holland, no questions asked, but I tell you most of it is worthless. Look for yourselves, it's all in a trailer locked in a garage near our apartment in Denia.'

Van Doorn jumped forward and pulled Hagemans away from the table.

'Shut up, Wil, you've said enough.'

Michael spoke briefly to Jose Luis and then turned again to the two men.

'You can tell the Captain where the garage is and give him the keys.'

'Yes.' Hagemans obliged, despite Van Doorn's furious scowl.

'How do you account for the blood stains at the finca?' said Michael, watching the two men to gauge their reactions.

Van Doorn didn't flinch, but Hagemans was visibly unnerved by the question. A look of panic crossed his face, his lower lip quivered and he started to babble as his eyes filled with tears.

'Look, Mr Fernandez, I swear to you, I don't know how that blood got there. We've told you the truth. We met Harrington at the finca for just a few minutes and then he left. That's it, end of story. We're not murderers. Please, you must help us, otherwise the Spanish police are going to fit us up. You know what they're like, don't you?' He pleaded with desperation, tears rolling down his cheeks as he reached out for Michael's hand.

It was a pity to scare the young man further, but this wasn't on. Michael pulled back. 'Tell me, Wil, has Johan ever been to the finca without you?'

Hagemans' expression changed as he pondered the question. Before he could answer Van Doorn shot forward from his slouching position and banged his fist on the desk. Jose Luis started in surprise.

Van Doorn pulled Hagemans away from the table again and forced him against the back of his chair.

'Don't answer, Wil. You can see what he's up to. Well, it's not going to work. The interview's over. We'd like to see our solicitor now.'

There was silence for a moment and Hagemans was still looking confused when the door opened and Colonel Cardells strode in with Ramirez at his tail.

'Thank you, Michael, that was most useful,' the Colonel said.

Van Doorn sprung from his chair and lunged at Michael. 'You bastard,' he shouted as Jose Luis pinned him to the desk. 'You set us up.'

Hagemans cowered in his chair, still not sure what was happening. Two uniformed policemen entered the room and took the suspects toward the door. Cardells turned to Michael.

'You'd better tell these two that we've just found the Harringtons' hire car in an old garage about five hundred metres from the finca in Orba.'

Michael managed to restrain himself from swearing at the Colonel and spoke to the two Dutchmen in English.

'It's a set up,' said Van Doorn calmly. 'These bastards have set us up.'

Hagemans was not so unperturbed. He twisted his head around to look at Michael, straining the sinews in his neck as he spoke.

'Please Mr Fernandez, you've got to help us,' he begged, as the policemen led him away.

The look of wide-eyed panic hit Michael like a bolt from a crossbow, but he could offer no more than gentle nod by way of reassurance.

'They weren't the only ones who were set up, were they?' Michael stared directly at the Colonel's grinning face.

'I think you'll find that your Chief Superintendent wants to talk to you,' he replied, ushering Ramirez and Jose Luis out of the room.

Jose Luis looked briefly back at Michael and shrugged, but Michael already knew he was not complicit in the deceit.

'What the hell do you think you are playing at, Fernandez?' Bowater said as soon as Penny put the call through. 'Colonel Cardells is furious.'

'It's all a set up,' said Michael.

'What is, the case against the two Dutchmen?'

'No, Cardells. He set me up. He pretends to be indignant about my involvement, but he just used me to get to the suspects. He was listening to every word while I spoke to them. I was trying to be friendly, you know, someone they could trust. I think I was getting somewhere, with Hagemans at least. Then he bursts in with the news that they've found the Harringtons' car. I swear he knew it before I spoke to them. Now I've lost them. They'll never want to talk to me again, and who'd blame them?'

'I doubt you'll be talking to them again, in any event. Cardells wants you called back. He says it's an open and shut case and there's more than enough evidence to convict them.'

'Well, he's wrong. Van Doorn could be lying, but Hagemans is just his puppy. Even Van Doorn doesn't seem stupid enough to kill the Harringtons and hang around afterwards. There are too many unanswered questions. Besides, they haven't found the bodies yet.'

'So what do you want to do?'

'I'd like to stay around for a while, if that's all right, sir? I'll have to talk to John and Linda Harrington anyway. And I think I can keep in touch through Captain Perez. I don't think he believes the Dutchmen are guilty, but he's afraid to challenge Cardells.'

'I thought you didn't want to be in Spain, Michael.'

'I don't, but I don't like unfinished business and I've got a few other matters to attend to.'

'Such as what?'

'It's personal, sir.'

'Tread carefully Michael, whatever it is you're up to.'

'Don't worry, Sir, I will.'

The meeting with John and Linda Harrington at their Benidorm hotel was bound to be difficult. If he shared Colonel Cardells' belief that the two Dutchmen were guilty of abduction and probably murder, it was bad news. If he expressed his doubts, it only prolonged their anxiety. And how could he explain the bloodstains without leading them to fear the worst?

They met at three o'clock in a quiet corner of the hotel bar. Linda took a Coca-Cola in response to Michael's invitation. John asked for beer and the hotel obliged with cold *Cruzcampo* in a dimpled glass tankard. It was not John's first of the day. He was shirtless, sticky, and by the looks of the cherry-red skin beneath grey-brown chest hair, he'd become accustomed to an after lunch siesta in the sun. A dark sweat stain showed below the elasticated waist of his baggy shorts. He was shoeless and his feet were grubby. His eyes were bleary and he looked ready to snooze at any second. Linda was tanned and neat in strappy sandals and a thin cotton dress that showed the outline of a pale yellow bikini.

Timothy Middleton joined them, every inch the staid civil servant. Michael felt that even he would like to suggest dispensing with the jacket and tie for once.

'Are they looking after you?' asked Middleton, after the usual pleasantries.

'Food's not up to much,' said John, 'but apart from that it's okay. You are paying the bill, aren't you? I mean, everything's included?'

Linda nudged him.

'Don't worry about the bill, Mr Harrington. It will be taken care of. Apparently, Inspector Fernandez has some news for us.'

Michael coughed. 'Ahem... er… yes. The Guardia Civil have arrested two Dutchmen on suspicion of abducting David and Alison.'

'Are they all right?' Linda grasped the arms of her chair.

Michael shuffled in his seat. 'I'm afraid I can't say for certain. You see, they've found bloodstains at an old finca – a farmhouse – near Orba and they match David's and Alison's.'

'Oh, my God.' Linda gripped John's hand, though he sat as stiff as if he'd just been set in concrete. Even his eyes were frozen.

'Look,' said Michael, 'I know it sounds pretty awful, but there could be all sorts of explanations. There's no need to fear the worst at the moment. The Guardia Civil are making further inquiries.'

John suddenly moved. He took a gulp of beer and wiped his lips.

'Don't give us that "further inquiries" crap. Are they dead, or what?'

Michael was not surprised by the abruptness and replied equally brusquely, 'They haven't found bodies yet, if that's what you mean.'

'These Dutch geezers, they've confessed, then?'

'They've admitted meeting David at the finca, but not Alison. They were working a scam, pretending the place was theirs to sell and trying to get people to hand over a deposit. But they deny anything more. Oh, and the police have found David's hire car in an old garage nearby.'

Linda gasped and raised a hand to her mouth. Middleton passed her a handkerchief.

'Sounds like they're bang to rights,' John said, returning to the *Cruzcampo*. 'Did they get David to part with any money?'

'No, they say they just met him and showed him round and then he left.'

'They would say that, wouldn't they? What do the police think?'

Michael sat back. 'Well, they seem pretty certain the two were involved and I must admit there's a lot of circumstantial evidence...'

'You don't believe it was them, do you?' said Linda, hopefully.

'I know this sounds cold, but until there are bodies, it's impossible to be certain.' He realised how grave these words sounded and tried to recover. 'But of course, there's a real chance they're still alive. It's just best to keep an open mind until the Guardia Civil finish their inquiries.' He recognised his own police-speak and added, 'I've interviewed the two suspects and from my experience there's a great deal of room for doubt.'

'Sounds to me,' John broke in, 'like you're trying to get them off the hook. Typical of British police, soft on everything. The Guardia don't mess about. You've got bloodstains and the hire car and these two blokes admit they met David. They don't want to go down for murder, that's all. They're just trying to save their skins. Are the Guardia going to charge them?'

'If they have evidence,' said Michael.

'With murder?'

'I expect so.'

'There you are. I told you the Guardia don't mess about, so why do you come here with this talk about further inquiries and reason to hope? They're dead and you know it. I just hope those bastards are topped.'

'Capital punishment no longer exists in Spain, Mr Harrington,' Middleton said.

'More's the pity.'

Linda had been weeping into the handkerchief, but now she looked up at Michael with pink-rimmed eyes.

'Do you really think they're dead?'

'I just don't know, Mrs Harrington. I hope not,' Michael said, trying to sound sincere. He would have reached forward to comfort her, but didn't think John would take kindly to the gesture.

John returned to the offensive. 'So where do we go from here?'

To Michael's surprise, Middleton decided to lend a hand, reciting helpfully, 'I think we shall all just have to await developments. I'm sure the Inspector will keep us informed, won't you Inspector?'

'Of course.'

'In the meantime, the Consulate will do everything it can.' Middleton smiled, and for a second, Michael expected him to add, *to make your stay a pleasant and happy one.*

'Just so long as you cover the bills here, Mr Middleton,' John said. He stood up. 'Where's the barman?' He turned back to Michael. 'You just make sure those Dutch bastards get what they deserve.' He strode towards the bar.

Linda looked up. 'I'm sorry,' she said. 'He's really very upset.'

Michael felt like commenting, *he has a funny way of showing it,* but settled for, 'I'm sorry too, Mrs Harrington.'

Michael's next move was to call Jose Luis on his mobile phone, deliberately avoiding the office number.

'Can you talk?' he asked.

'What do you mean? Of course I can talk.'

'I mean the Colonel's not listening in, is he?'

'What do you want?'

'You don't really think they're guilty, do you?'

'I have my doubts, about Hagemans at least.'

'Then what are you going to do about it?'

'What do you suggest I do, open the cells and let them out?'

'I'm serious. The Colonel's going to railroad them into court and he'll probably get a conviction. Two innocent men could go down.'

'That's for the courts to decide. It's not my problem.'

'You need to talk to Hagemans. He's the weak link. Find out if he was ever away from Van Doorn long enough for him to go back to the finca alone. And see if you can check the numbers called from Van Doorn's mobile. He could have contacted David Harrington again. Oh, and another thing – do your lab people have any idea how old the bloodstains are?'

'I didn't see anything in the report, just the results of the blood tests.'

'See if they can find out, will you?'

'You don't ask much, do you? Have you any idea how long all this will take?'

'I'm sure you can manage it, Jose Luis.'

'I'll see what I can do, but if the Colonel finds out I'll be in deep shit.'

'So be careful. And do me another favour, if you can? Let me know if you find anything at the garage in Denia. I'll call you in a couple of days.'

The next call was to Rosana. 'Are you free for dinner tonight?'

'I'm not sure.'

'Good, book somewhere nice. I'll be back about seven-thirty.'

An hour later he was explaining, 'No, thank you, Grandma, I'm having dinner with Rosana.'

'Oh, that's nice. By the way, Julio was here looking for you today.'

'Was he?' Not hard to guess what that was about.

After several dress rehearsals, Michael settled for a pale yellow, short-sleeved shirt with button down collars, beige chinos and a brown leather belt. He almost dispensed with socks, but when he couldn't quite bring himself to go through with it, put on a pale brown pair, inside an almost new pair of tan loafers, which he buffed to a lustrous sheen.

Walking to Rosana's house, a curious sensation overcame him, of nervousness, excitement, anticipation. After a deep breath to bring him back to calm, he knocked at the door.

'Michael-Ángel, come in.' Rosana's mother led him awkwardly into the house, dragging her left foot along the tiled hallway. Her cotton dress was covered by an apron, tied in a bow at the back. 'Rosana won't be long.'

'Thank you, Mrs Ferrando Moll,' he said uneasily.

'Please, call me Isabel. You remember Asunción, don't you? Rosana's grandmother. She and your grandmother are cousins, you know.'

'Pleased to meet you again, Mrs… Asunción,' he said, hesitant about being so informal. He shook the old woman's hand, noticing she was dressed in black. She returned his smile, but remained in her chair.

Isabel gestured him towards a wooden chair with a tapestry cushion.

'Please sit down.'

The chair typified the rest of the room, rustic and homely. Nothing matched, but everything blended perfectly and the smell of furniture polish mingled with the aroma of cooking. But the tapestry cushion sagged as he sank into the chair, as if trapping him and about to say, *What are your intentions towards my daughter?*

He was rescued by footsteps on the stairs and turned to see a heavy velvet curtain pulled aside. Rosana paused briefly on the final step like a model at the end of a catwalk. Her dark shiny hair flowed in carefully sculpted waves across one side of her face and down onto her shoulders. A narrow gold chain hung around her neck and glistened against her olive skin. She wore a simple khaki cotton dress that buttoned all the way from the rounded neck to the calf-length hem. It clung to her bust and hips and was gathered at her slender waist by a narrow black belt. Her shoes had thin straps around the ankles and toes with a cut-out flower in black leather sitting on the top of each foot. He returned his gaze to her face, conscious, but not caring, that he was staring. She met his smile with her own and spoke through glossy lips.

'Well, Miguel-Ángel, will I do?'

'You look... ' He struggled to rise from the sagging chair.

'Don't say, very nice,' she said with a grin, 'or I'll kill you. Come on.'

At Restaurant La Tasca on the edge of the village they were greeted in French by the waitress, Celine. She kissed Rosana before being introduced to Michael. They walked through the restaurant to a walled courtyard at the back. A few tables were occupied, but Celine led them to a corner shielded by night-scented jasmine. She lit a candle in a small glass holder and left the menus.

'I like it here,' said Michael in the break between the main course and dessert, adopting the tone of a restaurant critic and pretending to read from the back of the menu. 'The food is pleasant with fresh seasonal ingredients neatly presented without over-elaboration. The atmosphere is tranquil and relaxed...' He replaced the menu on the table and looked directly into Rosana's face. '...and what's a girl like you doing in a place like this?'

'I come here quite often,' Rosana said, trying not to giggle.

'I meant in Parcent.'

'I was born here.'

'The witness is being evasive.'

'Okay, I left here for university, moved to Madrid, rented an apartment, took a job as trainee account manager at Banco de Bilbao, became a branch manager and married Vicente, an investment broker. We lived a very high life with expensive cars, international travel, a yacht in Barcelona. It was great for a while, but we both burned out in a couple of years, tired of chasing the next buck. And it turned out that wasn't all Vicente was chasing.'

'Children, that sort of thing?'

'"That sort of thing"?'

Michael shrugged.

'No, nothing of that sort.'

'And?'

'And then my father died and soon after mother had a stroke.

Grandmother is not at all strong, so I came back. I guess it gave me an excuse to end the marriage, but it was over for me in any event. Now I have a part time job in an insurance office in Jalon and the rest of the time I look after my mother and grandmother.'

'Happy?'

'Happy enough.'

'You don't find it quiet? After Madrid and Barcelona.'

'Sometimes you come to realise what's really important. Material possessions and status symbols are all very nice, but there's something that means more than all of that.'

'Like family?'

'You are perceptive,' Rosana said with a hint of sarcasm.

Michael realised where the conversation was heading and anticipated the next question.

'And what about your family?' Rosana asked.

'I didn't realise I had one,' he said, 'until recently.'

'And now? Are you evading the question?'

'Only because…' He spotted Celine approaching. 'Ah, here comes dessert.'

After placing dessert on the table, Celine paused. Customers were thinning out and it seemed curiosity might be getting the better of her. 'So you are the long lost grandson. I didn't know Maria Carmen had a grandson until this week. What suddenly brings you to Parcent?'

'Just visiting.'

'Oh, what do you…' A shouted instruction from the kitchen pulled Celine away before she could finish her question.

'Is that true, then?' Rosana asked.

'What?'

'You're just visiting.'

'Maybe. I don't know. A few days ago I was an unattached British policeman and now I'm in Spain with a family. I own a house, land, and problems.'

'And?' Rosana stroked her hair away from her face.

'And I've met this beautiful woman who seems to know my thoughts before I do and who has a way of getting me to do things

I'd rather avoid.'

Rosana's lips formed a thin smile. 'So tell me all about your life in England. How did someone with so much Spanish blood become so antagonistic towards his father's homeland?'

'You know most of it.'

'I know your father left Spain rather than stay in Fontilles. I know your mother left with him, but I don't know anything about you.'

'You want the whole story?'

Michael recounted how his father had effectively been expelled from Parcent and how he had left Fontilles with his nurse, Susan. They later married in England and he was their only child.

Rosana listened attentively, but her curiosity was far from being assuaged.

'But what about you, yourself? Your own story, please.'

Michael sighed.

'My childhood was no different to anyone else's, Rosana. But one afternoon I went to my best friend's house and his mother came to the door. She said Andy couldn't play and I must never come to the house again. I was fourteen years old at the time and I didn't understand why, but Mum said they were not nice people and we should ignore it. A few weeks later, we moved house and Mum transferred to another hospital.'

'And then?'

'We had been in the new place a couple of months and I'd just started at a new school when the same thing happened. Some of the other kids shunned me and then they started calling me a leper.'

'What did you do?'

'I confronted my parents and my mother told me what had happened, about this village and about Fontilles. She didn't blame anyone. She accepted that she and Dad could never live a normal life. But I was worried I might have the disease, or I might catch it from Dad. I could see how much she loved Dad, how close they were, but... well, after that I couldn't bear to touch Dad and once I stupidly told him he'd ruined my life.... Dad had no self-pity. But it hung over me. We moved a third time, to Derby and their secret remained safe there, but I never settled. I left home at eighteen to go to university and then I joined the police. I met Aurora at university. She was Argentinean and we married a year later. I should have told her about Dad, but she found out when he died a couple of years after we married. She thought I was deceitful, which I was, in many ways. We were both relieved, I think, when the divorce came through. Mum died last year. That's about it.'

'Your father gave you a Spanish name and he taught you Spanish, so why do you profess to hate Spain?'

'It was the language of my father, not his country, as far as I'm concerned. He never quite mastered English, so we always spoke in Spanish at home. But he must have hated Spain for what it did to him.'

'You don't know that though, and from what you've said, the people in England were no better.'

'Some, possibly. But at least they didn't lock him up.'

'You think Fontilles is a prison?'

'It was, essentially, which is why my father ran away.'

'Attitudes were different then and your father was young. But Fontilles is not the place you make out.'

'How would you know?'

'I visit. The sanatorium's open to the public. I'm planning to take you there tomorrow.'

Michael sat upright. 'No,' he said firmly.

'Why not?'

'No, look, these are my problems, Rosana. It's not a good idea to force people into doing things they'd rather avoid. Let them take their own time. In the long run, this sort of thing never works out, where people are forced to do things before they're ready, in their own minds. That's my last word.'

'But...'

'No buts, Rosana, I mean it. And it's time we left.'

'But we haven't had coffee.'

Coffee came and went, Michael paid the bill and they strolled in silence through the narrow streets back to Rosana's house. The night air was still and warm and the sky was sprinkled with stars.

'Thank you for a nice evening,' Rosana said unconvincingly when they reached her door. 'Sorry if I spoiled things. It's just that, if we're going anywhere, you need to be sure of your feelings.'

'Going anywhere?'

'I mean, if we're going... '

The meaning was clear. He moved to her, placed his hand around her back and pulled her close. She returned his kiss, her hand around the back of his head, her fingers running through his hair. Footsteps sounded on the other side of the door and he pulled back.

'So?' Rosana said.

'What?'

'So are we going to Fontilles tomorrow?'

'Will you give that up? I can't go.'

'I'll see you in the morning,' said Rosana, drawing her door key from her purse. She lifted a hand and touched his cheek. 'And file your prickles before you come.'

'Don't exaggerate.'

But she had manipulated him with great finesse. Either that or he'd had too much wine.

CHAPTER TEN

'Ah, Michael, I was about to call you this morning, but you've beaten me to it.' Jose Luis sounded serious.

'Any news?'

'Yes, and it's all bad for our Dutch friends, especially Van Doorn.'

'What's happened?'

'We searched the garage in Denia and it was mostly junk. Some probably nicked in Holland, but nothing of any real value. But here's the best part. We found almost ten thousand euros hidden in a metal toolbox.'

'And you don't think it was their life savings?'

'No more than you do. It gets better – or worse – depending on your point of view. We interviewed them both again last night, separately. Hagemans seemed genuinely surprised and very scared when he realised the implications. He broke down again, I tell you he was squealing. If he knew anything about the money I'm sure he would have told us. Van Doorn was a different story, his usual defiant self to begin with, but when we pressed him he came up with a different account. He says that David Harrington contacted him again about a month ago and said he was interested in the place at Orba. He admits that he went there to meet him, on his own, and that Harrington paid him a deposit of ten thousand in cash. But he still claims that he only took the money. He says he gave Harrington a set of keys to the place – just one padlock – because Harrington said he wanted to get an architect in to draw up some plans and then Harrington left. Van Doorn says he promised to get the paperwork to Harrington in a couple of days, but of course he never did.'

'What do you think?' asked Michael, still considering this information.

'It's looking pretty grim, at least for Van Doorn. I can believe that Hagemans might not have known about Van Doorn's last meeting with Harrington, otherwise I'm sure he would have told us. He's like a frightened rabbit and when we told him about Van Doorn's story he was shocked, you could see it in his face. He remembers Van Doorn disappearing for a day about four weeks ago, but he says he doesn't know where he went. Van Doorn just told him he had some business in Calpe.'

'I don't know, Jose Luis, Van Doorn's story just doesn't add up. Surely no one would be so stupid as to hand over ten thousand to a virtual stranger.'

'Like I said, Michael, people do the strangest things. Who knows?'

'What's going to happen to them now?'

'We're very close to charging Van Doorn.'

'With murder?'

'What else? We've got the prints, the car and the bloodstains. Oh yes, I almost forgot. The lab boys say the bloodstains are between two and four weeks old. It's difficult to be more precise.'

'So they could date back to the time when Van Doorn says Harrington met him again?'

'Yes, if what Van Doorn says is true.'

Michael was still thinking. 'Like you say, it's looking pretty bad for Van Doorn. But if his story stacked up, you'd expect David Harrington to have reported the con when he realised he'd been had. And yet you still haven't heard from them, or found them... or their bodies.'

'We've widened the search area around the finca in Orba. It seems the most likely place to look.'

'Do you think they're dead?' Michael asked.

'It looks that way. Even if the Dutchmen have got them tucked away somewhere, we've had them in custody for three days now. Without food and water I dread to think what state the Harringtons would be in.'

'Unless they have an accomplice we don't know about.'

'Surely the Dutchmen would say if they'd locked them away

somewhere. It's better than going down for murder.'

'You'd think so, wouldn't you? But who knows?'

No. Something was wrong, Michael was sure. The Dutchmen had been caught too easily and they'd made no attempt to hide the evidence against them. Perhaps they thought the finca was too remote for anyone to find it. But leaving the prints and the car and the blood was just too inept, even for a couple of bunglers like Hagemans and Van Doorn.

'Any chance I could interview them again?' he asked.

'I don't think the Colonel would be too happy. And after last time, I'm not sure the Dutchmen would want to see you. Look Michael, I'm grateful for your help, but for the time being it's best if you stay away. If anything happens, I'll let you know and if you think of anything give me a call.'

Michael sat back. The evidence was stacked against Van Doorn, and even if they never found the Harringtons there was enough to charge him with murder. Michael had to admit that he would do the same if he were running the case in England.

'Miguel-Ángel,' called Maria Carmen from the bottom of the stairs. 'Rosana's here.'

Rosana met him at the door with a questioning smile. 'Are you all right?'

He'd been telling himself he was, but now he wasn't sure. 'I'm fine.'

'Come on, then.' Rosana held his arm on the way to her car. 'It's only about twenty minutes. I'll drive.'

In other circumstances, Michael thought, he would have approved of Rosana's faded denim jeans, the knife-edge crease that ran down her long slender legs and her broad brown leather belt with a gold buckle. Her brown, Cuban heeled boots might also have attracted his attention, as would the blue silk blouse that revealed a hint of white bra beneath. But in the circumstances, if she was trying to take his mind off where they were going, he hadn't noticed a thing.

Up from Parcent, the road toward Orba swept over the

mountains before plunging down a series of hairpin bends into the next valley. As green as the Jalon valley, it was dominated by orange groves and vineyards – and scarred by urbanisations that clung to every hillside.

They fringed Orba and then, from a Val de Laguart signpost, the road climbed into pink and white blossoms which were gradually fading into green leaves.

Rosana explained that cherries were the main crop in this part of the valley. Normally, the blossom would have disappeared by now, but an unusually cold winter had held it back.

'Fontilles, straight ahead,' she said at last, lowering her head to look up through the windscreen towards the top of a hill in the distance.

A cluster of yellow stone buildings stood on the summit. On a bright day, the scene might have evoked a hilltop castle. But the clouds had thickened and they descended into a forest where pine trees clung to steep slopes. A steely grey haze covered a long stone wall, about two metres high, that snaked its way up the mountainside, encircling the sanatorium.

Ahead, a pair of stone towers interrupted the line of the wall. Obviously, Michael thought, this was the entrance. There would be a gate, barred and bolted.

But Rosana drove straight between the twin pillars and on into the complex, heading for a small car park. Opposite, a building of church-like design with a tall bell tower looked as if it housed the administration block.

Rosana turned off the engine and looked at Michael. His face was white and sweat trickled down the collar of his shirt.

'Perhaps this isn't a good idea,' she said.

'It's fine.' Michael tapped her hand. 'Thanks for bringing me.'

She nodded and took a firm grip on his arm as they walked toward the building.

Through the mist, an old man in cardigan, jeans and faded pink baseball cap looked up from sweeping pine needles off the road.

Rosana clasped the man's arms, kissed him and turned.

'Miguel-Ángel Fernandez, this is Juan Garcia.'

Juan propped his broom against a tree and offered his hand. His fingers dug into Michael's palm and he looked down. Juan's fingers were bent and truncated and his thumb was missing. Michael resisted an instinctive almost overwhelming urge to yank his hand away. He held firm. Juan released his grip. Their eyes met, and Juan smiled.

'Dr Santos is waiting in the reception wing,' he said.

Juan led the way through a hall and up a broad staircase to an office dominated by a bow window that overlooked a deep tree-lined ravine.

Dr Santos sat behind a low table with his back to the window.

A man determined to disguise the onset of middle age, Michael surmised; a designer suit that was just a little too tight to fit comfortably and chisel-toed brown shoes that looked equally incommodious.

But Santos's tone was friendly enough and he came straight to the point.

'Welcome to Fontilles, Miguel-Ángel,' Santos said after Rosana made the introductions. 'I understand you want to know more about leprosy. In particular, what happened to your father.'

Rosana had obviously given Santos some forewarning.

'Thank you, Dr Santos,' Michael said. 'I appreciate it very much.'

'Please, call me Eduardo. It's no trouble at all.' He sat back in his chair. 'Leprosy,' he began, 'is present in over one hundred countries around the world, mainly India, China, Nepal and South America, but also Europe, even the United States – few people know that. More than twelve million sufferers have been cured in the last twenty years, but seven hundred thousand new cases are diagnosed each year, including two hundred and seventy last year in the USA.

'Theoretically, we can eradicate it. The biggest problem is the stigma. Since Biblical times, lepers have been shunned – you remember the film Ben-Hur?'

The scene where the champion charioteer finds his mother and sister in a leper colony hidden away amongst caves flashed across Michael's mind. He straightened and loosened his collar. It was getting hot.

'Well, some people associate leprosy with a lack of cleanliness or hygiene and others still believe leprosy is a punishment from God. This means, in some parts of the world, sufferers don't even see a doctor, mainly through fear. And yet modern treatments are highly effective.'

Dr Santos stood up and moved to his desk. He switched on an intercom and asked for coffee, then returned to the low table and sat down. 'Where were we? The bacillus, Micobacterium Leprae, which was discovered by Dr Armauer Hansen in 1873 is what causes leprosy. That's why it's also referred to as Hansen's Disease.

'It's actually very difficult to transmit and has a long incubation period,' Santos went on. 'Years. We are not entirely sure how it's transmitted. The microbacterium is found in the respiratory tract, so it's possible it's passed through droplets when people cough or sneeze – but it's not proven. The disease can be spread through prolonged contact and the most common contact is within the family. For that reason, many believed leprosy was hereditary, but we know now that it is not.

'Most people, ninety-five percent, have in-built resistance, so they're immune, even with prolonged contact. This makes the disease difficult to research. We just don't have all the answers, I'm afraid.'

Michael sat forward. 'What about treatment?'

'I'll explain.'

A young woman came into the room with a tray holding cups and a pot of coffee. Rosana took over and filled the cups. Michael hadn't realised how dry and tense he was. He gulped his coffee then sat back on the soft cushions of the armchair. 'I'm sorry,' he said, 'I must seem very ignorant.'

'There's no need to apologise. Most people know very little about the disease apart from the fallacies that surround it. Basically, there are two categories of leprosy. The milder form is tuberculoid which causes dry or discoloured skin, loss of sensitivity, particularly to the face, arms or legs where it can cause enlargement and lesions. Seventy percent of patients suffer from this form.

'The more serious form is lepromatous leprosy. This is characterised by large lesions all over the body. Sometimes it affects the eyes, nose and throat and can lead to blindness, voice change and putrefaction.

'Both forms attack the nervous system. Untreated, it can cause neurological damage – sensory loss in the skin and muscle weakness. People with long term leprosy often lose parts of their hands and feet, though that is often caused by the absence of sensation, rather than the disease itself.'

'I see,' Michael said. 'You were going to tell me about treatment?'

'Treatment is highly effective in curing and preventing the spread. We use dapsone, rifampin and clofazimine, usually in combination as a multi-drug therapy. A cure takes six to twelve months though this depends on the spread of the disease at the time of diagnosis. Occasionally, the drug therapy has to be repeated at intervals to prevent a recurrence or as a precaution. Following treatment, patients are normally non-contagious within a few months, but treatment can't reverse damage done before diagnosis.'

'What about my father? Was leprosy treatable in the early fifties?'

'Certainly. I've just been looking at his records.'

Michael nodded. He sat up and took another sip of coffee.

'Your father suffered mild tuberculoid leprosy. He had significant lesions on his arms and right leg and a couple of smaller lesions on his face and chest. He also had minor muscle damage in his right leg. I expect he had a slight limp.'

Michael nodded again. 'It didn't seem to trouble him.'

'No, it wouldn't. Anyway, he was given multi-drug therapy. The drugs then were different, but I see from the notes that they worked for him – were working when he left. He'd have been non-contagious and if he continued treatment, he would have been cured. Do you know if that was the case?'

Michael shifted in his chair. 'Yes, he continued treatment. But there was a minor recurrence of the disease a few years later and he was treated again. I think more than once.'

'Very possibly,' said the doctor. 'Especially with the earlier drugs. Still, he was unfortunate to have to repeat the therapy.'

Michael wanted to move on. 'My grandmother mentioned that he was locked up here at Fontilles.'

The doctor looked uncomfortable now. 'There's nothing in his records, but it's possible. Even today, the key is immediate isolation and treatment. But attitudes were a lot different in the 1950s. The stigma was much worse and practitioners tended to impose their will upon patients with enforced isolation. It was well intentioned, but mistaken. Today we know so much more about the disease and we have better support and counselling.'

'I see.' Michael finished his coffee. 'Thank you, Doctor Santos, I'd better not keep you any longer.'

Rosana also put down her cup.

Dr Santos stood up and smiled, holding out his hand as they rose after him. He shook hands with Michael.

'Well, thank you, Rosana, for bringing Miguel-Ángel to visit us. I'm pleased to have met you. Now, Juan will show you around and if you'd like to know anything else, I'll be here. Be sure to call in on your way back if you have any further questions.'

'I will. And thank you again, doctor.'

Juan conducted the tour of Fontilles, reciting as if from a script. 'Sanatorio San Francisco de Borja was founded in 1902 by a Jesuit priest, Father Carlos Ferris and a lawyer, Joaquin Ballester, whose dream was a facility for care and treatment of leprosy sufferers.' Juan stopped to pick up a few leaves and put them in a bin. 'In the late nineteenth century leprosy hit many rural villages. This area was badly affected, though no one knew why. At first the sanatorium was just a place of isolation, but over the years, patients found work to do and it grew into a village.

'Gradually the sanatorium became self-sufficient, growing much of its own food. There was a bakery, a carpenter and a cobbler and they even had their own winery pressing grapes grown on the estate. At one time, Fontilles accommodated three hundred sufferers, but now it has just sixty patients and one hundred and fifty out-patients.

The main work now is training and research. Doctors and nurses visit from all over the world to attend training courses and Fontilles runs programmes in China, Asia, and Latin America.'

The sanatorium could not have been more different from what Michael had always imagined. Like the grounds of a vast country estate, tree-lined groves were punctuated by small gardens. Tiny alcoves held statues of saints, or distinguished figures linked with Fontilles. Juan reeled off the names as if he knew them all personally.

The main building was a huge quadrangle of three storeys with a tower at each corner. With white painted walls and a terracotta tiled roof of castle-like proportions, it resembled some of the Spanish Paradors Michael had seen on television.

Inside, a marble-floored lobby was lit from a high vaulted ceiling and further on, a sunny courtyard featured a garden and a fountain.

A few people wandered around, others basked in the sunlight that had broken through the clouds. They looked as if they might be on holiday.

Michael asked Juan why no one looked ill.

'Fontilles is now a residential home for the elderly or infirm, not just leprosy sufferers. And there's a short stay centre for people recuperating after illness.' Juan hesitated and then continued. 'I was sorry to hear about your mother and father. I met your father, just before he left. I knew your mother, too. I had great respect for her.'

Michael looked surprised. 'How long have you been here?'

'Over sixty years. I was fourteen when I arrived.'

'And you've never left?'

'I could have left, but in the early years I had nowhere to go, so I stayed. I go outside now and again, but Fontilles is my home and I'm always glad to return.'

'I see,' Michael said, not knowing what else to say.

Juan seemed to understand Michael's unease. 'Your father's contributions were, of course, greatly appreciated,' he said after a pause.

'Sorry?'

'Your father – he was a fervent supporter of Fontilles. His

donations must have totalled thousands of euros over the years.'

Michael was dumbstruck, his mind a frenzied muddle of thoughts and emotions that induced a state of panic.

'I have to leave now,' he said suddenly, prompting a look of puzzlement from Juan. Embarrassed, he shook Juan's hand and said, 'I'm sorry. Thank you for showing me around.'

Sensing Michael's inner turmoil, Rosana said nothing on the drive back down the mountain, leaving him to wrestle with his own thoughts.

For years he'd believed his father had left Spain to escape incarceration. But far from being a medieval dungeon-like place, the sanatorium was friendly and welcoming. True, it had changed over the years, but there were no bars at the windows or locks on the doors and the place had transformed itself into a world renowned centre for the treatment and understanding of leprosy, combating ignorance and prejudice where it still existed. Worse still was the realisation that his father knew this, but had said nothing.

And Michael's belief that the people of Parcent had shunned his father and excluded him, was also unfounded. It had been the work of an ignorant old priest.

Michael had used the oppression and cruelty of Fontilles and the callous heartlessness of the villagers to feed his resentment toward Parcent and Spain. Now he realised he had been misguided.

Everything he'd believed in, everything that had influenced his attitudes, his personality, his being, felt wiped away. Like someone with amnesia, it would be a struggle to rediscover who he was and where he came from. Most disturbingly, he now had to view the world afresh, without prejudice and resentment and he felt a profound sense of pointlessness about his life.

'Shall we stop for coffee?' Rosana said.

'Yes, if you like.'

She stopped a minute later at a small roadside café and went inside. Michael headed for a shady corner of the terrace. Two boys and a girl romped around a playground at the side of the bar, watched by their parents sitting on the grass nearby. Gentle sunshine filtered through the trees as the children squealed and shouted. Sunlight on a half-turned face, dappled branches in the shade... red soil, flushed cheeks... Michael pictured a young man at a window, looking up at the mountains, the sun setting through the smoke of burning leaves, warming the mist along a ravine. His thoughts turned to his childhood when he'd played happily with friends, before the discovery of his father's illness. The father of the playing children was about the same age as Michael, and he contrasted the family with his own purposeless life.

Suddenly he could find nothing worthwhile to raise his spirits; nothing to look forward to; nothing worth living for.

Rosana returned to the terrace, carrying two cups.

'Was I wrong to press you to go to Fontilles?'

'Not wrong, no.'

'It wasn't what you imagined, was it? But it's best to know the truth.'

'Sometimes it's easier to build your life on things you believe in.'

'But what if they're false?'

'Yes, even if they're false, it's easier – no, that doesn't make sense. I'll put it another way... As far as I was concerned, I may not have been aware of it, but the past was like another country, psychologically and physically... and I was not ready to visit it.'

'I understand. So – where do you go from here?'

'Back to England, I guess. It looks like the case is as good as solved, so my job here is finished.'

'What about last night?' Rosana said, with a glance across at him.

His mobile phone rang and, as if distracted, Michael looked to one side. 'Last night,' he said, 'perhaps I got carried away.'

Rosana stared coldly as he spoke into the phone.

'Jose Luis... What?... Are they sure?... When will they know?... Where are you?... I'm coming over – no, I insist, I'll be there in twenty minutes.'

Michael switched off the phone and turned, oblivious to the disappointment on Rosanna's face. 'I need a lift to the finca. It's not far from here. They've found a body. I have to get there right away.'

He stood from the table without glancing at her and moved toward the parked car. Rosana followed.

On the road to Orba, Michael talked – deliberately and detachedly – about the latest development. 'This is the final nail in their coffin. It looks as if this is Mrs Harrington – they won't know until tomorrow – so that's it for the Dutchmen – at least for Van Doorn. If they find Mr Harrington, that will wrap things up... though I still don't get it. It's been too easy. But, as Jose Luis says, people do some strange and stupid things. I'll have to speak to John and Linda Harrington later on. I'm not looking forward to that – oh, I think it's over there somewhere,' he added, pointing to a track ahead on the left. 'Yes, you can see the police cars. Turn in here.'

Rosana pulled into the track. Brambles scratched the roof as she negotiated potholes. About seventy-five metres down the track she stopped, confronted by two Guardia Civil officers.

'Drop me here, thanks,' Michael said. 'I can make my own way back.'

He turned to Rosana as if to kiss her cheek – surely she could understand he was in no condition to make decisions, let alone a commitment, and that this was for the best – and that he'd spent so long being self contained, ignorant and self deluding, he was no good to her – or to anyone, even himself.

But Rosana stared straight ahead in silence and a kiss could only be patronising and dismissive, so he got out of the car.

Rosana crunched the gears as she slammed into reverse, swung the car around and headed back down the track.

Before she'd disappeared, Michael was trying to persuade the officers to let him pass on the strength of his civilian ID card, but it took Jose Luis to get him through. They walked past the dilapidated finca and continued along a track to a clump of almond trees and a roughly pitched tent. The forensics team in white overalls and latex gloves were busy. Two uniformed men lifted a stretcher with a black plastic body bag.

'Can I have a look?' asked Michael.

'Are you sure you want to?' replied Jose Luis. 'She was wrapped in a plastic groundsheet so the body is reasonably well preserved, but if you ask me it's been buried for quite some time. Are you sure you want to look?'

'I think I need to.'

Jose Luis nodded to the two men as they placed the stretcher on a collapsible trolley. One of them unzipped the front of the bag. He pulled the seam apart to reveal remnants of skin over bone and red earth. The blonde hair was tangled and matted and stuck to one side of the face by a clot of dry black blood. Michael winced. Then he saw the eyes. Those soft doe eyes from the photographs were now cold and lifeless, staring into infinity.

Michael turned. 'Any sign of Mr Harrington?'

Jose Luis appeared pale and nauseated. 'They're still looking,' he said, 'but there's a huge area to cover. It could take days unless the Dutchmen help us out. I'm heading back to Alicante now to talk to them.'

'Can you give me a lift? I need to pick up my things from Parcent.'

Jose Luis parked in the square outside Bar Moll and Michael asked him to wait.

As he walked past the bar, someone shouted, 'Hey!'

Julio, in overalls and boots splattered with paint and plaster, swung the door open. He strode up, reeking of alcohol. 'I've been trying to talk to you. About the house and the land.' Julio grabbed Michael by the arm.

'I don't see where you come into it.' Michael pushed his hand away.

Blood rose in Julio's cheeks. 'I've been stuck in this village all my life, working hard to earn a living and build a business and then you... you turn up fifty years after that leper father of yours disappeared and expect to take over.'

Michael displayed a measured calm. 'When and if I decide what to do, I'll discuss my inheritance with your father.'

Julio grabbed Michael by the throat and shoved him against the wall.

'No you will not. You don't deserve a thing. Why don't you just piss off back to England and...'

Michael's knee slammed into Julio's groin. He crumpled to the ground.

Jose Luis joined the scene. 'Is everything all right?'

'This is my little cousin, Julio.' Michael dusted off his hands. 'Julio, this is Captain Jose Luis Perez of the Guardia Civil. Tell him everything is fine.'

Julio uttered a long low groan.

'Good, because I have to dash.'

His grandmother's house was empty. He had his suitcase packed in seconds and was heading along the hall when Maria Carmen appeared in the doorway. She saw the suitcase.

'I've got to get to Alicante, Grandma. Something's cropped up. It's urgent.'

He kissed her cheek and moved to one side for her to pass. 'It's business. If anyone asks for me, can you let them know?'

'When are you coming back?'

'I'll phone.' He stepped outside and walked on, not looking back.

He reached Rosana's house, paused for a second to think what he might say to her and then continued down to Jose Luis's car.

Back at police headquarters, the two Dutchmen were lined up for interviews in separate rooms. Colonel Cardells was strutting.

'Still think they're innocent, Fernandez?' he said in the corridor.

'Can I be there when you interview them?'

Cardells hesitated, considering the request.

'You can sit in with us, but don't say a word. Ramirez will interpret and if you want to speak, ask first. Understood?'

'That's fine by me.'

In the interview room Van Doorn slouched back in his chair, as if nonchalant, but he looked less arrogant than earlier.

His solicitor, Erik Mohl, sat up straight beside him, crisp and business-like in cream shirt and striped tie.

'What's that bastard doing here?' Van Doorn looked up at Michael.

'He's here as an observer, nothing more,' said Ramirez.

Mohl nodded his approval.

The Colonel slammed a photograph onto the table. 'Recognise her?'

Van Doorn dropped his eyes and glanced at the picture without leaning forward. Michael tried to gauge his reaction, but saw only indifference.

'Means nothing to me.'

The Colonel smiled. 'It means you're going down for murder. That's what it means. That's Alison Harrington and guess where we found her?'

Now he had Van Doorn's attention.

'I have no idea.'

'Just a few metres from the finca in Orba where you admit you met David Harrington and say he gave you ten thousand euros. The finca where we found the bloodstains and your fingerprints. Now why don't you tell us where you've buried Mr Harrington and we can all get out of here.'

Van Doorn's face displayed a mixture of anger and fear as he pushed the photograph back towards the Colonel and knocked the solicitor's file to the floor. He stared hard at the Colonel.

'Look, I've told you everything. I admit I conned Harrington out of money, but I know nothing about murder. I've never met Mrs Harrington.'

'That's your final word?' the Colonel asked, 'You're not going to tell us what you've done with Mr Harrington?'

The solicitor intervened, as if to appear useful. 'My client has denied murdering anybody, Colonel, and unless you've further questions I can really see no point in continuing this interview.'

'So we'll just have to keep digging around the finca until we find Mr Harrington, won't we? Then perhaps your client will want to talk to us.'

The Colonel was ready to leave.

'Can I ask a question?' Michael looked at the Colonel and then at Erik Mohl.

The Colonel glowered but didn't object and the solicitor nodded.

'Did Wil know about the money you got from Mr Harrington?'

'I never told him.'

'Could he have found out?'

'It's possible, but he never said anything.'

'Did Wil ever go to the finca alone? I mean after you met Mr Harrington and he gave you the money?'

Van Doorn turned the possibility over. Suddenly he was interested and keen to talk. 'He could have done, yes. We're not together all the time. He's had plenty of opportunities to go over there without me. What are you thinking? He might have gone there alone and done them in?'

Mohl had just about caught up and interrupted. 'Wait a minute. What are you suggesting? That my other client, Mr Hagemans, did this?'

'Of course, I forgot, you represent both suspects.' said Michael.

'Colonel Cardells, I must object to this,' said Mohl. 'Inspector Fernandez is trying to drive a wedge between my clients.'

'I'm sure he's only trying to get to the truth,' the Colonel said. 'Now, shall we talk to Mr Hagemans?'

Between interviews the Colonel pulled Michael to one side.

'I'm not sure what you're up to here, Fernandez. Of course they'll blame each other, but where will that lead us?'

'To the truth perhaps,' said Michael.

Hagemans was nervous and almost as straight-backed as the solicitor. The photograph of Mrs Harrington produced horror on his face. Once again he pleaded whimpering ignorance.

This time the Colonel picked up Michael's lead. 'Mr Van Doorn says you could have found out about the money he got from Mr Harrington and gone back to the finca. Perhaps you met Mr Harrington again? Perhaps you met Mrs Harrington as well? We think you had an argument and killed them both.'

Mohl folded his arms, but his eyes were alert.

After hesitation, Hagemans suddenly metamorphosised from timid and twitchy to angry and resolute, showing a side to his character previously hidden. He leant forward and stared coldly into the Colonel's eyes.

'I can see what Johan's trying and it isn't going to work. He took the money from Harrington. He's the one with a motive to kill the Harringtons, not me.'

'Can you account for your movements over the last two weeks?'

'What do you mean?'

'Well, if you say you never went back to the finca, perhaps you can prove it by telling us where you've been?'

'Two weeks? It's impossible. How the hell can I remember everything I've done in the last two weeks?'

'I'm sure you can if you try, Mr Hagemans and we'll be asking your friend to do the same. We'll leave you to think about it.'

The Colonel returned to his office with Jose Luis and Michael in tow.

'Well, gentlemen, I'm not sure where that takes us, except that now they're blaming each other. I guess we'll just have to charge them both with murder then see if one of them squeals and gives us something positive against the other. In the meantime, we let them stew. Perhaps we'll know more when we see the results of the post mortem and the forensics report. And we'll just have to keep digging at the finca until Mr Harrington turns up. I'm sure he's buried round there somewhere. Anyway, thank you for your help, Michael. I expect you'll be on your way back home before long?'

'Oh, I'll be here a while yet. As you say, there's the post mortem and forensics report. Have you told John and Linda Harrington about the body?'

'I was hoping you'd do that,' the Colonel said with a hint of a grin. 'That's what you're here for, I believe, liaising with the family, that sort of work?'

'Amongst other things.'

'Anyway,' said the Colonel, 'it's all coming to a conclusion and when we find Mr Harrington's body it'll wrap things up nicely.'

The Colonel was a smug, detached sort of a bastard, Michael thought 'Not so much for the Harringtons,' he said

'No... well, perhaps not, but at least we've got the culprits.'

'You're sure of that, Colonel?'

The Colonel bristled. 'Of course I'm sure. What more do you want?'

Michael hesitated, but set his shoulders and pressed on.

'Haven't you wondered why bloodstains from both Mr and Mrs Harrington were found in the finca, but only Mr Harrington's fingerprints? If the Dutchmen held the Harringtons, it certainly wasn't at the finca. So where was it? If the Harringtons weren't abducted, but were killed more recently for their money, where were they hiding? Why were they hiding? And what's happened to the money? We know Mr Harrington had a lot more than ten thousand euros. There are just too many loose ends.'

The Colonel exploded. 'Don't muddy the waters now, Fernandez. This isn't England, where you cross all the T's and dot all the I's because some judge will throw the case out on a technicality. We've got enough evidence to convict them. In fact, I don't want you here again. Your involvement is at an end. You can speak to John and Linda Harrington and then I suggest you book a flight back home.'

Michael opened his mouth to protest, but the Colonel cut him off.

'Goodbye, Inspector Fernandez. Thank you for your help. You can leave your ID card at the desk on your way out.'

The meeting with John and Linda Harrington went as expected. He broke the news about the body, leading them to fear the worst about David.

John was indifferent, or pretended to be, and his main concern seemed to be how long they should extend their stay in Spain. Linda was tearful, genuinely distressed. Even so, she agreed to identify Alison's body when John declined the responsibility on the grounds that she was not his blood relative. Michael made no mention of his doubts about the two suspects, allowing John and Linda the scant comfort of thinking the culprits had been apprehended.

Just after ten Michael arrived back at his hotel in Alicante and returned the phone call from Chief Superintendent Bowater.

'I hear you've been upsetting the Colonel again.'

Michael explained his reservations about the case and found the Chief Super surprisingly sympathetic. 'All the same, I don't see what more you can do. The Colonel's made it clear he wants you off the case.'

'I'll just hang around for a while, if that's okay with you. I'll take leave if you'd prefer it that way. I want to see what the post mortem turns up and if forensics can shed any light.'

'Stay on, then. There's no need to take leave, but be careful. And if nothing occurs in the next few days, you'd better think about coming home.'

A couple of brandies failed to bring sleep. He tried to concentrate on the loose ends of the case but his mind drifted to Fontilles and his grandmother's story. Had his father ever hated Spain? What about Maria Carmen, Uncle Pepito, Julio, Pedro? The house and the land?

He drifted back to the rooftop terrace where he'd marvelled at the setting with Rosana. He recalled the night at La Tasca and their walk back to Rosana's house. Couldn't build a life on one kiss… or his senses when they touched... Drowsy thoughts gave way to perpetually deep, dark dreams he could never clearly recall.

CHAPTER ELEVEN

Next morning, Michael killed time around the hotel since it was too early to contact Jose Luis to see if there'd been any further developments.

He strolled outside to a kiosk where he bought the *Daily Telegraph* and found a small piece on page four:

FEARS GROW FOR COUPLE MISSING IN SPAIN
Spanish police have discovered a body believed to be that of Alison Harrington, missing in the Alicante province of Spain for over four months.

Mrs Harrington and her husband David, from Nottingham, disappeared in January this year after they failed to return from a trip to buy a retirement home on the Costa Blanca. The body was found buried near a remote farmhouse on the outskirts of Orba. It had been the focus for police inquiries after the arrest last week of two Dutchmen believed to be involved in a property fraud. Mr Harrington is still missing and police are continuing to search the land near the farmhouse.

A British Detective, Inspector Michael Fernandez from Nottingham CID, has been helping Spanish police with their search. He was unavailable for comment last night. Last year a British couple were murdered in the same area after travelling to Spain to look for a retirement home.

Back at the hotel, there was a message from the *Daily Mail's* reporter and another from a reporter for *The Sun*. He ignored them both.

He'd hoped for news from Jose Luis. He'd also hoped there might be a message of some kind from Rosana. He was disappointed on both counts.

By six that evening he could wait no longer and called Jose Luis.

'I've got some news, but I can't talk to you now,' said the Spanish detective in hushed tones. 'I'll call you back in an hour.'

For ninety minutes Michael stayed by the phone, wondering what further twists had emerged. Perhaps they'd found David Harrington, or his body. Perhaps the Dutchmen had confessed. Perhaps the real killers had been found. The news when it came was devastating.

'Jose Luis, what's happening?' Michael asked.

Jose Luis spoke in excitement, 'The post mortem confirms the body is Mrs Harrington. Killed up to four weeks ago. The cause of death appears to be a single blow to the head. And we've found the murder weapon. A rusty old mattock in a clump of bushes about thirty metres from the body. It has bloodstains and we lifted prints from the stave – and guess what? We've matched them to the Dutchman.'

'Jesus. It looks like curtains for Van Doorn then,' Michael said, still taking in the damning evidence.

'No, not Van Doorn, Hagemans. We lifted Hagemans' prints. Looks like your hunch was right.'

'What hunch?'

'Well, you suggested he found out about the money Harrington gave Van Doorn. Our theory is, Hagemans went back for more and ended up killing them both. That explains why we can't find the rest of the money.'

'And you still haven't found David Harrington?'

'No. We've scoured every inch of land around the finca, but no sign.'

'So what happens now?'

'The Colonel plans to charge them both with murder tonight. He might reduce the charge for Van Doorns if he comes clean, but if not he'll try to make the murder charge stick for both of them. He's hoping one of them will crack and tell us where Mr Harrington is. Oh, and he's arranged a press conference for tomorrow morning.'

'Does he want me there?'

'What do you think, Michael? He's speaking to your Chief Superintendent tonight. He'll say there's no need for you to be there.

He will acknowledge your assistance at the press briefing, but say there is no further need for your involvement. John and Linda Harrington have been invited and Timothy Middleton will support them. Of course, he'll promise to keep searching for Mr Harrington for as long as it takes, but he'll hint that Harrington is presumed dead and the case is as good as closed.'

'What do you think, Jose Luis?'

'Look Michael, I've tried to help as much as I can, but we've reached the end of the road. Even you will admit the evidence is overwhelming.'

'I guess so,' said Michael without conviction.

'What will you do now?'

'I suppose I'll get back to England. Look Jose Luis, thanks for your help. I mean it. I know we haven't always seen eye to eye, but I appreciate you've gone out on a limb for me a couple of times. I hope it all works out for you and that I haven't marred your record with the Colonel.'

'Don't worry about me, Michael. The Colonel's just happy to have wrapped the case up. It's been good to work with you and if you ever come back to this part of Spain, be sure to look me up.'

'That's kind of you, Jose Luis, but I doubt I'll be coming back.'

The first flight back to East Midlands was on Sunday afternoon. Today was Friday. For a moment he thought of spending Saturday sightseeing in Alicante – after all, he'd hardly seen anything of the place – but...

In the end he made the call.

'Oh Miguel-Ángel, I'm so glad. Are you coming home?'

'I'm coming to Parcent, grandma, if that's what you mean, but the case is over. I'm booked on a flight to Britain on Sunday afternoon. I thought I'd come up in the morning, and stay the night. I need to talk to you and Pepito.'

'Of course. I just wish you could stay a bit longer.'

'Grandma, I need to get back to work. I'll talk to you in the morning.'

'Are you going to talk to Rosana? She's been asking about you.'

'I'll be back as soon as I can.'

The hotel booked him a hire car, to be delivered early on Saturday and returned to El Altet airport on Sunday afternoon. He rose early, breakfasted on the terrace and checked out of the hotel with all his belongings.

It was a warm spring day with only a few puffy clouds interrupting a clear blue sky. The sun had gradually risen earlier and higher during his stay as June approached and the shade dwindled in the middle of the day.

The drive north took him once again past the distant skyscrapers of Benidorm. He never did get to visit the package tour centre of the universe, but somehow he wasn't bothered. He left the A7 at Benissa and followed the twisting road through Senija and the one-way chicken run in Lliber. Emerging into the flat bed of the Jalon valley, he glimpsed the church tower of Parcent in the distance and wondered if this was last time he would see it.

Uncle Pepito and Maria Carmen were waiting on the terrace. They greeted him with smiles, but anxiety showed on their faces as he approached them.

Michael decided to skip formalities. 'Grandma, Uncle Pepito, I've been giving some thought to my inheritance. I understand the empty house is worth a sizeable sum for foreign buyers, but I don't want to sell. I'd like to keep it and visit from time to time. It needs some repairs and it will have to be furnished. I'd be grateful if Uncle Pepito could organise that work. I'll pay for it myself.'

Pepito nodded acceptance.

'As I understand it, this house passed to my father and Pepito when my grandfather died and my father's share belongs to me. Of course you, Grandma, must live here – that's what I want, as does Pepito. As for the land, I understand nothing can be disposed of unless Pepito and I are in agreement. I'm happy to let Pepito decide.' Michael looked at Pepito to see his reaction. 'You can sell some or all if you want, Pepito, it's up to you.'

Pepito burst out, 'I'll never sell any.'

'Fine,' replied Michael. 'Then I want Pedro to keep working the land and taking income from it. My share is his, for the time being at least.'

Pepito stepped forward suddenly and clasped Michael in a hug.

Maria Carmen looked up from her weathered wicker chair. She lifted her gold-rimmed spectacles and wiped away a tear as Michael bent to crouch at her side.

'I thought you would be happy with my decision.'

'I wish you would stay here.' She touched his hand softly. 'We lost Francisco all those years ago and now you are leaving, too. Your family want you here Miguel-Ángel. What is there to back to in England?'

He wanted to say he was sorry to disappoint her. He wanted to tell her that he had to take possession of this new life at his own pace. He wanted to explain his feelings about his father, about Fontilles, the village and the land. But words could not express the way he felt and, to his dismay, he simply maintained his steadfastness, knowing the pain it caused.

'Grandma, I've made up my mind. I'm going back to England.'

Silence fell, finally interrupted by Pepito. 'It's the people's dinner tonight to mark the end of the fiestas. Everyone in the village will be there. Will you come?'

He wanted to say no, but his grandmother's face made him wilt.

He wasn't sure why or what he was going to say, but he decided to call at Rosana's house only to discover she was working that morning at the insurance office in Jalon. He greeted the news with what he thought was relief, but turned out to be disappointment.

On the spur of the moment he decided to drive to Jalon.

The roadside verges, he noticed as he approached the bridge into town, were littered with abandoned cars. Michael queued to cross the one-way bridge, but was delayed by cars trying to get in and out of an unofficial car park on the far side. The weekly Rastro market was in full swing.

Driving slowly along the riverside road, he passed almost a kilometre of rickety tables and blankets set out on dusty ground. Between trees that fringed the dried-up riverbed, ladies' underwear fluttered over cracked clay urns, tarnished brass, leather belts, knitwear, shoes, handbags and second hand tools. The sound of a Venezuelan nose flute wafted through his open car window, accompanied by the aroma of hot dogs and fried onions and the sweet scent of *churros* sizzling in hot oil. The fish and chip shop was doing a roaring trade and the Brits looked to be out in force, along with the Dutch, Germans and a few Spaniards.

A row of parked coaches slowed his progress and, just as he'd cleared the blockage, a yellow-clad workman turned his table tennis bat from "go" to "stop". A construction crew had decided Saturday morning was the ideal time to lay the tarmac to a new roundabout. He waited at the head of the queue for five minutes, watching the confusion of the market. A local policeman chatted to the yellow overalls and pulled on a cigarette.

Michael searched for a parking spot. A Land Rover drove out from a rough patch of land and he pulled in. As he stepped from the car, a layer of cement dust puffed beneath his feet and covered his freshly polished shoes with a film of fine white powder.

By the time he reached the insurance office he was sticky, hot and flustered. He was also out of breath, having jogged the last hundred metres, concerned that it was approaching one o'clock and the office might already be closed.

He pushed open the double glazed door and went up to the counter.

Rosana sat talking on the telephone and tapping a computer keyboard. She glanced up and returned to the screen without changing her expression. Her soft, white silk blouse hung loosely round her waist and shoulders and her dark wavy hair, brushing gently against her cheeks, looked – well, like the hairstyle on the cover of a magazine.

At the end of her call, she said, 'We offer travel, health, motor and life. Which is it you want?'

'Lunch.'

'I'm sorry, Miguel-Ángel, I don't feel like lunch today.'

'Can you recommend the local fish and chips? I'll bring some in if you prefer.'

'No, anything but fish and chips. I know a little tapas bar... it's just around the corner.'

Bar Rull nestled nearby in the corner of a small square with white plastic tables and chairs spread beneath the shade of a billowing jacaranda tree. Rosana ordered the tapas which arrived quickly in small dishes. As the condensation on a bottle of chilled *rosado* wine turned to droplets, Michael explained that the case was as good as over and he was booked to return to England the next day. He outlined his decision about the house and the land and looked for signs of approval, but Rosana's face showed only indifference.

'Am I telling you something you already know?' he asked.

'Not at all,' replied Rosana. 'I'm just not sure why you're telling me at all.'

If that was meant to sound dismissive, it hit the mark. 'I just thought you deserved an explanation, Rosana, that's all.'

'An explanation? You're a free agent. You don't have to justify yourself to me. So we met and... well, nothing. A brief interlude, a dalliance. As you said the other day, perhaps we got carried away. We're both adults, we don't have to make excuses. Let's leave it that.'

Michael almost said that was fine by him, but somehow he didn't want that. It was just... he couldn't think straight. And... he didn't like being rejected. 'Is this how you really feel?' he asked after a short pause.

'What do you care how I feel? You've made up your mind, you're returning to England. Go home. It's clear I don't figure in your plans, so why should you care about my feelings?'

'But I've told you, I'll be coming back. That's why I asked Pepito to do some work on the old house.'

Rosana's hackles rose. 'Well, good for you, Miguel-Ángel, you'll have a nice little holiday home for two weeks a year. You can pop in on the old relatives and admire your quaint little olives and oranges, drink a few bottles of your own wine. You can take off your jacket and tie and swap them for overalls and a straw hat. Won't that be fun? Only please, don't bother to look me up.' She turned, crossed her arms and raised her chin.

'Just what is it you expect of me, Rosana? Two weeks ago I'd never set foot in this country; never been to Parcent. I never even knew I had family here.'

Rosana swung round. 'And how did you reach the age of forty, or whatever, without knowing your family? Why did you never ask about them? Weren't you even curious?'

'You know why.'

'No, I do not.'

'Because of my father.'

Rosana's eyes narrowed, her voice hardened.

'So your father was a leper. But he wasn't rejected by his village as you believed, but by a stupid, nasty old priest. And he wasn't incarcerated in a dungeon. He chose to leave Spain for his own reasons. Just as you are about to do.'

'What do you mean?'

'Face it, what happened to your father has been an excuse to deny your Spanish ancestry. What was it, really? Did the other kids pick on you because you have latin looks and a funny name? Is that why you call yourself Michael? Is that why you act and dress like some sort of superior English gentleman and look down your nose at everyone? Is that why you rejected your father? – not because of leprosy, but because he made you half-Spanish.'

Michael sat up. He was angry, but more than that he was hurt. 'Perhaps you have a point. But this is not the time or place. I just wanted to let you know my plans. Come on, it's time we left.'

Rosana hesitated and then placed a hand on his. 'I'm sorry, Miguel-Ángel... I just wanted to get you to face a few misconceptions and think about…'

'I know, but let's leave it, Rosana. I can make up my own mind.'

Outside Maria Carmen's house, the tables and chairs took up most of the street and food was being passed from every doorway when Michael came downstairs. Flat coca breads laden with peas, tomato paste or anchovies were being torn apart by hand. Spicy sausages sizzled on a gas-fired barbecue, hot tortillas were carried out in heavy pans and warm pasties filled with spinach and tuna were piled high on trays alongside mountains of bread, plate-loads of sliced serrano ham and chunks of hard cheese. Baskets of fruit lay in waiting and jugs of wine were passed from one end of the table to the other. The village band played cheerful music that wafted through the warm night air.

He had spent the afternoon brooding in his room. Now he was late, tired and unenthusiastic. He would have preferred a quiet night before his early departure in the morning, but the hubbub from the street reminded him of expectations.

His emergence from the house seemed to go largely unnoticed as everyone continued talking. Maria Carmen shuffled along a short bench and made a space for him to sit. Pepito thrust a glass of red wine into his hand, a plate arrived, piled high, and cousin Pedro presented him a grin and a slap on the back.

Rosana, with her family further down the street, looked up briefly, but gave only a cursory nod of recognition. Closer by, Julio offered a malevolent glare.

Everyone else looked happy – possibly too happy to be convincing. But eating, drinking, chatting with family and friends, they seemed to belong there; from old people, revered by their younger relatives, to small children who were fussed over and encouraged to join in the festivities. With the exception of Julio, everyone around the table exchanged smiles and warm greetings. This was kinship, friendship and fellowship beyond anything he had known in his life... a celebration of life itself. A part of him wished he belonged there.

At one in the morning, the party began to wind down. The band retired and revellers sauntered home through the narrow streets. A rocket lit the sky, sending a boom around the mountains. Michael used this as his excuse to retreat. Rosana had already left. He should have made an effort to circulate in her direction – if only to pay his respects to her mother and grandmother – but the opportunity had passed.

Sleep evaded him. The noise from the street below gradually faded to silence, punctuated by occasional bursts of conversation or laughter. Finally, he drifted into a vague dream with images and scenes flashing like disjointed film clips. A loud crash disturbed the dream, followed by a thud and the tinkling of glass. He blinked, but saw only darkness. He turned on the lamp at his bedside, swept back the bed clothes, blinked again, and looked around the room. The windowpane at the side of the wardrobe was shattered. Shards of glass were spread over the bedside rug and the surrounding wooden floor. A rock the size of his fist rested at the foot of the door wrapped in white paper and tied with a knot of string. He reached for his shoes, shook them to release a few small splinters of glass and slid them on. He crunched over more broken glass to reach the rock and remove the paper. Even looking at it upside-down, the single word written in capitals with a heavy, black felt-tip pen was easy to decipher – LEPER.

He left early next morning after sweeping the bedroom floor as best he could. He said his farewells to Maria Carmen, mentioning the rock but not the note. Cutting short their parting hug, he kissed his grandmother on both cheeks then picked up his case and stepped out of the door. He hated goodbyes and there was no point in prolonging this one.

Most of the village was asleep, the streets silent as he wound his way down to his parked car. The sky was a clear sapphire blue, like most of the mornings since his arrival in Spain and the temperature was already rising. He walked in shade where he could and looked up now and again at the swallows weaving in and out of rooftops. A cock crowed in the distance as the church bell rang out a nine-thirty chime. Strings of plastic bunting fluttered as he passed along the painted road outside the town hall and an ancient set of fairy lights, now dimmed, formed the words, "*Bones Festes*" in Valenciano.

He paused to look back and raised his eyes to the white church tower silhouetted against blue. That image would haunt his dreams and he wondered if he would ever see it again.

Slowly he continued the walk to his car, parked near a pollarded maple tree, one of twelve in front of the Coopertiva bar. In the circle of dark shade beneath the tree, he could just make out a figure leaning against the trunk. He didn't need to look twice to recognise the silhouette.

'You weren't going to leave without saying goodbye?'

Once again she confronted him; pricking his conscience and forcing him to reflect on his behaviour. Why must she do this? Did she think she had the right to rule his life? Why couldn't she simply leave him alone to live his life the way he wanted instead of acting like a domineering big sister?

Defence strategy. Answer a question with a question.

'Would you care if I did?'

'Yes, I would.'

'What?'

'I would have cared, if you hadn't said goodbye.'

He stepped closer. 'Okay, I'll say goodbye.'

'Oh, this is stupid. I couldn't let you leave without saying goodbye. I know I've pushed you and cajoled you into doing some things you would rather not have done, but I never meant to hurt you.'

'You're not going to ask me to stay, are you?'

'Would there be any point?'

'No.'

'Then I won't.'

Michael was almost disappointed. Almost.

'Rosana, you know perfectly well I can't stay. I don't belong here.'

'I said I wasn't asking you.'

'I know, but I want you to understand.'

'It's all right. I do understand.'

'We're still friends, then?'

'Always.' She stretched up and kissed him softly on the lips.

He moved back, resisting the temptation to pull her in.

'Would you like me to come to the airport, to see you off?' she asked.

'It's kind of you, but I hate protracted goodbyes. I'm glad I came, glad we're still friends. Let's leave it at that and I'll keep in touch.'

'I'd like that.'

Michael glanced in the rear view mirror and returned Rosana's waves until he reached the junction at the edge of the village. He looked for a smile from her, but didn't see one.

The afternoon flight to East Midlands was only three-quarters full and Michael found a window seat with no one at his side.

Someone on the in-bound flight had left a copy of the *Daily Mail* in the pocket in front of him and he browsed the pages as the plane taxied. It was an abrupt reintroduction to England and English politics.

The front page was dominated by: NEW TAX HIKE. Page two proclaimed: RECORD VIOLENT CRIME and on page four: PM PROMISES IMMIGRATION CONTROLS.

By the time he reached page six, the plane was beginning to level off. Michael felt his eyes grow heavy, his head slumped to his chest and the newspaper fell to his lap waking him abruptly. He was about to return the paper to the pocket when something on page six caught his eye: SPANISH POLICE CHARGE COSTA MURDERERS.

Three full columns spelled out the case against Hagemans and Van Doorn and reported the continuing search for David Harrington. Photographs of David and Alison Harrington appeared beneath the headline.

Lower down the page, there was an interview with John Harrington announcing his return to Britain and full of vitriol about Spain and the Spanish police who had refused to investigate the case for so long.

No mention of Michael Fernandez, thank God. At least he'd be spared celebrity status when he got back to the office.

According to John Harrington, it wasn't safe to buy a house in the Costa Blanca because you were likely to get murdered in the process of looking.

Michael folded the paper and returned it to the pocket in front. For a moment he thought about Hagemans and Van Doorn sweating it out in Alicante prison and awaiting their trial. He still felt uneasy about the way the case had turned out, but at least the villains had been apprehended. As for the newspapers, it was already yesterday's story and he doubted there would be much more coverage. Unless, of course, David Harrington was found.

CHAPTER TWELVE

A charcoal grey sky and heavy rain greeted Michael's arrival at East Midlands airport. After the constant stifling heat of Spain, he almost loved it. The colours were drab and dismal, but there was freshness in the air and a smell of damp earth as he descended from the plane. Even the taxi driver's predictable rant about asylum-seekers and the health service made him want to laugh – or it would have, if he'd had the energy.

He climbed the steps of the small apartment block where he owned a flat and had to think for a second, to remember the entry code for the security system. A patch of fresh graffiti was posted at the side of the door – a multi-coloured tag that must have taken at least twenty minutes to complete. Scorch marks at the foot of the metal door suggested someone had set a small fire, as if the artist had needed to keep warm. He unlocked the box and collected his post – mostly unsolicited brochures, and bills – and climbed the stairs to his front door. Inside, the room was cold and uninviting, illuminated by the phosphorescent glow of street lamps outside the window. It didn't look much better with the lights on, but he dropped his case, removed his soggy jacket and kicked off his shoes before slumping, completely relaxed, into the leather recliner in front of the lifeless television. Within five minutes he was asleep.

He woke just before seven and the idea of getting back to work was suddenly exciting. He showered and shaved, noticing a hint of a tan. An image of his father flashed across the mirror.

His desk was surprisingly clear apart from a few memos, bulletins, and *The Job* – the police magazine. A yellow post-it note attached to the phone said: 'Please see the Chief Super.'

Penny Edwardes blushed when he entered the outer office. 'Welcome back, Michael,' she said without further comment. 'The

Chief Super's waiting. Go right in.'

Michael tapped on the door and stepped inside to a smell of paint and wallpaper paste. He stumbled on the new beige carpet. The desk was the same, but in a different position and a new coffee table with couch seating occupied the corner where a bookcase had stood. Everything else was pretty much the same, including the family photos and the bravery award.

'Welcome back, Michael, take a seat.' Bowater gestured towards the chair by the desk. This was not going to be a coffee table chat. Bowness was in full uniform with three shiny crowns attached to the epaulettes of his jacket and a row of coloured ribbons sewn above the breast pocket. His peaked cap with chequered band rested on a pair of brown leather gloves on the corner of the desk. Michael sat down and crossed his legs.

'Been a few changes since you left. What do you think?' Bowater scanned the new décor.

'Very nice,' Michael said. *Glad the budget stretched to it.*

'I just thought you ought to see this. It arrived yesterday by email.'

He handed a sheet of white paper to Michael, who spotted the crest of the Guardia Civil straight away.

'It's from Colonel Cardells. You'll understand it better than me, but it's clear he was grateful for your help in solving the case. It says something about tact and diplomacy, doesn't it? Anyway, I've passed a copy to the Chief Constable. Thought he ought to know. What do you say?'

'Just doing my job, sir.'

'You're too modest, Michael. I know you were thrust into a potentially tricky situation over there. You handled it very well. Pity about Mrs Harrington, but at least they got to the bottom of it. Things would have been much more difficult if they hadn't arrested the killers. It's just a shame they haven't found Mr Harrington yet. What do you think?'

'They might never find him.'

'What, you think they've hidden him better than they hid his wife?'

'He's certainly well hidden, that's for sure.'

'And what about the two Dutchmen, do you think they'll go down?'

'All the evidence points that way.'

'But you're not so sure?' Bowater frowned slightly.

'There's just something not quite right. Oh, the evidence is pretty overwhelming, but there are still too many loose ends.'

'That's typical of you Michael, always want things neat and tidy. I thought you'd realise by now that life isn't like that where the criminal fraternity is concerned. Anyway, it's all done and dusted and it's good to have you back. We've got a new assignment for you.'

Michael straightened, curiosity mixed with suspicion.

'Don't look so worried, Michael, we're not sending you back to Spain. A new team's being set up as part of the Community Safety Partnership, to tackle youth crime and anti-social behaviour. Vandalism, graffiti, yobbism, truanting, glue sniffing, that sort of stuff. You see, the Council's research boffins have been talking to Youth Offending and they reckon there are twenty to thirty young yobs, "prominent nominals" I think they call them; the key players responsible for most of the trouble. Council elections are next year and the politicians know this kind of crime is top of the voters' concerns, hence the new team. What do you think?'

Michael tried not to let his scepticism show. 'What is this team supposed to do?'

'Well, everyone says the right hand doesn't know what the left is doing. You know, we catch them, the Courts let them go, or refer them to social services and then we catch them again. It's a merry-go-round and the little buggers know it. So this new team, did I tell you it's called "The Frequent Young Offenders Forum," will bring all the agencies together to co-ordinate their efforts.'

Michael cringed at "co-ordinate," an excuse to swap stories, discuss strategies and argue over responsibility. A recipe for inertia.

'Who exactly will be involved?' he asked.

'Just about everyone – police, that new woman the council have just appointed as Community Safety Officer, social services, magistrates, probation staff, housing associations, environmental services, education welfare officers, the whole shooting match.'

Michael was already picturing endless hours in fruitless meetings, piles of paper passing backwards and forwards, pointless debates about supporting young people rather than punishing them. He was already thinking of excuses for not being able to get to meetings. He'd send a sergeant or a constable instead. This wasn't criminal investigation. It was an exercise in petty politics designed to show that everyone was pulling together when they were going in opposite directions. It would look good in the Force's Annual Report and in the politicians' election literature, but the yobs would still be creating havoc out on the streets.

'And what's my role in this?' He tried to sound interested.

'You're in charge, Michael. You will be Chairman – or should I say "Chair" – of the Forum. You'll report directly to the Community Safety Partnership, through me of course. And, as Chairman – sorry "Chair" – of the Partnership, the Council's Chief Executive will be taking a personal interest. You've met Colin Deakin, I think.'

'I have.' *Ruthless, self-seeking egomaniac who'd stop at nothing to please his political masters, since his knighthood depended on it.*

'It's a great opportunity, Michael, and very high profile. This is the future of crime reduction. Catch them young, divert them from crime and steer them towards more productive forms of recreation.'

Michael recognised the words from the latest Home Office research.

'Any questions?' Bowater asked.

Michael thought for a moment.

'Good,' said Bowater, 'I know you'll make a good job of this. I have every confidence in you. Penny's got all the details and you'll find a few dates pencilled in your diary already. I have to dash now. I'm standing in for the Chief Constable at an award ceremony for cadets. Keep me posted and remember this is very high priority. We need results and fast.'

Penny handed him a pile of papers and files topped by a glossy one hundred page document: Home Office Crime Reduction Manual – Supplement Twenty-Three – New Strategies for Tackling Youth

Crime and Disorder. The enthusiasm he'd felt at returning to work had evaporated. Catching murderers, robbers, rapists and thieves was what he did best, not heading up a talking shop to deal with a few petty yobs.

Worse was to come. A meeting had been arranged with Colin Deakin and Adrienne Forrester, the Community Safety Officer, for six o'clock that evening. There would be a presentation to councillors on Thursday night and weekly meetings of the Frequent Young Offenders Forum had been scheduled for every Wednesday morning. There was a file on each of twenty-three named young offenders with patchy details from all the agencies involved. None of it amounted to a solid case against any of them.

He tired of the paperwork in half an hour and did not read beyond the executive summary of the Home Office blurb. He leant back in his chair, laced his fingers behind his head and gazed from the window across the roof of the nearby shopping centre, glistening in the rain. Traffic crawled along the Broadway, being overtaken by empty buses cruising, unhindered, along the bus priority lane. He could just make out the spire of St. Martin's church in the distance, blurred by drizzle and merging with the drab, cold dark clouds. He snapped forward in his chair and re-shuffled the files on his desk.

Over at the Civic Offices, the meeting with Colin Deakin started fifteen minutes late and lasted for all of five minutes before Deakin's secretary called him out for an urgent consultation with the Leader of the Council. Michael found himself being chaperoned along the corridor to a smart office signed "Community Safety Team." Inside Michael surveyed a collection of six brand new desks, each topped with a computer console and keyboard. The walls were plastered with coloured graphs and bar charts. Only one of the desks, the largest, was occupied and Michael headed in that direction, taking a seat opposite the caramel-complexioned, sleek-haired Adrienne Forrester, Community Safety Officer, dressed in a dark blue trouser suit over an open necked pale blue blouse. This was a woman who liked to wear the trousers and she quickly moved to take control of the discussion throwing out words like "integrated strategy to tackle cycles of deprivation and develop latent potential." It took all Michael's will power to restrain a yawn.

The first meeting of the Frequent Young Offenders Forum was spent pouring coffee for late arrivals, amid jokes slotted into arguments between agencies and refusals to divulge confidential information.

Thursday night's presentation in the Council Chamber was a slick affair, though from what Michael could see, only half the councillors had bothered to put in an appearance. Deakin and Ms Forrester put on polished performances backed by a Powerpoint slide show with elaborate graphics full of bar charts, statistics and key phrases. The word "Partnership" was repeated ad nauseam. Michael was introduced from the background and was relieved that none of the councillors could think of anything meaningful to ask.

As he left the Town Hall, a uniformed attendant wished him goodnight. He turned to respond and a notice board caught his eye. It was cluttered with department names and direction arrows, but something stood out: PRINTING DEPARTMENT, GROUND FLOOR, ROOM 317.

'Who's in charge of the Printing Department these days?' he asked.

'That's Mr Brooks,' the attendant replied. 'Alan Brooks.'

'Has he been here long?'

'As long as I can remember. He took over when Mr Harrington left. Have you heard about him? He went to Spain to look for a house and now they say he's dead.'

'Yes, I read about it.'

When he arrived next morning, the Printing Department was not what Michael expected. No darkroom, no machines with metal plates clanking around drums and rollers spreading ink. Instead, a pair of giant *Xerox Ducutecs* almost five metres long stood in tandem, each with its own computer console. They purred quietly, spitting out printed pages. A machine in the far corner dispensed paper at a slower pace, but in full colour.

'It's all changed since Harrington was here,' said Alan Brooks with pride. 'We've moved entirely to digital printing, directly linked through the Wide Area Network to four Word Processing Centres and to the Graphic Studio upstairs. Our work all comes straight down the line. We farm out the wet printing to specialist companies. Our old fashioned presses were years out of date and we just couldn't compete with commercial printers. Now we concentrate on short-run work – rapid turn-round, straight to the post room and out.'

'Very impressive,' Michael said.

'Anyway, you didn't come here to talk to me about printing, did you? Let's go into the office.'

The small glazed cabin in the corner of the print room mirrored the high-tech appearance of the print operation. The only exception was a notice board, littered with bulletins, fire drill procedures, a leave chart, bits of paper and photographs, mostly curling at the edges and gathering dust.

Alan Brooks adjusted the blind to deflect the sun and sat behind the gleaming desk. He removed his thick-lensed glasses and rubbed his eyes, as if to steady them. Michael took a seat on the other side of the desk.

'You were out in Spain, weren't you? Do you really think that David is dead?' asked Brooks, now fiddling with his bushy brown eyebrows as if to straighten them. 'That's what the papers claim.'

'The evidence seems to point that way,' replied Michael. 'Though we can't be sure. I'm afraid we won't be, until they find him or his body. The Spanish police are still looking. What was he like when he worked here?'

'As a person or as a boss?'

'Both.'

'As a boss he was very pleasant, perhaps even too pleasant. He hated confrontation. He was from the old school in terms of printing. There was nothing he didn't know about the insides of a *Heidelberg* print press. They're the Rolls Royce of small presses, you know. We had three, about ten years old but good for another ten. Although he was the manager, he was never happier than when he was on the machines and if anything went wrong, more often than not he'd roll his sleeves up and fix it. I imagine that's why he resisted the latest digital equipment for so long. Oh, he could have run the new machines all right, but if anything goes wrong – and it does – you have to call out an engineer and wait. It would be like losing control to David, you just punch a few buttons and the computer does the rest. A lot of the traditional skills disappear with digital machines. Camera work, plate making, ink mixing, fine tuning the machines, it's all defunct.'

'You said he hated confrontation?'

'Yes. Well, you see, David worked his way up from the shop floor, so to speak. He was never really cut out for management. He was a good organiser, but he'd never put the staff under pressure. He hated having to say no. Some of the staff knew it and took advantage. Not in a big way, but if you know your way round a print workshop there are all sorts of dodges to get out of doing some of the – let's say – less interesting work. David knew them all, but still he let some of the staff get away with it. You'd think the staff would respect him for it, but it didn't work that way.'

'Were you surprised when he took the offer of redundancy?'

'I'll say. Don't get me wrong, I wasn't unhappy when he left. Not because I didn't like him, I did, but it gave me the opportunity for promotion. And it gave the Department a chance to modernise, which might never have happened under David.'

'So why were you so surprised?'

'Well, that he could afford it, that's all. Okay, he got a nice redundancy package, but no pension. He was just forty-eight, you see, and under the Local Government Pension Scheme, if you're redundant before fifty, you don't get your pension until sixty. That's a long wait, unless you have another job to go to, or plenty of savings. I was surprised he didn't hang on for a couple of years, then look for redundancy. That's the deal everyone's looking for. Early retirement, redundancy package, lump sum and immediate pension.'

Michael looked at the frayed cuffs of Brooks' pin striped shirt. His greying hair and moustache suggested he was in his mid-forties, and Michael wondered if he was working towards his own early retirement.

'Did he have plenty of savings, do you think?'

Brooks scratched his chin and paused a moment before answering.

'Never given it much thought... He was careful. Not tight, just careful. He never splashed out on clothes, though he did like expensive shoes.'

Michael's ears pricked.

'What do you mean by expensive shoes?'

'I don't know exactly. Leather brogues, made to measure, hand stitched, that kind of thing. A bit old fashioned for my taste.'

Michael looked down at Brooks's cut-price rubber soled shoes.

'I see. Anything else he liked to spend his money on?'

'Holidays in France. He was a bit of a wine connoisseur by all accounts. Not in a big way, I don't think he could afford it, but he knew what he liked.'

'France, then. Regularly?'

'Definitely France, every year for as long as I can remember. Tell you the truth, we were all a bit dumbfounded when we heard he was looking at houses in Spain. I thought perhaps property was cheaper out there.'

'Would it surprise you that he and Mrs Harrington were looking at houses in Spain that cost around three hundred thousand pounds?'

Brooks shot forward in his chair. 'My God – yes, it would. I never imagined he had that sort of money. Perhaps he had a windfall, old uncle died or something.'

'What part of France, do you know?'

Brooks was still wondering about the three hundred thousand price tag.

'Er, sorry. Erm... Gascony, I think. He and Alison used to tour. Just set off in the car. Sometimes they went camping, sometimes they stayed in those little country places, what do they call them?'

'Gites?'

'Gites, yes that's the word.'

'Did you know Alison?'

'Not really. I met her at a couple of Christmas parties, but that's about it.' He glanced around the room, fiddled with his tie and stretched the muscles in his neck. 'Cracking bit of stuff. Have you met her?'

Only in a body bag. 'No, but I've seen photographs.'

Brooks seemed to be losing interest in the discussion. He moved back from his desk, turning. 'Bit stuffy in here, I'll open the window?'

Brooks lifted the aluminium window frame to slide it open a couple of inches and the blinds fluttered in the draught.

Michael continued as Brooks returned to his seat. 'Did he have any special work mates he was particularly friendly with?'

Brooks fingered his moustache. 'Not that I know of. He'd chat with lots of people, especially some of the office girls who used to bring down work for their bosses. But then we all did. There was a bit of a game we played if the girls had an urgent job and we were busy. Some of them flirted a bit to get the work done quickly, though we'd have done it anyway.'

'Anyone in particular?'

'No. Like I say, we all did it, and more often than not David was tucked away in his office.'

'Did he meet friends after work? – a beer on Friday night, that sort of thing?'

'Not to my recollection. He just packed up work, got on his bike and cycled home.'

'He cycled to work?'

'More often than not, yes. They only had the one car, a beat up old Honda, and I think Alison used it most days.'

'Perhaps he was a saver after all,' Michael mused.

'You could be right. You hear of these people, don't you? They live like paupers, then die and leave a fortune to the cats' home.'

The discussion was coming to an end and Michael was not sure it had served any purpose.

'Well, thank you for your time, Mr Brooks. If you think of anything else, please get in touch.'

They rose and shook hands across the desk and Michael moved toward the door. As it opened, the breeze from the window lifted the papers on the notice board and Michael glanced in that direction.

Something caught his eye – a photocopy of a lottery ticket with six rows of six numbers. A similar sheet was pinned to the wall in the Crime Prevention Office back at the police station. The old boys in the office, mostly ageing constables waiting for retirement, had often joked with him about what they'd do when they won the jackpot. Then he remembered the lottery ticket found in David Harrington's jacket at Gleeson's storage depot.

'Office syndicate?' Michael asked, fingering the corner of the sheet and looking back at Brooks.

'Oh, er – yes. We've been doing it for years.'

'Ever win anything?'

Brooks pursed his lips and let out a short puff of air.

'Couple of ten pound wins – oh, and four numbers one time, just over a hundred pounds. Waste of time really, we'd be better off putting the money in a box and having a good party at Christmas.'

'Do you always use the same numbers?'

'Yes, for years now. Sometimes we do a lucky dip as well.'

Michael thought for a moment, mulling a remote possibility.

'Do you mind if I have a copy of this?'

Brooks looked bemused.

'Not at all, I suppose not, but...'

'Don't worry, I'm not going to use your numbers. It doesn't sound like they've been very lucky anyway. Who keeps the ticket?'

'I do, in my wallet. It wouldn't be safe, leaving it around the office.'

'And before you?'

'What? Oh, I see what you mean. David kept it. But there's no way anyone could fiddle it. Every week I take a copy of the ticket and pin it on the board. Someone, usually Andy, checks it first thing Monday morning. He brings his newspaper in and goes through the numbers. You'd hear the shout from here to the police station if we ever won any serious money.'

'Andy?'

'Yes, Andy Fielding, he operates one of the big *Xerox* machines. Been here years. He's on leave this week, otherwise you could talk to him.'

'Would he remember all the numbers, do you think?'

'What? Andy? I doubt it. He has a job remembering what day it is sometimes. Look, you don't think...?'

'I don't think anything, Mr Brooks, just covering the angles, that's all.'

Alan Brooks placed the sheet on the small desk-top copier in the corner and waited until the copy slowly emerged. He passed it to Michael.

As he crossed the floor of the CID office a sergeant shouted.

'Hey, Michael, this arrived for you this morning.' He waved a large manila envelope, about two inches thick. 'Pretty little thing from the Council brought it over and insisted she handed it to you personally, but I persuaded her it would be safe in CID. I suppose we can expect a few visitors from the town hall now you're moving in higher circles. What's that new Community Safety Officer like, Adrienne someone-or-other?'

'She'd eat you for breakfast.'

Michael took the envelope to his desk and noticed the heavy red letters: PRIVATE AND CONFIDENTIAL. He tore it open and pulled out a sheaf of papers: FREQUENT YOUNG OFFENDERS FORUM: AGENDA. Beneath it was another bundle of paper, stapled at the corner: COMMUNITY SAFETY PARTNERSHIP: INFORMATION SHARING PROTOCOL – FIRST DRAFT. He thumbed through the thirty-two pages, shoved them back into the envelope and slid it into a bottom desk drawer. He had other things on his mind.

Michael found the website for The National Lottery and searched through previous results for the main draw. Now he hit a problem. The results on the website went back only six months and he doubted that was long enough for his purposes. He reached for the phone.

An hour later, all he'd got was the run around. He decided to pull rank, quoted the Chief Superintendent's name and mentioned a murder enquiry. It did the trick and he finally got through to Jeremy Catterall, Head of the Claims Department. Michael explained his suspicion, not mentioning that it was nothing more than a hunch, and outlined the information he needed.

'So...' said Catterall. 'You want me to check a series of numbers for the main draw to see if any of them won over the last twelve months.'

'Exactly. Can you do that?'

'Not personally, but I do know a man who can.'

'Great. Thanks. How long will it take?'

'It's urgent, you say?'

'Very. A man's life may depend on it.' This was a bit melodramatic, but tended to get results.

'Give me the numbers. I'll call you back in about half an hour.'

Michael could have used the time to read the INFORMATION SHARING PROTOCOL, but his thoughts were on how you might swindle your workmates when the numbers were pinned on the board every week.

He stared at the sheet of paper Alan Brooks had provided – a copy of a copy of an original lottery ticket. Then he looked at the ticket Sergeant Rawlinson had recovered from the jacket at Gleeson's. It was dated for the draw on Saturday 20th July last year. Both tickets contained six lines of six numbers, but on David Harrington's ticket, one line was different.

Michael recalled his days as a young constable and the two weeks he'd spent in the Registry, filing records, extracting information, photocopying reports. It took him about five minutes to figure out the answer.

The phone had barely completed its first ring before Michael snatched it from the cradle.

'Jeremy Catterall here, about those numbers you gave me.'

'Any luck?' Michael said, excitement rising in his voice.

'Well, it's interesting. We ran back over the past eighteen months to see if we could match any winning sets of six numbers for a jackpot. Nothing came up.'

'I see.' *Damn*.

'Then we did a more selective search to see if just some of the numbers had been drawn and we found one of the sets of numbers you gave me matched five out of the six numbers drawn on 8th May last year.'

Michael sat up. 'How much would that have won?'

'One hundred and eleven pounds.'

'I see.' *Dead end.*

'But here's the really interesting bit,' Catterall said with a sense of satisfaction, 'We added in the Bonus Ball number and came up trumps. On 13th July last year there were eleven winners with five correct numbers plus the Bonus Ball, including one of your sets of numbers.'

'And?' *And, and, and?*

'Oh, sorry, you want to know how much, of course. Three hundred and fifty thousand pounds.'

'Each?' Michael asked incredulously.

'Each.'

'Tell me, are the winning numbers – 12 14 21 33 40 and 49?'

'Yes, that's right. They all came out of the draw except 33 and that was the Bonus Ball. But how did you know?'

'A lucky guess,' said Michael, smiling as he looked at the line of numbers he'd highlighted on the photocopy Alan Brooks had provided. He took a moment to consider the implications. £350,000. A lot of money for one man but split six or seven ways, about fifty grand apiece. Well worth ripping your mates off. Worth killing for? People had died for much less.

'Can you give me the names of the winners?'

'I thought that might be your next question, Inspector,' said Catterall. 'There's no problem with nine of the names. They didn't ask for anonymity, so I can release them subject to an official request.'

'And the other two?'

'There's a bit of a problem.'

'How big a problem?'

'Well, when winners ask for anonymity, we protect their privacy. That means we won't disclose details to the media or in response to casual inquiries. But there is a precedent where there's a suspicion of fraud.'

'Tell me about it.'

'Well, it wouldn't be for me to decide you understand. But if we get an official request, explaining the grounds for suspicion, then the-powers-that-be will consider it. But I can't make any promises.'

'What sort of official request are we talking about?'

'I don't wish to appear rude, Inspector, but I think it would need at least a letter from your Chief Constable.'

The meeting in Bowater's office began cordially, as Michael outlined his progress with the Young Offenders Forum. Bowater was impressed.

'I knew we had the right man for the job. Succeed with this project, Michael, and you could be set for stardom. Anyway, you asked to see me.'

Michael coughed. 'Well, sir, it's about David Harrington. It's just...'

'What?' Bowater exploded. 'I thought you understood, Michael. That's over. Case closed. This young offenders stuff is your number one priority. You haven't got time to be raking over the embers of the Harrington case. Just let it drop and get on with your job. Is that clear?'

Michael was not going to be dissuaded. He outlined his discussion with Alan Brooks, pressing on through several attempts by the Chief Super to pull him up short. Finally he explained what Jeremy Catterall had told him about the winning numbers.

'All very interesting, but it doesn't prove anything. Maybe the syndicate in the print department just forgot to check their numbers that week.'

'No sir, Catterall has confirmed that all prizes were claimed. So – don't you see? It means that someone, almost certainly David Harrington, took the winnings and did a runner. It puts a whole new perspective on the case. It means the Harringtons didn't disappear, they went into hiding. No wonder they were looking at property that seemed way out of their price range. They had a three hundred and fifty grand that no one knew about.'

Bowater was fighting his instincts, dreading the thought of

reopening the case and upsetting Colonel Cardells.

'It still doesn't prove anything. Maybe they just got robbed of more than we knew about. That would be poetic justice, don't you think?'

'It would indeed, but what if they weren't robbed? What if they set up Hagemans and Van Doorn to make it look like they had been abducted?'

Bowater looked up, incredulous. 'And Mrs Harrington just happened to get killed along the way? It still doesn't make sense.'

'But what if it was all part of Harrington's plan? Suppose he wanted to get rid of his wife. What better way to cover your tracks than fake your own death as well and set up Hagemans and Van Doorn to take the rap?'

Bowater was finally beginning to consider the possibilities.

'So where would we go from here? We still have no proof.'

'I need a letter from the Chief Constable to get the National Lottery list of winners' names, including the two who asked to remain anonymous. I'll bet you anything Harrington's name turns up. Then we have to reopen the investigation because the whole basis of the disappearance has changed.'

'I don't know... '

'Sir, there's real kudos to be gained from all this. The British police solve the real crime and get one over on the Guardia Civil. Even the Foreign Secretary would be impressed.'

'That's... an angle.' The Chief hesitated. 'Something still baffles me, Michael. How could Harrington fool his colleagues? You say a copy of the ticket was pinned on the notice board and someone always checked it.'

Michael took a sheet of paper from his folder and passed it over.

'What do you think that is?'

Bowater gave the sheet a cursory glance, as if reluctant to take part in a guessing game. 'It's a photocopy of a lottery ticket.'

'Actually, sir, it's a photocopy of a photocopy of a lottery ticket with six rows of numbers for this Saturday's draw to be precise.'

Michael reached into the folder and removed another sheet of paper which he thrust across the desk. 'And what's that?'

Bowater was becoming irritated at being treated like a trainee detective. His eyes focused on the date of the ticket.

'Same thing.' He threw both sheets back in Michael's direction.

Michael pushed them back. 'Look again, sir.'

This time Bowater studied the two sheets more thoroughly, but refused to look puzzled. 'Okay, so one line of numbers is different. So you bought two tickets.'

'Yes... but how would I know which line to change until after the draw had been made?'

Bowater's frustration finally boiled over.

'Just get to the point, would you?'

'The first sheet I gave you,' Michael continued with a flourish, 'is a copy of an original ticket for this Saturday's draw. It contains six lines of six numbers including, in the fourth line, the numbers 12 14 21 33 40 and 49. As it happens, those were the numbers that won last July. The second sheet is a copy of two different tickets which I cut, then stuck together. Or rather, I copied them. I cut the copies then pasted them together, then copied the pasted sheet. The top half is from the original ticket, with this Saturday's date. The bottom half is from a different ticket – and you'll see that the fourth line is completely different. If you look carefully, you can just about see the join, but it's imperceptible unless you're looking for it.'

Bowater fiddled with his spectacles and took a closer look. Michael continued, producing another photocopied sheet of paper.

'This is the sheet Alan Brooks gave me with all their regular numbers. And this is the ticket we found in Harrington's jacket for the draw on 20th July last year. They're identical, except for one line.'

Bowater compared the two and found the line that was missing from Harrington's ticket – 12 14 21 33 40 49.

'Mmm... I see what you mean.'

Now Bowater had to demonstrate that the penny had finally dropped and he launched into an explanation.

'So after the draw on Saturday night, Harrington, or someone, bought a virtually identical ticket for the next draw, but with a different set of numbers substituted for the winning line.' He paused, for this to sink in. 'Then he put the two together, keeping the original date, to make a composite copy without the winning line. Next he switched the sheets on the notice board in the printing department sometime before Monday morning. So long as no one remembers the numbers, he's got the winning ticket in his pocket and off he goes to claim the prize, asking for his anonymity to be protected...'

'And if all this happens just as you're offered a redundancy package, you can see why he'd be tempted,' Michael added.

Bowater took on a superior air. 'Leave this with me, Michael. I'll speak to the Chief Constable as soon as I can. In the meantime, you pay full attention to the Young Offenders project. Is that clear? If anything comes of this, we'll inform the Spanish police and let them handle it.'

'But, sir...'

'No buts, Michael. Get on with the project. After all, you've made such a good start we can't possibly take you off it now. Can we?'

The question was purely rhetorical.

Michael waited for news until the following week. He went through another meeting of the Frequent Young Offenders Forum, this time dominated by squabbles about the content of the Draft Information Sharing Protocol and nothing else. On Wednesday afternoon he received the call.

'Chief Super wants to see you. Soon as,' said Penny. 'He sounds grumpy. What have you been up to?'

Bowater was back in civvies: crisp pink shirt, patterned silk tie and pale grey suit. 'Well, Michael, here's the list you asked for, but there's no sign of Harrington's name.'

He passed the sheet of paper across his desk.

Michael nodded. 'Probably too risky for him to use his own name.'

'So he..?'

'Either he used a false name, which isn't too easy given that you need to produce some proof of identity in order to claim a prize.'

'Or?'

'Or he claimed through someone else.'

'Someone he trusted,' added Bowater firmly.

'With his life. And it has to be someone on this list, because we know that someone claimed that prize.'

'So where do we go from here?'

'Can I keep this list a few days? For a few more inquiries. My guess is, it's one of these last two names. The two who asked for anonymity.'

'All right, Michael, you can look into it, but don't neglect the Young Offenders stuff. Understood?'

Stuff the young offenders. This is real police work.

'Understood.'

Back at his desk, Michael focussed his attention on the last two names: Paul Makin with an address in St. Ives, Cornwall and Sandra Marlowe with an address nearer home, in Derby.

Makin checked out. He was on the St. Ives Electoral Register and registered to pay Council Tax.

Sandra Marlowe was a different story. She'd been registered at the address in Derby until late last year. A one-bed flat in a converted house. But a new name now appeared on the Register of Electors, which meant that Sandra Marlowe had moved some time before 10th October last year when the new register was compiled.

Michael's nose twitched for a moment, but then he thought again. It was hardly surprising she'd left a one-bed flat if she'd just claimed three hundred and fifty grand from the lottery.

He doodled on a writing pad as he tried to assemble his thoughts.

13th July – syndicate wins lottery.

August – David and Alison Harrington go on holiday to Benidorm.

Late October – Harringtons' house sold.

Late November – David Harrington takes redundancy and leaves job.

7th January – David and Alison leave for Spain.

It all seemed to fit together like a timetable, but something was missing. Michael's next call was to Alan Brooks.

'Thanks for seeing me the other day, it was very helpful. I'd just like to ask, do you know when Mr Harrington was first offered redundancy?'

Brooks thought for a moment. 'Let's see, he left at the end of November and they had to give him three month's notice, so I guess it was around the beginning of September.'

'But it didn't just come out of the blue, it would have been talked about before that. Am I right?'

'Oh, yes, sorry. It had been on the cards for a while.'

'Since when?'

'Let me think. I believe... some time around June. We were all called to a meeting with Dave Richardson. He's the Assistant Chief Executive who has overall control of the printing department. He said that the Best Value Team would be carrying out a review of the department and he doubted the results would be very favourable unless we modernised and focused on – "our core activities" were his words. He mentioned slimming down and we all knew what he meant. I think David spoke to him privately after the meeting because he sensed the writing was on the wall.'

'And this was June, you say?'

'Hang on a minute. I've got last year's diary here, I can check.'

Michael listened to the pages being flicked.

'Yes, here we are. The meeting was on 27th June. Of course there were formalities to go through. They had to call for volunteers for redundancy in the first instance. Anyone who was interested was given an estimate of their redundancy entitlement before they made up their mind. I think they made the decision some time in August and the formal period of notice started at the beginning of September.'

'Did anyone else volunteer?'

'Besides David, you mean? Only Steve Boynton. He was fifty-eight, one of the old print machine operators. It came as a godsend to him. He couldn't wait to get out and took his pension at the same time.'

Now it all made sense. When David Harrington realised they'd won the lottery, the prospect of redundancy had already been raised. The redundancy money and the money from the sale of the house, plus his savings, wouldn't be enough to live off for long. But an extra three hundred and fifty grand...

'Is that all, Inspector?'

'Yes... Oh, does the name Sandra Marlowe mean anything to you?'

'Sandra? Yes, of course, she used to work here in the Housing Department. Secretary to the Director. I knew her quite well. She was always popping down with rush jobs at the end of the day, especially Fridays.'

'You said "used to work here"?'

'That's right, she left last year.'

'When exactly? Do you know?'

'October or November I think, but I can't be sure.'

'How old was she?'

'Now you're asking. Difficult to say. She was very attractive, very efficient, and – well, slim, elegant, and a bit superior. If I were to hazard a guess I'd say late twenties, but she could have been a bit older.'

'Would you say she was particularly friendly with Mr Harrington?'

'What?... You don't think...'

'I don't think anything. Really. Just – did she know Mr Harrington?'

'Well, of course she knew him, like I said she was often bringing work down. But I never saw anything out of the ordinary between David and her, if that's what you're getting at.'

'I'm not getting at anything. And do me an important favour, would you? Don't mention a word about this conversation to anyone. It wouldn't do to talk about police business. And I'll be wanting to get in touch again.'

'Mum's the word. I'll stand by then, Inspector.'

'Thank you very much.'

It took the best part of an hour on the phone to persuade the

Council's Personnel Manager to reveal information about Sandra Marlowe. Aged 29, she'd worked as Secretary to the Director of Housing for the last five and a half years. She left on 5th October last year, saying she was taking up a job in the private sector. The address on the file was the same flat in Derby given by Sandra Marlowe when she claimed the lottery prize. A photograph on the personnel file was taken last year for the ID card that operated the automatic entry system installed at the offices. Michael asked for a copy and sent one of the constables over to collect it.

The flat, number 3A, was on the top floor of a converted Victorian villa on the outskirts of Derby. The house had recently been painted and the small front garden was planted with pansies and begonias. A column of doorbells was attached to the wall inside the porch. Michael pressed each of the bells and came up with two responses. A male student in 2B looked nervous at the sight of Michael's warrant card and made no move to invite Michael in. He thought he knew the lady in the top floor flat, but that was about all he knew. They'd spoken only briefly on a couple of occasions and he had no idea why she had left or where she'd gone.

The old lady in Flat 1A, Mrs Montgomery, was considerably more helpful and only too happy to give Michael, over tepid tea and digestive biscuits, the benefit of her observations after identifying Sandra Marlowe from the photograph Michael showed her. Yes, Sandra, it turned out, had lived in the flat for two years. She was a model tenant, clean, smart, professional and very quiet, who always kept regular hours, leaving and returning at the same times every day for her job with the Council in Nottingham. She didn't go out much, perhaps Saturday nights and sometimes on Sunday, but was never late back home.

Visitors? Oh yes, a man sometimes picked her up and dropped her off in a silver car, but he never went up to the flat. The description was gathered from behind curtains, but yes, he used to kiss her goodbye as she got out of the car. Probably her boyfriend, surmised Mrs Montgomery, and he seemed like a very nice man, though quite a bit older than her. Michael showed her another photograph from which she confirmed that Sandra's regular visitor was David Harrington.

So where was Sandra Marlowe now? Mrs Montgomery didn't know for sure. Sandra left rather abruptly, but there'd been quite a flurry of post just before she left. The post for all the tenants came together and, more often than not, Mrs Montgomery had the job of sorting it and leaving it on a table in the vestibule for individual tenants to pick up. In fact, post had continued to arrive after Sandra left and Mrs Montgomery had thoughtfully kept it in case Miss Marlowe came back.

Michael had all the information he needed and prepared to leave.

'What do you think I should do with the post,' Mrs Montgomery said lifting a bundle of letters from a sideboard.

Michael was about to tell her to hang on to it when he spotted a large printed envelope containing a company logo jutting out from the smaller letters and bills. Curious, he thumbed through the bundle and confirmed what he first thought.

'I'll take it away if you like,' he said and pass it on when I find Miss Marlowe.

Back in the office, Michael opened the envelope and read the covering letter. It began: "Further to your recent interest in renting a holiday villa in the Costa Blanca, we have pleasure in enclosing our latest brochure and price lists." The letter was signed: Susan Shaw of Saunders & Shaw, Spanish Villa Rentals.

Thirty minutes later, Michael trudged through drizzle along Nottingham's Broadway, head down, raincoat collar up, heading for Saunders and Shaw. It was a mid-June mid-afternoon and the pavement glistened in the murky light. He passed the latest piece of civic architecture, a water feature in grey marble and steel. Detergent foam rippled over the pool forming clouds that broke off and rolled down the street like clumps of tumbleweed.

At the side of the fountain, under a canopy over the entrance to a shopping mall, a gang of youngsters in school uniform congregated, seemingly pleased with their achievements.

Michael shivered and hurried past. Five minutes later he hit the jackpot at the office of Saunders & Shaw. Susan Shaw, ostentatious as ever, explained that Sandra Marlowe had rented – was still renting – a villa in Altea Hills between Benidorm and Calpe in the northern Costa Blanca.

'What?' exclaimed Chief Superintendent Bowater.

'I'm going back to Spain.'

'You're bloody not, Inspector, you're staying right here. You're getting on with this Young Offenders project.'

'But sir, it's obvious. David Harrington and Sandra Marlowe conspired to claim the lottery money then ran off to Spain.'

'So pass the details to the Guardia Civil and leave it to them. There's no need for you to go rushing off to Spain again. They can handle it.'

'I can't sit around and wait for the Guardia Civil to mess things up.'

'And what if I order you to stay here?'

'You may have my resignation, if you need it.'

Bowater's eyes flashed and his face turned a deep, angry crimson.

Michael jumped in his chair as Bowater's fist slammed the desk, making the new Royal Worcester cup rattle in its saucer.

'If you defy me, Fernandez, it won't be resignation. I'll have you fired. If you go to Spain, you might as well stay there.'

Hoping to appear calm, Michael returned Bowater's stare.

'I might do that,' he said quietly before closing the folder on his lap, rising from the desk, and walking out of the office.

CHAPTER THIRTEEN

Michael booked the earliest available flight out of East Midlands which was at 4.30 the following afternoon. Next he made a call to Spain and then to Jeremy Catterall at the National Lottery. The prize had been paid to Sandra Marlowe by cheque and Catterall was sure it had been cleared or he would have heard about it.

'Is there any way you can find out where the cheque was paid in?' asked Michael. 'It must have gone into a bank account somewhere.'

'It's a bit unusual, but I expect our bankers will be able to tell us,' Catterall replied. 'It could take a couple of days, though. I'll need to get authority from someone senior in our accounts branch.'

'That's fine. I understand. Just see what you can do. Oh, by the way, if you get the answer, don't call me. I'll contact you in a couple of days.'

Michael landed at El Altet in the middle of a fierce electrical storm that left a torrent of water rushing along the road in front of the arrivals hall. Jose Luis was there to meet him, full of smiles.

'I thought we'd seen the last of you,' he said with false disdain. 'You never give up, do you?'

By the time they reached the A7, the sun was shining and steam was rising from the road as the patches of moisture shrank to nothing.

'We've had her under surveillance since you called yesterday, but there's been no sign of Mr Harrington,' Jose Luis announced as they sped northwards past Benidorm once more. 'But there is a man with her and they seem to be very friendly.'

'What do you mean by friendly?' asked Michael.

'They've been sunbathing by the pool, rubbing sun cream on each other and there's been an occasional kiss. Of course we can't see what's going on inside the villa, but it's safe to assume he's more than just a friend.'

'Any idea who he could be?'

'No. He looks Spanish, though it's difficult to tell.'

'Age?'

'Difficult again. Younger than her, perhaps early twenties, very slim, skimpy swimming trunks, gold chain. Could be a beach bum.'

'What do you mean?'

'Come off it, Michael, don't tell me you don't have them in Britain. Young men with deep tans, hanging around the beaches, preying on single women who want a little holiday romance... Age no barrier, so long as they have money. They move in for a couple of weeks, enjoy spending the ladies' money, show them a good time while the holiday lasts. Then it's back to the beach to find another willing victim.'

'That wouldn't work in British weather – but a gigolo, you mean?'

'Well, not exactly, but you're on the right track. Anyway, this is all supposition until we talk to the guy and find out who he is.'

They left Benidorm behind them and rounded a long curve as the mountains rose up from the narrow coastal plain. The old town of Altea loomed on the right, its ancient colour-washed houses engulfing the mound of rock that overlooked the bay and once offered protection from pirates. On their left, a jagged ridge rose into the sky, peppered with hundreds of villas huddled together and clinging precariously to the side of the slope. The once-barren mountainside, home to little more than a few drought-resistant trees and bushes, now accommodated a vast collection of houses fighting for space and a glimpse of the Mediterranean.

'Welcome to Altea Hills,' said Jose Luis as they left the motorway.

They zigzagged their way through the warren of almost identical villas until they reached a villa about half-way up the slope.

'We were lucky,' said Jose Luis. 'We found this empty villa above Casa Emelia, the place Sandra Marlowe is renting. It's not perfect, but there's a good view of the terrace and pool. Come on, I'll show you.'

They descended the steps from the road and walked inside. The spacious villa was cool and light with pale grey floor tiles and white-painted walls. The furniture and curtains added vivid colours, but failed to combat the mortuary-like atmosphere. Outside on the edge of the terrace, Sergeant Ricardo Ruiz sat beneath a hastily erected canvas pergola with curtained sides that shielded him from prying eyes above and below, right and left.

Michael was introduced to the sergeant and enquired about recent developments. There were none. Sandra Marlowe and her boyfriend had spent the whole afternoon by the pool. Sandra had been reading, the man had listened to a stereo through headphones. They'd talked at intervals and Sandra had brought drinks from inside; a beer for the man and a long clear drink for herself. They'd remained on the terrace until half an hour ago. It was now almost eight in the evening and they were still indoors.

The sergeant's radio crackled and he listened to the message.

'Mariela says they're leaving the house,' he reported to Jose Luis.

'Tell her to stick with them and keep us posted.'

As the sergeant relayed the instructions, Michael prepared to move. 'Who's Mariela?' he asked.

'Officer Poquet,' said Jose Luis. 'She's been keeping watch in a car outside the villa for two days now.'

'Shouldn't we go, too?'

'Relax Michael, let Officer Poquet do her job. There's no need for us to go tearing around after them. Pour yourself a drink, have something to eat. The fridge is fully stocked, courtesy of the letting agent.'

Michael took a cold Coca-Cola for himself and poured a beer for Jose Luis. Sergeant Ruiz was released for the night and they sat in the naya watching the sun slowly sink. The Mediterranean gradually turned from turquoise to indigo and then to black.

Officer Poquet reported by radio that Sandra Marlowe and friend had taken a table outside Cafe Mozart on the Altea sea front. Mariela, in a next door restaurant, had ordered dinner so as not to appear conspicuous.

'So, Michael, what do you think happened?' asked Jose Luis as he relaxed in a padded armchair and sipped his beer.

'To the Harringtons? I'm certain David Harrington was having an affair with Sandra Marlowe. Whether it was serious or not at the time I'm not sure, but when the office syndicate came up on the lottery, he saw his opportunity. He knew he was likely to be offered the redundancy package and I think he took his chance. Sandra claimed the money and came to Spain to wait for Harrington. David and Alison Harrington arrived later and we still don't know where they stayed after they left the hotel in Benidorm while they were supposedly looking for a house to buy.'

'So what do you think happened to Mrs Harrington?'

'I'm not sure it was part of the original plan to get rid of her. Who knows, perhaps he planned to buy a house with his wife and keep his mistress nearby. In the end, I suspect she was just getting in the way so he decided to get rid of her. But their disappearance became headline news and then I arrived to intensify the search. Perhaps then, he realised that he would always be a hunted man and so he had to find a way to fake his own death as well. That's where the two Dutchmen came in. I still think they're a couple of small time crooks – amateurs – but Harrington saw an opportunity to use them. I think he planted the evidence to make it look as though they killed his wife and then made sure her body would be found. At the same time, he left enough evidence to convince everyone he was dead as well, even though his body would never be found.'

'A clever plot,' mused Jose Luis. 'Especially if you're willing to sit back and watch two innocent men go down, probably for life.'

'Where there's money and a woman involved, some men are capable of anything given the right encouragement.'

'That's all well and good Michael, but that doesn't square with what we have now. Sandra Marlowe's living it up with her toy boy and there's no sign of Harrington.'

'Yes. That's why we need to talk to her. When do you plan to go in?'

'What's the rush? All the cards are in our hands. The moment we go in, we blow our advantage. I think we should just keep an eye on her for a few more days and see what turns up.'

Michael was not inclined to be so patient.

'And what if nothing turns up?'

'Then we'll have a chat with them. In the meantime, we're doing a few background checks on Miss Marlowe. Let's see what we can find out first.'

'I think we should go in now, tomorrow at the latest. We're just wasting time.'

'You sound as if you're in a hurry, Michael, but I can't see why. From what I've heard, you don't have a job to go back to.'

Michael sat forward and cocked his head to one side.

'What have you heard?'

'Your Chief Superintendent was on the phone to the Colonel this morning. He said something about your return to Spain being unofficial. Against his orders.'

Michael sat back again. 'Things will sort themselves out. I just want to get to the bottom of this as soon as possible. What did Cardells have to say? I don't suppose he was too happy at having me back on the scene.'

'Actually, he didn't seem too bothered. I guess he'd rather get to the truth than have the conviction of two innocent men on his conscience.'

'I didn't know he had a conscience.'

'You've got the Colonel wrong, Michael. I know he comes across as a bit of a tyrant, but he's a good cop. He built his reputation on one of the best investigative records in the force. He's feared but respected and no one will be happier if we find out what's really happened here. Besides, it will look much better for the authorities if it turns out the Harringtons weren't abducted, tortured or killed by a band of local gangsters. Better for the property market and tourism, if you see what I mean.'

'That's a bit cynical, isn't it?'

'Perhaps, but it's the truth. Anyway, like I said, there's no rush for the moment. I thought you might want to pop back up to Parcent for a while. I gather you're a big landowner in those parts.'

Michael tried to hide his surprise.

'It's just an old house and a bit of land.'

There was a glint in Jose Luis's eyes when he asked the next question.

'Are you sure there isn't another reason for you to get back...?'

Michael raised his eyes to meet Jose Luis's expectant glance.

'You've obviously been busy while I've been away.' He returned his gaze to the horizon.

The hiss of the radio interrupted the silence.

'They're leaving now,' said Officer Poquet. 'I'm on their tail.'

Fifteen minutes later the lights went on at Casa Emelia. Soon after, Sandra Marlowe and friend were relaxing by the pool on a swinging seat with coffees and brandies on the table in front of them.

They sat, swung, talked, and drank for the next half-hour before locking in a long kiss. Michael watched through the binoculars feeling like a Peeping Tom as they writhed, touching each other into arousal, constantly readjusting in a search for the right position. He was relieved when they finally ran, giggling, into the house.

Jose Luis dismissed Officer Poquet and announced his own departure.

'There's no point in me staying, Michael. I might as well get home to the wife. You'll be all right alone, won't you? It looks like our friends have gone to bed for the night, so it should be quiet until morning. No need for you to stay up. I suggest you get some sleep. I'll be back first thing in the morning.'

'Fine,' Michael said, though he'd have preferred some company.

'Just remember, Michael, don't do anything stupid. This time you're not even an honorary member of the Guardia Civil. If anything happens, call me. Okay?'

Nothing did happen. Michael sat on the terrace watching the villa below. The outdoor lights had been left on, but the rest of the house was in darkness. His eyes grew heavy and, half asleep, his thoughts drifted to Pedro's necktie, booming fireworks and Rosana... until sleep took over.

Jose Luis returned next morning to resume the watch. Officer Poquet was back outside Casa Emelia. The morning passed without incident and at Michael's suggestion, Mariela joined them for lunch. This was the first time he'd met her. Oversized black-rimmed reflective sunglasses dominated her appearance and gave her an air of mystery as she entered the house. The remainder of her face was perfectly proportioned with high protruding cheekbones, a narrow nose and soft pouting lips. Long shiny blonde hair, parted in the centre, framed her features. Without seeing her eyes, Michael reserved judgement. But the sunglasses remained firmly in place for the whole of her short visit and her conversation was confined to the briefest of pleasantries until she returned to the car.

Casa Emelia was quiet until Sandra appeared on the terrace at four in the afternoon to give her boyfriend (if that was what he was) a wave through the window as she headed toward the car parked in the road above the villa. Presumed boyfriend emerged and stretched out on one of the sun beds by the pool.

Mariela was in pursuit and reported the details when Sandra Marlowe returned about forty-five minutes later. This time officer Poquet removed the sunglasses that had veiled her features as effectively as the Lone Ranger's mask. It confirmed what Michael already knew: this was a very attractive young woman with an approachability factor of zero. She delivered her report without excitement or emotion.

Sandra Marlowe had parked in the underground car park by Altea's railway station. Her first call had been to the tobacconists on Calle St. Carlos from where she'd emerged with a carrier bag appearing to hold two cartons of king-sized cigarettes. Her second destination, which she reached on foot from the tobacconists, was the CAM Bank on Calle Vicente. She had used the ATM in the entrance lobby to withdraw an unknown amount of cash. Mariela had watched her insert a card into the machine, punch in some numbers, then remove cash and a printed slip of paper. Miss Marlowe had driven directly back to Casa Emelia where she was now enjoying a poolside drink with the boyfriend.

Jose Luis was already on the phone and half an hour later his call was returned.

'The CAM Bank, are you sure?'

There was a pause before he continued.

'How much?'

Another pause.

'Okay, thanks.'

Jose Luis flipped the cover of the mobile phone.

'That was HQ. Sandra Marlowe has an account with the CAM Bank, Altea Branch, with a current balance of 8,650 euros. The account was set up in January this year with an opening balance of seven thousand euros. Another deposit was made on 14th April – 8,000 euros – in cash.'

'Mmm,' Michael murmured, 'but we still haven't found the lottery money.'

'Perhaps she has another account,' said Mariela.

'Then why haven't your people at HQ found it?'

'Perhaps they will, given time. But the account could be in a different name, in which case we might never find it.'

Michael thought for a moment.

'I need to make a call to England. Is the phone here connected?'

'Sorry, no,' said Jose Luis. 'It's standard practice in rental villas. Prevents abuse. You have a mobile, don't you?'

'Yes, but I don't get expenses on this trip.'

He made the call, but kept it brief.

'Damn!' he said. 'That was my contact at the National Lottery. Sandra Marlowe paid the winner's cheque into an off-shore branch of the National Westminster Bank in the Isle of Man.'

'So?' said Jose Luis. 'Phone them up, see if the money's still there.'

'I wish it was that simple. These off-shore banks are extremely reluctant to give details of their clients' accounts.'

'But I thought there were new rules, to say that they had to.'

'Well yes, but only if there's a suspicion of a crime or fraud.'

'So, what's the problem with that?' Jose Luis asked.

'The problem, my friend, is that I don't have any authority and I can't really ask Chief Superintendent Bowater for his help, can I?'

'Perhaps we can ask. I could speak to the Colonel, if you want.'

Jesus. 'That could take forever. I know you mean well, Jose

Luis, but why don't we just go down and have a chat with Miss Marlowe?'

It was Jose Luis's turn to show his irritation.

'Look, Michael, we still don't have much to go on here. All we have is your suspicion that the Marlowe woman claimed a lottery prize that didn't belong to her.'

'It's more than just a suspicion.'

'Even so, the real crime is the murder of Mrs Harrington and we're no nearer to solving that than we were before. I still think we should sit tight for a while. We've only been watching them a couple of days.'

Michael was in no position to argue. 'Okay, but I hope we're not wasting our time. And could someone please check whether the CAM Bank registered that withdrawal Sandra Marlowe made this afternoon.'

Mariela didn't wait for instructions. 'I'll get on to it right away, but the banks will be closing soon and we may have to wait until the morning.'

'Spain!'

Jose Luis forsook his family that evening and remained with Michael. Sergeant Ruiz kept watch until he was dismissed at ten. Michael and Jose Luis chatted on the terrace whilst keeping an eye on the villa below.

At nine-thirty next morning, Officer Poquet, still hiding behind the dark glasses and icy as ever, returned.

'Any news from the bank?' Michael washed down a stale croissant with the last of a cup of coffee.

'They don't open until ten-thirty,' Mariela said, 'and we'll have to wait for someone in the bank to authorise release of the information.'

She flicked her blonde locks behind her shoulders as Michael's eyes flicked skywards for the merest fraction of a second.

'I'm sure it would take just as long in England, Inspector Fernandez.'

Sandra Marlowe was first to rise at Casa Emelia. She took the car to the bakery on the outskirts of Altea and returned with a long thin carrier bag. She breakfasted alone on the terrace. Concern was rising about her companion when he emerged and plunged gracefully into the deep end of the pool. He came out after two lengths and joined her on one of the white chairs at the table. There was a brief conversation before Sandra removed her bathrobe to reveal a bright yellow bikini, the top of which she also removed as she stretched out on her back to lie on the cushioned sun bed.

It was past midday when Mariela took the call from HQ. At 5.07pm the previous day, three hundred euros had been withdrawn from the ATM at the Altea Branch of the CAM Bank on the account of Sandra J Marlowe.

'Damn,' said Michael.

'You hoped the withdrawal was from another account, didn't you?'

'Exactly. The rest of the money must be somewhere and I was hoping the withdrawal would show that – but now we're no further forward than before. I still think we're just wasting time, Jose Luis. Why don't we go in there and have a look round? I'll go in myself, if you want. I'll wait until they go out and find a way to get in.'

'You've been watching too much television,' said Jose Luis. 'We don't do that in Spain and I'd hate to arrest you for house breaking.'

Michael sat back and folded his arms. Jose Luis looked at Mariela and shrugged. 'Okay, Michael. If nothing happens tonight, we'll go in first thing in the morning. But remember, it will just be for a chat. We won't be arresting them and we don't have a warrant to search the place.'

'About time.' Michael sat up and poured another coffee.

Delivery of a pizza to Casa Emelia was the highlight of the evening. Michael slept well and rose early, ready for action, but it was at ten-thirty before Jose Luis arrived with Mariela who still emitted a frosty edge behind her shades.

'I thought you said first thing?' Michael said.

'What? You didn't expect us to charge in at the crack of dawn and suprise our two lovebirds in their nest. Are they up?' asked Jose Luis.

'No signs of life as yet.'

'Good. Let's have coffee and then we'll take a stroll down there.'

They walked the short distance down to Casa Emelia and entered the garden from the road, descending precariously steep terracotta tiled steps. The steps were edged by natural stone walls retaining the reddish earth on either side which had been planted with a dozen or so orange trees that sparkled with small green fruits. A short, crazy-paved terrace led to the front door of the villa.

Sandra Marlowe's head appeared around the door after a second push on the bell. Her wispy blonde streaked hair was ruffled and damp as if she'd just climbed out of the shower and her green-blue eyes were half open under thick lashes. She squinted and restrained a yawn as Michael began to speak.

'Sandra Marlowe?'

'Yes?' Her eyes widened and seemed to sparkle. Behind her, a mobile phone began to ring.

'Detective Inspector Fernandez of Nottingham CID. I'm helping the Guardia Civil with inquiries into the death of Alison Harrington and the disappearance of her husband. This is Captain Perez and Officer Poquet of the Guardia Civil. I wonder if we could ask you a few questions.'

Now fully alert, Sandra opened the door wider, pulled up the collar of her bathrobe to cover her cleavage and tightened the dangling belt, knotting it firmly around her waist. Michael looked for signs of panic, but saw only concentration as she hesitated before speaking.

'Yes, of course, Inspector. Why don't you come through to the back terrace?' She stepped inside and led them along a hall, across the lounge and through double doors to the terrace, now bathed in bright sunlight.

'Over here,' she said, pointing to a hardwood table and chairs beneath a vast canvas parasol. 'You'll be cooler in the shade.' The phone was still ringing. 'I'd better get that,' she said, turning back toward the house. Mariela followed discreetly. The phone stopped ringing just after she entered the house and Sandra returned to the table on the terrace with the phone in the pocket of her bathrobe.

As they took their seats around the table, a ripple of water signalled Miss Marlowe's companion emerging from the pool. He grabbed a towel from a sun bed and vigorously rubbed away droplets of water from his deeply tanned body. After wrapping the towel around his neck he approached the table with an inquisitive look.

'Good morning,' Armando said slowly in a rich baritone, in English. He glanced across at Sandra.

'I'd like you to meet a friend of mine, Armando Bertomeu,' she announced. 'Armando, this is Inspector Fernandez from England, and his colleagues from the Guardia Civil.' She added, 'Would you like coffee?'

'That would be very nice,' Michael said quickly. 'Perhaps Mr Bertomeu could make it – and Officer Poquet, here, could help.'

Mariela looked up icily, but responded to an official-looking nod from Jose Luis.

'I'll let you know when we're ready for the coffee,' Michael added. 'We'll have a little chat out here first, Miss Marlowe, if that's all right.'

Sandra gave a nod and Armando smoothed his hair back as he headed for the house with Mariela in tow.

'So how can I help you?' Sandra said.

Michael opened the questions, leaning forward slightly.

'Miss Marlowe – '

'You can call me Sandra.'

'Sandra – we'd like you to tell us about the Harringtons.'

Sandra lit a cigarette. She sat stiffly for a moment, deeply drawing in then exhaling smoke in roughly equal proportions from her nose and mouth. Then, suddenly, her shoulders relaxed and she slipped back in the chair, physically letting go as she came clean, at last.

'I've been expecting someone to come round. To be honest, it's a relief. I know I should really have come forward before now. I've been agonising over it for a couple of weeks, but it's very difficult.'

'In what way, difficult?' Michael asked.

She frowned and hesitated. 'Well... I expect you already know that David and I were having an affair...'

'Were you?'

'Well – why else would you be here?'

Michael smiled. 'Quite,' he said. 'Perhaps you'd care to explain.'

'David and I had been seeing each other for about eighteen months.' She took a hard pull on her cigarette. 'We met at work, and became friendly. I saw him in the office when I took papers down to be printed. He was nice, everyone thought so. We flirted a few times when I needed things printed in a rush. One day, he asked me out for lunch. I was quite surprised, but I saw no harm in it so I agreed. He was interesting, easy to talk to and we seemed to enjoy each other's company. We met quite regularly after that.'

'You knew he was married, of course?'

'He was open about it. He didn't complain about Alison, just said they didn't have much in common. He was a serious person; intelligent and thoughtful. He liked eating out in good restaurants, going to the theatre, that kind of thing – which I do myself – but he said Alison wasn't interested.'

'She didn't like going out?'

'It wasn't that. She was – well, if she stayed in it was for beer and soaps on the television, and if she went out, she liked a noisy pub or dancing. Gradually, he told me all this. At first, mostly, we talked about work, and – well, news and books and films and theatre. I got the impression Alison wasn't interested in these things.'

'You met him for more than just a few meals out, though?'

'To begin with, that was all. But I liked his company and I knew – I sensed – he liked me. I'd broken up with someone a short time earlier and I was still getting over it when David came along. We got on so well and I really appreciated his company. He gave me ridiculous little gifts and I think I found that reassuring. Then he asked me to go with him to a conference in Harrogate. I made no promises, but he was never a pushy sort of person, so I wasn't worried, and I thought it would be a nice to share a few days together. That's when it became more serious. He talked about leaving Alison, but to be honest, I think he was frightened of her and then of course, there was the money.'

'Money?' Michael said with mock surprise.

'Yes, David was concerned about the cost of a divorce and having to give her a share of the house and their savings.'

'Yes, go on – I interrupted you,' said Michael.

'Oh, yes, well, then the offer of redundancy came through and that changed everything. At first I thought David would think again about leaving Alison, but it had the opposite effect. He was worried she'd claim half his redundancy money and that would hurt him even more. To be honest, it almost broke us up. If he was fully committed, that was one thing, but the only thing stopping us being together was his fear of how much money he would have to pay to Alison if they divorced.'

'You argued?'

'Yes we argued. I'd fallen in love with David and he said he loved me, but I was living like his bit on the side and he just didn't want to make a commitment. I guess I nagged him quite a lot and that's when he came up with his plan to come to Spain.'

'I see,' said Michael. 'What exactly was this plan?'

'It was David's idea. Alison had wanted to live in Spain since they came on holiday last year. So David went along with the idea though he was never really interested. To begin with he tried to come over to Spain on his own so that he could get an understanding of the property market, but Alison insisted on coming with him.'

Michael was bemused. 'But if he planned to leave Alison, why go through the charade of looking at homes together?'

'I've told you he was obsessed with money. You see, all their money in England was in their joint account, so it would be difficult for David to take it all. His idea was that if he could get Alison interested in buying a house in Spain it would give him an excuse to transfer all the money over here into an account in his name only. Once the money was safe, he planned to tell Alison he wanted to divorce her. He hoped she would return to England without him and that it would be much more difficult for her to get her hands on the money here in Spain. Especially if he disappeared for a while and moved the money around.'

'I see,' said Michael. So how come you ended up in Spain as well?'

Sandra looked sheepish. 'That was partly my fault. You see when David told me of his plan, I wasn't happy. He said he might be away for a month or two while he set things up and had the money transferred. I didn't want to be left on my own in England for that length of time and I was worried he might come to Spain with Alison, buy a house and start a new life with her.'

'So basically, you didn't trust him?' said Michael.

Sandra looked chastened. 'I guess you could say that, but I was in love with him. I just didn't want to be away from him. So I nagged him and in the end he agreed that I should come over here as well. He gave me enough money to be able to give up my job in England and rent this place. It also meant we could continue to see each other.'

Michael pretended to look puzzled. 'And how exactly did that work, Sandra?'

'At first he took Alison to see quite a few houses – even properties they clearly couldn't afford, telling her they had to understand the market before making a decision. He new she'd soon get bored. She was quite happy to view properties with David while they were staying at the hotel in Benidorm, being waited on hand and foot. But then David suggested they rent a villa in Altea la Vella, not far from here because it was cheaper than staying in the hotel. It was a nice place, a bit like this villa, and while David continued to 'research the market" as he put it, Alison lost interest and preferred to lounge around the pool, enjoying the sun and tanning herself. Most of the time when David said he was looking at properties, he was here with me.'

'When exactly did you arrive in Spain?' Michael asked.

'That was in the middle of January.'

'And when did David rent the villa in Altea la Vella?'

'About the same time.'

'So your plan was coming together nicely?' Michael said with barely disguised sarcasm.

'You could say that,' Sandra replied looking slightly embarrassed.

'This is all well and good, Sandra, but what I don't understand is why David and Alison never told the family back in Nottingham that they had moved from the hotel and into the villa. According to our records David spoke to his brother more than once after they left the hotel and Alison spoke to her sister-in-law Linda as well.'

'That was all David's idea. He was worried that if his brother knew they were renting a villa over here, he and Linda might just turn up for a free holiday. John was a bit like that, David said. He insisted that Alison should say nothing and let the family assume they were still at the hotel.'

'I can see that,' Michael said, 'But after that they just stopped calling; there was no contact at all. Surely David must have realised that suddenly losing touch would cause alarm?'

Sandra reached for another cigarette. 'Just a minute.' Her cheeks hollowed as she sucked the flame of a pink plastic lighter. 'I don't usually smoke so much.' She pursed her lips and exhaled. Suddenly she looked furtive. 'Alison found out. You see, in the few weeks at their villa, David was always making excuses for not buying property – too expensive, too far from the coast, too close to the neighbours, that sort of thing. I think Alison was becoming suspicious. Then, on 10th of April, a Thursday, David left his phone in the car when he popped into a supermarket for a bottle of gin and some tonic water. Alison stayed in the car. He was only gone a couple of minutes, but I just happened to text him at the time and Alison saw the message. It was nothing really, I just asked when I would be seeing him again, but Alison put two and two together.'

'Then what happened?'

'Alison was furious. She argued with him at their villa and said she was going back to England. That's when David told her he wanted a divorce. She said that was fine by her, but she would take him to the cleaners for every penny she could get. David told her she could try if she wanted, but that all their money was now in Spain in his name and she'd never get her hands on it. Apparently they fought, David walked outside onto the terrace by the pool and Alison lunged at him.'

Sandra stubbed out her cigarette in a small ceramic ashtray that was already overflowing with dimps.

'And…' Michael said, encouraging her to continue.

'Look, I know David, he'd never hurt anyone. He's not a violent man.'

'So…' Michael prompted.

'David pushed her away and began to walk towards the gate in the corner of the garden. Alison chased after him and tried to stop him from leaving. David pushed her out of his way and…' Sandra shivered and hesitated.

'Yes?'

'She was only wearing a pair of flimsy flip-flops; she slipped and fell back heavily. Her head smashed on a rock in the garden at the side of the terrace. David could see it was serious; there was a lot of blood he said. He took her inside and tried to resuscitate her, but she was dead. Then he came straight here.'

'With the body?'

'No, of course not. But I told David immediately that he had to go to the police. It was an accident, it would be all right. Poolside terraces are notoriously slippery, especially if you have wet feet. The police must have seen it happen before. But David was terrified. He was worried that if the police started sniffing around they might find out about the two of us and that would look bad. He was ranting and raving, on the verge of panic. I tried to reassure him that everything would be all right. I poured him a drink and he calmed down for a while, but I could see he was thinking things over. Then... after a while he suddenly sat up and said it could all be for the best...' Sandra lit another cigarette, her hand shaking. 'He was calm; almost calculating. He thought for a while and then came up with a plan to get rid of the body at this old farm house he'd seen near Orba.'

Michael said quietly, 'I'm sorry, could you explain?'

'Yes. It was a rough old place – a finca I think they call it. David had been to view the place a few weeks earlier. He said it was very ramshackle and needed far too much work to make it into a decent home. And it was very isolated; miles from anywhere, which is probably what gave him his idea. Anyway, David went back to his villa, put Alison into the car and took her out to the old finca. Then he came back here. I was worried and asked what would happen if anyone found the body.'

'And what did he say? Michael asked.

Well, I was shocked. He was like a different person, so cold and calculating. I'd never seen that side of him before. He said he'd set things up so that if the police found the body they would pin the blame on the two Dutch people who showed him the finca in the first place. He'd smeared blood on a spade or something to incriminate them and even cut himself to leave traces of his own blood so that it would look like he had been killed as well.'

'Did this seem like a sound plan to you?'

'No, not at all. To be honest the whole thing just seemed so far fetched, like something out of a book or a movie. But David was so... it was almost as if he was excited, like he was on a mission and enjoying the challenge.'

'And how did you feel?'

Sandra's blew her nose and her voice trembled. 'I was horrified. I said we should have told the police the whole story in the first place.'

'And how did David respond?'

'He said, very calmly, that I must never say anything to anyone. He said it was too late by then and if we went to the police now, I'd be implicated as well.'

'So you went along with his plan.'

Sandra suddenly looked angry.

'No Inspector, I did not. I've told you I was terrified, especially when he said I'd be implicated. Okay, I did nothing and said nothing, but Alison's death had nothing to do with me.'

Sandra drew a long, shuddering breath. 'Though I knew it was an accident, things had gone too far. I told him we had to stay apart for a while and he should go back to his villa and stay there until things calmed down. But he was worried. Although he hadn't told anyone where he was staying he thought Alison might have said something to somebody.'

'What happened after that?'

'Just a minute.' She gasped and wiped her eyes. 'He went back to his villa because he said he had to clean up – get rid of the blood stains, I suppose. He was there for a few days and he came here only once. He wanted to stay the night, but I wouldn't let him. To be honest, I was frightened of him; he'd changed so much from the David I'd met and fallen in love with. Then we heard that you'd arrived in Spain and he became frantic. The final straw was when the police found Alison's body. He was already stressed out, but when that happened he just went crazy. He turned up here one night and said he was getting out.'

'What did he mean?'

She sniffed, reaching for the cigarettes. 'Well, he said he was going to France and he'd send for me when everything died down. I wasn't sure I wanted to go anywhere with him at that stage, but I didn't say anything, I just pretended to go along with his plan.'

'He was determined to go, however?'

'Yes, he knew you were in the country and that the search for him had been stepped up, especially after Alison's body was discovered. He was terrified he would be spotted by someone and picked up by the police. He said he had to get out straight away. I told him to just go ahead, and as for me, we'd see how things worked out later.'

'And is that where he is now – in France?'

'As far as I know, yes,'

'Did he say where in France?'

'He said something about Gascony; he'd been there before on holiday.'

'And have you heard from him?'

'Not for almost two weeks.'

'But you have heard from him since he left?'

'He telephoned just after he left and then again about... a week later, but he didn't say where he was. He'd read in the papers that the Dutchmen had been arrested and he knew the police were still looking for him. I told him the papers here were saying that he was probably dead, too.'

'And that's the only time he's contacted you, since leaving?'

'Yes.'

'You didn't agree to join him in France then?'

'No, I did not. I've told you, I didn't want to be with him anymore. That's one reason I invited Armando up; to put David off if he returned – if he was fool enough to. When he called, that last time, I told him clearly I didn't want to go to France. I had nothing to do with Alison's death and I knew that if we were ever found together, I would be implicated in her death and the subsequent cover-up. On top of that, he'd changed dramatically after all this happened. He became very self important and acted as if protecting himself and his money was all that mattered. And he even looked different, with that ridiculous beard.'

'He'd grown a beard?'

'Yes, a hideous goatee thing. He grew it before he left for France, but it looked stupid because it was pure grey and his hair is sandy.'

Michael looked over at Jose Luis. He appeared to be have been keeping up with the conversation and he said something now in Spanish.

'Ah, yes – Captain Perez just reminded me. The money.'

Sandra's head lifted wonderingly. She stared at Jose Luis.

Michael continued. 'Mr Harrington had quite a lot of money, as we understand it. His redundancy payment as well as his savings and the money from the sale of his house in England. We know he drew most of it out in cash. Do you know anything about that?'

'He took it with him to France, I think.' She thought for a moment, and continued. 'Well, most of it. He gave me fifteen thousand euros because I had rent to pay and other expenses to cover. It's in my bank account, what's left, you can check if you like?'

'We've already done that.' Michael studied Sandra's face,

looking for and finding signs of apprehension. 'So you're saying, Sandra, that after the accident and hiding Alison's body, David went to France, saying he'd come back for you or tell you where he was so you could join him, though he knew you had misgivings. He gave you only the fifteen thousand euros – to keep you going, is that right?'

'That's right.'

'You realise, Sandra, that you could be in serious trouble.'

'But I've told you,' she looked up, tearful again. 'I had nothing to do with Alison's death. I didn't even know her.'

Time to ratchet up the pressure. 'I mean,' Michael said sternly, 'at the very least, you're guilty of helping to cover up Alison's murder.'

Alison jerked upright. 'Murder! But I've told you, it was an accident.'

'We only have your word for that – at the moment.' Michael leaned forward and lowered his voice. 'You've already told us of your affair with David – an affair that Alison had discovered after you sent that unfortunate text message. It seems to me, Sandra, that in the circumstances, David had a very good motive for getting rid of Alison. Come to think of it, so did you.'

Sandra froze, her face white with panic.

'But I've told you, I had nothing to do with Alison's death. You must believe me.'

'What I believe or don't believe will depend entirely on the evidence. Now, think for a minute. Is there anything else? Something about David? No matter how small or insignificant you think the information is, it could help us – and help you, even at this late stage.'

It was Sandra's turn to study Michael's face, as if to look for a hidden purpose to the question. She spoke again. 'I... I can't think of anything.'

'You're absolutely sure of that, Sandra? It's just that it always puzzled me why, right from the outset, David was looking at properties that were priced considerably in excess of the budget he had available, especially bearing in mind he would need money to live on since he had no income after his redundancy. Perhaps he had more money that we first thought. Do you think that's possible Sandra?'

Michael cocked his head to one side and raised an eyebrow.

Sandra seemed to recognise Michael's derisive gesture and her shoulders sagged.

'The lottery money, you mean?'

Michael pounced. 'Yes, Sandra. I did wonder when you were going to tell us about that.' The sarcasm in his tone was undisguised. 'Perhaps you'd care to explain.'

Sandra straightened. 'All right, David came up on the lottery just when he was offered redundancy. He was already thinking of leaving Alison to move in with me and this made that all the more possible. But it also made things more complicated because Alison might be entitled to half of the win, especially if they ever divorced. He was determined that Alison must never know about the lottery money and so we agreed that I should claim it for him. It seemed the ideal solution at the time.'

'And that's what he told you – that he'd won the money, but needed to keep it a secret from Alison.'

'Yes.'

'So there was no other reason why he would want to hide the fact that he'd won the money?'

Sandra looked genuinely perplexed. 'What other reason could there be?' she asked.

Michael ignored the question. 'How much money are we talking about, Sandra?'

'Three hundred and fifty thousand pounds... But I expect you already know that, Inspector.'

Michael ignored the suggestion and sailed on.

'That's a great deal of money. He must have trusted you implicitly. I mean, once you had claimed the money there was nothing to stop you hanging on to it.'

Sandra scowled. 'I've told you, Inspector, we were in love; we trusted each other completely. Perhaps that's something you wouldn't understand.'

Again, Michael ignored Sandra's retort. 'So what happened to that money?'

'We... I had it paid it into an off-shore account in the Isle of Man. Soon after David came to Spain he had me transfer it to a Spanish bank.'

'And whose account was that?'

'It was an account in David's name.'

'Just David's name?'

'Yes.'

'I see,' Michael said, 'So you were in love and trusted each other implicitly, but the money was banked in his name only?'

Sandra huffed and raised her eyes to the sky.

'I should tell you, Sandra, we've traced only one Spanish bank account for David Harrington, and there's no sign of the lottery money.'

'So?' She looked more angry than perplexed.

'So what bank account did you transfer the lottery money to?'

Now she went on the offensive. 'I only wish I knew. David arranged it all himself. I just signed some papers and they were sent off to the Isle of Man. That's the last I heard of it.'

Michael sat back and folded his arms. 'Another question then. Two men were locked up in Alicante prison for a murder they didn't commit. Did neither David, nor you, have any conscience about that?'

Sandra shifted her gaze, focusing on the far distance. 'I knew they were criminals, but I was sure they would get off.'

'Perhaps David made a better job of setting them up than you thought.'

Sandra ignored Michael's suggestion and looked away.

'Now, just one more thing, Sandra.'

She turned her head toward him.

'Your companion, the young man making our coffee. Who is he?'

'His name is Armando Bertomeu,' she answered.

'And what's Armando's part in all this?'

'He's just a friend. He knows nothing about this and I'd much rather you didn't tell him anything at all about it.'

'How long have you known each other?'

There was hesitation in her voice. 'He's been here for a few days.'

'He's a closer friend than that, isn't he? I think you can tell me.'

Her eyes fell to the ground. 'We met last year.'

'During your affair with David?'

Sandra tensed. 'Don't read anything into that, Inspector. I met Armando while I was on holiday in Fuengirola last year. We finished when I went back to England. When David left for France, I called Armando and invited him to visit for a few days. I was lonely and very frightened and I thought I might need, well, protection. So I called him. Nothing wrong with that, is there Inspector?'

There was a lot wrong, but it would have to wait.

'When exactly did Armando come here?'

'About ten days ago.'

'We'll be asking him, of course.'

'A week last Sunday. The 3rd I think.'

'Thank you, Sandra,' Michael said. 'Perhaps the coffee's ready now.'

Jose Luis took his cue. He went into the house, returning a minute later with Armando who was carrying a tray with glasses, a jug of iced water and a box of tissues. Mariela held another tray with a coffee pot and mugs.

Sandra helped herself to a glass of water and a fresh tissue and blew her nose with a vigorous blast, followed by a more refined attempt.

Armando had changed into white jeans, white slip-ons and a pale blue T-shirt. He glanced at Sandra curiously and then began to pour coffee.

Michael pulled out a chair. 'Why don't you join us, Mr Bertomeu? Miss Marlowe has been telling us all about you.'

Armando sat, said nothing, but smiled helpfully.

Michael said. 'You came here – when?'

'One week, maybe....'

'The 3rd, Miss Marlowe says, so that's almost two weeks.'

'I think – yes, is correct. Two weeks.'

Michael sipped his coffee. 'What do you know about the Harringtons?'

Sandra slammed her glass on the table. 'I've already told you, Inspector, Armando knows nothing about either David or Alison Harrington. I haven't even mentioned them to him.'

Very convenient, Michael thought. If Bertomeu didn't know anything, or if Sandra said he didn't know anything, he couldn't contradict her.

'If that's the case, I think we're finished here.'

Michael rose and then sat again as Jose Luis spoke in Spanish.

'Captain Perez reminds me you need to go to the police station in Alicante to make a formal statement. Now would seem as good a time as any. We'll need a statement from Mr Bertomeu, as well. And,' he turned to a slightly less nonchalant Armando, 'we'll need your address in Fuengirola.'

'Actually, I live in Malaga,' replied Armando, as if that were somehow better than Fuengirola.

Unimpressed, Michael turned again to Sandra. 'Oh, and you may want to contact the British Consulate.'

The comment was designed to cause alarm and it succeeded.

'Is that really necessary, Inspector?'

'I'm afraid so. After all, this is a murder inquiry. The Spanish police do tend to take murder quite seriously.'

'I've told you – it was an accident.'

'The problem is, Sandra, we only have your word for that at the moment.'

Sandra sneered. 'And I only have someone else's word.'

She did have a point, Michael thought, if – and it was a big if – she was telling the truth.

'In any case you need, at the very least, to explain your part in covering up Alison's death. You need to get changed into something more suitable, something warm, I would suggest. You could be there quite some time.'

'I'll do that,' Sandra said, struggling for bravado.

'And before we leave here, you'd better give us the address

where David Harrington stayed. The villa where the *accident* occurred.'

Jose Luis spoke and Michael turned back to Sandra.

'The Captain has pointed out we need to search this house. He can get a warrant, of course, but that would seem unnecessary in the circumstances, don't you think? I can do it now, with Officer Poquet, while you go and make your statement in Alicante and that would speed things up.'

'Help yourself.' Sandra said nonchalantly. 'You'll be wasting your time though. I would have thought your time would be better spent trying to find David.'

'All in good time,' said Michael with an air of coolness. 'All in good time.'

Another car was called in to take Sandra and Armando separately to Alicante. Armando sat quietly looking bewildered while Officer Poquet accompanied Sandra into the house to change. Meanwhile Michael and Jose Luis strolled around the garden of the villa, reaching the end of the pool and turning toward the front of the house.

'Did you think she looked nervous?' Jose Luis asked.

Michael shrugged. 'At times yes, but in parts she seemed confident, even cocky.'

'Do you think she is telling the truth?'

Michael thought for a moment. 'Her story is plausible. We know for example that David Harrington has been to France before, but that doesn't mean it's the truth. There was just something... I don't know... rehearsed. At times I got the impression we were witnessing a performance in which every line had been carefully scripted.'

At the front of the house, Jose Luis approached the steps leading up to the road above. The stone side walls of the steps were overhung by bushy lampranthus plants which tumbled from the red earth on either side. Only a few of the deep purple flowers remained in bloom, the rest having long since faded to withered brown seed heads. Jose Luis sat on the wall and Michael joined him on the opposite side of the steps.

'What will you do about finding David Harrington if he is indeed in France?' Jose Luis asked.

Michael sighed. 'To be honest, I have no idea. We could contact the French police, I suppose, or Europol, but first we need to search this place and the villa where Harrington was staying. Let's just see what turns up before we do anything else. If we can keep a lid on Sandra's information for now, there's no reason for David Harrington to become suspicious, wherever he is. Do you think you can do that, Jose Luis?'

'I think we can find good reasons for keeping Sandra out of the way for a few days at least, if that's what you mean.'

'Fine,' Michael said, rising from the wall. 'Come on, let's see if Sandra is ready for her trip to Alicante.'

As Michael stood, he stepped in a pool of water that had seeped from a series of irrigation pipes that meandered between the orange trees set in the bank on either side of the steps leading to the road above. The trees reminded him of the groves his uncle Pepito had shown him in Parcent and for a brief moment he was transported there, wondering how his own crop would be faring in his absence… and whether Rosana might be thinking of him as he occasionally thought of her.

'It surprises me, Michael said, turning to Jose Luis, 'that in such a dry climate, there's enough water to irrigate gardens like this.'

Jose Luis smiled. 'That's a fallacy that fools many of the foreigners who come here to escape the cold wet winters of northern Europe. They are all too easily convinced by the publicity that says we have three hundred days of sunshine each year here on the Costa Blanca.'

'You mean it isn't true?'

'Oh, it's true enough, and in fact we have just over half the annual rainfall here as in northern France or southern England. The difference is, nearly all of it comes in a few months in the autumn and winter time. The mountains trap the rain and it feeds into vast underground aquifers. Sink a bore hole almost anywhere round here, especially in the bottom of the valleys, and you'll hit water. That's why everywhere is so green and why oranges are one of the main crops. But you will know that for yourself, being a landowner in Parcent.'

Michael looked across the orange trees on either side of the steps and wondered what else Jose Luis knew of his new found family and fortune.

As they shuffled back toward the pool terrace, Michael noticed a withered tree with leaves shrivelling to brown. 'Looks like growing oranges is not as easy as it sounds,' he said, nodding toward the struggling specimen.

'That's something else you'll learn,' said Jose Luis. 'Even with rich soil and plenty of water, fruit growing is not without its problems. There's blight and insect infestation to worry about, frost damage some years and a need for expert pruning. Still, I'm sure you'll soon get the hang of it, and pretty soon you'll be complaining like the rest of the farmers about the meagre price paid for your crops.'

Michael doubted very much that the vagaries of growing citrus fruit would ever feature in his future. 'Sandra must have dressed by now,' he said, bringing them both back to more serious concerns.

Sandra emerged from the villa in an ankle length floral print dress with a white linen jacket draped around her shoulders and toting a large red handbag. Mariela hurried behind, her sunglasses glinting like headlights.

Michael paused at Sandra's side. 'Officer Poquet and I will search this villa, then the one David Harrington rented and we'll join you in Alicante as soon as we are finished.' He turned to Mariela. 'And we're going to need the forensics boys.'

'Actually,' Mariela said, 'our chief forensic scientist is a woman.'

'So... we'll need her, as well.' Michael moved over to Jose Luis. 'We'll need a couple of hours, I guess, and then we'll join you back at the police station. That'll give you time to get their statements and we can take stock from there.'

The search of Sandra's villa revealed little of immediate interest. A few bank statements found in the drawer of a dresser in the lounge confirmed the status of Sandra's account at the CAM Bank. A three-day-old *Daily Express* lay on a coffee table beside last week's *Costa Blanca News*. An electric percolator sat, as if banished from the kitchen, on a corner table next to the television.

The kitchen looked hardly used. At one end of the work-top a wooden chopping board stood in front of a block with slots containing six kitchen knives. At the other end, a pink plastic basket contained an assortment of utensils – a whisk, a fish slice, a ladle, two large serving spoons and a wooden spatula. A bottle of 'Lemony Soft' dishwashing liquid stood in a sticky stain on the window sill above the sink. Beneath the sink, in two musty-smelling cupboards, there was a dust-pan and brush resting on a sheet of old newspaper next to a small rubbish bin. A few Mediterranean cookery books were stacked on an open wall shelf. The fridge was empty but for a large carton of skimmed milk, one of orange juice, half a dozen eggs, a bunch of wilting parsley and two steaks in a polystyrene tray wrapped in clingfilm.

Two of the three bedrooms appeared entirely unused. The wardrobes contained only a couple of empty suitcases and folded bed linen. In the main bedroom, the queen-sized double bed was rumpled. Four pillows were scattered over a duvet cover that rested on the floor to one side. Michael approached the dressing table. Hairbrush, nail varnish, cleansing lotion, and perfume – *Anaïs Anaïs*.

He opened a drawer and found a collection of underwear. Some items were white, some red, many were black, and all of it was extremely skimpy.

'Officer Poquet – I think you had better continue over here.'

Mariela looked inside the drawer, withdrew a pair of black thong-like panties and held them stretched in front of her hips.

'Not embarrassed, are you, Inspector?' she said, with a slight smile that revealed, for the first time, perfectly even, perfectly white teeth.

For a second, Michael couldn't help staring. He looked away, his face reddening. 'Not at all. It's just that they look most uncomfortable.'

'Appearances can be deceiving.' Her smile broadened to a grin.

Michael turned his attention to the en-suite bathroom.

A shelf above the wash basin held his and her tooth brushes, *Adidas* after-shave, a twin-blade razor, some Spanish toothpaste and *Eucryl* Smokers Toothpowder. In the medicine cabinet Michael found a box of *Ibuprofen* tablets, a bottle of aspirins and another bottle containing mouthwash.

He returned to the bedroom and Mariela tossed a foil strip in his direction. 'Contraceptive pills.'

'You don't say?' He tossed the strip back. 'Anything more revealing?' he asked, immediately realising his mistake.

'Like this?' She held a short see-through negligee against her body.

'Catch your death of cold in that,' he said, not knowing what else to say.

'In Spain? I don't think so.'

Michael opened the first of two louvre-doored wardrobes and slid garments along the rail – light-weight summer dresses, tops and skirts, with one thick woollen jacket. The base of the wardrobe was home to five pairs of shoes, all in leather, high-heeled and very elegant; nothing heavy or clunky. All very tasteful in the shoe department.

The adjoining wardrobe was obviously Armando's, though there was barely enough to fill a hold-all, let alone a suitcase. Two pairs of jeans, three short sleeved shirts, five coloured T-shirts, one pair of shorts and several pairs of *Calvin Klein* Y-fronts. For a second he thought of holding them up for Mariela, but only for a second.

On the floor of the wardrobe Michael found a pair of leather loafers. He checked the size and replaced them. On the other side of the wardrobe he spotted a pair of brown leather brogues. He picked them up and examined the leather-lined inners to find a gold embossed stamp inside each heel: LOAKE SHOEMAKERS ENGLAND. He turned them over to see the hard leather, hardly worn soles were stamped with a figure 8.

'I don't suppose you know the European shoe size for an English size eight, do you?' he asked, not really expecting an answer.

'Common knowledge, Inspector. It is a size forty-two.'

As Michael replaced the brogues, his finger rubbed over one of the highly polished toe-caps and disturbed a faint layer of dust. He set the brogues down carefully and closed the wardrobe door.

By the time Michael and Mariela arrived at the villa used by David and Alison Harrington, the forensic team was crawling over every inch.

Mariela had contacted the letting agent who confirmed the villa was rented from 17th January to the end of May in the name of Ronald Fletcher. (No, he hadn't checked the man's identity. Why should he? The rent had been paid monthly in advance in cash and a sizeable deposit had been paid – which had not yet been reclaimed. Fletcher had not contacted the agent when the rental period expired, so it was hard to say if he'd left before the due date. The agent had checked the inventory and nothing was missing.)

There had been two lettings after Mr Fletcher and the villa had been thoroughly cleaned between each letting. Although it was surrounded by other holiday homes they were all a good distance away and did not overlook the villa. Mr Fletcher had originally made use of the weekly maid service, having the villa cleaned and the bed linen changed, but he had cancelled this after the first two weeks.

Michael opened the door of the villa and stepped inside.

'Where do you think you're going?' The voice came from a cotton-suited figure with a white facemask that left only a pair of bespectacled eyes glaring out from beneath a hood pulled over the brow.

Mariela intervened. 'Sorry, Alicia. This is Detective Inspector Michael Fernandez. Inspector, this is Alicia Llopis, chief forensic scientist.'

The facemask was removed to reveal unsmiling, glossy red lips. 'So this is our meddling English detective.' The hood was pushed back and boyish, glossy, spiky brown hair sprang to attention.

Michael got straight down to business.

'Found anything useful?'

'Too early to say just yet. Usual stuff. Fingerprints everywhere, hair in the plugholes, pubic hair in the bottom of the shower. No sign of blood, at least not in the house.'

'What about the garden?'

'That's next, but have you seen it? There must be almost eight hundred square metres. It's going to take a while.'

'Miss Marlowe's hire car?' Michael asked. 'Have you been over that yet?'

'It's down in Alicante, but there's a problem. It was only rented ten days ago. She changed it from the original car she hired. She's given Jose Luis some excuse about a wanting an automatic.'

'Are you…?'

'Looking for the first one? No, actually Inspector, we're hoping someone will just pop it into the police station, save us the bother.'

Michael ignored the sarcasm. 'And when you've finished here you'll be going over Miss Marlowe's villa?'

'That's the plan,' said Alicia. 'Unless we get held up here. Now, if you'll excuse me, I need to get on.'

Michael and Mariela found Jose Luis in a dingy office at Alicante Police HQ where a small shaft of sunlight illuminated a beam of swirling smoke. Jose Luis stubbed out his cigarette in the overflowing ashtray and waved his hand in a futile attempt to clear the air.

'What news?' Michael asked, forcing out a deliberate cough.

'We've found the car. The first one Miss Marlowe hired. It's on its way here now, on a trailer. It's been hired out to a German couple in Alfaz del Pi for the past week or so. They were none too pleased when we took it away.'

'And forensics?' Michael asked.

'Going to take a while, I'm afraid... couple of days, at least.'

Michael frowned.

'What about our friend, Armando Bertomeu? What does he have to say for himself?'

'Very little. I interviewed him twice. He seemed nervous,

installed in an interview room, but that's to be expected. So far he's confirmed what Sandra claimed. He's a friend. He lives in Malaga and works occasionally as a singer in a nightclub in Fuengirola. When he's not working, he's on the beach. He says he met Sandra last summer and spent a week or so with her after which she phoned now and again. Then he came here two weeks ago when she phoned him and said she wanted company.'

'Have you got Sandra's statement?'

'Being typed right now.'

'Anything new?'

'Nothing. Except... I asked her how Harrington went to France. She said she drove him down to the centre of Benidorm where he was going to hire a car, but she doesn't know the make or model. It must be Spanish registered, so I guess it won't be too hard to find – in France, I mean. We're asking round the car hire companies to see if we can get a lead.'

'So what do you think, Officer Poquet?' asked Michael.

'About Miss Marlowe or Armando?'

'Both.'

'Sandra Marlowe is plausible,' Mariela said slowly. 'Quite convincing. I can see how she could be drawn in, lured by someone she totally believed in – attracted by money and a new, luxurious life abroad.'

'Even with Mrs Harrington on the scene?'

'Well, if her lover was everything to her.' Mariela looked up. 'Have you ever been in love, Inspector? Be honest now. Have you ever been totally besotted – deeply, truly and blindly in love?'

Michael reddened. 'What if I had?'

'You would know that such love can overwhelm rational thought, change your personality, alter your views and even override your conscience.'

'I'll take your word for that.'

Mariela continued. 'All I'm saying is, if Miss Marlowe truly loved David Harrington, I can easily believe she'd come here – simply to be near him and in the hope, however unrealistic, that they'd have a life together.'

'And when the accident happened, if it was an accident, and Alison died?'

'She'd be shocked. But inside herself, she'd possibly be relieved in a way. After all, it opened the door for her and David to be together.'

'So why didn't she go with him to France?'

'Perhaps, as she said, she saw a different person when he became cold and calculating. Perhaps she didn't like what she saw and became afraid of him.'

'And what about Armando, Mariela? What's your opinion?'

'He's just a playboy taking advantage of a lonely woman and her money. Extremely attractive, but he'd be straight back to Malaga when the money dried up. What do you think, yourself, Inspector?'

'I think we need those forensic reports. Right now, on the double.'

'Shouldn't you be heading for La Belle France, Michael,' said Jose Luis. 'Harrington has quite a head start.'

'Perhaps, but first I need a quick word with Sandra.'

Michael would have been disappointed if he'd planned an intimidating confrontation. The interview room was bright and airy with a large south-facing window at one end. Only the narrow bars at the window, criss-crossing the outer frame, gave a hint the room was intended for detention. Jose Luis seated himself in a corner behind Sandra Marlowe who sat on a hard grey metal chair that matched the desk in front of her.

'Did you find anything useful?' She pulled a cigarette from the packet.

'In a manner of speaking,' said Michael, pulling up a chair on the opposite side of the desk. 'There's a rather nice pair of hand-crafted brown leather brogues in your wardrobe. They're not Mr Bertomeu's, so they belong to David, I presume.'

'Yes – yes. Come to think of it, David left a pair at the villa one night.'

'And how did he happen to leave a pair of such fine calfskin brogues?'

'I think it was... not long before the accident.' She sent a ring of smoke drifting. 'One evening he'd been for early dinner with Alison and afterwards he told her he was going for a drive and a walk along the sea front.' She glanced up. 'He sometimes did that, but it was an excuse and he came up to see me. When he arrived, his feet were killing him and he had blisters. So he changed into a pair of flip-flops and didn't change back when he left. I meant to remind him about them, but once I'd put them away I forgot they were there.'

Jose Luis leaned forward, speaking in Spanish.

Michael sat up. 'That's all for now,' he said, 'but Captain Perez needs your passport. It's just a precaution, but you aren't going anywhere, are you?'

'No, but is that really necessary?'

'Yes. You have it, don't you? Only we didn't find it back at your villa.'

For the second time since they'd met, Michael thought he detected faint panic in her eyes as they flashed before she regained control.

'Yes, I have it here.'

She picked up the red bag from the floor by the desk, lifted it onto her lap and began to rummage deep inside, lifting items and putting them back. Compact, cigarettes, lighter, hairbrush, lipstick. She appeared to locate something and plunged both hands deep inside the bag, fiddling to extract a sheet of paper from the passport before producing it.

'Can I have a look at that, Miss Marlowe?' Michael said.

'What?' She dropped the passport onto the desk.

'The piece of paper you just withdrew from your passport.'

'Oh, that. It's just a photocopy.'

She thrust the folded paper down next to the passport on the table.

Michael examined the worn sheet. He unfolded it once, then again, and turned it round to study the details. His eyes were drawn first to the photograph – black-and-white, but identifiably clear. He picked up the maroon passport and compared the inside back page with the photocopy, then checked indistinct areas, especially across the folds, to satisfy himself that it was what it purported to be – a photocopy of the original. Next he turned his attention to the stamp at the edge of the page that read: AYUNTAMIENTO DE ALTEA, with an indecipherable signature.

'What's this?' He looked at Sandra.

'It's a stamp from the town hall, to certify the copy. It's a service they provide so you don't have to carry the original all the time. There's a big racket in stolen passports out here, you know, so I usually carry only the copy and leave the original in the house. It's much safer that way.'

'Thank you Miss Marlowe, you've been very helpful.'

'You're welcome. Does that mean I can go now?'

'We're going to have to ask you to remain here for just a little while.'

'Yes, all right.' Sandra picked up the cigarettes. 'I'll wait, but I hope I can get back to the villa before too long.'

Michael said casually, 'Are you sure you wouldn't like us to contact a lawyer?'

'Why would I need a lawyer?' Sandra met his eyes with a slight frown of puzzlement.

'No reason,' Michael said calmly, deliberately hiding his suspicions.

In Jose Luis's office, the mood was sombre. 'No progress then,' he said.

'Not at all,' said Michael with an air of satisfaction. 'We're a great deal further forward.'

'In what way?'

'Well, at least have a few leads to follow up. We've been told how Alison died and where the Harringtons stayed. We know that David grew a beard and that he went into hiding in France. And we've tracked down some of the money in Sandra's bank account.' He paused. 'And we know that Sandra has told at least one lie.'

'How do we know even that?' Jose Luis raised an eyebrow.

'You've never owned a pair of Loakes handmade leather brogues, have you?'

'I've never even heard of them.'

'Then you would not realise that such a fine pair of hand-crafted shoes would never give you blisters.'

CHAPTER FOURTEEN

The money was the key. Find the money, you'll find the answers, Michael told himself. David Harrington had taken £55,000 in cash from his building society account before he left England. Then he'd withdrawn all the cash from his Spanish bank account. That accounted for the redundancy money and the proceeds of his house sale. Sandra Marlowe's account held the remainder of the 15,000 euros she said David had given her, but that still left almost 200,000 euros unaccounted for. And what about the lottery money – £350,000. Even allowing for moderate spending since Harrington arrived in Spain, that still left around half a million euros unaccounted for.

The lottery money had been paid into the account in Sandra Marlowe's name in the Isle of Man. If Sandra Marlowe had told the truth, that money had since been transferred to an account in Spain. But the Spanish police had found nothing in her name or in the name of David Harrington.

Michael's attempts at careful, rational analysis were, for once, defeating him. The equation grew more complicated with each element he introduced. He was, as he'd once accused Sergeant Rawlinson, going round in ever-decreasing circles to assemble a jigsaw with missing pieces.

For a second he thought of asking Superintendent Bowater to track the money from the Isle of Man account, but he quickly dismissed the idea. He decided instead to enlist the help of Brian Small. He could do with a decent meal and Brian's knowledge would be cheap at the price.

Brian suggested Parcent, but Michael made an excuse, saying it was too far away. They settled instead for a return to the Calpe seafood restaurant.

'I heard you'd returned to England,' Brian announced, joining Michael who was already seated at a table in the shade of a canvas canopy.

'I did.' Michael said. 'I've already ordered, I hope that's all right.'

Brian nodded. 'So, to what do I owe the pleasure today?'

The food began to arrive and they both tucked in to an array of salads and seafood and a bottle of chilled white wine.

Michael smeared a blob of alioli on a torn crust of bread. 'Do you remember last time we met, you explained how a person might open a bank account in Spain, or get someone to open it for them?'

'Aha. You're thinking of buying a little place over here after all?'

'I already have a little place over here…'

'What?' Brian sat back, gaping. 'And you didn't buy it through me?'

'It's a long story, I'll tell you later. Now, what about the bank account?'

'All business today.' Brian sighed. 'Okay, the bank account's easy, as I told you. You fill in a form, present your passport, register for an NIE number and then you can just open a bank account.'

'I think you told me a photocopy of a passport is good enough?'

'Yes, it's quite usual, especially when people are buying a house in Spain and they've returned to the UK. They fill in the forms, return them by post with a copy of their passport and their asesoria does the rest.'

'And when the account's been opened by the asesoria, you can transfer money over from another account, say in the UK?'

'Or pay cash or a cheque into the account – or through an automatic transfer.'

'What about withdrawing cash from the account?'

'You just go along to the bank or use your card in one of those machines, if it's only a small amount.' Brian pulled the head from a jumbo prawn.

'No, before that, I was told that you'd have to present your passport.'

'Sorry, I was rushing ahead. Look, is there a point to all this?'

'I'll come to that in a minute. You were saying?'

'You'd have to present your passport the first time you went to the bank in order to get a cheque book and cards, before you could withdraw any cash.'

'The actual passport, not a photocopy?'

'Yes, yes, the actual passport. Are you going to tell me what this is all about?' Brian stabbed ring of battered calamari. 'The excitement's killing me.'

Michael pushed his plate to one side and distributed the last of the wine. 'Keep this strictly to yourself. Nothing official has been released. David Harrington had a great deal more money than we originally thought, some of it not his.'

'Strewth – you mean he robbed a bank or something?'

'Not exactly. But let's say it wasn't his to spend.'

'Well, he won't be spending it now, will he? According to the papers, like as not he's dead,' said Brian.

'Perhaps, but right now we need to account for the money.'

'Hence the questions about bank accounts. You think it's been banked somewhere?'

'We know some of it was banked, but Harrington withdrew all of that in cash. The "extra" money was also banked somewhere here in Spain, but we can't find the account.'

'I see.' Brian took a sip of wine. 'So what's all this about you having a place? I thought you didn't like poor old Spain. What changed your mind?'

'I never said I disliked everything about Spain. I've just found out I've inherited a house in Parcent, that's all. And some land.'

'What sort of house? How much land?'

'It's just a modest town house. The land is mainly oranges, olives and almonds. Oh, and a vineyard. I don't know how much exactly, but a good few acres.'

'Jesus, Michael.' Brian looked ready to burst. 'Have you any idea what that little lot's worth, especially around Parcent? The house alone must be worth a hundred thousand.'

'Who said it's for sale?' Michael said firmly, draining the last of his wine.

'Sorry... It's the property agent in me. I think in terms of values all the time. So are you thinking of moving in?' His tone was hopeful. 'Yes, you are thinking about it – I can tell.' Brian leaned forward, clutching his glass. 'I tell you, Michael, you won't regret it. Spain's a wonderful country and the Jalon Valley is really special. I just hope you're coming because you want to.'

'What do you mean?'

'I told you, some people are just fed up with Britain. They don't integrate and so they never get to appreciate all that Spain has to offer. But you already speak the language and you're half-Spanish.'

'Yes... ' Even now, half-Spanish rankled, as if he was carrying it round like a placard at the airport. But this time he didn't protest.

Brian went on. 'So what will you do? You could take up farming, I suppose, if you're not going to become a property speculator.'

'No – this is all in the realms of fantasy, Brian.'

'Exactly. Just my point. This place is Fantasy Island. You can make of it just what you want. The opportunities are boundless, and like I say, you have an advantage over most people.'

'You're getting a bit carried away here. All I want to do is solve this case and right now I'm a long way from doing that.'

Fresh pineapple arrived, coffee followed and then the bill. Michael picked it up. 'That's strange... There's no wine, dessert or coffee on the bill.'

Brian smiled. 'You'll find it's all included in the price. Like I said, Fantasy Island.'

Michael set down a generous tip and pushed back his chair.

'Where are you staying?' Brian asked, standing up.

'For the time being I'm in a rented villa in Altea Hills, but I'll probably have to move out before long if the case isn't solved quickly.'

'What do you think of it? Altea Hills, I mean.'

'Nice villa, but it's all too built up for me. Actually, it reminds me of a seventies housing estate in Britain, except there are palm trees and the sun shines.'

'Altea is not at all like Parcent, is it?' Brian added with a grin. 'As a matter of fact, I'm going to Altea Hills tomorrow with a couple of prospective purchasers, a Mr and Mrs Jaines. No, not Jaines... Haines. That's it, James Haines. Funny name – easy to get mixed up.'

Michael's eyes widened and his expression froze for a moment.

'Are you all right, Michael?' Brian asked. 'What on earth is it?'

'Brian,' Michael said, his face melting to a grin. 'In policeman's terms, you've just squared the circle with a missing piece of the jigsaw. But I have to go now.'

'Any time. It's been a pleasure.' Brian looked bewildered.

'Believe me, Brian,' Michael called back, 'the pleasure's all mine.'

Michael sped towards Alicante, thoughts on anything but driving. All he could think of was Harrington – Carrington. He went through the alphabet – Barrington (possible) Farrington (possible) Larrington (doubtful) Marrington (doubtful) Warrington (possible). He was breathless when he entered the police station, to be greeted by a startled Mariela.

'Where's Jose Luis?'

'What?'

'I need you to get in touch with him right now.'

'What's the problem?' Mariela asked.

'I said now, Officer Poquet. This is urgent.'

At eight-thirty in the evening they were still awaiting news.

'So what makes you think we'll find the money in another name?' Jose Luis asked, picking up his coffee cup and swirling the dregs.

'It's just a hunch,' said Michael. 'When I first looked at the interview notes with Hagemans and Van Doorn, they said that the man they met at the finca in Orba called himself Carrington. At first we thought it was just a typing error or even a mix up in pronunciation – you know how guttural Dutch is – but do you remember, Jose Luis, they confirmed it when I spoke to them later? He used the name Carrington, not Harrington. Something Brian Small said to me this afternoon set me thinking. If you are going to use a false name, why use one so close to your real name?'

'And the answer is?' prompted Jose Luis.

'David Harrington needed to open a bank account to get the lottery money over here. A professional might have arranged forged documents, but Harrington's not in that league, so he had to do the next best thing.'

'Which was?' Mariela asked.

'A subtle alteration to his name. You remember the copy of Sandra Marlowe's passport? It looked very official, stamped by the town hall. As Harrington knows, a photocopy is very easy to alter. All he does is alter the initial letter of his surname and he's got a document good enough open a bank account in a different name. No one would know what to look for.'

'But surely you'd need to produce some original documentation at the bank in order to withdraw money?' Mariela said.

'Of course. The bank would ask to see your actual passport, not a copy.'

'So how could he get away with it?' asked Jose Luis. 'Assuming you're right, of course.'

'What's the first thing you look at in someone's passport?' Michael said.

'I don't know. Photograph, I suppose.'

'Exactly. You look at the photo, then at the person presenting it. If the photograph matches, that's usually enough. Even if you glance at the name you might not notice the initial letter of the surname is different. It takes some nerve, I know – but if it all went wrong you could bluster your way out of it by saying someone at the bank had made a mistake.'

When the phone rang they all froze. Michael tried to make sense of the muffled words as Jose Luis scribbled in his notebook.

'Damn!' Jose Luis ended the call.

'Well?' Michael asked.

'They've found it – that is, they've found an account in the name of David Warrington at the Javea branch of the Banco de Valencia. It was set up on the 2nd of February this year with 420,000 euros, transferred from the National Westminster Bank in the Isle of Man. That's roughly £350,000. It has to be our man.'

Jose Luis's voice told Michael that this was not all good news.

'So what's the problem?' he asked.

'The problem is, Michael, we're too late. The money was withdrawn yesterday – all of it, in cash. The bank received a faxed request last week and they needed five days' notice. Someone, presumably David Harrington, called in yesterday and walked out with the lot.'

'A fax, you say. That's old fashioned technology, don't you think?'

'It's standard practice because they need a signature. An email isn't good enough.'

'Where did the fax come from?' Michael asked.

'They're checking now. We should know in a few minutes.'

The call came and they were no further forward. The fax was sent from a busy newspaper and stationery store in Benidorm. An officer had been to the store and shown a photograph of David Harrington to the two girls who work there; neither of them recognised David Harrington.

'We've got to interview the bank clerk in Javea,' said Michael.

'I agree,' said Jose Luis. 'But the bank is closed now so that will have to wait until morning.'

'This is where I mutter something unintelligible,' Michael said.

'Go ahead – but do you think it was David Harrington?' asked Mariela.

'It had to be,' said Jose Luis. 'After searching for weeks... and now we've missed him by just one day.'

'At least we know he's still around,' said Mariela, sounding hopeful. 'Still in Spain. At least...' her optimism evaporated '...he was yesterday.'

Teresa Carreres looked up nervously when Michael and Jose Luis entered the private office in the Javea branch of the Banco de Valencia.

The assistant branch manager, she was dressed in impeccable black patent leather loafers and charcoal grey trousers. A dazzling, fuchsia pink silk scarf tucked down the front of her bright white shirt almost matched the crimson flush that rose in her cheeks as they browsed the documents on the desk. The Branch Manager, Señor Alvarez, hovered, catching the glances Teresa threw in his direction through her designer spectacles, as if trying to assess his mood.

The signatures of "D. Warrington" on the fax and the receipt for the cash were more or less identical, but David Harrington's signature H was vaguely adjusted to appear like a W.

'Tell me,' said Michael, 'did you check Mr Warrington's passport?'

'Yes, of course. It's standard procedure,' Teresa said.

'And did the man resemble the photograph in the passport?'

'Well, yes. But you know what passport photographs are like. They're very small and often out of date. Put it this way, there was sufficient resemblance for me to be satisfied.'

'And did you check the name on the passport?'

'I'm sure I would have done. Again, it's standard practice.'

'Is it possible you could have missed spotting a discrepancy between Warrington and Harrington?'

Teresa shuddered. 'I suppose I could have done.' She looked anxiously towards Señor Alvarez, who felt obliged to assist his junior colleague.

'You must understand Inspector,' he said, 'we probably handle around ten large cash withdrawals a week. They're quite routine at this branch. Normally a faxed request and production of a passport is enough to confirm someone's identity. I don't think we can blame Miss Carreres if she failed to spot a very subtle deception.'

It was Michael's turn to reassure.

'No one's blaming you, Miss Carreres. We just need to ask what happened. What did he look like? I know you checked his passport photograph, but can you describe him?'

Teresa hesitated. 'Well, he was middle-aged. I see so many people...'

'Perhaps this will help,' said Michael, placing a photograph of David Harrington on the desk. 'It was just yesterday, so perhaps...?'

Teresa studied it. 'Yes, that's him, I'm sure. Only... his hair was longer, I think, and his face was a little thinner.'

'You didn't happen to notice what was he wearing?'

'Yes, I did notice his clothes. In fact, I spotted him sitting in the waiting area in the foyer. He looked a bit out of place because most other customers were tourists dressed in casual clothes. Before he came to my desk, I was thinking he must be a businessman. He was wearing a smart summer suit; pale grey, I recall, with a blue shirt and a blue striped tie.'

'What about his demeanour? Did he seem nervous or anxious at all?'

'He was sweating a bit, but I put that down to the suit and tie, though he didn't have his arms in his sleeves – he had his jacket over his shoulders. He seemed quite relaxed in his manner.'

'Anything else?' Michael asked. 'About his appearance?'

'No, I think that's everything – blue shirt, striped tie, pale grey suit and white trainers.'

Michael raised an eyebrow.

Teresa continued. 'I just remember he looked quite smart. When he came to my desk, I was surprised he was British.'

'Why do you say that?'

'Well, most of the British people I deal with are more casually dressed; they're here on holiday, I guess, so they don't even pack a suit. And then there was the way he had draped the jacket over his shoulders. It's rather a continental thing, I think. I've seen Spanish businessmen dressed like that, especially in the summer time, but not the British.'

Michael understood what she meant. 'Did he have a beard?'

'No, definitely not. He was clean shaven.'

'And what about the money? How was it packaged?'

'It was all five hundred euro notes, as requested in the fax, wrapped into bundles of ten thousand euros and sealed in polythene.'

'Miss Carreres, what does 420,000 euros look like?'

'I'm sorry, I don't understand.'

'The bundles, I mean. How big a package is that amount of cash?'

'Oh, I see what you mean? About the size of a briefcase, I'd say.'

'Did he count it?'

'No, each ten thousand euro bundle was sealed in polythene and initialled by one of the clerks. Most people accept it like that without counting.'

'And what did he do with it?'

'He signed the receipt, I handed it over and... oh, I remember, he asked for a bag. It's not uncommon. You'd be surprised how many people come unprepared. So I found him two of our Banco de Valencia carrier bags. I helped him put the money into the bags and then he left. He was very polite. He shook my hand and thanked me for my assistance.'

Michael stood up.

'Thank you, Miss Carreres, you've been very helpful. Is there a room I could use? I need to make a call to England.'

'Yes, of course,' Alvarez replied. 'You can use my office.'

As they followed Señor Alvarez along the corridor, Jose Luis tapped Michael on the shoulder. 'Where do you think he's gone? France?'

Michael walked on. 'I don't think David Harrington's gone anywhere.'

Alvarez left the two detectives in the privacy of his office and Michael made the call, ignoring Jose Luis's pleas for an explanation.

At the mention of Penny Edwardes' name Jose Luis glanced away sheepishly as Michael talked, then hung on in silence as he waited.

The response came after a few minutes. Michael asked another question then closed his phone with a satisfied smile.

'Come on Jose Luis, we're going to the airport and we need to get our skates on.'

'What's going on?' said Jose Luis.

'I'll explain on the way.'

Jose Luis raced southwards along the A7, flashing lights to clear the outside lane.

The horn was blaring so loudly that Penny's return call to Michael's mobile phone was barely audible, but he got what he wanted.

The car screeched to a halt in front of the departure point at Alicante's El Altet airport. Michael leapt out and ran towards the automatic doors.

Inside the hall people scurried this way and that. Queues progressed towards the check-in desks and then on to the security scanner staffed by two uniformed officials.

Michael glanced up at the electronic notice board and found the check-in desks he wanted. He strode across the hall and stood to one side scrutinizing the three dwindling queues advancing towards the desks handling the 13.20 EasyJet flight to East Midlands Airport. These were just the last few stragglers for the flight and he failed to spot what he was looking for.

Jose Luis caught up, panting and demanding to know what was happening.

'I expect he's gone through already,' Michael said. 'Can you get us through security and into the departure lounge?'

'He's with me,' Jose Luis said, flashing his Guardia Civil badge to the security officer at the metal detector. As they rushed through, the alarm sounded with a high pitched wail. 'It's my gun,' Jose Luis said to the officer, pulling back his jacket to show the leather holster attached to his belt.

'I hope you're not going to use that thing,' said Michael as they rushed towards departure gate twenty-two.

'Only if I have to,' Jose Luis replied.

'Wait a minute,' Michael said, pulling Jose Luis back. 'If he sees us rushing in, he'll do a runner. Let's just slow down and walk normally as if we are regular passengers.'

'But what if he's spotted us already?' said Jose Luis.

'That's a chance we'll have to take.'

They found a position beside a coffee kiosk overlooking the seating area at gate twenty-two.

A few passengers were already gathered, though the first call had only just been announced. From their position at the kiosk they could view passengers as they arrived at the gate after the long walk down the concourse.

Jose Luis studied the backs of heads, wondering how he'd recognise their man.

Michael looked for something else and it wasn't long before he spotted it.

Amidst the steady shuffle of passengers, a man stood out. He was wearing smart grey trousers with a matching jacket draped over his arm. Michael cast his eyes downwards and found what he was looking for – a pair of white trainers. He tapped Jose Luis on the arm and nodded. They approached from behind.

'Mr Harrington?' Michael asked.

The man froze and his knees seemed to buckle slightly.

'Hello, Mr Harrington. You know Captain Perez, don't you? Jose Luis, you remember John Harrington, David's brother?'

CHAPTER FIFTEEN

'So, now... Are you going to finally tell me?' Jose Luis said, driving back to Alicante police headquarters. 'How could you know it was John we had to look for at the airport?'

'Sandra told us that David Harrington had left for France in a hurry because he was terrified of being identified. He was in such a hurry that there was no time to withdraw the lottery money from the bank. In any event, he had the other cash and that was more than enough to keep him going for quite a while.'

Jose Luis was still baffled. 'But I still don't understand what led you to suspect John Harrington.

Michael pressed on. 'I couldn't help thinking that if David Harrington skipped the country in such a rush, leaving the lottery cash in the bank, why would he come back now and risk being identified and picked up? As I said, he couldn't be short of funds just yet. But he must have been worried that we'd find the account with the lottery cash and freeze it. Then he would have lost almost everything he'd worked so hard to achieve. So I wondered, if he was desperate to get the cash, but afraid of being picked up, how would he go about it? The answer was simple – get someone else to collect it for you. Then Teresa Carreres said the man who collected the cash had longer hair and a thinner face.'

Jose Luis sighed. 'People change, Michael. Their hair grows; they lose weight.'

'And then there was the jacket. Remember Teresa said the man had the jacket round his shoulders and his arms weren't in the sleeves.'

'So?'

'It may be quite a normal thing in Spain for a man to wear a jacket like that, but it's virtually unheard of in England.'

'Even so, what does that tell us?'

'It tells me the jacket didn't fit, it was too large. John Harrington bears a reasonable resemblance to David, facially at least, but he is much slimmer.'

'That's very flimsy.'

'You're forgetting the shoes,' Michael replied. 'When Teresa at the bank described who collected the cash, it could have been David Harrington, especially when she said how smartly dressed he was – suit, shirt and tie – but then she mentioned the trainers.'

'So?'

'Why would someone so immaculately dressed be wearing trainers with a suit?'

'I don't know, some people wear them all the time.'

'Not David Harrington. Look, you remember those photos we have of David Harrington? In almost every photograph he wore brogues – they're his trademark. And when Mariela and I searched Sandra's villa, I found two pairs of men's shoes in the wardrobe. One pair belonged to our friend Armando – size 41, English size 7. The other was a pair of size 8 brown brogues, hand-made by Loakes of England. The brogues were obviously David Harrington's and Sandra Marlowe confirmed that. They were slightly dusty which suggested they had been there a while.'

'So?'

'So someone was posing as David Harrington, wearing one of his suits, but not his shoes.' Michael paused dramatically and looked at Jose Luis who still appeared baffled.

'The brogues didn't fit did they? You can get away with wearing an ill-fitting suit, but John Harrington has much bigger feet than David – I'd noticed it before when I first met him and then again at the hotel in Benidorm – and you can't squeeze your feet into shoes that are a size too small.'

'Do you really notice such things, Michael? You need to get a life. So once you realised it might be John Harrington posing as his brother, that's when you phoned Penny.'

'Exactly. I asked her to find out if John Harrington was in England. She spoke to Linda Harrington, who said John came back to Spain six days ago and was to return this afternoon. Hence the rush for us to get to the airport. I also asked Penny to find out where John was staying and see if he'd checked out. She contacted Linda again and then me called back just before we got to the airport. John had been staying at a hotel in Albir, just down the coast from Altea. But he hadn't checked out. The receptionist told Penny his clothes were still in the room. So I figured he spent last night somewhere else, which meant he would still be wearing the outfit that he wore to the bank. '

'Including the trainers?'

'Of course, including the trainers.' Michael sat back triumphantly.

'Mind you,' Michael said 'all this begs a question. How and why did David Harrington leave Spain without his passport – and more importantly, how did he have the foresight to leave behind a suit and his best shoes?'

'That's two questions.'

John Harrington and Sandra Marlowe were in separate cells at Alicante Police headquarters.

The money from the bank – recovered from John Harrington's suitcase (taken from the hold of the plane and causing considerable disruption) – was in safe custody.

Sandra was willing to talk, while John insisted on the presence of Timothy Middleton from the Consulate.

Michael was in no hurry. He needed results from forensics and Alicia Llopis of the white overalls was on her way.

When she arrived, she appeared taller in high heels and looked quite different, breezing across the office in a navy blue trouser-suit with a bolero jacket over a stiff-collared green shirt. She joined Michael, Jose Luis and Mariela at the long conference table and slapped a bulky file down.

Michael offered a hand in a greeting and, unsure of his ground, opted for safety. 'Señora Llopis,' he said carefully, 'thank you for coming over.'

Alicia shook his hand perfunctorily and sat down. 'There's more to do, but we have the basics. DNA results will take a little longer.'

She placed a pair of frameless half-moon spectacles on the end of her nose, tossed a brief glance in Michael's direction and opened the file.

'We found blood samples on a rock that formed part of a border to the poolside terrace at David Harrington's villa. There was blood on the terrace as well. The whole area had clearly been scrubbed and hosed down, but it's just not that easy to wash away every trace of blood. There were minute particles on the rock and blood had seeped into the gaps between the tiles on the terrace next to the rock. We're still waiting for DNA tests, but the blood group matches that of Alison Harrington.'

'So the accident to Alison Harrington could have happened just as Sandra described?' Michael surmised.

'I think you know better than that, Inspector Fernandez,' Alicia replied. 'All this proves is that Alison Harrington suffered some kind of wound on that terrace. Whether it was an accident or whether she died there remains uncertain.'

'I take your point,' Michael said, chastened. He thought for a moment. 'This rock, the one with the blood samples, how big is it, do you know?'

Alicia turned a page in her file. 'I can tell you exactly. It is roughly oblong, slightly rounded at one end and with a jagged square edge at the other. It measures twenty five centimetres in length, twelve centimetres wide and fourteen deep. It is igneous rock with a hard, abrasive surface, red-brown in colour and containing small particles of a crystalline material. It weighs four point three five kilograms. Here, I have a photograph.' She passed a glossy print across the table. 'It's in the lab now. As I said, we have blood samples matching Alison Harrington and we're doing detailed DNA analysis at the moment. We've also lifted several of the tiles from nearby on the terrace for further tests.'

'I see,' said Michael, thinking things through.

'And before you ask, we've reviewed the evidence collected from the finca in Orba, especially the wound to Mrs Harrington's head and the blood stains found on the mattock previously assumed to be the murder weapon. It's inconclusive. There's grime, local earth, and evidence to prove the mattock was indeed in contact with Mrs Harrington's skull. But there's nothing to prove, or disprove, that the skull fracture was caused by the mattock. Equally, there is no forensic evidence to suggest it was caused by the rock. The rock itself is extremely hard and it is unlikely that traces of it would be dislodged if it had been in contact with Mrs Harrington's skull. However, we know from the post mortem that the blow caused a fracture of the temporal bone which dissected the external carotid artery and lead to almost instantaneous death.'

Michael had already reached the conclusion to which Alicia was leading. 'This means that unless Alison suffered some other wound, which we know she didn't, then the blood on the rock proves it was the cause of the injury which resulted in her death.'

Alicia nodded to indicate her concurrence, but continued. 'What it does not prove, however, is whether Alison's death was accidental or the result of a deliberate blow.'

Jose Luis interrupted. 'But it does mean that the mattock was probably not used as a murder weapon.'

'Indeed.' Alicia was anxious to move on. 'There's much more interesting news from Sandra Marlowe's villa,' she said, turning another page in the file with a flourish. 'We found further traces of blood in the kitchen tiles at Sandra's villa. Again they had been thoroughly scrubbed, but it had soaked into the grout. And there were identical traces of blood on one of the kitchen knives. That, too, had been washed, but we found tiny traces where the hilt of the knife is set into the handle. The tiles, the grout and the knife are all back at the lab being checked for DNA.'

Michael gaped, trying to compute this new information.

'So Alison Harrington could have been wounded or even killed at Sandra Marlowe's villa?' Mariela suggested.

'No, no, that can't be right,' Michael exclaimed. 'We know that Alison died of a head wound, she had not been stabbed.'

Alicia raised a hand. 'If you would just allow me to continue, I might be able to clear up the confusion. You see, the blood we found at Sandra Marlowe's villa did not belong to Alison Harrington. It was David Harrington's.'

'What?' Michael almost choked as he sat forward. 'Are you sure?'

Alicia looked exasperated as she opened her mouth to speak.

'You don't need to answer that,' Michael said.

Silence reigned for a few moments before Alicia spoke again.

'I'm intrigued, Inspector Fernandez, as to why you asked us to examine Miss Marlowe's car?'

Michael felt a smug twitch coming on, but suppressed it. 'Oh, it was just that Sandra Marlowe told us that after Alison had died – in the accident at the villa – David Harrington took her body to the place in Orba. In the original forensic reports, there was no evidence of blood in his car. Not surprising at the time, since we were working on the theory that Alison was killed at the finca. But when Sandra told us her version, it made me wonder.' He paused. 'We found David Harrington's car in an old garage near the finca, so how did he get back from Orba to Altea? It must be forty kilometres and I imagine there's no bus service in those parts.'

Alicia looked across at him with what could be interpreted, Michael thought, as either appreciative admiration or disgruntled irritation.

'Well, your hunch was right. Sandra's first hire car had been thoroughly washed, inside and out. The hire company had even valeted it before the next hire. But, as I said, it's not that easy to obliterate evidence. We found blood samples in the fibres of the boot lining. We're still waiting for DNA tests, but we've matched the blood type to Alison Harrington.'

'And what about Alison's second car, the one she hired later?' Michael asked.

'Nothing, it was clean,' Alicia replied.

'Anything else?' Michael inquired.

'That's it for now,' said Alicia.

The four of them sat in silence for a while; no-one, it seemed, wanting to draw conclusions from the evidence they now had before them. It was left to Michael to try and bring things together.

'So,' he said, 'let's go through this.' He paused. 'The blood found on the rock and on the terrace at David Harrington's rented villa matches Alison Harrington's. Her death was virtually instantaneous, so almost certainly she suffered the fatal blow, accidentally or otherwise, in that location. Her body had been buried near the finca in Orba. David Harrington's car, recovered nearby, contained no evidence that it had been used to transport Alison's body to Orba. On the other hand, Sandra's first hire car did reveal samples of Alison Harrington's blood. We can reasonably conclude, therefore, that after her death Alison was placed in Sandra's car and taken to Orba. We might also surmise that David Harrington went to Orba at the same time in order to bury the body and set the false evidence to incriminate the two Dutchmen. Having abandoned his own car nearby, he needed a lift back to Altea, probably in Sandra's car.'

Mariela interjected as if to show she was keeping up with the plot. 'And realising her car might contain incriminating evidence, she changed it for a different hire car.'

'Exactly,' Michael said, pressing on. 'But the most crucial new evidence is the discovery of David Harrington's blood on the kitchen tiles and the knife at Sandra's villa. What does that tell us?'

Jose Luis was quick to respond. 'That David Harrington was, at the very least, wounded in Sandra Marlowe's kitchen. Of course it could have been just a simple kitchen accident.'

Michael thought for a moment – *another accident?* 'But what if it was more serious? What if he had been stabbed; killed even?'

The idea that David Harrington might be dead seemed to shock them all; it was contrary to everything they had been working on up to that time and, if it was true, then Sandra Marlowe's story about Harrington running off to France was a complete fabrication. What other lies might she have told?

Michael returned to his summation. 'I suppose there could be some other explanation for the blood at Sandra's villa, but, let's just for one minute imagine that David Harrington is dead. How does that lead to John Harrington coming back to Spain to collect the lottery money from the bank?'

Mariela chipped in. 'Well, Sandra knew the money was in an account in David's name. If he was dead she needed a way to get hold of that money. She couldn't pose as David herself, so that's why she arranged for John Harrington to come back to Spain to collect it.'

'Yes, but why now?' Michael said. 'Even without the lottery money, David had the best part of two hundred thousand euros in cash. We haven't found any of that money, so if Sandra had it, why the rush to get hold of the lottery cash. Why not wait until things died down?'

Alicia had been sitting quietly listening to the three detectives hypothesize. 'Forgive me,' she said, 'but I'm a scientist. Your theories and postulations are all well and good, but I prefer to deal in facts and it seems to me you have very few of those. All your speculations and suppositions are based on the idea that David Harrington is dead, but without a body your theories cannot be tested.'

The forensic scientist's statement brought them all back down to earth and a vacuous silence settled on the group.

After several minutes, Michael sprung to his feet. 'Of course,' he yelled. 'Why didn't I think of it before? Come on, we need to get back to Altea.'

It took less than fifteen minutes to locate the body of David Harrington buried under the withering orange tree in the garden of Sandra Marlowe's villa. It was wrapped in four large black plastic rubbish bin liners that has been split down the sides and opened out into sheets. The cause of death was easily established as a single stab wound to the chest that penetrated the heart. The pathologist's preliminary assessment was that he had been dead for at least two weeks, possibly a little longer.

'How did you know we'd find him there?' Jose Luis asked.

'Well,' Michael said, 'Alicia was right. Facts are all important, but there's nothing wrong with theorising if only to distinguish been the possible and the probable. Based on what we knew, it was possible that David Harrington had been killed at Sandra's villa. We know of no one else with a motive to kill him, so Sandra seemed the most obvious suspect, even if his death was not intentional. Then

Alicia reminded us all that without a body everything else was supposition. So I asked myself, where was David Harrington's body? We knew that neither of Sandra's two hire cars contained traces of David's blood. That left two possibilities. Either she hired a third car, which seemed improbable since carrying such a dead weight up those steps and lifting it into a car would have been virtually impossible for someone as slight as Sandra; or the body had been hidden closer to home. Based on this second possibility, I imagined the best that Sandra might be able to manage would have been to drag the body out of the house and into the garden. Most of the garden is hard landscaped with steps, pathways and terracing, leaving just a small area planted with trees.'

'And then you remembered the withering orange tree we talked about yesterday,' Jose Luis said.

'Exactly. You said that trees could suffer blight or insect infestation, even frost damage. But all the other citrus trees in the garden seemed so healthy, and when I thought about it, I just couldn't understand why that one tree could have withered and died.'

'We'll make a farmer of you yet, Michael,' Jose Luis said with a smile.

Surprisingly, Colonel Cardells indicated he didn't want to be involved in the interviews. They decided, then, to start with Miss Marlowe and Mariela joined Michael in the interview room. They agreed beforehand to start with the lottery money and keep in reserve the discovery of David Harrington's body. The theory was that the more Sandra tried to explain away the recovery of the money, the more she might incriminate herself.

Sandra was waiting and today her face was white.

Michael sat down immediately opposite her with Mariela at his side. 'You'll be pleased to know we have found the lottery money.' Michael said abruptly.

'Why would I be pleased about that? It's not mine,' Sandra snapped.

Michael ignored the question. 'And guess who we found with

the money?'

Sandra shook her head and blinked. 'I'm not in the mood for guessing games, Inspector.'

'We found it on John Harrington.'

'Oh? Did David give it to him?'

'I think you know that's not the case, but John certainly knew where to find it. He withdrew it himself from an account at the Banco de Valencia in Javea.'

Michael watched closely, looking for any sign of surprise, but Sandra's face was deadpan. 'You know something about this, Sandra. You told us David had you sign some papers to transfer the money from the Isle of Man, but you didn't know what account that was. Isn't that right?'

'I can't remember, exactly.' She looked up. 'Honestly, I'm confused.'

'Perhaps John will be able to help us when we talk to him. He's waiting in a cell downstairs.'

Sandra said nothing though her eyes seemed to narrow in concentration.

'Something else is puzzling me, Sandra. John had David's passport with him when he went to the bank. I wondered where he'd got it.'

'I haven't got the faintest idea. Perhaps David gave it to him?'

'But you have told us David is in France. He'd need his passport to get there, I think.'

Sandra shook her head, eyes wide.

'When John collected the money, he was wearing one of David's suits; I just wonder how he came by that.'

She looked even more surprised.

Mariela said softly, in slightly-accented English, 'Sandra, we've shown your photograph to the assistants in the stationery shop in Benidorm. That's the shop where a fax was sent to the Banco de Valencia requesting the cash withdrawal. One of the women assistants identified you from the photograph and she was able to confirm the date you were in the shop. It's the same date that the fax was sent to the bank.'

Still Sandra remained silent.

'It's fairly obvious,' Michael said, breaking the silence. 'You colluded with John Harrington so that he could pose as David and collect the money.'

Sandra slumped back in her chair and sighed. For a moment Michael thought she was about to capitulate and come clean. But she paused and Michael noticed a look of intense concentration as her eyes narrowed. Eventually she flicked her hair to one side and began to speak.

'All right, I'll tell you. I knew John was going to the bank; I helped set it up, but I didn't want to say anything before now because I thought perhaps he had got away with the money. But if you have found it and John as well, I might as well tell you the truth. After Alison died and then you found her body, David was in a frenzy. He was ranting and raving, terrified that he'd be blamed for her death. I tried to calm him down, but he wouldn't listen and then he just disappeared.'

Michael couldn't disguise the smirk that crossed his face. 'Disappeared, you say. So the whole escape to France was just a fabrication on your part?'

'I was just trying to help him, that's all.'

'I see. So now your story is that David disappeared, leaving behind his clothes and his passport. Is that right?'

'I told you he was panic-stricken. He wasn't thinking straight at the time.'

'I can understand why he would be worried,' Michael said, trying, and just about managing, to sound convinced by Sandra's story. 'But now I'm puzzled, Sandra. Why did you feel it was necessary to arrange for John Harrington to come back to Spain to collect the money from the bank?'

Sandra straightened in her chair.

'Why do you think?' Her voice was tinged with anger. 'Because David just buggered off and left me high and dry. I had a few thousand euro's that's true, but I helped him claim all that lottery money and I was entitled to a share at the very least. When he disappeared I was worried that he might come back and collect it and keep it all for himself and then where would I be?'

'So you are telling us now that you knew where the money was all along. Is that right?'

'Yes, I knew. I'd signed the forms to have it transferred from the account in the Isle of Man.'

'But you couldn't collect it yourself, so you contacted John and suggested he pop back to Spain to pose as David and collect the money?'

'Yes.'

'And how did you know he would agree to that?'

Sandra scowled. 'You think you're so clever, Inspector, but you know nothing. There was always friction between John and David. John's never had any money and he was always jealous of David, especially when David left Nottingham for a new life here in Spain. All I had to do was suggest a way for John to get his hands on some of David's money and I knew he would jump at the chance.'

'It was that simple?'

'Pretty much. John knew by then that Alison was dead and I told him David was worried about being incriminated and that's why he had disappeared.'

'And what was the deal between you and John?'

'We were to share the money. I should have met him outside the bank in Javea, but unfortunately you turned up and dragged me down here.'

'I see. What about Armando's involvement?'

'He wasn't involved. I'd told him I had my own money.'

'That's what he said, so now we go on to... '

'Just... ' Sandra crushed her cigarette packet. 'I'm sorry, I'm feeling a bit overwhelmed by all this. Could we take a break, just for a second?'

'Of course, let's take a break, and perhaps Officer Poquet can find more cigarettes.'

Mariela displayed her familiar frown of disapproval before she turned and left the room with Michael.

'Why stop there?' Jose Luis said when they joined him in the adjoining room where he had been watching through a one way mirror and listening in. 'I thought you were going to hit her with the fact we have found David's body. I'm sure she would have capitulated.'

'All in good time,' Michael said. 'She's dug a big enough hole for herself, I thought we could just leave her to wallow for a while in the pit of her own lies. In the meantime it might be useful to corroborate her story so far with John Harrington. I suspect he'll say much the same thing since they were obviously working together and I expect they concocted a fall-back position just in case they got caught. At least this way we can prove they conspired to obtain the money fraudulently and then we can move on from there with the real story of what happened to Alison and David Harrington.'

Ninety minutes later Michael and Mariela rejoined Sandra and she seemed relieved to rip away the wrapper from a packet of Fortuna Lights.

'I'm sorry, they're not your usual brand,' Mariela said, taking a seat at the side of the table.

Sandra dragged hard on her first cigarette and inhaled deeply to fill her lungs before raising her head to exhale a cloud of smoke towards the ceiling. She coughed.

'These are a bit strong,' she said before taking a second drag.

'You'll be pleased to know,' Michael began, 'that John corroborates what you have told us about how he came back to Spain at your suggestion to collect the money from the bank.'

'So you believe me?' she said hopefully.

'Oh, it's a very believable explanation,' Michael said, trying to sound sincere. 'But there's one small problem.'

'Oh?' Sandra looked curious.

'The problem, Sandra, is the body of David Harrington we found buried in the garden of your villa in Altea Hills.'

Sandra shuddered, her shoulders slumped and she sunk in her chair. Her eyes closed and her head flopped forward causing her hair fall about her face as she began to snivel.

Michael handed her a tissue and spoke in a soft voice. 'It's time to come clean, Sandra. You've led us all on a merry chase, but your lies are getting you nowhere except into more and more trouble.

Sandra looked up, dabbing at her eyes which were now bloodshot and streaked with mascara.

'If I tell you what I know, will it help me? I mean, I've done some bad things, but murder isn't one of them.'

Michael avoided the temptation to be smug, but did not want to let Sandra off the hook.

'Any help you can give us would stand in your favour, but as David's body was found in the garden of your villa and since the murder weapon was a knife from your kitchen, you'll understand why you are top of our list of suspects.'

'It wasn't me. It was John.' Her voice was tinged with desperation.

'John, you say? But we know that David was killed at least two weeks ago. That's before John came back to Spain.'

Sandra sneered. 'How little you know or understand, Inspector. John killed David just after Alison's body was found – while he and Linda were staying in that hotel in Benidorm pretending to be so concerned about the missing couple.'

Michael had to admit his surprise. 'But how did John know where to find David?'

'Like I said, he fooled you all along. John found out about me and David before David left England. When David announced he was coming to Spain with Alison, John threatened to tell Alison unless David gave him twenty-five thousand pounds. David might have called his bluff if it wasn't for the lottery money. But John didn't know about that so David paid him off.'

'That doesn't answer my question, Sandra. How did John know where to find David?'

'They were in contact all along. David had a mobile phone – I bet you didn't know that did you?'

Damn, Michael thought. Of course he had a mobile phone – the text Sandra sent him that Alison saw.

'And John knew the number?'

'Of course he did.'

'And Linda as well?'

'No, she knew nothing of this.'

'So John contacted David from the hotel in Benidorm, but why?'

'Because you found Alison's body, of course. John knew straight away that David must be implicated and he seized the opportunity to demand more money.'

'How much more?'

'Another fifty thousand pounds.'

'And what was David's reaction?'

'What would you expect? He was furious. That's when John came to my villa to meet David and try to get the money. David was so angry, there was a blazing row and...'

Sandra's whole body shuddered and her voice dropped to a whisper. 'They fought. John grabbed a knife in the kitchen. They struggled and David fell to the floor. There was blood everywhere it was terrible...' She began to weep.

Mariela pushed a box of tissues under Sandra's drooping head. She grabbed a bundle and held them to her face, sobbing.

A more sympathetic person might have allowed her time to compose herself, but Michael pressed on.

'And then you buried David's body in the garden?'

Suddenly Sandra looked up. 'Not me, no. That was John. He managed that all by himself.'

'I see,' Michael said. 'And after all this; after David had been murdered right in front of you, you never once thought of calling the police?'

'Of course I thought about it, but John threatened me. He said he would do me serious harm if I said anything and in any event I knew I could be incriminated.'

Poor Sandra, Michael thought. An innocent bystander to two deaths, but always worried about being incriminated.

'And did John get his money; the money he came for in the first place?'

'No he didn't.'

'So what happened to all that cash? Even without the lottery money David still had almost two hundred thousand pounds.'

'David never brought it with him to the villa.'

'So where is it?'

'I honestly don't know, Inspector. John searched David's villa from top to bottom afterwards, but we never found it.'

'You say "We"?'

'Yes, well, I helped him but we never found a penny.'

'And that's when you decided to concoct the story about David going to France.'

'Yes, we cleared his villa and I took away all his clothes so that it looked like he had just disappeared.'

'And John returned to England empty handed?'

'Yes.'

'And so you remained here in Spain with just a few thousand euros left from what David had given you, but knowing all the while that the lottery money was left sitting there in the bank and you had no way of getting hold of it.'

Sandra nodded.

'And that's why you conceived the plan for John to come back and pose as David?'

'Yes. I told you he's a greedy man; I knew he jump at the chance.'

'And so he did, Sandra. So he did.'

'Yes, well, it serves him right. If he hadn't been so greedy in the first place, David and I could have been together now, living the life we dreamed of.' Sandra snivelled again. Her story was at an end – for now at least.

'Of course we'll have to corroborate your story with John Harrington,' Michael said, bringing the interview to a conclusion.

John Harrington was stubborn, even belligerent, until it was suggested to him that tests were being carried out on David's body and on the plastic sheets in which he had been wrapped and, unless he had been meticulously careful, there would almost certainly be traces of material and DNA that would link him to the death.

John crumbled and confessed to killing his brother claiming it was an accident in the frenzy of a struggle, he said. As for the rest, he corroborated Sandra's story of how he had tried to extort money from his brother and went along with the plan to pose as David and collect the lottery money from the bank. It was only when Michael asked him how he planned to share the lottery money with Sandra that John came up with his most devastating revelation.

'Share the money with that bitch?' he stated emphatically, 'No way. I wouldn't have given her a penny.'

'But how could you get away with it? She would have shopped you, surely.' Michael said, confounded by John's vitriolic statement.

John sneered and snorted loudly. 'Because she killed Alison, that's why.'

Michael hid his surprise. 'And how do you know that?'

'David told me. After I heard that Alison's body had been discovered, I admit I took my opportunity to get a bit more money from David – it was nothing more than I deserved after covering up for him all the time he was in Spain. But he refused to give me any more and that's when we argued and fought. He told me then that Sandra had been at his villa when he and Alison argued. David was always weak, especially where women were concerned. Sandra had him wrapped around her little finger, or so she thought, but when Alison pleaded with David to stay with her, he dithered. That's when Sandra picked up the rock and hit Alison over the head. I didn't know anything about the lottery money then, but I guess that's why Sandra was so angry – she would have lost everything she had worked for if David dumped her to stay with Alison.'

'But even when David told you this, you still fought with him and killed him?'

'I never meant to. I deserved the money and I wasn't going to back off just because David said Sandra had killed Alison. As far as I was concerned the two of them were in it together. When I refused to back off, David attacked me and tried to throw me out of the villa. He was yelling and flailing out with his fists. I hit back, only to protect myself, and punched him in the face. He fell over towards the kitchen worktop and when he turned round he had the knife in his hand. He lunged at me and I grabbed his arm to protect myself. We wrestled together and both of us fell to the floor. When I got up I saw the knife in his chest. That's when I realised…' John's head slumped to his chest and he began to sob.

Michael remained silent for a few moments, trying to assess the situation. 'Did you believe David when he said that Sandra had killed Alison?'

'Yes, I believed him. Why would he lie?'

'No reason, I suppose. But despite this, you still came back to Spain when Sandra told you about the lottery money.'

'Yes, well, we were even, I guess. And if the money was just sitting there in the bank I thought, why not? Sandra said it would be easy with virtually no risk so I went along with her plan. I wish now…. That bitch, she's to blame for all of this. Right from the start.'

'What did Sandra say after David told you she had killed Alison.'

'She denied it of course, but she would, wouldn't she?'

'So we only have your word as to what David said and unfortunately he's no longer around to substantiate that story.'

John lowered his head again and continued to sob.

'So that's it,' Jose Luis said when they returned to the office. 'It will be her word against his.'

'Not necessarily,' said Alicia who had joined them a few minutes earlier to pick up the tail end of the conversation. 'I told you before that the rock which killed Alison was extremely hard and that it was unlikely that traces of it would be found in the wound to Alsion's head.'

'Yes, yes,' Michael said impatiently.

Alicia's lips tightened to a faint smile. 'But it was always likely that the opposite would be true.'

'The opposite? What are you talking about?' Michael's exasperation was clear.

'I also told you that the rock was very abrasive. So although particles of the rock might not be dislodged in the wound, particles of flesh would very likely have adhered to the rock. And that indeed proved to be the case.'

'But where does that take us? We already know it was the cause of the wound.'

'Yes, Inspector. But we have found two different skin samples on that rock. The detailed DNA results will be with us shortly, but it seems likely that one sample will be from Alison Harrington and the other will be from someone who had picked up that rock and used it with such force that it caused an abrasion or contusion to their hands.'

Of course it was always possible that Sandra might have grazed her hand on the rock if she had simply picked it up, though Alicia was willing to argue that simply handling the rock would have been unlikely to have caused that to happen. In any event Sandra scuppered that theory herself when she denied any part in cleaning up the scene of the crime. But the more damning evidence was the faintest trace of an old contusion to the thenor (the heel) of her right hand.

The initial paperwork out of the way, Michael, Jose Luis and Mariela sat down to coffee and bocadillos in the staff canteen. Suddenly ravenous, Michael ground his jaws on the dry bocadillo and then put up a hand to pull at three long strands of stringy Serrano ham that dangled down his chin.

Mariela smiled primly. 'I think the English inspector is thinking that a sharp knife would be handy.'

'Spanish teeth must be sharper than British ones,' said Michael as he swallowed the ham and brushed crumbs from his face.

'Well, a satisfactory result all round, I think,' said Jose Luis.

'And to think,' Michael responded, 'if it wasn't for a pair of carelessly discarded shoes we might never have got to the bottom of the case.'

'Shoes!' Jose Luis said. 'What is it about you and shoes?'

'Listen, it's quite simple. You can fake *Calvin Klein* jeans, or *Lacoste* shirts. You can even buy a passable *Louis Vuitton* handbag or a fake *Rolex*, but you can't fake good shoes. And shoes say more about a man than anything else he wears.'

Jose Luis was still trying to understand.

'Sorry to interrupt the happy gathering,' Sergeant Ramirez said from the door, 'But the Colonel would like to see you, Michael. Right away?'

'Ah, Fernandez, nice to see you again. Take a seat.'

Colonel Cardells was in full uniform, three silver shields glistening on the epaulettes of a rumpled white shirt. A large oil painting on the wall depicted the Capitan General of the Guardia Civil, King Juan Carlos, in full uniform. The portrait seemed to frame the Colonel's head. The massive oak desk made him look smaller, but the scowl had been replaced by a benign smile, making him look almost jolly. He smiled for about two seconds then sat down and leaned forward, elbows on desk, flabby chin resting on intertwined fingers.

'Now then, Detective Inspector. You're in a bit of trouble?'

The tone was light, but Michael didn't answer.

'I've been talking to Chief Superintendent Bowater,' Cardells went on smoothly. 'He tells me you resigned just before you came back to Spain.'

'In a manner of speaking.' Michael straightened his back.

'It's all sorted.' Cardells nodded. 'I've told him what a help you've been and what a smart detective you are. He should be proud of you.'

Michael nodded. 'May I ask what Chief Superintendent Bowater said?'

'Well, I won't go into the detail, but your job is waiting for you.'

'I see, sir. Thank you.'

'But...' Cardells leaned forward and lowered his voice. 'But how would you like to work for the Guardia Civil, instead?'

'The Guardia – sir?'

'Yes.' He stood up and marched over to a map on the wall, spreading his arms. 'Something like four hundred thousand expatriots live permanently on the Costa Blanca – most of them British – and literally millions more come every year for their holidays. Sadly, there's a corresponding crime wave out here. Much of it involving the British, either as victims or villains. For some time we've been thinking it would be useful to have a fluent English and Spanish speaking trained detective on the force. And...'

He crossed back to the desk and sat down. 'The job's yours, if you want it. We'd rank you as a captain and help you with relocation expenses, that sort of thing. What do you think, Inspector Fernandez?' He beamed.

'I'm honoured... truly honoured. But it's a big decision.'

'Of course it is. But we'd love you to join us. Think it over.'

Cardells stood up. 'Take as long as you like.'

'Thank you, Colonel,' Michael said, standing for his hand to be vigorously shaken. 'I will, sir – I certainly will, sir.'

Cardells added, 'By the way, if you took the job, we'd assign Officer Poquet to work alongside you.' An ominous twinkle lit the Colonel's eyes.

Back in the canteen, Jose Luis and Mariela looked up, grinning.

'Bastards. You knew all along what that meeting was about.'

'What did you say?' Jose Luis asked impatiently.

'I said I would think about it.' Michael sat down and reached for coffee.

'What's to think about?'

'I don't know. It's just me, I suppose. I have a lot to think about – more than just the job.'

Standing up, Michael took the hand offered by Jose Luis, knowing they might never work together again, and squeezed it firmly. When he saluted, Jose Luis laughed, clapped him on the shoulder and saluted back.

Michael walked over to the door where Mariela was waiting.

She held out her hand and, as he shook it, her hazel eyes sparkled behind a watery film. She reached up to kiss him lightly on the cheek. Her lips felt softly moist.

'We could have dinner tonight,' she whispered.

He opened his mouth and found himself saying, 'Mariela – you're absolutely not going to believe this, I can hardly believe it myself, but there's something I've simply got to do. And besides, you still need to find the missing money. David Harrington must have hidden it somewhere'

CHAPTER SIXTEEN

Michael's destination was about an hour and a half away. He knew that if he didn't go now he might never go. He thought about confirming his return flight to England, but that could wait.

With a few belongings in a suitcase in the back of a hire car, he hit the A7 motorway in familiar territory. At Benissa he left the motorway, paid the toll and took the turning for Senija. The sun was starting its westward descent and he headed directly toward the shallow beams of light that radiated from yet another cloudless sky. The shadows were beginning to lengthen as he neared the traffic lights at the approach to Lliber. Green changed to red and he thought about following the three drivers in front of him who jumped the signal, but didn't. Instead he stopped, waited, and admired the scenery.

The pastel painted houses seemed little changed by the tide of development in this part of the Jalon Valley or by the influx of foreign residents. But who could really know what went on behind the closed front doors of houses that, within living memory, had echoed to the slow clip-clop of over-burdened mules and the creaking of wooden cart wheels? Mechanisation in the form of chugging, rattling, smoking diesel engines had changed the resonance, as well as the volume, but had not greatly increased the pace of life or changed the values people held. Yet just as the images of yesteryear were crystallising in his mind, the next convoy of traffic approached in the distance, led by a German-registered Audi. Michael studied the oncoming cars as they filed past, noting their registrations. After the Audi came cars registered in Spain, Britain, Britain, Holland, France, Spain, Holland, Britain, Spain, and Belgium. Where else in the world, even in capital cities, could you see such a multi-national collection of vehicle registrations? And yet here it was, streaming through a two-donkey pueblo in the middle of nowhere.

As he passed between the houses, two lurid lilac walls stood out from the standard sandy beige, as if to announce foreign ownership. Not that he cared – 'He Who Hated Spain.'

A lone pursuer in a white van emblazoned with the letters, 'STEVE JONES – PLUMBER,' overtook him as he left the village.

The wide-open space of the valley unfolded before him and Jalon came into view. Parcent stood in the far distance. Along the road, vines stretched out at angles, their leaves maturing in the heat of early summer. Tight bunches of tiny, pale green grapes were just beginning to swell.

Approaching Jalon, his eyes were drawn to the vast urbanisation of Almazara that loomed high on the northern mountain like a giant concrete avalanche. It seemed to have expanded horrifically since his last visit... But why should he care? He hated Spain.

As he fringed the town, the riverbed looked as dry as ever. The bodegas were doing good business as usual. Day trippers lugged heavy plastic flagons across the road and staggered towards their coaches. The fish and chip shop was doing a roaringly British trade, serving tourists happy to eat within inches of passing traffic. He began to speculate about the forces at work in the valley that had brought about such changes in just a couple of decades. Economic necessity? Subsidising of a struggling rural way of life? Greed? Corruption? – Why should he care?

He crossed the bridge, left Jalon behind and pressed on for Alcalalí. The direction sign had been amended in dribbling black spray paint to read: ALCANALÍ. It seemed that perhaps the Valenciano protesters were concerned about more than just the demise of their regional language.

The landscape changed as the valley narrowed and vineyards were replaced by orange groves. The blossom he'd seen wilting on his last visit had given way to tiny oranges, barely visible within the deep green foliage of sculptured trees. Already the fruit was beginning to swell, absorbing the warm summer sunshine as if storing it up for the winter harvest.

Michael pulled over at the side of the road. He'd been drifting off to sleep. He blinked, stretched, and lay back in the seat.

A silver-haired old man trudged by in ragged clothes; rope-soled espadrilles laced around his ankles. His back was bent under a canvas sack; a tattered straw hat shielded his eyes from the amber glare of the sun. He passed a pile of discarded builders' rubble and an unsightly set of overflowing rubbish bins, apparently without regard, and continued on his way, tracing steps he'd probably taken for most of his life. For a moment Michael began to resent the unstoppable progress that now marred a once idyllic rural environment. But then he realised; this is not the Cotswolds or the Lake District, where order and tidiness are essential ingredients of life – and where conservation is of paramount importance, and it's easier to buy a mohair scarf than a loaf of bread. This is Spain, where life is more important than order and tidiness. What did it matter if perfection was marred by progress? Life continues. The sun rises and sets, the seasons come and go. Life is not about neatness and congruity. Life is friends, fellowship, family and food on the table.

Michael sat up and stretched. The old man had long gone. Nobody was on the road ahead. He turned the ignition key and pulled out. A few corners later, Parcent came into view with its narrow streets of houses huddled together around a knoll, watched over by the fretwork church tower.

He parked on tree-lined Avenida de la Constitución and climbed the hill. The Placa del Poble was crowded with vans and cars. Bar Moll was packed; the buzz of conversation as difficult to penetrate as the smoke-filled atmosphere. As he approached the counter he reached into his pocket. Withdrawing his hand, he pushed his way through a group of men. Silence spread across the room as he faced Julio.

'Yours, I think,' he said.

Amongst the group by the bar, all eyes turned to the stone wrapped in a crumpled piece of paper and tied with string which Michael slammed on the bar in a pool of spilt beer.

He picked up the heavy brass knocker on the solid oak door and banged it hard, perhaps too hard. The door opened and Rosana stood before him. Her eyes widened.

'What are you doing here?'

'I had to come back to Spain, to complete my investigation.'

'Was that the only reason?'

'Why else would I come?'

Her expression grew in intensity. She took a deep breath as her elbows rose in unison and she planted her hands on her hips.

'Miguel-Ángel Fernand...' was all she could say before he kissed her.

*****

BY THE SAME AUTHOR

SPANISH LIES

Detective Inspector Fernandez returns to Spain to investigate a tangled web of murder, corruption and immorality on the Costa Blanca. Meanwhile, in the village where he has inherited a home, the tentacles of local life engulf him in an irresistible intrigue and a mystery that has its roots in the aftermath of the Spanish Civil War.

"This is an excellent detective novel with lots of twists and turns to keep you thinking right to the end! Just the right balance between the plot and background of the main character's private life. Really enjoyed it!"

A SPANISH AFFRAY

The third Fernandez novel. When the body of a British ex-con is fished from the Mediterranean, Michael Fernandez is once again called on to investigate. Now a captain in the Guardia Civil, Michael must face his own doubts and demons as he unravels a case that leads him back to an unsolved robbery and murder from ten years earlier. His pursuit of one of "Britain's Most Wanted" takes him to the limit of his powers but he refuses to back off. But what motivates him to put his own future on the line when a desperate situation get out of hand?

"After reading the first of the Michael Fernandez series and enjoying it immensely I went straight onto reading books two and three and neither disappointed. I like the area of Spain in which they are set and the Spanish family background and customs provide an interesting aside to the underlying crime story. Mark Harrison doesn't fall into the trap of over complicating or lengthening the stories which made them an enjoyable read for me. I hope that the sequel isn't too long in being released."

A SPANISH PACT
(An historical novel)

Spain 1939. In the immediate aftermath of the Civil War, General Franco seeks to strengthen his tenuous grip on power by suppressing and eliminating all opposition whether real or imagined. When Eduardo Ripoll is unjustly arrested and consigned to prison in Alicante, his wife, Vicenta, embarks on a perilous journey to fined him and secure his release. Constantly under threat of arrest and railing against the forces of fascism and anti-feminist dogma, Vicenta fights for her own survival and the right to bring up her new born child.

Against all odds, Vicenta refuses to accept that Eduardo is dead and she can never forget or forgive the injustice he has suffered. Finally the truth is revealed and Vicenta is presented with an opportunity – if not for justice, then for revenge.

"A spellbinding storyline with deep descriptive passages creates a smouldering effect that combines with some quite brutal action to increase the pace. The dialogue is clear and concise; quite clipped and snappy. There is good background information and the novel draws you in very early on. A sense of time and place are created from the first page. There is atmosphere and tension and emotional impact. Well

worth a read."

I WANT TO LIVE IN SPAIN
(Non fiction)

In the middle of a dreary drawn out English winter, Mark Harrison and his wife Vivien suddenly took stock of their lives and decided it was time for a change.

Ten months later they had resigned from their jobs, sold their house in leafy Surrey and moved to a new home in the mountains inland from Spain's Costa Blanca. This is the story of how they got there and how they fared in their new surroundings.

I want to live in Spain will make you laugh at their innocence and cry at their misfortunes. It is essential reading for anyone who has ever dreamed of moving out of the fast lane to find a new life in the sun.

"My first thought was, 'it's all been done before,' but this is different – fresh, funny and unpretentious. I just couldn't put it down."

IN PURSUIT OF THE PERFECT PAELLA
(More advents from a new life in Spain)

Ten years on from an impetuous "lock, stock and barrel" move to the Costa Blanca, Mark Harrison recounts the events that exemplify his new Spanish lifestyle. From a serious skirmish with developers, to an encounter with wild boars and the vagaries of the weather, the story paints a humorous and yet poignant picture of life in foreign land as viewed through his own eyes and those of his stoical wife, Vivien. The story is interwoven with a series of paella experiences that epitomise Spanish culture and tradition and give a taste of everyday expat life.

Forget the guides and manuals, this is real time, real life experience written with true insight and honesty. Essential reading for anyone who has ever dreamed of exchanging the rat race for a new life in the Spanish sun.

Printed in Great Britain
by Amazon